UNBOUND JUSTICE

THE SANDSTONE TRILOGY, BOOK 1

MICHAEL BEASHEL

UNBOUND JUSTICE

Michael Beashel

ISBN: 979 8 6913550 04

Publishing and Marketing Consultant: Lama Jabr
Website: https://xanapublishingandmarketing.com
Sydney, Australia

Cover by Mark Thacker, Big Cat Design
Front cover photograph: Getty Images

THE SANDSTONE TRILOGY

Three novels, *Unbound Justice*, *Unshackled* and *Succession*, span 37 years of Sydney life in the second half of the nineteenth century. They follow the fortunes of 20-year-old John Leary, who in 1850 leaves his rural home in Ireland and sails as an assisted immigrant to New South Wales.

His trade is carpentry but his ambition is boundless. By hard work, talent and opportunism he manages to create his own construction company, never ceasing the struggle to become the biggest and the best. The building industry becomes a metaphor for his chosen city, with its mixture of squalor and grandeur, of corruption and high ideals.

The Sandstone Trilogy is a historical drama with a rich cast of compelling characters. It is also a family saga, in which love, revenge and tragedy all come to influence the Learys' destiny.

'Well-written and thoroughly enjoyable. It's a love story with a vivid background of those early days of European settlement—and all the drinking, hard work, treachery and jostling for position that was mandatory in those times. You warm to the characters as they make their way in this new land. More of it!'

Wendy O'Hanlon
Australian Provincial Newspapers

PRINCIPAL CHARACTERS

The Leary Family
John Leary
Richard Leary, John's father
Maeve Leary (née Riordan), John's mother
Alf, Mervin, Vincent and Kieran, John's brothers
Maureen Murphy (née Leary), John's sister

The McGuire Family
Clarissa McGuire
David McGuire, Clarissa's father
Christine McGuire, Clarissa's mother

The O'Hare Family
Beth O'Hare
Jim O'Hare, Beth's father
Anne O'Hare, Beth's mother
Olivia and Sarah, Beth's sisters

The Baxterhouse Brothers
William Baxterhouse
James Baxterhouse

CONTENTS

CHAPTER ONE

John Leary stood at the crossroads, waiting for the coach. There was still time to back out of this venture.

His mother was watching him from the farm; he felt certain of that. He wanted to stay in Ireland, but his father insisted that the opportunities in New South Wales were massive for a twenty-year old journeyman carpenter with ambitions to become a builder—one day he might even have his own building company.

His mother had wanted him to stay, wanted him to train as an architect and set up his shingle in Dublin, joining his twenty-two-year-old brother Mervin as a professional man. Two of John's other brothers, Kieran twenty-four and Vincent, born a year before John, were farmers on the family's land, while Alf, twenty-three was a priest. Their only sister, twenty-five year old Maureen, the eldest sibling, lived in Dublin, where John would see her soon, if only to say goodbye.

If he were to travel, his mother would have preferred him to travel as a paid passenger with money and comfort. But that was expensive and some of the family farm would have needed to be sold to pay for it, and that wouldn't happen. What it came down to was that he wanted to stay, his mother wanted him to stay, but his father wanted him to seek out opportunities elsewhere, opportunities that Ireland didn't offer.

The Bianconi coach rolled up to him, its dust making him turn his face away. It was decision time. He could defy his father and stay here and work, or he could get on board. It wasn't worth labouring the matter. There really was little choice.

He loaded his trunk, climbed aboard, nodded to the passengers and closed the door. As the coach moved off he looked out onto the Leary farm, perhaps for the last time. In the June sunlight, his father's land was an oasis in Kildare. Its grass shone bottle green and lush on the one hundred acres, its cattle were fat and content. And it was owned, not rented—a rarity. In the distance, on lots bare as a beggar's pocket, neighbours struggled to survive. Those farmers had had but one crop: potatoes. Blight was killing the potatoes and, over the last four years, the failure of the crop had led to starvation and deaths. All over the country there were stories of deaths in their hundreds of thousands, numbers that sounded impossible to be true. John Leary felt for his country. His mother had nursed many local families. She had prayed over their children, while John had fixed their chairs and mended their stables. But their efforts were a single grain in a full mill of pain and suffering.

The coach gathered speed, climbed and cleared another hill, providing John with an opportunity to admire his handiwork. Three hundred feet of top and bottom timber rails running along the edge of a drainage ditch were squared and finished with pride, and his labour paid for in cash by the county. This in a time when coin was rare and food was the main currency, because only jobs away from the farms 'paid' anything. The rocking coach bumped against his shoulder as he looked out at the mill on the hilltop. Its sails had seen fifty summers, but its wheel would be idle now with no wheat to grind.

As his view of the family farm receded, John became more aware of the cramped conditions in the carriage—he felt like he was in a vice, his six-foot-three-inch frame squeezed between the other passengers. The thought of sitting so long like this added to his discomfort as did his jacket and trousers of broadcloth. He longed to swap them for working clothes. He was at ease when building. All his actions had purpose and logic. When he scanned drawings, swung a hammer or shifted timbers, his movements were confident and lithe. Outside of his job, he felt different and was conscious of his size. Now that awkwardness made him irritable and he kicked himself for not opting for the cheaper seats outside the coach.

The people around him were talking.

'It *is* high, I tell you,' the passenger beside him said. 'Even an eagle couldn't land on it.'

The man opposite had hair as red as a terracotta mortar mix. He laughed. 'So you said before, Declan.'

'No, it can't be that high!' A woman flashed a bold look at John that lingered for a second over his left eyebrow. John was conscious of his prominent scar, caused two years ago by a flying nail spun from an errant hammer. She said, 'What do you think, young sir? Is Dublin's Customs House taller than St Paul's? St Paul's in London I mean.'

'Don't know, ma'am. I've never been to London.'

The woman sniffed. 'Neither have we. But nothing could be taller than the Customs, nothing.' She turned to the red-haired man and continued chatting.

John looked at the man's hair, so different from his own untidy gold locks, and thought about his uncertain future. New South Wales. What he'd read about the place made him pause—heat, flies, snakes. But there was money to be made there; carpenters were well paid and work was plentiful. Sydney was a growing town. New people meant more houses and carpenters were needed to help build those houses. Melbourne was another place he could work. It was— no, it couldn't be six hundred miles from Sydney, no, that had to be wrong. Pulling out papers from his jacket pocket, he read the lists of wages he'd be likely to earn and tried to work out what he'd need to live on. The wages for a stonemason caught his eye. He noticed they compared well with carpenters' pay.

John's Uncle Gerry had been a stonemason, but he knew nothing about him because the family had never heard from him after he'd been transported to New South Wales in 1828, for murder. His mother had always maintained his innocence. Might this uncle have been released, in Sydney or Melbourne? Or, after twenty-two years, was he still in jail for his crime? The rocking motion of the coach made it hard for John to think. He extracted a book from another pocket and started to read, the action prompting a flash of home and how his mother had read to him as a boy. He would miss her.

An hour later, the coach stopped. He looked away from his book to watch the change of horses in the late-afternoon light. Getting out, he stretched his arms and legs and looked down the valley to the distant spires of Dublin and the Anna Liffey. By that ribbon of water he would meet his sister again—and then sail to the other side of the world. Kicking the dust in excitement, he leapt back onto the coach and willed it to go faster.

~

William Baxterhouse rubbed the watermark on the creditor's letter and placed it back down on his desk.

'Damned sniffing hounds. *Anomalies*, *inconsistences*, all fancy words for lack of cash.' He grinned. 'Well, I don't have cash for them!'

His business in imported goods had kept him solvent, but lately his debts had risen to exceed what he earned. One creditor had done a check and found *anomalies*. In ten days there would be an audit of William's books. That he couldn't have. If he owned up to not being able to pay his debts, he would be bankrupted, with nothing but beggary and thievery to follow. However, if he migrated, he could escape debts and disgrace. It would mean being separated from his brother, James but maybe James could follow him, at some point.

It was just the two of them, born to a wealthy Belfast family. Different they were as granite was to talc. James, slight of frame and fair of face, loved music and the theatre. William smiled. He himself favoured the rough and tumble of life and limb. And yet, they loved each other. Their early lives had been comfortable in 1830s Belfast, which was a dirty city with overcrowded houses. The family's company interests had comprised shipbuilding but primarily cotton and linen-making. After training as an accountant at Queen's College, William had entered the shipbuilding firm at age twenty-three. James joined the cloth company four years later. His brother's talents were well-suited for selecting fabrics that sold well and he was now propping up their father's faltering Belfast business, Elite Fabrics. The family's cotton division suffered from a general turndown in 1848 and their income, status and influence had mirrored the same unhappy downward slope as the change in demand. Bitter and angry at his misfortune, William suffered a massive blow that same year when their dear mother had died from cholera. Inconsolable at the dual calamities, his father George had suffered a breakdown and a stroke and had retired from both businesses.

The shipbuilding industry was booming in Belfast. However, as it had only been a small proportion of the Baxterhouse's businesses, the other shipbuilders had closed ranks and thwarted their growth. As senior manager William had been sent to Dublin to use his skills and had initially achieved a modest success, winning the odd tender for naval vessels. To supplement their income he'd opened an office for importing furnishings from England for ocean-going vessels. Over the past year and again squeezed by local competitors, William had had no choice but to cut costs and prices. The company's finances struggled and he was forced to live in the warehouse they owned near the Dublin docks.

Their biggest customer was the East India Company and William had been steadily overcharging them, in small amounts that now added up to a considerable sum that was lodged in the safe at his feet. He thanked his luck and congratulated himself that they'd never discovered his scheming. But this damned creditor was a worry. An audit would be his undoing. He had to act, now.

There were two folders on his desk. Opening the thick one, he picked up the top document, a letter of credit from Barclay's Bank of London for £2,000. Part of that amount was based on the value of his Dublin house (£500) and the other on the Mayor Street warehouse, in which he now sat (£1,500). Neither property, nor the smaller Belfast business, Elite Fabrics, had been mortgaged to the Dublin business so his creditors couldn't touch them.

So, to set himself up overseas, in addition to the cash in his safe he had Barclay's note. Not bad. At nearly thirty-five, he could still become rich, even if that meant leaving his country and his brother behind.

Was he running away? He'd never yet baulked at taking on an opponent! He glanced at an 1841 Dublin newspaper mounted on the wall and smiled at the article displayed. He'd been new to the capital then—a twenty-six-year-old trained accountant. He'd also been a boxer, and in twenty rounds, with a half-closed eye and a broken rib, he'd won the bare-knuckle final to become Queen's College Lightweight Boxing Champion, knocking out the star opponent, a protégé of Dublin's top trainer. Yes, he could fight. But fighting for his business was a different battle, perhaps better fought elsewhere. No, he was not running away—he was taking on a greater challenge.

He tapped the thinner file. Most of these documents described investment opportunities in Canada, America and New South Wales. He scanned them again and nodded. He'd decided on New South Wales, because of the growth potential there for boatbuilding, in which he would have few competitors. Sydney would be his destination. The last sheet in the file was an offer to buy his existing Dublin warehouse stock for £200—less than its value, but in this crisis William needed the money. Taking a pen, he wrote a letter to James in Belfast, telling him of his plans and instructing him to sell the stock after he'd gone.

Standing up, he walked from his desk to the window and looked down at the Anna Liffey, his escape route, shimmering in the afternoon heat. The capital was cleaner than his native Belfast and not so overcrowded, but it still crawled with beggars and starving people. A breeze wafted from the water, redolent of salt, waste and assorted smells from the endless coming and going of ships. William felt a surge of hope. A voyage to a new land, a new beginning. It was time for a drink.

Grabbing his hat, he walked from his warehouse to the nearby tavern. It was seldom quiet and now was no exception. As usual, sailors and dock workers rubbed shoulders with better-dressed patrons. Ordering a whiskey he sat down and observed the customers, noticing a nearby woman whose breasts nearly burst out of her blouse when she laughed. Her face had a tell-tale blush; she'd be carrying more disease than a plague-ridden city.

Tonight he'd come back here and play cards. Afterwards, he'd pick out a woman—but not like this one. He would take her back to his lodgings at the warehouse and enjoy her. A rousing goodbye to Dublin life, before he adopted a new one in Australia. *Have your fun here, man; soon you need to get married again.* Mary. He often thought about her. A slight figure, a gentle spouse and of good temperament. It had been eight years since her death and her passing had been senseless. A trip on a misplaced doorstopper and a fall down the stairs. In anger he'd sacked the servant who'd caused the hazard. Bitter that a life could be taken so, he'd been cautious in seeking a new partner and was satisfied up till now with short term dalliances. In Sydney though, once he'd planted feet, turned timber and sown money in a new land, he hoped to find a respectable woman, similar to his late wife. She would attend church every Sunday, raise his children and maintain his social standing.

His thoughts turned to Maureen Murphy. She was definitely worth getting to know better. He ordered another drink and allowed his thoughts to dwell on the delightful school teacher.

~

It was late in the afternoon and two young women, Jane Forde and Maureen Murphy, were walking homeward together through the Dublin streets.

Jane was talking about her brother. 'Liam knows where you can get that novel you were after. I've forgotten its name.'

'*David Copperfield.*'

'That's the one. Do you still want it?'

Maureen liked Jane Forde and she liked her brother Liam even more. She'd only met him twice but there had been a mutual attraction. 'Yes, I'd like to talk to him about it.'

'I'll tell him.' They turned a corner and Jane looked back. 'Your place is a fair walk from Portland Street. Do you still like teaching at the school?'

'I do, Jane, but I've only been a teacher for six months and it's all come at a cost.'

'Is your family still angry with you for staying in Dublin?'

'My parents are. My brothers understand, I think. Except for Mervin.' When she was widowed, Maureen had won a scholarship to train as a primary teacher, at The Kildare Place Training Institution run by The Church of Ireland. Her parents had disapproved, even more so when she chose to teach in Dublin instead of in the country. 'I don't regret it so far. The teaching standard's high, and Dublin's a far cry from Kildare.' Maureen stopped at her front gate. 'I'd invite you in but—'

'That's all right. You're expecting your brother. He's coming tonight, isn't he?'

'At about eight. I must run out and pay my rent beforehand. I've just got time to wash and eat, then I'll dash out.'

'Doesn't your landlord come round for your rent?'

'I don't want him to do that anymore. I feel a bit uncomfortable with Mr Baxterhouse. He might come again, so I'm going to pay him now at his office first before he does.'

'He's a good-looking man,' Jane said, 'and he knows it. Those piercing eyes and that smile.'

Jane didn't seem to mind Baxterhouse flirting with her, but Maureen was wary of him. She said quietly, 'I don't like his behaviour as much as you do. Isn't he married?'

'No, he's not! So he's ripe for the catching if you want him, though you'd better hurry—I've seen him with Frances Ferguson at church. You should get married again, Maureen. I'm surprised you don't have many suitors, with that curly red hair and all your curves. You're so attractive.'

'I'd like to get married again, but not yet and certainly not to Mr Baxterhouse.'

Maureen turned away to open her gate, stepped through and shut it, thinking of her husband. She still missed him terribly. Colin Murphy had been killed in Mexico in 1846, fighting for General López de Santa Anna. Under the green banner of the Irish republicans, he had fought for Mexico's independence, and been cited for bravery. She was lonely on her own. A child by her beloved husband would have been a gift to Maureen, but God hadn't blessed her.

In the silence, Jane gave Maureen a quizzical look.

Maureen managed a smile. 'If I'm to see to our *friend* Baxterhouse at his office before it closes I'd better not dally. I'll see you tomorrow.'

Jane laughed and walked off, waving goodbye.

Upstairs in her room Maureen half undressed, washed her upper body and checked her reflection in the mirror. Was Jane right? As a twenty-five-year-old widow, was she attractive? Her face was bright, with fair skin and clear eyes. Maybe.

The knocker on the front door thudded. Startled, she pulled up her gown, quickly doing it up. Hurrying down the stairs she wondered who it could be. Jane, perhaps? It was too early for John. The other tenant of the house was away and wouldn't be back until the next day. She opened the door a fraction.

'Good afternoon, Mrs Murphy.'

Maureen felt awkward and flustered. 'Mr Baxterhouse. I wasn't expecting you.'

Baxterhouse smiled. He *was* a good-looking man, suave and urbane. 'I was passing your way and decided to take my luck.' He leaned closer, and Maureen smelled whiskey on his breath. 'I hope I'm not imposing.'

She hesitated. She didn't want him in the house. Perhaps she could get his visit over quickly. 'Please come in. If you'll wait in the parlour, I'll get the rent.'

She stepped back and he entered and shut the door behind him. 'Thank you.'

Maureen hurried upstairs to her room and took the envelope from her chest of drawers.

A squeak on the floorboards outside her door made her turn.

Baxterhouse stood in the open doorway, smiling at her. 'I thought I'd save you the trouble of coming downstairs.' Maureen stepped towards him, expecting him to make way for her. But he stayed where he was. 'You're a handsome woman, Mrs Murphy. Has anyone told you that?'

Maureen held out the envelope. 'Here's your rent, Mr Baxterhouse.'

'Please call me William. I asked you to call me that, last time. Don't be shy.'

Maureen tensed, not liking his manner or the now hard look in his eyes. 'I'd be grateful if you could go.'

He reached out, took the hand that held the envelope and squeezed. 'A handsome woman, make no mistake.'

She disengaged her hand. 'There's your money. Now please leave.'

He put the envelope in a pocket, his confident figure still barring the doorway. 'And spirited, too. That's good. That shows you've missed a man, missed his attentions. Come, I'll be gentle.'

She backed away.

'Maureen. Come on, we've been flirting these past weeks. I know you want it as much as I do. Be good to me and I'll give you back the money.' He smiled. 'A week's rent, back in your hand for a quick frolic with me.'

'I asked you to leave!' He grinned again. 'I've power in Dublin. I'm on very good terms with the trustees of the Church of Ireland. Make a fuss and you'll be on the street, begging. Your choice. I could revoke your licence to teach, faster than a pickpocket can snatch a purse.'

'You wouldn't dare!'

He moved closer. The danger galvanised Maureen. She screamed, 'Get out of here!'

He gripped her throat with one hand, pushing her further into the room and onto the bed. Filled with terror, Maureen grabbed his strangling hand and tried to jab her knee into his groin. But he twisted away, still holding her with one hand. With the other he yanked her gown up to her waist and drove his hand between her thighs.

Breathless and blind with panic, Maureen fought him as hard as she could, but she was no match for her boxer landlord.

~

William Baxterhouse was at his lodgings in the warehouse. Maureen Murphy had been in his sights for some time and the deed was done but he was a little ashamed that he'd used such force to have his way. It surprised him that he had. It hadn't been his intention. He'd planned to woo her which he sort of had been doing these past weeks. Perhaps, it'd been the drink or maybe it was his anger at having to leave Ireland that had driven him. Now, he wasn't sorry to be leaving. He'd not be facing any possible repercussions, not that he thought there would be. He was too powerful for that. She'd wanted it, he convinced himself, even though she'd fought him. He'd done her a favour; she probably hadn't had a man for years.

Relaxing, he reached into his trouser pocket and took out the gold watch, admiring its craftsmanship. He'd seen it on Maureen's bureau on his way out and taken it.

'A fine piece,' he thought then laughed. He'd always wanted one and now he had one. Its connection with Maureen was easily erased from his mind.

~

The coach stopped in Talbot Street. John leaned forward and gazed out the window. The Dublin streets were busy in the evening, as people hurried by, but there was misery, too, in the starving, huddled groups with nowhere to go.

'At last,' the red-haired passenger said. 'The weather has been kind and I've enjoyed our talk on the poets. We could continue it? Over a pint?'

John grinned. It had been grand talking to another about the poetry he loved. Kieran had fostered his interest, his eldest brother delighting in the classics. 'I would down the first, sir, and steadily drink the next four—but I can't. I promised to go straight off and see my sister, the moment I arrived. I haven't seen her for six months.'

'You'll get a fond welcome, Mr Leary?'

'Indeed.'

The man nodded. 'All power to you and your future, then. Goodbye.'

'Farewell to you,' John said as he jumped out.

It took little time to retrieve his trunk and sign it into the depot for safekeeping. When he set out for Maureen's place on Temple Street, it felt good to walk again, to stretch his muscles. Along Sackville Street, folk made way for him and a few women glanced his way.

It was disorienting, too. Here he was in the city of Dublin, and this time tomorrow he'd be on a ship. He might have planned to have more time between his arrival and embarkation, but hanging around in Dublin would only make him miss Ireland all the more when he left. As long as he could stay one night with Maureen, he was content. He had no intention of seeing his brother, Mervin—Mervin took his parents' side against Maureen and believed she should never have become a teacher and chosen to live on her own.

When John saw the house where she lodged, he hastened his step. He knocked on the front door and waited. He knocked again and tried the handle, but it was locked.

'Maureen!'

He called again, louder, and waited. Nothing.

He went around to the back of the house and found a gate that yielded to him. A path led to the back door, which she sometimes left unlocked when she was in. It was open today and he went in.

'Maureen?' He listened but there was nothing. He looked around downstairs, then ran up and found her room. It was untidy, which surprised him.

He went downstairs and decided to wait for her. Ten minutes passed and he was beginning to get worried when he heard the key in the front door. He went to greet his sister—but found another woman on the doorstep.

'You're Mr John Leary?'

'I am. Who are you?'

The woman sighed. 'I'm your sister's friend, Jane Forde. I'm sorry, something terrible has happened to Maureen.'

John's concern returned. 'My God! Is she hurt? Is she—?'

'She's had an accident. I'll tell you on the way.'

The vestibule of the Rutland Street Hospital was busy.

The doctor standing before the desk said, 'You're John Leary, Mrs Murphy's brother?'

'I am.'

'Your sister's in a fair condition. The facial cuts and bruises will heal.'

'Are there any other injuries?'

'You may speak to her yourself.'

'That I will! Where is she?'

The doctor pointed down the corridor. 'In Ward Three.'

They found her alone in a four-bed ward. Her eyes were closed, her neck was swollen and discoloured. John leant over, close to her face. 'Maureen, it's me. Can you hear me?'

'Johnny . . . Johnny . . . is that you?' She opened her eyes and tried to turn her head. Her eyes closed and her forehead creased as the effort overcame her.

'What happened to you? Miss Forde tells me you *fell down the stairs*! Did you?'

Maureen managed to look at her friend, then back at him. 'I was so silly. It was my fault entirely.'

'Maureen!' Jane said, her voice stern.

'I fell, Jane. That's what happened.' Maureen closed her eyes. 'Please, let me just sleep.'

'But Maureen—'

'Please, Johnny. Come back when I'm rested. Jane has my key. Stay at my place. We'll talk tomorrow.'

John stroked his sister's forehead, then left. In the corridor he stopped and confronted Miss Forde, who saw his expression and said at once, 'I'm glad you've seen her. Now I can tell you, your sister didn't fall down the stairs.'

'Then what on earth happened?'

Miss Forde looked around in case anyone else was in earshot. 'She was assaulted. At home, in her room. Afterwards she just had the strength to go out in the street and get a man with a dray to bring her here.'

'She's been beaten half to death! Who did this to her?'

'Not only beaten but attacked as . . . as a woman can be. Do you understand?'

'God Almighty!' Shock and anger filled him. 'Who? *Who?*'

'She told me not to say. She won't tell you and she won't go to the police. He's a man with influence. She'd lose her job at the school. She'd be thrown out of the house.'

'She can tell me and I'll deal with him!'

'She doesn't want you to know and she definitely doesn't want your family to know. They're against her teaching and living away from home. She doesn't want to bring shame on them as well.'

Maureen had rebelled against her father. To him, she'd turned her back on her faith. God, what a mess. 'Did she know her attacker?' Jane began to walk away from him but he caught her up. 'She won't tell me, but you will! Who is he?'

Jane took one look at him and he sensed her weakening. 'William Baxterhouse, her landlord.'

John's anger mounted and he pressed his hands to his head. 'Where does he live? I'll kill him.'

Miss Forde gripped his arm; he was surprised at her strength. 'I'd like to kill him, too. I'd like to skewer the mongrel. But we've no proof against him. It's Maureen's word against his.'

John's anger turned to bitter frustration. He groaned and leaned against the wall.

'Mr Leary,' Jane pleaded, 'please do nothing stupid. You'll only hurt your sister if you try to do battle for her. She'll get over it, with my help. I've written a note on her behalf, explaining her absence from school for the next few days. Let her recover.' She pressed his arm again. 'Do nothing, Mr Leary, nothing. Let me help her. That's all she needs.'

After a restless night cramped on his sister's sofa, John made his way to the Emigration Depot. He had to ensure that all his papers were in order before he could think about hunting down the man who had raped Maureen.

But the name hit his eye the moment he entered the vestibule, on a faded advertisement tacked to a notice board. *Baxterhouse Company, Superior Ships' Chandlery, 16 Mayor Street.* Now he knew the address!

Pushing open a set of doors, he found a room filled with aspiring emigrants. There were three queues and John got on the shortest. A rumble of dialects rose and fell. For the first time that day, excitement replaced his anger. In his pocket, his hands closed around his Approval Circular from the Commissioners—his permission to emigrate. When his turn came, a doctor looked at his documents, gave him an examination and pointed him towards the counter where a clerk waited.

'Your papers, manifest and proof of identity.'

'Did my trunk come from the coach depot?'

'Give me your name and I will check it. Come on, come on, there are people behind you.'

With his documents approved and his trunk's arrival confirmed, John set out to find Baxterhouse. He'd make him pay.

The port was busy. Amongst its bustle, sights and smells he found the warehouse and walked through the front doors. The place was packed with crates and stock. He approached a worn counter where a man was adding up a list of figures. 'Is Mr Baxterhouse here?'

The man looked up. 'He's at the tavern just down the road.'

William Baxterhouse was having a drink and using his charm on the lieutenant of a Royal Navy vessel that was about to sail from Ireland with two pinnaces on board—pinnaces built, in fact, by the Baxterhouses. His best and most discreet way out of Dublin was as a civilian passenger aboard this ship, but the lieutenant was lukewarm about the prospect.

Eyeballing the officer, William put his glass down. 'Look, Mr Johnson, it's easy. You take me to New South Wales. I'm an experienced boatbuilder who wants to report on how my pinnaces perform on the voyage.' William rapped his fingers on the table. 'It's to the Navy's advantage and ours if we understand how they can be improved under real conditions at sea.'

'Against regulations, sir. We can't take on another civilian.'

'Come, I'm not just any passenger, my friend. I have links with the Navy. And you have a vacancy on board the *Defiant*. You gave a berth to a man going to New South Wales, and now he's fallen ill.'

'He's forfeited the fare for his passage.'

'So he has, Mr Johnson, and now you can tell your captain that I'm taking his berth at the last minute, therefore at a discount. And I'll pay the remainder to you on the quiet.' William smiled. 'You'll be richer and the Navy none the wiser.'

It never ceased to amaze William what debt could do to people. In February, William had tendered for supplying ten pinnaces for the Royal Navy and the young naval officer vetting the bids had been the Jack Johnson with whom he was now bargaining. Back then, Johnson had been short of cash to pay a gambling debt. William had paid what the officer owed, won the contract and supplied the ten eight-oared craft, two of which were now on the *Defiant*.

The lieutenant paused for a moment. 'I can't do it, Mr Baxterhouse.'

The boatbuilder pulled his chair nearer and leaned closer. 'You will do it, my friend, even if I have to reposition your facial features.' He grinned. 'I wouldn't mind doing that. You can take a beating and succumb, as they all do . . . or, keep your face as it is and I write to your flag officers and enclose the receipt I paid for your debt. On any reckoning, after your dishonourable discharge you'll be fighting the waterfront beggars for scraps.' More silence, and Baxterhouse was about to get up.

Johnson said, 'Our ship sails at sunset. Have your trunk at the dock. The wherry will take you out.'

'Good man.'

It was short notice, but William had all he needed and was ready. He stood up. 'I'll see you on board.' He put on his hat and left.

John walked up to the tavern. A barrel-access door stood open on one side and he stepped in, looked around and went up to the bar. He had no idea what Baxterhouse looked like, so he'd have to ask questions that might bring him face-to-face with the man—but John was angry and past caring about anything except punishing Baxterhouse.

'I'm looking for a Mr Baxterhouse,' John said to the barman. John eyeballed the man. Baxterhouse could be here and the barman was protecting him or the man just wasn't in the tavern.

'You've just missed him.' The barman turned and served another patron.

John's tension sank for a moment. He hadn't eaten all day, and hunger gnawed at him. He paid for and ate a meal and went to leave. Near the door he passed a lone drinker.

'Hey, big fella, you want to know about Baxterhouse?'

John turned and faced the wiry stranger. 'Do you know him?'

'Depends.' The man looked down at his empty glass and back at John. 'It's a hot day.' John returned with two ales and sat down. His fellow drinker brought his chair close. John had smelled everything on his father's farm but what filled his nostrils now was beyond words. 'He's a regular here. I hate the bastard, true. He sacked my brother for stealing from him but I can't touch him. I tell you, I'll see him hurt, if it kills me.'

John didn't care whether the man was telling the truth or not. 'What does he look like?'

'He's a gentleman, dresses fine, good looking.'

'Hair?'

'Black and straight.'

'Height?'

'About five foot nine and solid. Be careful, friend. He's a fighter.'

'A gentleman fighter? That's odd.'

'He is, bare-knuckle.' The man sipped his beer. 'But you're a giant.' He touched his forehead. 'It looks like you've had a round or two yourself. You'll give him a go.'

John had broken skin in scuffles during his apprenticeship. He would have Baxterhouse all right. John's ship sailed at seven that night. He needed to catch up with Baxterhouse beforehand. 'You saw him here?'

'Aye. He was deep in talk with an English naval officer.'

'Did you hear anything?'

'Too noisy, but I know the officer. He's the first lieutenant on the *Defiant*, name's Johnson. She's at dock now. Got the feeling Baxterhouse wanted something out of Johnson.' The man of odours finished his beer. 'Look son, that's it. If I've been a help to ya, then that's one step closer to nailing the bastard.'

John thanked the man and left some change on the table. His time in Ireland was running out.

~

Maureen was fighting for her life, her arms punching the air. Then she woke to the sounds of a trolley. She lay back, panting.

'Tea, love?' the sister asked.

Maureen nodded, took the cup and drank. It was good. 'Sorry, sister. Another nightmare.'

'Happens often here. The matron says you need watching. I'll help you. I've just started my shift.' She smiled and moved on.

Maureen sank back on the bed. On each side of her head the invisible vice grips were easing. Her head throbbed less, but between her thighs was still painful. Maureen shivered. It all came back to her—in the summer sunset, raped in her bedroom by her landlord. Tears came to her eyes.

~

John returned to Mayor Street ready to confront Baxterhouse. He would face him, demand that he admit his crime and if not, then John would beat him to a pulp. Then what? How could he prove the man's guilt to the police? He himself might be arrested for assault, and never be able to leave Ireland. What would that do but increase Maureen's pain, and that of the family?

The same clerk faced him. 'Back again, sir? Found the boss?' John just stared at him. 'Did you hear me?'

John's anger boiled again. 'Is Baxterhouse here?'

'It's *Mister* Baxterhouse and no, he's not here. But as you want him bad, leave your name and I'll tell him you came. Is it business?'

If John revealed that it was personal, the man's employees would warn him. 'I'll come back tomorrow.' John turned and left, shaking from head to foot with barely controlled rage.

~

'She's better, Mr Leary,' the matron said. 'Not a bad night, with the laudanum helping her. You can see her.'

John went into his sister's ward and Maureen welcomed him with a half-smile. He went to her. 'You're looking better. Did you sleep at all?'

'Yes, Johnny, I did. What about yourself? I was going to take the afternoon off school, to see you to the boat. And look at me, bedridden. But never fear, I'll be up tomorrow.'

She was putting on a brave face for him and he loved her for that. 'I wish I wasn't going and leaving you like this. But my ship sails tonight.'

A shadow settled on her face. She sat up and John helped her with the pillow. Maureen drew breath. 'What a voyage it'll be! How did you find the money for the passage?'

'I'm going assisted.'

'Ah, the full fare is so expensive. But you'll gripe sailing steerage.'

'There's no cash to spare. Da would have had to sell land to raise enough for the full fare.'

Maureen looked out the window. 'Does he ever speak about me?'

'No.' He saw her look of pain and burst out, 'It's not right for you to suffer so, Maureen. You *can't* let him get away with it!'

Maureen looked at him. 'Da?'

'No, Baxterhouse! Miss Forde told me what he did to you.'

Her eyes flashed. 'She had no right to tell you and I don't want to talk about it.'

John didn't understand. Maureen had always been a fighter, like him, and here she was just giving up. 'You must tell the police and make the bastard pay. I'll back you up. They'll have to take your word.'

'I'll do nothing and neither will you.'

'But you have to, Maur. It's—'

'He could get back at me. I need my job.' She lifted her chin. 'Johnny, I mean it. This is to stay with us. And Da must never know.'

'But it's unjust. That man gets to go free.'

Maureen shut her eyes. 'I don't want people knowing what happened to me. I'll deal with that man—my way.'

'How?'

She opened her eyes. 'Just leave it to me. Is that clear?'

He knew he had no time left to change his sister's mind. 'Yes, but I do so, very reluctantly.'

'Now, go back to the house and get my Colin's gold watch. It's no use to me, the big heavy thing. It's on the top of my bedroom bureau. I want you to have it, but don't you dare lose it—'

'Maureen, please.'

'God knows you might. If you do, remember it's inscribed on the back with "C.M.". Lock the house and leave the keys with Jane.'

She leaned over and John gently embraced her. 'I'll be all right. Now, off you go, with my blessing.' Her eyes filled and he kissed her on the cheek knowing he'd miss her terribly.

John left the hospital, torn between frustration and sorrow. At Maureen's house he searched for the watch. It wasn't on or in the bureau and he didn't have time to look anywhere else. The hall clock showed five-thirty; he should have been on the dock at five. He left the house and dropped the keys off at Miss Forde's place nearby. Jane told him not to worry; she'll look after Maureen.

At the docks, the Anna Liffey raised his spirits. Its water reflected the outlines of the buildings above as an easterly filled with sea air cooled the crowded docks. Sobs and cries competed with the screeches of the gulls as loved ones said their farewells around him.

He soon found his ship, the *Spirit of Dublin*. Easing his way through the crowd, John completed the formalities, then sat down on a bench and looked downstream. A warship departing under gentle sail caught his eye.

A merchant seaman joined him, squatting on a mound of rope. 'Good to see the arse end of that, eh?'

'Aye, English warship, isn't she?'

'You're a country lad, I'm guessing, and you guessed right! That's the *Defiant*, on East India convoy duty.'

John's memory jolted back to the conversation in the tavern. 'A naval vessel . . . where is she bound?'

'I'd put money on New South Wales.'

John gazed at the warship. The *Defiant*. Baxterhouse had been talking to a naval lieutenant on that ship. Why, he wondered.

'All aboard, last call,' came a voice from a loud hailer.

John walked to his ship, still thinking about Baxterhouse and the *Defiant*? What was their connection? A thought suddenly occurred to him—could Baxterhouse be on board the *Defiant?* Was he fleeing a possible prosecution for his rape of Maureen? Was he not so confident she wouldn't report his crime?

CHAPTER TWO

Leaving Dublin behind, the Plymouth-bound ship cleared St George's Channel while John Leary slept soundly. Now unprotected from a lee shore, the rollers of the Irish Sea thumped against the ship. During the night the weather changed: the banging sound of the shutters was precursor to a storm. Hands shortened sail. Rigging groaned as waves, springing up from grey-green plates of water, smashed against the side. John pulled his blanket closer, turned his back on the maelstrom and went back to sleep.

'Better move there, matey,' a sailor nudged him awake. 'Grub's up.'

The gale had subsided and the ship had returned to a steady roll. Porridge was served and John ate with appetite.

On the companionway the first mate brushed past him and hailed the passengers. 'Scilly Isles are dead ahead. Plymouth the day after tomorrow.'

'Sir,' John enquired, 'can you tell me if you've seen another ship?'

'No, my big fellow, with the gale last night, no sight of anything.'

The answer was disappointing. Surely, the *Defiant* had weathered the same gale? John had little knowledge of ships, but he thought that the *Spirit of Dublin* should have caught up with her. Disturbed, he went topside to the bow to think. He loathed having left Maureen. Would Miss Forde help her, as she'd promised? Would she get justice for her friend? Would she be able to keep her safe from Baxterhouse if he was still in Dublin? How he wished he'd been able to get his hands on him. He would one day, he swore.

Plymouth harbour was crowded. After completing formalities, John set out to explore. He had five hours before his ship, the *Emily*, sailed for New South Wales. Everything stamped Plymouth as a naval port. Ships' chandlery was abundant and the taverns beckoned. Shops overflowed with foodstuffs, and the streets were thronged with transports and carts, urchins, seamen and animals. John took his time exploring and then, protected from the passing parade, counted his money. He had enough to last the voyage, thanks to his mother's supplement and what he'd saved—he could afford a pint and a pork pie.

After eating, he took a stroll and came upon a gang of Royal Navy sailors. 'Do you happen to know the *Defiant*?' John said.

One sailor looked up. 'She's a ship of the line, ain't she?'

'I think so, just out of Dublin.'

'Well, if she's that, then Plymouth won't see her. The Gib will be her first call.'

'The Gib?'

'Gibraltar.'

'Oh. Thank you.' So the *Defiant* would be on a different course from his own.

All he could do was go and find his ship. The *Emily* was a three-masted two-decker. It was nothing fancy, but it would serve as home for the next four months or so. In the crowd he saw faces he recognised from Dublin but there were many strangers, some of them in fine clothes. Before he boarded the ship he was given a marker, worn at the neck to show on which deck he was housed.

Paint was peeling from some of the ship's woodwork. Despite the breeze, John's nose tweaked at the body odours as busy sailors going about their work added more activity to a crowded deck.

Well-dressed passengers were drinking glasses of wine, and John was about to approach one when he felt his elbow gripped.

'Steerage is this way, sir.'

John was about to reply when a young woman passed by. She was petite and dressed in high fashion, her arm entwined with that of a middle-aged woman. John caught her eye, just for a second, then stepped out of their way and as he did, the air lost the scent of stale waste and smelt like fragrant flowers.

He snapped at the sailor, 'What do you mean?'

The man let him go. 'I mean sir, that you belong in the steerage section, which is forward. Down the stairs.'

He preceded the sailor below decks and wondered who the lovely girl might be.

Darkness shrouded him, in contrast to the sunshine above. The trapped heat dampened his armpits and he recognised a musty smell . . . yes, tallow, regularly imported into Ireland. He took moments to focus and, when the gloom cleared, heads became visible—until an open porthole blinded his vision. Closing his eyes, he ran into someone.

'Steady there!'

'Sorry.'

John found a corner where he tried to stand, and cracked his head. The 'tween decks was bloody low he thought, rubbing his crown, especially for a man his height. Height was always going to be a hindrance here. Shapes dotted the space and a lamp illuminated a huddled group. Bunks became visible, laid out in a pattern, with screened sections for families, all arranged around an open space where people sat talking at benches and tables, some even laughing or singing.

He stumbled back to the person he'd bumped into earlier, a small middle-aged man. 'Excuse me, but are we stuck here the whole time?'

'Another young 'un seeking fame and fortune in the Antipodes? Donald Watkins is my name. Let me describe your floating palace, your commodious accommodation for the next four months. Keep doubled up that way and you be orright. Don't want to add another scar to that head of yours.'

John smothered a reply as Mr Watkins showed him the ins and outs of their surroundings, including the water casks, which had today's date stamped on each one. 'At least they will be fresh,' John said.

'They may all say the thirtieth of June,' his guide replied, 'because the water's not supposed to be older than the date of sailing—but I'll bet you a pound to a penny they have live stuff in them already. Now, give us a look at your ticket.'

Reading John's marker, he showed him to his bunk in the single men's quarters. John shook his head in disbelief. His bed for the next four months was just the width of his shoulders. Satisfied that the trunk underneath was his own, he followed his guide forward through an open door into an area filled with chamber pots.

'Men's,' his companion said. 'Women the other side. Bring plenty of paper with you. It's not so bad at the moment. They've just been cleaned.'

Watkins passed the segregated bath cubicles and climbed another ladder and once again John was forward in a section above the orlop deck where shutters were removed allowing the breeze to enter. 'Are all the passengers in this part of the ship?'

'No, this is for the assisted passengers. The paying passengers are up aft. The deck's just as low over their heads, but the accommodation's more spread out and they have different privies for their expensive behinds!'

John became irritated; he'd never had any choice but to travel steerage. He would have to make the most of it.

'Let's go and eat. I'll show you your mess table. Supper's up and it ain't bad.'

The messing area adjoined the accommodation section. The smell of soup and fresh bread rekindled his hunger. John farewelled his guide and squeezed between a mother and her children in a space lit by more lamps. He reached for a bread roll just as all talk stopped. His hand poised over his food as a voice came from the semi-darkness.

'Thank thee, Lord, for this food. May we be forever grateful.'

A loud noise made him jump again and he banged his sore head yet again.

'The Lord's given you long limbs, my friend, but don't fret.' His eating companion laughed. 'It's just the lines being cast off.'

John nursed his head and turned to face the source of this reassurance. 'I'm John Leary, from Kildare.'

'Luke Collins, Clare. I'm your mess captain.'

'Are you going to New South Wales, Mr Collins?'

Collins brought a bowl from under the table and reached for the ladle in the pot. 'No, Cape Town. I've family there and I'm going to make a new start. What about yourself?'

'New South Wales. There's building aplenty, I'm told.'

'Are you a tradesman?'

'Carpenter, yes.'

'Good lad. Just save a bit and don't spend too much on the ladies and the grog.' Collins addressed his soup.

'Thank you. Say, I haven't a bowl.'

Collins shook his head. 'Those officials, they never tell you everything. Lad, you're supposed to bring all your utensils. Tell you what, I've got a spare for the time being, until you can buy one from the ship. Here.'

John took Collins's offered bowl, thanked him and helped himself, as his eating companion turned to talk to another passenger. He gulped his soup, cleaned his bowl and wolfed down a thick stew. He then escaped topside to read. In the twilight, the *Emily*'s topsails were filling. Leaving the harbour, the ship cleaved into the Celtic Sea and he marvelled that somehow he'd got his sea legs without effort. Passengers crowded the aft section of deck, most of whom gazed back at the disappearing shore. John looked seawards. There was his future. Planting one foot for support he gripped the shrouds as he thought of Baxterhouse. Was he still in Dublin, going to New South Wales, Cape Town or elsewhere? What had that sailor said? The Gib?

God blast his soul! He punched the rigging in frustration and caught a movement of flashing colours passing close by.

A cry came from his left. 'Please catch it!'

John reached out over the water and snatched the object. He looked at his capture—a bonnet.

'Oh, thank you.'

John turned. There, screened from the steerage passengers by a rope, was the young woman he'd seen earlier. He walked to the barrier and held out the bonnet. 'You'll have to come and get it. I can't go any further.'

She moved with confidence across the swaying deck, to meet him and reclaim the bonnet. Just as he remembered; sharp blue eyes, nose a little thin but balanced by full lips. There was a birthmark high on her cheek—attractive, not scarring.

The young lady looked at him and blushed as he released the bonnet. She said, 'Thank you very much.'

John looked at her, then the bonnet. 'Very pretty.'

She smiled. 'Yes. It's a going-away present.'

'Well, goodbye.' John said and turned away.

'Wait.'

John turned, but having called him back, she seemed not to know what to say next.

'The lady you came on board with—is she about to join you?'

'No,' came the quick reply. 'That was my mother you saw and she is below. My name is Clarissa McGuire; may I know yours?'

John tried to place her voice. There was a Dublin lilt to it, for sure. She was a few paces away now, and he longed to step forward and join her, but the rope across the deck came between them. But for his father's penny-pinching, he'd be on that side of the rope, too, with the beautiful Miss McGuire in her tailored jacket and silk dress. He said abruptly, 'John Leary, steerage passenger.'

She looked puzzled at his tone. 'Well, Mr Leary, thank you once again. I'll keep you no longer.' With that she turned and walked aft.

John cursed his petulance. It wasn't her fault he was in steerage. He turned and headed forward, the book in his hand of no interest now.

Clarissa did not go below at once. She had sighted John the moment they'd boarded, and had felt drawn to him. A very tall man, somewhat awkward in his actions, and a country man by his dress, but with a neat appearance and handsome face, despite his scar. When she'd spotted him again on deck, she'd asked her mother to get her a shawl that she claimed she hadn't been able to find in the baggage—all in the hope of speaking to him alone.

She was glad that the introduction had been made, but distressed that he'd acted so poorly. Still, something told her he was worth another chance.

Her mother came up to her. 'I found it in no time, dear!'

Clarissa nodded and put it on. 'Thank you, Mother.' They strolled towards the lee side of the ship to escape the breeze. 'I'm looking forward to the milder Sydney winters. I may be able to wear my latest Paris dresses.'

Her mother shivered. 'So am I! We should go below. This breeze is too chilly. It's almost time for bed and it's been a long day.'

Clarissa had hoped she'd see Mr Leary again, but followed her mother to their compartment, where there was just enough room to house two smallish beds, separated by a chest of drawers. On top of the chest was a bowl filled with murky water. The lamp had been lit and the porthole opened.

Clarissa sat on her bed and started to undress. She noticed a chamber pot and laughed. 'At least there's some convenience.'

Her mother frowned. 'Really, Clarissa.' Clarissa smiled. Her mother loathed discussing bodily functions. When her mother was in bed, Clarissa turned out the light. 'Goodnight.'

But her mother was already asleep.

Clarissa woke in the night, terrified by a nightmare. Her nightgown was damp, her mouth was parched and her stomach ached. It was not because of the *Emily*—it felt nothing like seasickness.

Fierce bowel cramps sent her rushing to the chamber pot. Heavens! It must be either the water or the food. Returning to bed, she fell into a fitful sleep that did not last.

John slept well in his bunk amidships. A change in the watch woke him and he pushed off the covers. Grabbing his wash kit from his trunk, he headed forward, where an orchestra of snores and coughs greeted him. 'Good morning to you all as well,' he murmured. After relieving himself, he eschewed the baths and found a wash-deck pump installed behind the last cubicle. The scuppers had been opened to drain the water.

He stripped behind the bulkhead and used the pump. The water was cold and refreshing. It failed to lather, but it was enough to get him clean. After shaving he towelled himself and returned to his bunk, a new man.

He arranged his kit in his trunk so he could get access to all items. Besides his toolbox, four books and clothes there was his Ma's bag of home remedies. It brought back the night before he'd left, when she'd fussed over packing. John smiled; she'd be angry if she knew she'd forgotten the supper bowls. Shaking his head, he went topside. The sky was overcast and the air humid and still. *Emily* had all her canvas set.

John felt thirsty but he'd been told water was rationed.

Walking forward, he noticed the rope barrier where he'd spoken to Miss McGuire. He'd not made a good beginning there, and he hoped to be able to make amends. He was not of her class or breeding, but he told himself that that shouldn't bother him. It did, though. He turned back and bumped into Luke Collins, who smiled.

'Morning,' Collins said. 'Looks like we're in for it, muggy as hell.'

'Aye. Have you had your water ration yet?'

'Is that what you call it? I call it piss, even with the peppermint added. The captain, I'm thinking, got a bargain with those casks. The pots will be filled quicker than you can fart, with that lot going through you.'

John was about to reply when he saw Clarissa's mother talking with a ship's officer. She looked anxious. John walked up to the barrier to overhear.

'My daughter is very ill, Mr Jones,' Mrs McGuire said. 'She must have drunk or eaten something that disagreed with her.'

The ship's officer touched his cap. 'I'll see if the surgeon can look at her.'

The lady caught sight of John's looming figure and turned towards him. John couldn't resist the chance to help. He held the mother's gaze and tried to keep his voice gentle. 'Excuse me, Mrs McGuire, I have some very reliable medicine that my mother gave me for the voyage. Please allow me to help if I can. Is Miss McGuire feverish and does she suffer . . . you know . . . stomach pains?'

'Now, son,' Mr Jones said, 'let's leave this to the surgeon.'

John would not be put off. 'I'll get the medicine and bring it back here.'

Without waiting for a reply, he sped back down to his bunk, opened his trunk and grabbed the cloth bag of remedies. To his relief, Mrs McGuire was still there when he came back on deck. She was standing alone near the barrier, staring at the sea.

He approached and showed her a small bottle. 'Here, this is what I have. It's—' Out of the corner of his eye he saw Jones returning, with a severe expression.

At that moment, Clarissa appeared, leaning against the frame of the companionway. Mrs McGuire was alarmed. 'Clarissa! You shouldn't be out of bed.'

Clarissa moved forward, put out a hand in front of her . . . and fell. John pocketed the bottle, scrambled under the rope barrier and ran to her. He caught her just in time and lowered her to the deck.

Clarissa's mother cradled her head. 'Please help me carry her to her bed,' she said to both men.

Jones shook his head. 'Best not to move her. I'll get the surgeon, ma'am.' He walked away.

John didn't hesitate. He picked her up, Mrs McGuire led him below and he placed Clarissa on her bed in the compartment, where she lay with her eyes closed.

'Mrs McGuire,' he murmured, 'if I may be so bold as to give advice. Let your daughter drink only boiled water,' and he pulled out the bottle, 'with one teaspoon of this.'

Mrs McGuire frowned. 'We must *boil* the water?'

'Yes, for ten minutes. Let it cool and pour it into a clean boiled bottle. Then give it to her, mixed with the medicine. My family has used this treatment for generations, just for this sickness.'

Clarissa's mother looked sceptical. 'Thank you, but I'll consult the ship's surgeon before I make up my mind.'

'The lad's right.'

They both turned to the surgeon who came between them. He felt Clarissa's pulse and brow and looked up at her mother. 'How long has she been like this?'

'She's been sick through the night. Vomiting and . . .'

'Her bowels are deranged?'

'Yes, yes.'

'Has she taken any water?'

'Only from that glass by the bed.'

The surgeon stood up. 'Like I said, ma'am, the lad's right. Boil the water. We don't know why, but it seems to work.' He turned to John. 'What's in your bottle?'

'I think it has a variety of ginger root. It seems to work a treat when we have that . . . problem.'

The surgeon nodded. 'It's up to you, ma'am. But I'd back the boy's medicine.'

Mrs McGuire looked from the surgeon to John. 'I'll try your way, Mr . . . ?'

'Leary, Mrs McGuire, John Leary from Kildare.'

'Very well, Mr Leary. Leave the bottle.'

John gave it to her and left the cabin with the surgeon.

John didn't see Clarissa for four days. Late in the morning of the fifth, he'd had enough of idleness and reading poetry. The lack of physical work made him edgy, and the cramped conditions below deck added to his frustration. So he grabbed his toolbox and sought out the ship's officer. 'Mr Jones, I know about timber and I can use tools.'

'You can, can you?' the first officer grinned. 'How well can you use them?'

'Like Bernini with his chisels, sir.'

Mr Jones laughed. 'Right, I'll ask the carpenter, Mr Sheffield, if he needs a hand. There are always things to be fixed on a ship.'

Within an hour, John was in the space beyond the steerage area, using a block plane on a spare spar. If only the work gang in Kildare could see him doing an honest day's work in such a place. He said a short prayer that some of this hard work would be appreciated on the ship and make him wanted in the new colony. Success would bring money.

He began to sing to the rhythm of it. His voice was soft and full, cheering him further.

'You carry a nice note, Mr Leary.'

John dropped the plane on his foot and swore. He looked at Clarissa and grinned. 'I'm sorry. I didn't see you there.' She moved closer and he felt self-conscious. He touched his forehead. 'You're looking better. Was it my ma's medicine that did it?'

'I came to thank you for that.' She handed him the half-empty bottle of herbs. 'Yes, and the water, what a good idea. My mother insisted on it, against opposition. The captains don't like boiling it, worried their ships will go up in smoke.' She laughed, her teeth white. John smiled in return. She did look improved. Her face had better colour and her movements were lithe: signs of a healthy girl.

She said, 'You look like the ghost from the well, with all that dust over you. Why are you doing this?'

He became defensive. 'It passes the time and I'm keen to improve my skills.'

'Oh! You're a carpenter?'

'I am. What's wrong with that?'

Her eyes widened in surprise. 'My, Mr Leary, it's rude you can be at times.'

Again he'd stumbled. She was right, and he decided to control his temper. 'I should try not to be.'

She sat on a sawhorse and looked seawards. The *Emily* was on her best behaviour and the sky was a deep blue. Clarissa closed her eyes and breathed in the air. Opening her eyes, she found him looking at her. She didn't look away. 'Indeed, for if you're going to respond that way to every question you don't like, you'll make few friends on this voyage.' The sides of her mouth turned up as if concealing some joke.

John's smiled back, but wondered whether she was laughing at him. Nonetheless, she had come looking for him. 'You're right. It's good of you to visit here. I'm sorry, I've got work to do.'

She rose. 'You have, and I must go. Can you come to the barrier after dinner sometimes?'

'The barrier,' he murmured. 'It'll be always there.'

She turned away. 'Please yourself.'

'Wait! Yes, I'd like to come.'

She was not smiling but she wasn't frowning either. 'I'll see you, then.'

When John had filed the holes for the braces on the last spar of the day, he picked up his tools and went below to his second task. Armed with a coping saw, drill and hammer, he started cutting a section for a replacement bulkhead. All the while he thought about Clarissa and the irritating mixture of attraction and unease he felt with her. In his part of the ship, living so close together tended to break down barriers between people. No one seemed to care about differences in their backgrounds. John could see that they mingled to overcome the boredom. But once they were on land again the lines of social difference would be drawn again.

He put down his saw and prepared nail holes with timber plugs. The difference between him and Clarissa was even greater. Her way of speaking, her dress and above all her mother's manner, all indicated wealthy middle class. The Learys were not poor, but they could never be considered country gentry. Somehow, everything he said to her made him feel even more of an awkward country fellow. If he'd paid full passage, would he still feel this difference with her? Yes, he would. He shook his head to concentrate on the job in hand, and two hours later asked the ship's officer and carpenter to look at his work.

Mr Jones examined the bulkhead. 'It's good, Mr Leary. Mr Sheffield?'

Angus Sheffield inspected the work with a professional eye. 'It'll pass, Mr Jones.'

'Excellent,' the first officer replied. 'If you're up to it, Mr Leary, there's plenty more. Right, Mr Sheffield?'

The ship's carpenter smiled. 'I'll have this big lad busier than a beaver, sir.'

The first officer nodded. 'Be here after breakfast tomorrow, John.' He grinned. 'I suppose you'll want to be paid for all this.'

'I would.'

'I'll speak with Mr Sheffield about a fair wage. Let's talk in the morning.'

John felt satisfied. He cleaned up and went up on deck near the cow cage and chicken coop. There he heard his name called. Luke Collins and Donald Watkins were sitting on the deck with another man, ready to play cards.

'We need another hand,' Collins said. 'Sit yourself down John, next to Tom here.'

Tom Semrot nodded to John and dealt the cards. They played four hands. During that time they were surrounded by activity, while a cooper and his mate made new barrels. John felt lucky: he had work and cards to break the boring shipboard routine. What if there was something else that could break the barrier between steerage and the other passengers, raise spirits and loosen some laughter, even just for a few hours. A reckless idea came to him. A dance! That was it. There were plenty of young people for it, on both sides of the barrier. Yes, he would suggest it to the captain.

Semrot threw down his hand. 'That's me.' Semrot didn't like to lose.

'We should be at the Canary Islands tomorrow night,' John said. 'Reckon the captain should let us have some kind of celebration, for the whole ship?'

'The whole ship, eh?' Collins said shrewdly.

John studied his hand and it was his turn to deal. The others looked at him.

'Seen you talking with Miss McGuire,' Tom said at last. 'Like her, don't you?'

John looked at the man's leering face. 'What's it to you, Tom?'

'Now John,' Collins said, 'don't get upset, and Tom, don't be asking rude questions of the lad.'

Semrot continued to leer. 'She might come looking for you, but she's way above your station. She's a Dublin toff, related to the Fitzgeralds.'

John rearranged the cards in his hand. 'Who I keep company with is my business.'

'She sees you as fun,' Semrot continued. 'But d'you think if you were walking by the Anna Liffey she'd say good day to you?'

John became furious. 'If it's a fight you want, I'll have you. Just leave the girl out of this.'

Tom's eyes opened wide and his mouth twitched. 'Hang on! I'm not out to fight you, Leary. You're too big for me—me and my game leg.'

Everyone around them stopped working or talking and John realised he was in a foolish position, challenging a weakling. 'All right then, but hold your tongue.'

They finished the game in silence.

'Come with me, John,' Collins said as he packed away the cards. 'I want to talk to you.'

John stood up and followed him to the ship's side.

'Tom's a simple man and, because of his leg, he's an unhappy one. Don't worry about him.'

'I won't,' John replied.

'You've no kin on board and I've a liking for you. You're a good lad. So here's a word of caution.'

John folded his arms. 'And what have you got to say?'

Collins grinned. 'Now, don't be like that. I want to save you from making a fool of yourself. Miss McGuire—'

'What about her?'

'She's a nice young lady, but this is a sea voyage. It will have an ending and then things will go back to what they were. She to hers, you to yours. Don't get too deep with your feelings.'

'Not you, too! She and I have spoken for a few minutes! That's all.'

Collins looked at him for a time. 'If that's all, then good.'

John lost patience and moved away. 'I'm going to see the captain. I'll say good day, Mr Collins.'

John got permission to go aft, and requested a word with the captain, and Mr Jones escorted him. It felt grand to be addressing the captain face to face. 'Excuse me, sir. I would like to talk to you about something. Is now convenient?'

'Your name again?'

'Leary sir, John.'

'Ah yes, our new carpenter.'

'Sir, I thought, you know, with the good weather and all and with the Canary Islands near, we might, well . . .'

'Get to it, lad.'

'Well, sir, I'm thinking of a dance or a social gathering.'

The captain threw a glance at Jones and smothered a smile. 'Is this your own idea?'

'It is sir, something to break the routine, get people into the fresh air. Keep people's spirits up, you know.'

The captain and Jones moved away from John, and were soon deep in conversation. After a few minutes, the captain walked away to stand by the rail, and Mr Jones came over.

'The captain has given the all clear. It'll be tomorrow night. Now, you're expected to put in some good work for this, Leary.'

'That I'll do, sir.'

Invitations went round the ship. On the Saturday afternoon, many volunteers chipped in to help. The deck was cleared. Rigging was festooned with bunting and tables set. The cook's special punch was laced with rum. Everyone either got involved or looked on.

John was tying a lantern to the rigging when Clarissa came up to him with her mother. 'Mr Leary, what a grand idea! A dance in mid-July.'

'Aye.' He smiled at her and greeted her mother, but somehow didn't dare to say more.

A space was made for the orchestra: a drum, two fiddles and a washboard. Dusk settled in and eager people went below to prepare for the festivities.

Clarissa put on her favourite ball dress. She was determined to dance with John Leary, but she knew her mother wouldn't approve. Clarissa couldn't help liking him. The way his eyes twinkled when she got him to smile! He could be abrupt . . . no, rude . . . at times, but underneath she sensed a softness that he didn't want to reveal. She made her final adjustments to her toilette and went up on the deck.

A surprise greeted her—perfumes overlaid the usual smells of the ship, and laughter and music filled the air. If she closed her eyes, she could imagine she was at a Dublin society ball. This was grand! People were milling about, chatting and smiling, for tonight the barrier was removed. Two brave couples were already dancing to a jig. Clarissa moved through the groups, acknowledging greetings and stopping to chat.

John watched her from the sidelines. This reminded him of Dublin too, where he and Clarissa McGuire could never have expected to meet. He was an assisted immigrant, bound for God knew what in Sydney. He didn't know what kind of work he might do there. He was supposed to be enjoying himself, but for some reason his thoughts kept turning to the wounded sister he'd left behind, and William Baxterhouse. Was he still in Dublin or on the *Defiant,* bound for Gibraltar? Thoughts of how to avenge Maureen preoccupied him.

Lost in turmoil and frustration, he didn't hear Clarissa's first hello. He felt a tap on his shoulder and whirled around, ready to take on the world.

Clarissa stepped back in alarm. 'Mr Leary, what's wrong? You look awful.'

'I'm all right, thank you,' he said abruptly.

'I don't think you are. Are you ill? You're perspiring!'

'No, no, I'm just...thinking.'

'And you don't believe I can share those thoughts?'

He shuddered. 'No. I'm sorry. After the next dance, may I ask you to dance? Will you permit me?'

'Very well.' Clarissa sighed and walked away.

John watched her go and took a deep breath. He had the whole voyage to think about Baxterhouse! He would have some punch, banish his funk and try to have some fun. He needn't take it too far with Clarissa McGuire. Collins had advised friendship only. Surely he could achieve that?

Twenty minutes later, John was laughing at a funny story Luke Collins was telling, his black mood gone. He was on his third glass of the punch and looked across the now crowded deck. Clarissa was looking at him with interest as he approached her before the next dance. That look made him think. Was she really concerned for him? If she was, then it was nice to know. 'Evening, Mrs McGuire. Miss Clarissa.'

'Good evening, Mr Leary,' Mrs McGuire said. 'It is certainly a fine night.'

'That it is. Mrs McGuire, may I ask Miss Clarissa for a dance?'

'It's up to Clarissa.'

Clarissa smiled. 'Thank you, Mr Leary.'

They walked to the centre of the dance area and John was conscious of eyes upon them. Stopping, he bowed and put one tentative hand on Clarissa's waist. His left hand held her gloved hand and he waited for the beat. Confidence flowed through him. His parents had always loved music, and dances were a big thing in his farming community, so dancing was something that came naturally to him.

Familiar faces around him smiled their greetings and he enjoyed having Clarissa in his arms. She was a good dancer, too.

'Mr Leary, just a while ago you seemed not well at all. Are you all right now?'

'Thank you, yes.' He searched for a subject. 'Have you left other family and friends back in Dublin? I'd like to hear about them.'

She smiled. 'If I may hear about yours in return!'

He agreed, vowing to himself not to mention Maureen or any of the disharmonies in his family. In fact, if he kept asking her questions, he needn't get onto the subject of his family at all.

They danced four more reels, which he enjoyed, then he made way for an officer who requested a dance with Clarissa.

The breeze was constant and balmy and the *Emily* skipped along under topsails. In the shadows near the rail, John stood looking out to sea. His head was full of the talk with Clarissa, his eyes mesmerised

by the phosphorescence on the wake. He was now glad to be bound for Sydney. He felt as if his course was set. He would make a new life there as a builder, and he was thrilled to think of everything that that might bring him.

Clarissa's dance with the officer was over. She rejoined her mother and looked around for John. 'Have you seen Mr Leary?'

'He's nowhere in sight and that's a good thing, in my view. I think you've seen enough of him tonight. We shall go below.'

'But Mother, the night's young! Please!'

'Below, Clarissa. Come.'

Clarissa took a long time to go to sleep that night. She'd enjoyed dancing with John. The feelings she got when he was holding her were ones she'd not forget. A mixture of security and excitement that was quite intoxicating. She wanted to be held in his arms again.

At mid-morning a pilot guided the *Emily* into Tenerife. The passengers were cheerful at the prospect of having fresh fruit and water, and time off the ship. Clarissa confronted her mother with an announcement she'd been turning over in her mind all morning. 'For the rest of this voyage, I intend to speak courteously to John Leary, whenever I wish.'

'So, it's *John* now, is it?' Her mother sighed. 'That ranks with informality and you will do no such thing. Mr Leary is not for you.'

Clarissa was not to be moved. 'Mr Leary is a fellow passenger, mother. I'm bound to see him from time to time.' She paused and prepared herself for a lie. 'It may develop into a friendship, but that's all.'

'A friendship? I don't think so. I saw the way you danced with him. Friends don't dance four dances in a row. I was embarrassed for you, but I didn't want to draw more attention to your behaviour by intervening. I will not have you showing partiality to that man.'

Clarissa pressed her lips together and counted up to five. Her resolve was firm, but it was fruitless to fight her mother's convictions outright. 'I'm ready to go ashore.'

'Of course. You'll accompany me.'

'I'm not meeting him there, if that's your concern.'

Her mother relaxed somewhat. 'Excellent. I want to see the sights and it will be good to stretch our legs on dry land. Come on.'

~

Two weeks out of Tenerife, the *Emily* pounded along. John, hard at work on deck, revelled in the exhilaration of the bow crashing into the sea, sending out sheets of spray. The equator was near and the weather was hot, though in the evenings there was a welcome cool breeze.

John felt wetness between his shoulder blades as he repaired a rack for the belaying pins. Nearby was the cow pen. Laying down his tools, he looked at the mournful animal. 'You poor, weak thing. Spending twenty-three hours a day cooped up. You should be out on a farm with grass under your feet.'

He hadn't seen Clarissa since the ship had left Tenerife. He had the feeling her mother was preventing her from seeing him, so he never lingered long at the barrier. Still, he went there every day.

But today was different. She was there, within speaking distance, and alone. He was glad. 'Good day, Miss McGuire.'

There was no smile and she glanced behind her. 'I haven't much time. Mother will be here shortly.' She drew nearer to him so they were both standing beside a bulkhead—within touching distance. He was surprised and thrilled. 'Tell me about yourself.' She smiled more openly now. 'I didn't learn a great deal about *you* at the dance! Now you owe me answers to some questions. I know you're a carpenter, but not from Dublin. Where, then?'

'Kildare. A farm near Kilcullen.'

'So your family are farmers?'

'We run a dairy herd, on one hundred acres of our own land.'

Clarissa's eyed widened. 'That sounds unusual to me.'

'What, the herd or the tenure?'

She looked serious. 'I know little of farming. But I hear most farms are leasehold, and there's great suffering in the country because most of the land is in potatoes, and they're failing.'

John smiled at her. 'None of that for us. So you see, the Learys are someone.'

She said with mischief, 'Ah, that's important to you, isn't it?'

He felt she touched on a raw nerve, but she was smiling. He said evenly, 'It's important to your mother, I sense that.'

Clarissa seemed on alert again. 'Ah, yes, my mother. I must go, before she catches me out, gallivanting on deck! But I hope we'll meet again?'

'If you want to.'

'Of course—I have so many more questions to ask.' She smiled and walked away.

John watched her go, and wondered if her playful interest was real. If it was, could he keep this to a friendship? He went below to have his meal and then came back on deck again, though she wasn't there. The stuffiness of 'tween decks had begun to stifle him.

~

Mrs McGuire closed the door to their cabin and folded her arms. 'Have you seen him since the dance?'

Clarissa knew she meant John and she wouldn't lie. 'I have, but I see a lot of people. It's a small ship, if you haven't noticed.'

'I won't have sarcasm, thank you. Did you speak with him just now?'

Clarissa berated herself for her rudeness. She had to keep her mother on her side but would keep certain facts to herself. 'Just in greeting.'

'That is more than sufficient.'

'You still think him beneath me?'

'I do.' Her mother sat down on her bed. 'We know nothing about him, dear. His breeding is unacceptable and his behaviour another matter altogether.'

Clarissa stood her ground. What John had told her about his family hadn't indicated poverty, and his conversation was intelligent. 'That's a prejudiced view.'

'Don't be impertinent. You are your father's daughter, there's no doubt about that, and you have his wilful qualities. I won't discuss this further.'

As Clarissa and her mother prepared for bed that night, she thought about how to see John again. What was this feeling she had for him? Might it be just a short-lived attraction? Her mother was right about one thing; they didn't know a lot about him and maybe he had some faults—some big ones. He might even be prone to violence; that scar wasn't a good sign! Perhaps it would be best not to see John for a while, and then see how she felt when they met again.

~

John was standing at the rail with Luke Collins as a sailor took the log beside them. John turned to his friend. 'Well Luke, it's nearly the end of August and the voyage is half over.'

'Aye, it is and Cape Town must be near.' Collins patted him on the shoulder. 'And you've rebuilt half the ship it seems.'

John grinned. 'Well, maybe not half. But there are spars, cabin partitions and deck repairs, all done to the highest quality of Kildare tradesmanship.'

'Go on with you.'

'True. Ask Mr Sheffield or even Mr Jones if you don't believe me. He's right behind you.'

The first officer touched his cap and smiled. 'Morning, gentlemen. I heard my name mentioned. I hope it wasn't in vain?'

'Not at all, sir,' Collins said, 'but this lad boasts of his work and I want to hear your views.'

'Put your mind at ease Mr Collins. It's all good.'

John swelled with pride. There was only one thing that would make this morning better—talking with Clarissa. He hadn't spoken to her for so long. She was avoiding him, he could tell. Because of her mother?

'You might offer this man a job,' Collins said to Jones, 'permanent, like, in the merchant marine.'

'I think Angus Sheffield may have a say on that! And it's New South Wales he's making his home. That's right, Mr Leary?'

'That's it Mr Jones. Sydney.'

'Land ahoy, off the port quarter!' the lookout shouted above them.

'The Cape!' Collins said.

They were joined at the rail by other passengers who chattered away excitedly. In the next five hours the *Emily* warped into Cape Town harbour, which was crammed with ships. John asked for the telescope from Mr Jones and looked at one group of ships in particular. He turned to the first officer. 'Is that a naval convoy over there?'

'Yes, those are all supply ships, except the one on the end. I recognise her: she's an English warship, the *Defiant*.'

The *Defiant*! What if Baxterhouse were on board? As John returned the telescope to the first officer, all his revengeful thoughts about the man who'd raped his sister crowded back into his brain. He'd get on land as soon as he could. If Baxterhouse was in Cape Town, he'd hunt him down.

CHAPTER THREE

LUKE COLLINS SHOOK JOHN'S HAND. 'GOODBYE. I KNOW YOU'LL GO all right in New South Wales. You're a likely lad with a bright head and a kind heart.'

John gripped Collins's hand as his friend of only weeks prepared to disembark in the late afternoon. They had become close in the *Emily's* confines and he would miss him. 'Thank you. Good luck to you as well.'

The *Emily* started the task of victualling. All manner of foodstuffs were brought on board, including new casks of fresh water. In the background, Cape Town and Table Mountain entranced him—but he'd explore them another day. In the warmth of a fading winter sun his gaze drifted from the mountain to the *Defiant.* He decided to snoop.

Standing behind a tree near the wharf, John looked at the warship's decks, which were deserted except for a crew repairing a foremast spar and a sentry. Could Baxterhouse be a passenger? John moved onto the dock and caught the eye of the sentry.

'Afternoon.' The sailor nodded to him. 'Can you tell me if William Baxterhouse is on board this ship?'

The sailor was about to reply when an officer approached. 'And who might you be, my tall young man?'

'John Leary, sir, from the *Emily*.' John chastised himself; he should have used another name.

'We're not permitted to release names of passengers to the public. I'm sorry, Navy rules.'

This might be the officer who'd met Baxterhouse in the Dublin tavern! 'Are you a lieutenant?'

'I am. One of three on this ship.'

So it mightn't be the officer. 'Is your name Jack Johnson?'

The other man stiffened. 'Lieutenant Johnson, to you, sir. State your business, please.'

'Where is William Baxterhouse?'

Both the lieutenant and the sentry were glaring at him now. If Baxterhouse was on their ship, they seemed ready to protect him. And now Johnson knew John's name, he could warn him, too.

Johnson's mouth firmed in a straight line. 'If you have legitimate business with the Navy, sir, please report to the offices at the end of the dock. And since you've none with *Defiant*, I must ask you to leave. Now.'

John walked away, seething. If Baxterhouse was on the *Defiant*, he'd never get at him while he was on board. What did Johnson's reaction tell him—that Baxterhouse was in Cape Town, and he was protecting him? He couldn't be sure. All he could do was spend the day in town, see the recommended sights and meanwhile keep his eyes open in case William Baxterhouse was ashore doing the same things. He'd go to the post office and mail a letter to Maureen and others to the family—those he felt like corresponding with. Maybe he'd come across Clarissa McGuire and her mother in town. He gave a bitter smile. Probably as likely as finding Baxterhouse . . .

Much later, he gazed at the harbour from the *Emily*'s deck. Lights twinkled everywhere and the fresh evening breeze blew inland against his cheek. It had been an interesting but tiring day. Frustrating, too, for he'd spent it alone and made no discoveries in the streets of Cape Town. Suddenly the dark shapes of a line of ships caught his attention, and to his dismay he spied the *Defiant* amongst them. He swore.

The friendly voice of Mr Jones came from behind him. 'That's a thundering great oath on such an evening Mr Leary! It can't be against the weather.'

John turned. 'Your pardon. No, it's not. Are we still due to sail the day after tomorrow?'

'Aye, on the twenty-sixth, if this breeze behaves.'

Well behind the *Defiant* . . . John suppressed another oath.

John woke at dawn the next day and took his shower at the wash-deck pump. He shivered at the first drops, cursing that though it was August, he was now in winter. After breakfast, he hoisted his toolbox and two sheets of timber and went to the skylights amidships. There he set to work making new storm shutters to cover the glazed frames, concentrating on the measuring and fixing to ensure squareness and watertightness.

During the first hour, Baxterhouse came to mind but John forced him away. He would get his punishment, John hoped. Meanwhile, doing good work on the ship and then getting himself a job in Sydney were more important. If the captain, Mr Jones and Mr Sheffield were satisfied, he would ask them for a reference. The hours passed and he finished securing the last of the brass hinges to the shutters just as Angus Sheffield came up to him.

'Looks good, Mr Leary.'

'Thank you. Could I ask a favour?'

'Aye.'

'Could you go below and stand beneath the storm shutters? I'm going to pour water over them so you can check to see if there are any leaks.'

'I was going to suggest that very thing. I'm on my way.'

John filled three pails of seawater and gave Sheffield time to get below before flinging the water over his work.

When Sheffield returned he said, 'Drier than a desert in Arabia.'

'Just have to varnish them now.'

'I'll get that seen to. You've done enough.'

John packed his tools and cleaned up. Later, after supper, he went on deck in the cool of the evening breeze. He stood alone by the barrier, thinking of Clarissa. Would she ever come up again and speak with him? He longed for her company.

~

William Baxterhouse counted the money from his gambling sprees in the hotels of Cape Town. Pushing the notes into his pocket, he made his way to the captain's cabin, smirking. What easy pickings! In two days he had cleaned up with tricks he'd never have got away with in Dublin. He knocked at the captain's door.

'Come.'

Heat swamped him as he entered and he squashed himself into the small space; the captain's penchant for candles added to the haze. Perspiration filmed on William's forehead as he acknowledged the greetings from the officers, including Jack Johnson. So far the lieutenant had kept out of his way on board and shown him no special preferences, so no one thought they were connected. The captain invited William to sit down.

In front of him were baked chickens sitting like islands in gravy, lean slabs of lamb, their red centres stained in blood, baked potatoes, crisp vegetables and fine wines. 'Good evening, sir. It looks like the cook's been busy grabbing the best from Cape Town.'

'Indeed, Mr Baxterhouse. Make the most of it, because in the next ten weeks the fare will certainly pale. The next feast you'll see like this may be in Sydney.'

A young lieutenant on the captain's left asked. 'Sir, have you been to New South Wales?'

The captain smiled. 'Yes, Mr Fosdyke, my first visit was in '38, as a captain of a convict transport. Not an enjoyable passage. Tell me Mr Baxterhouse; was your stay in Cape Town fruitful?'

'It was indeed.' William glanced at the other officers who (not including Johnson) had been among his card victims on shore, and who were worse off as a result. He chuckled to himself.

'You're a deft card player, Mr Baxterhouse,' the first lieutenant said. 'I bet you make a good living out of your dexterity.'

William looked at the barrel-chested officer, who'd been suspicious of his run of luck that afternoon. 'It's a natural talent, Mr Walgrove. Happy to let you win your money back, any time.'

'Thank you, no sir. I know when I'm beaten by an . . . honest man.'

The implication was blatant and William, angry now, was about to reply.

'Now, gentlemen,' the captain said. 'The card game is over. Leave it there.'

'There was a man enquiring after you yesterday, Mr Baxterhouse,' Jack Johnson said. 'A tall young man. Does the name John Leary ring a bell?'

William felt very relieved that it didn't. 'No. What did he want?'

Johnson glanced at the captain. 'As ordered, I didn't tell Mr Leary you were on board.'

William went on with his dinner.

The captain said to him, 'I'd like to run the pinnaces when we get to calm waters. Mr Fosdyke will command one crew and Mr Johnson the other. We'll race them, and you, Mr Baxterhouse, can review their seaworthiness.'

'Thank you, Captain. I'll look forward to that. Now, I must thank you for a fine meal and take my leave.'

Clean air buffeted him as he closed the door behind him, a pleasant change from the stuffy cabin and its even stuffier occupants. Making his way back to his bunk, he thought about New South Wales. Money to him was everything and a solid cash flow was what he wanted, gleaned from a number of businesses, of which boatbuilding would predominate. He'd never return to those pride-sapping days he and his brother James had had to endure when the family's cotton business had collapsed. Or scrape and pinch pennies in Dublin trying to build a business against long standing and entrenched companies. Then there was Maureen

Murphy. Quiet she'd be, he was convinced of that. Her job and salary were more important to her than a forgettable tumble in bed. He thought of James again, younger than William by two years and dear to him. There'd be a place for his brother in the colony, but not until William had established himself.

The *Defiant's* captain had told him that land ownership and land occupation were the key to power in New South Wales. Owners of property were the men he needed to mix with; that's where a person could make money and have influence. With his boatbuilding expertise providing a steady profit and his gambling tricks making up the shortfall, life would be good.

As the *Emily* slipped out of Cape Town on the evening tide, John was alone on the port side. Two women came on deck, chatting. One of them reminded him of Bridget, a woman he'd been with only two days before he left Kildare for good. This young woman laughed, flashing white teeth, the moonlight outlining her full figure. As she grabbed her wind-blown hair, her breast rose and swelled against her blouse.

John turned around to face the sea. Clarissa's face appeared before him, the one he'd seen in his dreams. When she came to him in the middle of the night, he could feel her in his arms, her mouth on his.

He remembered Bridget. She was gentle, soft hands and Christ! Enough! He went below and slept and dreamed Bridget was in bed with him, grasping for him with her soft hands, but when his lips moved up from her breast the flushed face he saw was Clarissa's.

Three weeks on from Cape Town, life on board the *Emily* had settled down to the same monotonous patterns. During that time John continued to work, and now he was mending bunks.

He put down his saw to wipe his forehead and said to the man standing over him, 'Ten more to do, Mr Sheffield, and we're done.'

'When the officers aren't around, you can call me Angus. Been meaning to ask how you got that scar? Not in a fight?'

'No. A flying nail. Nearly took my eye.'

'It makes you look right menacing, though Miss McGuire don't seem to mind it.'

'No.' Angus was right. It didn't seem to worry her, and she was still prepared to talk to him. It didn't happen often—only three times in the last three weeks—and her mother had been there every time. He longed to be alone with her.

'Right, let's keep going,' Angus said. 'House the end of this.'

John slipped the tenon end, the narrowed point of the bunk rail, into the slot, the mortice. He checked the firmness of the completed joint then secured it with nails.

Angus examined the job and nodded. 'We'll make a master joiner of you yet.'

'I like the work.' John was glad the captain had agreed to keep paying him wages until journey's end. He would need every penny in Sydney.

Angus swept up the sawdust and chips into a neat pile. 'You'll get good work in the colony, I'll be bound.'

'I hope so. I'll have to put my mind to it.'

'And your body.'

John laughed.

Angus emptied the sawdust into a bag. 'Now take this topside and get rid of it. We'll kick off again tomorrow after breakfast.'

The ship picked up the roaring forties and these accelerated the *Emily*'s smooth passage. At a Sunday service the captain said it was 22 September—four weeks since they'd left Cape Town.

That same afternoon, John saw Clarissa alone on deck. Reassuring himself that her mother was nowhere close, he walked up to her and was greeted with a gracious smile.

'Well, Mr Leary, and to what do I owe this pleasure? From all I hear, you've been busy rebuilding this ship.'

John smiled in return. 'I have, but I'd rather be talking to you,

Miss McGuire. It's nice to see you alone. Your mother's been your shadow since Cape Town.'

Clarissa became solemn. 'My mother is not well. She's lying down.'

This may have been the reason Clarissa had stayed away from him. 'Is it bad?'

'No, thank you. I'm not seriously worried about her. I tell you though, I'm getting bored! I've read all my novels, written umpteen letters and discussed everything with every woman aboard. Even the gossip's so old it's got cobwebs.'

John laughed. How he'd missed her banter. It made it easier for him to ask personal questions. 'Do you like poetry?'

Her eyes widened. 'I do.'

'I have two books. A Coleridge and a Byron. Would you like to borrow them?'

'That would be grand, thank you.' She smiled again.

'I'll get them both to you. Next time I see you.'

She exclaimed, catching sight of a school of dolphins accompanying the ship. For a while they both leaned on the rail, entranced.

'Playful creatures,' Clarissa remarked.

'Yes, and the flying fish are beautiful.' John paused. He wondered whether they would ever have this easy kind of conversation once the *Emily* got to Sydney. 'When the voyage is over, what will you do in Sydney? How will you spend your time, Miss McGuire—apart from reading? Will you embroider? Give tea parties?'

His curiosity was genuine, but Clarissa frowned. 'I won't be doing any such thing. My father has a business there, and I want to help him in any capacity he may choose for me.'

John was startled. 'You told me he had a business, but I never thought you'd be working with him.'

'Why not? I was of great assistance to him in Dublin.' Clarissa turned from the sea and sat down on a nearby chair. John kept looking at the water.

She looked up at him quizzically. 'I'm not ashamed of hard work, and I don't think you are, either.'

'No. I'm content with what I do. I love to build and I will succeed.'

'Good,' she said. 'You like what you do. But sometimes I suspect you're not content with what you *are*.'

He became defensive. 'That's nonsense. I'm not ashamed of who I am. I'm travelling steerage but I don't have to. In fact, my family could have afforded to pay for my passage.'

'Forgive my inquisitiveness, but why didn't they?'

'My father wouldn't spare the cash. He thought sailing steerage would strengthen my character.'

She laughed lightly. 'And has it?'

He couldn't help smiling at her. 'I've been too busy to notice!' He gripped a shroud, looming over her, but she looked quite unintimidated. He teased her. 'But no doubt you're right. I'm a lowly body beside your social standing and wealth.'

Her smile faded. 'You know practically nothing about my background. How can you form such a picture of me?'

'I know enough to be sure your family wouldn't have struggled in the famine. Compared to most people, you have everything: money, power, all the food you can eat.'

'Yes, everything I've wanted all my life. Except life has not given me the one precious thing that I longed for: a little brother or sister.'

'Oh!'

'Yes, "Oh". You have a big family, I assume?'

He was still so surprised by her answer that he said at once, 'Aye, four brothers and a sister.'

'Gifts from God that were not granted to me. I always wanted a brother or a sister, someone to talk to and confide in. Are you close to your sister? You haven't mentioned her once.'

Thinking of Maureen, and reasons why he hadn't said her name, brought a tightening to his throat. 'Yes, she's very dear to me.'

'It seems she is.'

She is perceptive, John thought.

Clarissa kept her eyes on his face. 'And so, you'll understand that

I'll never know that kind of love.' She rose and stood close to him. 'Is there any money on earth that could buy me a brother?'

He wasn't sure how to answer. 'No . . . of course not.'

'Indeed. So you see, my *wealth* is of no use to me in that regard.' She paused and looked sad. 'You seem to dislike people like me. You do, don't you?'

Donald Watkins and another man walked by, and John waited until they had passed. Her question seemed very important to her. He had to be honest in return. 'If you want to put it that way, I suppose I do. Yes.'

She shrank back a little. 'Why?'

He struggled for an explanation. 'Well, they get everything they want without having to work for it.'

'My father worked for all the things he has. He didn't inherit anything! In fact—'

'But a lot of people do inherit. They can count on it. They belong to a certain class and—'

'We're talking about *me*, Mr Leary. My grandfather struggled in his ironworks business and my father left Dublin to build his own, from the ground up. Just like you want to do.' Clarissa sat back down. 'For anyone who has money, it does make things seem easier on the outside, but on the *inside* you and I are the same as anyone else. We have illnesses and worries; our parents make things difficult for us. We share other problems, too.'

This was too much. 'What problems? You don't have any problems.'

'If you're going to be rude, I'll go below.' She stood up and began to move away.

He reached over and took hold of her arm. 'I'm not being rude. I just want to understand. You say you and I are alike. That's not how it looks to me.'

She gazed at him, clear-eyed, as though they *were* equals.

It moved him. He let go her arm and said, 'Please, I'll listen.'

'A woman in my position has very little freedom to show her feelings, to talk frankly. But *you* can say what you like, when you like, and be glad doing it.'

'That's hardly true! The moment I talk frankly, you tell me I'm rude!'

'It's confusing, I know. I'm talking about my upbringing. I was raised to always say the right thing, not to offend anyone. Even with our close friends, we have to guard our behaviour. Talking freely is out of the question.'

'So you've grown up thinking like your mother.'

'Mr Leary, if you understood me at all, you wouldn't say that to me.'

He said in despair, 'Well, I *don't* understand you.'

She smiled. 'That might be the case, but if you were brought up like me, you would never have stated it so frankly. *Now* do you understand?'

Light dawned. 'Ah. I think so. But look at yourself. You're being wonderfully free with your thoughts right now—but you are of that class.'

'That class, that class. All right. That class, as you call it, has to conform to convention—and sometimes it strangles me. I'm supposed to follow the customs and behaviour of a well-brought-up young lady. Not to *think*, not to have a future other than marriage to someone I most probably won't love.'

She held his arm and gave him that clear-eyed look again. 'Don't judge all people with money the same way. We're *not* all the same. Do you understand that?'

'I think I do.'

Her face lit up. 'Mr Leary, I'm talking with you because . . . you're interesting.'

Interesting! That might have disappointed him, but he was surprised instead. 'I haven't heard myself described like that before.'

'I want to talk to you because what you do interests me; yes, as a *woman*. Is that so hard to understand?'

It was quite heady, all this frankness. 'It is. Very. I'm a builder. That's not usually interesting to a woman, especially one like you.'

She laughed. 'There you go, Mr Leary, with your prejudices again.'

John was amazed. Could she really be so different from what

he'd imagined? There had been clues. From the start of the voyage she'd never snubbed him. She'd danced with him. She wasn't scared of his scar and she'd chatted with him within earshot of the well-to-do passengers. He tested her. 'I thought . . . perhaps you were only polite to me because you were bored with being on ship. And being at sea away from your usual society—doesn't it give you a bit more freedom?'

Her eyes sparked with challenge. 'Then why, if I have so much freedom, haven't I been able to see you these past weeks?'

See him? She had wanted to see him! John was excited. 'You mean your mother prevented it?'

'Yes, sir.'

'But when you get to Sydney, won't you have to . . . conform again, as you say?'

She smiled, a cheeky smile. 'I'm expected to. But I won't.'

'You won't?' *Was she playing with him or was she encouraging him?*

She took a deep breath, as though she'd just run a race. It had certainly been one almighty conversation. 'I have to go below.' She half turned. 'But I'll try to see you again. That's if you want to see me?'

'Of course! And you're forgetting; I have to give you those books.'

She laughed and walked away.

Below, Clarissa found her mother still lying in bed. She tried to look surprised at her first question. 'Mr Leary? Oh, I passed him on the companionway to dinner. I told him you were unwell.'

Her mother seemed unconvinced. 'And you didn't spend long with him?'

'No.' Clarissa adjusted her mother's bedclothes. 'I hope you're feeling better tomorrow. The ladies have organised a glee club to fill in time. I told them you'd be interested.'

'Thank you, dear. I'll see how I feel in the morning. It's time for bed.'

'I'll read for a while.' Clarissa picked up her book and tried to focus, but the words didn't register. Her mind drifted to John. Seeing him this afternoon had proved one thing; despite the separation she'd forced on herself, she still had strong feelings for him. Was it love? From the few novels she'd read on the subject, she'd suspected it was a shipboard type of romance—but the separation had only increased her interest. She wanted so much for him to understand her. Surely she could bring that about in time? They were from different worlds, but the difference was small—it was simply that John had a prejudice against her. By contrast, she knew she had none against him. But she felt there were deep feelings underneath everything they said, and that brought her hope. She thought back over their meeting today. Surely that had cleared up some things?

It was the way he smiled at her, by his impulsive reactions, that she knew he was attracted to her, but he'd never crossed the line of propriety. They'd been alone on occasions, and she had wanted him to show his feelings physically, he hadn't. Shyness, she presumed. A shocking thought crossed her mind that she wouldn't refuse him a kiss. Some of her dreams had surprised her too, making her blanch the next day at her body's response. Did other girls dream the same way?

She longed to find out more about him as a man. He seemed strong and capable . . . and he liked poetry, which she never would have guessed. But she'd seen him in a black mood at times—where did this spring from? She dismissed from her mind the idea that he might be violent. On the contrary, she thought that, deep down, he was kind. Especially to those he loved, like his sister. Sighing, she closed her book and glanced at her mother, who was sleeping. Getting undressed, she revelled in being free of her corsets. Slipping her nightdress over her head, she blew out the light.

Drawing the bed covers over her, she reached to pull down her nightdress that had got caught up. Bringing her hand back, she brushed her thigh, sending a pleasurable jolt through her. Her hand wandered back and she closed her eyes and saw John's handsome face smiling at her.

On 11 October, the captain announced that, with fair weather, the ship would reach New South Wales in two weeks.

Passengers started talking excitedly and John shared the news with Donald Watkins. 'Well, Donald, not long to go now.'

'No, indeed. It's been a good voyage and everyone seems to have got along. I suppose it's the cramped quarters, you either smile or you're considered a grump.'

'True. The people with the money and class, you'd think they'd snub you, but they've been mostly grand.' He was smiling, but he was wondering about Clarissa, even as he spoke. Would their new openness last after they reached Sydney?

Mr Jones took him aside. 'Your wages have been calculated. You'll be pleased to know that it's six pounds.'

John pumped the first officer's hand. 'That's grand. Could you hold onto it, sir and give it to me on the day I leave the ship?'

'I will.'

The weather held, and John was often on deck letting the warm spring weather sink into his bones. The sunshine made his uncertainties seem unimportant. Three days later he was at the barrier, looking around the deck where the passengers mingled.

As soon as Clarissa appeared, she came over to him. Her face was drawn.

He said, 'How's your mother?'

'She's still not better. The surgeon calls regularly but he can't seem to help her. She is drinking and eating small portions only.'

'You look after her so well.'

'It's just so frustrating watching her. I hope there's a doctor in Sydney who can prescribe a tonic.'

'The food will be better on shore. That might do her the world of good. And in the meantime you have my poetry books to comfort you.'

'They do. Thank you.' Her hand touched his for a moment and it sent a thrill through him.

'My pleasure,' he said teasing her. 'You won't need them or me for much longer, you'll soon be in Sydney charming all the beaux.'

Clarissa grinned. 'Mr Leary, the way you talk, you'd think half of Sydney's eligible bachelors will be queuing to meet me.'

'What do you mean, half? I'm thinking all of them.'

A vision of Sydney docks came before him—the place where they must part.

Clarissa lost her smile. 'What's wrong?'

He shrugged. 'I'm just thinking about what *I'll* do. I'll have to start looking for a job, the moment we land.'

'With the work you've done on the ship,' she said and smiled, 'that shouldn't be too hard.'

He was grateful for her encouragement. 'No.'

With a butterfly touch she indicated his scar. 'Forgive me for asking, but I must. How did you get that?'

He put his hand around her wrist for a second. 'Protecting the honour of a lady.'

Her eyes widened in surprise. 'Really?'

He smiled and let her go. 'Nothing as gallant. A flying nail found my head.'

'Thank goodness it didn't do worse. You were fortunate.'

~

William Baxterhouse grabbed his suitcase and went topside, where the *Defiant's* topsails filled as she ran before the wind. He caught the attention of Jack Johnson and they walked to the bulwark. 'You've kept your side of this arrangement. I like my people to do as they're told. '

'I'm not one of your people, Mr Baxterhouse, and I want that copy of that gambling receipt. As you say, I've done my part.'

'I'll just hold onto it a little while. Why, there may be another opportunity to help each other.'

'No. A deal's a deal. Please give me that paper.'

William's eyes widened. 'The voyage out has given you a spine, my friend.' He moved close to the lieutenant. 'Be careful. Spines break easily. Well, Jack?'

Jack Johnson exhaled. 'So when? When will this blackmail end?'

'Don't be coarse, Jack. Our arrangement, if you have to use a term, will end when I say it does. Don't look so glum. It could be soon. Now, let's see what mischief we can get up to tonight. Find out from the boys where we can have some fun.'

'I've a few days' leave, then the ship sails to Norfolk Island.'

'Then you've got time tonight.' William left him to make his farewells to the captain.

'Sir, I take my leave of you,' he said. 'The voyage has been made more enjoyable by your company and gracious assistance.'

'Thank you, Mr Baxterhouse, the feeling is mutual. I trust you will succeed admirably in this town.' The captain walked to a canopy rigged at the stern, to escape the sun, and William followed. 'I agree with your report's positive conclusions on the pinnaces and will forward same to the Admiralty. I've also made a copy of my report on the boats, which is with these.' He handed William a brace of documents. 'There are influential merchants and respected men of business in Sydney who would, I believe, benefit from your acumen. These are letters of introduction for you.'

'Thank you, captain, that is much appreciated. I bid you farewell.'

~

A loud squawk from above sent John leaping from his bunk. He rushed towards the source of the noise and through sleepy eyes caught sight of a bird perched at the top of the companionway. A seagull!

He raced on deck. It was early dawn. Some miles distant to the west, where the sea stopped, was the brown-ribboned boundary of his new home.

The *Emily* met the nor'easterly on her starboard tack as she approached the northern cape of a large bay. On the way up the coast John had savoured the wave-gouged sandstone cliffs and sparkling beaches. The passengers decked themselves in their fancy gear, a bit musty since Cape Town, and clustered together with him on this October morning, eager, like he, not to miss a thing. John turned to Donald Watkins. 'It's a different kind of green to home. The trees I mean.'

'Aye, it's not a rich green, rough like, but still dense. Maybe it's this strong sunlight. The place has a touch of the tropics too.'

Even on this mild day, John's brow and shirt were damp with perspiration. The captain had said the cape they were approaching was one of the pillars to Sydney Harbour. All hands made sail to go about and the ship turned to run before the wind. The inner harbour was like the seaward side except for smaller bays, outcrops of buildings and the occasional well-tended house dotted among the tall trees. Beaches blazed in the sunlight and John gasped at the scene; feeling proud he was the first in his family to see such a wonderful sight. And yet maybe his Uncle Gerry had stood in chains on this very spot and like him had been overcome by the beauty.

'You look astonished, Mr Leary.' John was surprised at the salutation. Mrs McGuire stood by her daughter's side. Her face was animated. John suspected as the voyage was at its end, Clarissa was soon to be free of him.

'Morning Miss McGuire, Mrs McGuire. It's indeed a beautiful place. You're looking a little better, Ma'am.'

This was flattering and John knew it. Clarissa's mother still looked pale and she'd lost weight.

'Thank you, Mr Leary. I *am* feeling a little better although my sleep is still restless. A permanent home in Sydney with good food may help me.' Clarissa gave her mother a troubled look.

'I'm sure it will.' John hoped so for Clarissa's sake.

'Clarissa, I'll go below for some final packing.'

John tipped his hat. 'Ma'am.'

The *Emily* clawing close to one headland caught the perfume of lemon-scented flora, making Clarissa close her eyes and sigh.

'How heavenly. I'd like to bottle that and have it by my bedside.'

John agreed. They enjoyed the vista and said nothing for some time. Sweeping his shaded eyes around, the magic view was spoilt by the grin of Tom Semrot leaning on the taffrail. Their journey's end would be a mixed blessing. He'd miss the developing friendship of Donald Watkins and others, but not Tom Semrot.

The ship had tacked again and now swung around a gun battery to lower its sails and prepare to land in the lee of a medium sized cove. Sheltered from the wind, the heat took over and soon everyone was in the shade. John stood beside Clarissa feeling self-conscious. The end of the voyage brought a reality, one of status, class, money and power. A world now split into the boundaries of social life, which the voyage, by fortunate circumstance, had blurred. 'Miss McGuire, I'd like you to know that the trip has been made more enjoyable by your company. You've spoken to me on many occasions and I'm grateful for that. I hope that our paths may cross in Sydney, although it's doubtful that they will.'

'I'd very much like to keep our friendship in Sydney. Indeed I'd like you to call on me there.'

John's eyes expanded. 'You can't mean that? Not in town, no.'

'I don't lie,' she said, her eyes clear and wide.

'But your family, your mother's friends. What will it look like?'

She looked down then back up at him. 'Do you want to meet me again?' He did. But where would it lead?

She smiled. 'You're hesitating?'

He smiled also and his breathing eased. 'Of course I want to,' and he again felt an urge to hold her.

'Good. I shall make sure we can remain friends. My father is an influential man and who knows what assistance he may be able to offer.'

John bridled at the thought of help and his face became a stolid mask, but Clarissa wasn't fooled. 'There now, I'm not standing on your Kildare pride. Everyone can use a hand but it'll still be up to you to pull your weight.'

John laughed outright. 'You know me too well, Miss McGuire.'

Clarissa's eyes softened. 'I'll say goodbye now. Mother wants me below and I've things to do before disembarking. You'll have to check your trunk as well.' She put out her hand.

John looked from her face to her hand and took it. 'Goodbye, Miss McGuire.'

She kept hold of his hand and drew him closer. 'It's Clarissa.' He breathed in the fragrance he remembered from the day he first saw her. Her cheek was glowing and tanned and without thinking he kissed it. Her cheek moved and her mouth met his. My God! John involuntarily broke free and looked at her closed eyes just for a heartbeat then she opened them to look into his. She smiled. 'As they say in France Mr Leary, à *bientôt.*' John's face creased in confusion and Clarissa giggled. 'It means I'll see you soon. You'll want your poetry books back, won't you?' She turned around and went below.

Clarissa assisted her mother with their belongings, doing things by instinct because a part of her was still on deck with John. She knew she'd been brazen and passengers would have seen them but she didn't care. This was farewell and she wanted him to know how she felt.

'That doesn't belong there.' Her mother remonstrated. Clarissa corrected the placement of the article. Her skin tingled from his lips and her body still felt his closeness. Thank God it was in the middle of a crowded deck during daylight. What would have happened in other times? A pleasant shudder went through her. She grabbed her immigration papers and helped her mother up to the deck just as the *Emily* docked.

'There's your father.'

Clarissa scanned the crowd and waved to him. He grinned in reply and her excitement mounted. As paying passengers, they were accorded special treatment and left the ship first. They made their goodbyes to the captain and left the *Emily* for the last time.

On the foredeck, the Immigration Agent was calling out the steerage roll for those leaving the ship. John was only half listening to the Agent, his attention taken by the last of the paying passengers passing by him at the bulwark: men and women of means, families all ready to begin a new life.

Donald's voice broke his reverie. 'John, the Agent's nearly up to your name. Come over here so he can spot you. Me being Watkins, I'm always near the end.'

John joined the group in front of the official reminding him he was an assisted passenger. He envied Clarissa's group, their money opened all doors. The roll completed, he queued to finalise the formalities and with the hot sun on his back, bent over the table and signed his name and date, 25 October 1850.

The official handed him his New South Wales papers. 'It includes all the details as well as the barracks' rules, bunk location, meal times, everything you'll need to know.' He pointed to the top left of one paper. 'That's the coach number that'll take your trunk to Bent Street, the immigration barracks. Here are directions to show you the way to get there.'

'Cheers, my big helper.' Angus Sheffield squeezed John's hand.

'Thank you, Mr Sheffield.' John moved on and made his farewells to the captain and shook his hand.

'Good luck young Leary, here's Mr Jones who wants a word.'

The first officer put out his hand. 'And I wish you good fortune too, lad. Here is your money and also references from Mr Sheffield attesting to your good workmanship. Let's hope they'll assist you to find suitable employment.'

'Thank you indeed, sir. I'm sure they will.' John was sad to be leaving but he sought out Donald Watkins. 'We're to walk.'

'We are and it's not far.'

Their coach set off in front of them. The steaminess was oppressive and the docks were frenetic with all manner of goods being handled, wool being the main one. Derricks loaded the bales of fleece from bullock-pulled wagons to the waiting ships. Further down the dock other ships offloaded much needed supplies from England. The tone of the singing rigging, the squeaking of pulleys, the hissing of steam derricks and accents from many countries bombarded John's ears. His moodiness was gone; overtaken by the bustle and smells of the dung and dust of a new country and the hive of activity. Sydney looked like it was rebuilding following an earthquake. He turned to Donald. 'Where's your bunk?'

'Section "A".'

'I'm in "C" the building trades group.'

'We'll still see each other. Now, I've got a map in my pocket.

This is George Street we're on; it's one of the main streets of Sydney.'

The style of residential houses was not dissimilar to parts of his old country. 'Plenty happening, my friend. That's good for me.'

Donald nodded. 'You'll be all right. I'm the same. The clerkship I've lined up with a merchant is just the go. I'd like to start my own business some time.'

'There's time for that, just settling in first is the key.'

They went up Alfred Street. 'There's not plenty of time,' Donald remonstrated. 'Your money won't last long, so get cracking and get that job. I mean it John. There's work here for sure but it won't come to you. You have to hunt it down.'

'I will Donald, I will.'

'There's Government House.' Donald pointed to a sandstone building on a promontory. 'Not sure if his Excellency is at home but I'm certain he'll send us a note of greeting!' They crossed into Castlereagh Street and were silent as they absorbed all that was happening around them. 'This must be Bent Street,' Donald said. 'We're here.'

They stopped in front of a three-storey building with an entrance full of people coming and going, children and adults alike. Their coach had just arrived and Donald took his trunk, which was one of the first offloaded.

'We'll split up now I'm thinking,' John said. 'I'll see you at tea.'

Donald waved and went his way. John waited till his trunk was offloaded, grabbed it and followed the official to the single men's C section where the bunks were laid out like on board ship but with more room and with a permanent lockable foot chest.

'Ablution blocks are in the corner,' the official said.

All in all, John felt at home. Strange, he mused, he didn't know a soul except Donald. Clarissa and Luke Collins, all gone. Well he thought, he must keep thinking of a job.

He sidled over to the window and gazed out over Sydney's streets. My future is out there and I'm going to make it.

CHAPTER FOUR

WILLIAM BAXTERHOUSE FORCED ONE EYE OPEN AND LOOKED around. Opening his other eye flashed pain through his head. Dropping his arm out, he felt something in his bed and he turned and squinted at the sleeping woman, the night before coming back to him. He'd bagged a lease on a site in Kent Street near Miller's Point for a boatbuilding business and had celebrated with the agents into the early morning. William nudged the woman in the side. 'Get up, my darling. I've things to do.'

The woman got out of bed naked and looked at her clothes scattered on the floor. She dressed looking at William. 'You promised me more money last night for what I did. Can I have it?'

'You were good, I'll admit.' He lifted a note from his wallet. 'Don't spend it all at once.'

The woman smiled, approached the bed, palmed the money and placed a hand on his thigh. 'I can be grateful.'

He grinned. 'You could be, but I've got things to do.'

Thirty minutes later, seated in the eating area of the Hero of Waterloo hotel, he felt better. He devoured eggs, bacon, toast and tea. The *Sydney Morning Herald* lay at his side and he glanced at the headlines.

Removing his gold watch, he passed a finger over its face as if caressing a lover. He grunted satisfaction. His Letter of Credit was safely in the Bank of New South Wales, digs here at the hotel—for now—and letters of introduction all answered. Not bad for two weeks in the new colony.

~

A nor'easter cooled John's face as he scanned the harbour. 'It's a brilliant scene and does the Sabbath justice,' he said to Donald.

'You going to Mass?' Donald asked.

'St Mary's was at ten o'clock and I've missed it. I've been filling in forms for jobs.'

'Better go next week, then and I'll join you. We can't have the Lord grumpy at us.'

John pointed to Campbell's warehouse. 'That's one building site. See the cleared left side. I'll be here tomorrow at first light to see if they'll have me.'

'And the rest of the sites?' Donald said.

'There's another one along here, George Street North. Then there's Pitt Street, Miller's Point and Day Street.'

'Pitt Street is where I'll be working. You want to see them all today? Why not wait till the morrow?'

'Taking your advice, remember. I don't want to waste time trying to look for them tomorrow. By finding where they are today, I'll have a better chance of winning that job.'

Donald smiled. 'Good. You know, just last night I got me land legs back. It's taken me two days. Now I'm steady as a Presbyterian at a wake.'

'Come on. I've got to post some letters home and if you're lucky, I'll buy you a feed.'

'Lead on, young sir.'

~

The following morning at breakfast John was sitting opposite a man, a carpenter. John wasn't the only one looking for work.

'Which jobs are you going to?' the man asked.

'Just a few.'

'Oh aye, well the head man here gave me the same list as you got.'

'That's so?'

The carpenter smiled. 'He did, so it'll be first in best dressed.'

'I've got a few things to do,' John lied, 'then I'll set out.'

But the man had his head down and was filling his mouth.

John finished his breakfast, gathered his plates from the table and left the barracks, keen to be ahead of his competition.

Miller's Point was a no go as was Campbell's warehouse extension. Both had their quota of tradesmen. There were three sites left and John was still confident but he knew time was not on his side. Each hour that passed lessened his chances of getting employed.

The George Street North site was busy as well with carpenters and masons competing for space. Not good.

A big man caught John's eye and sauntered over. 'Help you?'

'Are you the foreman?'

'Aye.'

John reached into his pocket and withdrew his references. 'I'm after a job as a carpenter.'

The foreman smiled. 'Just off the boat?'

'Three days ago.'

'County?'

'Kildare.'

'I've got relatives there.'

John was impatient. 'Can you use me?'

'Like to, son. Got me full site team. But I've another job starting in three weeks. Is your bunk at Bent Street?'

John was disappointed. 'It is.'

'I'll drop up and see you, if I want someone.'

John walked away. 'Thanks.'

It was eight-thirty and there were only two sites left. John stepped out along Pitt Street towards Liverpool Street where double-storey houses stood on each side, some of them swanky. He counted the house numbers and stopped on the footpath at a vacant site. There was no one there. Odd. He was told the site had started, yet not a trench had been dug or a wall pegged out. A wagon pulled up near him with four men in its tray—one of whom was his breakfast companion from that morning. The driver alighted, walked across the street towards John and went up to the site where he undid the gate and pushed it open. He signalled to the men on the wagon who jumped down, trooped onto the site and gathered round him. John went over and joined them.

The driver took off his hat and wiped his brow. 'I'm the builder, Don McGlinchy. I need two chippies and two masons to start. Bricklayers will do.'

'I'm a plasterer,' one man said.

'You're no good to me yet. Come back in a month.' The man touched his hat and left.

'I'm a mason,' another said.

'Good,' McGlinchy said. 'You can start today. Let me know the cement you'll want for the footings. Have you a mate who's a brickie?'

'Might know of one,' the man said.

'Bring him with you tomorrow.'

'I'll try.'

McGlinchy scratched his head. 'I might still be short of one then if you have a doubt.'

John saw a chance. There were two men left. 'I'm a carpenter, Mr McGlinchy.'

One of the men turned to him. 'So am I.'

It was his breakfast companion who nodded and smiled at him. 'Leary.'

'These two were here first, shorty,' McGlinchy said to John. 'They get the jobs. Can you lay bricks?'

'Not like a bricklayer.'

'Then I can't use ya.' He hesitated. 'Campbell's might want a chippy.'

'Tried them.'

'Sorry,' McGlinchy said.

John nodded and started running. He had one site left.

'So you think you know something of building, do ya?' The sweating overseer said.

The Day Street site was the last one and John's confidence had waned. But the excavation had commenced and he hoped the building would take many months to complete. 'I've got papers, from my ship.'

The man shook his head. 'Words won't mean much to me, son if you can't lay a straight trench.'

'I can work a hard day and the one after that. So have no fear.'

'Oh, I won't. If you're no good, you won't last a week. Any road I need a chippy's mate and you're big enough to tote a load. I'll—'

'But I'm a carpenter.'

'So you say.' The overseer scowled. 'But I'll give you a try.' John breathed out. A job at last. 'The wages are three shillings a day for six days work and you'll be here six tomorrow sharp.'

'That I'll be.'

John left and walked back up Erskine Street. Turning into George Street he stopped at a shop and bought a hat and laces for his boots. The shirts he had would do for now. Returning to the barracks he attacked his boots with dubbin and elbow grease. A job! He had a job.

The next day, the street lamps twinkled in the morning mist and Darling Harbour was just visible. John reported to the overseer, who seemed surprised.

'Turned up eh?'

'Aye, what's my job?'

'My name's Fruin, Dick Fruin.' He pointed to a bear-sized man twenty feet away who was sawing a scantling, the handle unsighted in his paw. 'You'll work with Doug Mullins on the footing shuttering for the rest of the week. Concrete's going in them on Saturday.'

John dropped his tool kit and barracks-supplied midday meal in the lean-to then went to meet his workmate. The foundations' carpenter had a pock-marked weather-beaten face. The man's smile showed two teeth. 'New lad, eh?'

'Aye.'

The man nodded. 'Know anything about carpentry?'

'Yes.'

Mullins sighed and placed his saw on the horse. 'Ambitious too, it sounds. Well for the time being, what's your name, big fella?'

'John Leary.'

'For now John you can help me. I'm building shutters for the footings. See that trench?' John looked over to a cut in the sandstone ground two feet wide and one foot deep and about twenty feet in length. 'That trench will be filled with concrete. The footing joining it at right angles is out of the ground and has to be formed up. That's why we're here.'

John nodded and grabbed the end of a plank ready for sawing. They got stuck in and the sun was high when Mr Fruin called out, 'Smoko.'

The pair moved to the lean-to where a billy boiled, its steam disappearing into a cloudless sky. John grabbed a cup and poured himself a big helping and ate half his meal.

Mullins sat beside him. 'Been in Sydney long?'

'Arrived last week. Still in the barracks.'

Mullins waved an arm at the timber pile. 'This hardwood's a bastard. Blunts the teeth from the sharpest saw and you'll build muscles trying to punch three inch nails into it. Give me English oak any day.' He flung the dregs of the tea into a rubbish pile and stood up. 'Back to work.'

They continued the rest of the day with John relieving the carpenter at sawing. At four o'clock they had enough timber formwork for the next day. Mullins downed tools and he and John cleaned up under a mason's tap.

Splashing water onto his face, Mullins muttered. 'Not bad for your first day. See ya tomorrow.'

John trudged back to Bent Street. His neck and back muscles ached as if he'd shouldered two bags of cement from Dublin to Cork. He swapped his kit to share the load on his blistered fingers. But he felt at home. From years of labouring he knew the secrets to easing strained muscles and damaged hands. That he would do tonight.

For the rest of the week John completed the footing formwork and helped Mullins build a timber site fence along the Day Street frontage. Saturday came and the labourers mixed the concrete, its odour familiar to him. This was gut-breaking work and John itched for the steam mixer he'd used at home, but he'd keep his own counsel and wait for the right moment to tell Mr Fruin. The team slogged to finish the pour, and it was mid-afternoon before the last batch was levelled and trowelled and Mr Fruin called a halt.

'Righto men, place sand over this lot. The sun will dry out our good work quicker than a sailor's first frigging on leave.'

Fruin got John's attention. 'You're done orright, Leary. Keep this up for a month and I'll fix it with the builder to put you on permanent. While the concrete's curin' next week you can work with Mullins cutting the floor timbers. Coming for a beer?'

'Aye and thanks.'

~

In the parlour, Clarissa sipped her tea. She was getting used to the smaller rooms in their Hunter Street house, which was half the size of their spacious Dublin home. She placed her cup down. 'Please elaborate, Father. Corrugated iron, wool and fencing wire?'

David McGuire, respectable middle-class merchant, sat opposite her in a chair that seemed like it was part of him. They had dined alone, her mother had retired to bed. Clarissa looked affectionately at her father who was nearly six feet tall, slim, with twinkling eyes and an easy smile. 'It's the same as we did in Dublin. There, the distances, customers, volume and opportunity were known. Here it's different. I had to come to Sydney to see for myself what opportunities there were. I travelled vast distances and saw the need for wire, wool and iron sheeting. Here's where our fortune lies, here in New South Wales. If I wasn't convinced I wouldn't have brought you and your mother out.'

'It's that lucrative?'

'The growth for all three is exponential! Both the iron and wire come from our Norwich supplier who's licking his lips over our prospects. I've also got a shareholding with a broker managing wool to export.'

'What generates the most cash?'

Her father smiled. 'Wire. The colony's screaming for it and the size of the orders boggles the mind. They don't measure fencing here in yards like back home,' he said slapping the chair in emphasis. 'It's chains.'

'Extraordinary. Wool?'

'Merino, superfine. It's a smaller clip than the rest of the fleece but twice as profitable. Nearly as good as wire. Sheeting is wanted too. Look, put simply I need you to assist me as my 'arms and legs' so to speak. There's so much demand. I'm not on top of it and that's one thing I abhor. All three companies: iron, wool and wire need planning on how we've going to build our businesses to cope with the demand. I'm going to do that. What I want you to do is to make sure our orders go out, on time and at the right price.'

A frown replaced his smile and she realised her father was serious.

'But I know nothing about these businesses.'

Her father stood and went to the fireplace where he took a pipe from the mantel. 'That's not quite correct. You're a shrewd judge of character, have an eye for a deal and the ability to lead. I saw that when you did that stint with me the year before last. I need to have a trusted person to know how all the businesses are at any time.' He ran a hand through his thick hair and filled his pipe. 'There are clerks and accountants to teach you the ropes. What do you think?' He lit the pipe, then ploughed back through the smoke to his chair. Clarissa sat still, thinking. What her father was asking was revolutionary! Yes, there were colonial 'helpmeets', women who assisted their husbands, but not to the extent that she would be helping her father. The weight of responsibility felt heavy on her shoulders. Would she have the courage to make decisions let alone *know* the businesses? And how would she face her father's workers? No woman had taken on what her father was contemplating.

David McGuire seemed to sense her thoughts. 'Yes, I dare say I'd be kicked out of the Australia Hotel Club tonight if they heard such radical views. God, a woman in business!'

Clarissa smiled. She could see in her father's eyes his trust in her. She couldn't let him down. 'I'll do it.'

John's site was going to be a hotel, public bars on the ground floor and accommodation rooms on the first floor. Its brick walls rose from their foundations as spring blurred into summer and he acclimatised to the sunlight and steaminess. Mullins had moved to another site. At the end of November, John was lugging the last of two sawn-to-length timbers with the help of his labourer, Harry Dickson, when Mr Fruin stopped them.

'The carpenter job's yours Leary, permanent. I squared it with Mr Jenkins the builder.'

'That's grand, thank you.'

Pleased, John continued on his way, the timber in his hands seemed a bit lighter somehow. Christmas was four weeks away and it felt odd to celebrate yuletide in near century heat, another wonder of this land.

The drain-layer was about to dig a trench in line with a row of brick piers. He caught John's eye and pointed to the timber. 'Don't put them anywhere down here, Tiny. I'm ready to dig.'

There wasn't much space left. The timbers John held, the bearers, would be the last to sit on top of the single low-height brick piers and would form the bottom layer of support for the floor. Fixed on top of the bearers, at right angles, would be the next layer of smaller timber beams, the joists, then fixed to the joists would be the floor boards. 'I've got to put them somewhere, just for a tick.'

'Just not here,' the drain-layer said and cursed.

Fruin looked around and raised his voice. 'There's no space to swing a bloody hammer. Finish laying those bearers on the brick piers, Leary. Check the set out then place the joists at right angles on them at sixteen inch centres and nail them.'

'Come on, Harry,' John said to his labourer. 'Let's strike a blow.' Sawing the eucalypt joists was just as tough as sawing the bearers. But John got stuck in. Every strike brought back Mullins's warning on the stubborn timber. It seemed John was an executioner meant to kill every nail he banged home.

He'd tucked away ideas about making the site more efficient. After he'd nailed ten joists an opportunity came when Mr Fruin called him over.

The overseer stood beside a man no more than five feet three tall with a shock of russet-coloured curly hair and a flushed face that had refused to tan, but with a build as tough as the hide of John's nail bag. 'Boss, meet the new carpenter. Leary, this is Mr Jenkins.'

John shot out his hand. The builder's eyes were friendly and John's hand was gripped with strength.

'God bless Ireland, but you're a big one!' Jenkins said. 'Mr Fruin's been telling me about you. You've settled in all right?'

Loud words distracted them. The drain layer and John's labourer Harry were pushing and shoving each other. Mr Fruin went to set things right. Jenkins and John watched as the overseer returned.

'It's the same problem, boss,' Fruin said. 'The site's too small, too many things happening. The drainer needs the space to lay his earthenware and the timbers are in the way. We'll lose half a day double handling.'

Jenkins swore and John saw his opportunity.

'Sir, it might be better to lay the drainage first and also to cut the timbers to length —away from the site.'

Fruin shot John a filthy look. 'You keep to your job, Leary and let us do the organising.'

Jenkins looked at both men in turn. 'Go on, Leary.'

John plunged in. 'From the architect's plans you cut all the flooring timbers away from the site in a shed somewhere. This can be done in dry weather and the time saved on site will more that make up for the rent you'll pay. There'll also be more room for other trades to work.'

Jenkins placed his boot on a foundation wall. He looked down in thought then back at John. 'Good idea, I've a shed which I'm setting up as a joinery shop. There'll be some room left over. I'll give it some thought.' Fruin and Jenkins walked away and John was about to return to his joists when Fruin glared back at him.

John wasn't worried about the overseer's attitude. He'd win over Mr Jenkins with other ideas. Back at his timber work, he helped Harry lay out more joists. 'I'll set out the last of these. You have a go at nailing them. I'll help you.'

'Grand,' Harry said. 'What did ya say to the boss? Dropped me in the shit, I suppose.'

'Just small talk,' John lied.

'He's a Freemason you know. You're a tyke?'

'Aye.'

'Well you're gone then. Freemasons have the secret sign.'

John smiled. 'Like our Sign of the Cross?'

'Yeah, but there's a square in theirs, not a trinity.'

John laughed. There were Freemasons in Ireland but mainly in the cities. As long as Mr Jenkins had no prejudice against Catholics, there was still hope. 'You're one then Harry?'

'Not bloody likely.'

'Come on, let's get this finished.' John looked forward to the day when he could give orders but not yet. He started nailing and thought about life away from work. After he knocked off, he had few hours to spare, Sunday was his one day off. Hard work gave him less time to think about absent friends, but his evening thoughts were a mixture of Clarissa and Baxterhouse. The *Defiant* was in Sydney, that much he'd learned. But was Maureen's rapist in the colony or was he still in Dublin? Until he'd seen the passenger list and had proof either way, he couldn't be sure. But, if he had to put money on it, he thought Baxterhouse was still in Ireland. Becoming angry at the thought made him miss-strike a nail that flew out of the timber and flashed close to Harry's eye.

'Jesus Christ, mate, watch what you're doing!'

'Sorry,' John said. Harry had come close to getting a scar like his own. He cleared his mind and concentrated on work for the rest of the day.

Walking back to Bent Street, thoughts of passenger lists returned. Efforts to find his uncle and where he lived had proved fruitless, but at least John had seen his relative's name on the convict transport list.

In the barracks, he washed up and went to the office where a letter with a Dublin address awaited him. It was from Maureen. She'd written a month after John had left Dublin and it contained good news. Maureen was back at school and she'd formed a friendship with Liam the brother of Miss Forde, the teacher who'd helped Maureen. His sister was happy and closed by sending John all her love and wishing him good health. John folded the letter, and placed it in his footlocker. It had said nothing about Baxterhouse. Damn.

Donald came up beside him. 'Hey ho. Have you time for a beer?'

'I have and it's my shout.'

William Baxterhouse was sitting in the office of Thomas Higgins at the Bank of New South Wales.

'Would you like a cup of tea, Mr McCreadie?' Higgins asked the man sitting on William's right.

'Thank you, no,' John McCreadie said. 'I want to review this contract again. Please give me some time.'

'Of course,' the banker replied, picking a loose thread from his suit.

Higgins wore the constant frown of someone who'd lost his wallet and couldn't find it. He was polite to William at first then effusive when he'd learnt that the bank would manage William's funds. The Baxterhouse boatbuilding business was the bank's first financial venture with him and today's would be the second.

William Baxterhouse smiled to himself. Higgins managed McCreadie's accounts and had told William the wool broker was interested in raising capital by offering shares in his company. By way of introduction, Higgins had invited both McCreadie and himself to dinner the previous Saturday. Business hadn't been discussed there but William had got to know the man. Now sitting in the banker's George Street office, he took stock while McCreadie concentrated on the sheaf of papers in his hand. The ticking of the clock and the turning of the pages were the only noises in the room.

McCreadie looked at him. 'Mr Baxterhouse, we would consider selling some of our shares but not thirty per cent. Fifteen is our limit.' William was hopeful for ten so the extra was welcomed. The Bank of New South Wales would provide the loan funds for that investment and it required the shares for security for the loan.

William leant forward. 'Mr McCreadie, thank you. I see growth in wool exports. The land's being opened up at a pace and I'm prepared to back my judgement. Fifteen per cent is acceptable.'

The broker took time to respond and looked at the banker. 'Mr Higgins, thank you for the introduction to this gentleman. You know our brokerage house and its secure financial position. Is there any comment you'd like to make?'

Higgins looked at William. 'Mr McCreadie, Mr Baxterhouse has only been in the colony a short time but his funds are sound.'

McCreadie paused then nodded. 'Very well. The documents I have here are explicit, concise and appropriate, I'll send a response in three business days.'

'Thank you,' William said. 'But I've had discussions with other brokers, and will evaluate all investment options by the end of the week. That's the tenth of December.' A lie. But it wouldn't hurt to keep McCreadie on the hop. 'The company who'll offer the lowest price for their share value will secure my business.' The merchant frowned and William plunged in. 'But price will not be my only benchmark. The honour and integrity of your company is regarded very highly by myself and the bank.'

A smile creased McCreadie's face.

Donald Watkins shook John's ankle. 'Look lively if you want to get to ten o'clock Mass.'

John stretched on his bunk and glanced out the window. Another hot day was on the way. 'Aye. How was the eight o'clock?'

'Fair. The priest gave us a serve on the perils of gambling. It's a lost cause. There are more card games here than at home. I'm off soon.' He smiled, 'Meeting a lady.'

John got up and grabbed a towel. 'Don't let me stop you. Just remember to be a gentleman, as I am.'

'You need to get out and about yourself.'

'I do.'

'I wouldn't call going to two dances getting out. You're not a priest, John. There are women out there who would like to meet you. Think about it.'

Donald waved him goodbye and John showered and shaved, dressed in his best moleskins and left the barracks. Donald wasn't a young man but he had found female company and John knew he should seek like companionship, but there was Clarissa. Seven weeks he'd been here and he missed her, but she would have no cause to see him. So there was little likelihood they'd meet again.

He crossed Elizabeth Street, the sun beating down and he concentrated on what money he had. Capital could only come from him being in charge of his future. He would give himself at least a year before having a go on his own and building for others.

A group of Church of England parishioners stood outside St James Church. Thankfully, his workmates didn't seem to care whether he was a Catholic or a Pillar of Fire, nor did his boss, even though he was a Freemason.

St Mary's Church lightened his mood, its lines and strength outlined against the sunlight. Brushing the dust from him he climbed the steps and entered the church. The transition humbled him as a coolness shrouded his shoulders and the smell of incense complemented the choir. Across the nave, stained glass lit by the sun cast a coloured pattern on the pews. After crossing himself with holy water he walked down the aisle to a seat.

There was solace in the absorbing Latin cadence. Memories of childhood and family filled his thoughts and he prayed for loved ones in Ireland. With the Mass completed he left the church to again confront the heat. Looking down to see his way, he heard a voice from behind, its lilting tones familiar.

'Mr Leary.'

John turned and Clarissa smiled, her gloved hand resting on the arm of a tall, middle-aged man. John was surprised at first then reached up to doff his cap but dropped it in the action. 'Miss Clarissa,' he said picking up his cap and brushing it against his trousers. What must he look like compared with Clarissa's partner?

'Father, I'd like to introduce you to Mr Leary whom I met on the voyage.'

Clarissa's father put out his hand. John reciprocated and found his own hand gripped firmly. 'McGuire.'

John felt self-conscious. Here was *class* in all its reality. 'How do you do, Mr McGuire?'

'Very well, thank you.'

'Is this your normal Mass?' John asked.

'No,' Clarissa replied. 'We usually go to the eight o'clock one, but today we decided on a change.' She grinned. 'Anyway, how are you?'

David McGuire interrupted 'It's very hot. There's an ice vendor close by which serves the best I've tasted. If you don't have any plans, Mr Leary?'

'No, no. I don't. That would be grand.'

Shaded by a gum tree with its lemon-scented perfume, they sat around a table and enjoyed the flavoured ices. Clarissa's father seemed at ease and John started to feel more comfortable.

Clarissa's face was healthier and her smile was just as sweet while her blue dress matched her cobalt eyes. She finished half her glass before breaking the silence. 'So, Mr Leary, how are you settling in?'

'All right I think, Miss Clarissa, thank you. The barracks in Bent Street are different from the ship and I can save more.'

'The barracks are close to us. We live in Hunter Street.'

All these weeks and he'd not been four hundred yards from her.

'And your work?' she asked. 'Have you been able to find some?'

'Aye, thank you. A good site in Day Street. It's for a new two-storey hotel.'

'Cochrane's Hotel, I think,' McGuire said. 'I don't know if it's named after the boatbuilder of the same name in Darling Harbour.'

'I don't know, sir, but it's got seven months to go so I'm glad.'

'You are a carpenter?' McGuire said.

'I am.'

'Architecture interests me,' McGuire said gesturing towards the cathedral. 'That will be modified next year to a design by Augustus Pugin, a great English architect. I know some architects here. Most have told me they always need skilled hands on their sites.' John sensed a hint of assistance in those words, but why would this man help him? No, he was just being polite. McGuire stood up. 'Mr Leary, we must go. Come Clarissa.'

Clarissa rose from the table. 'Father, if Mr Leary is going back to the barracks he might like to accompany us.'

McGuire frowned for a moment and then seemed to recall his manners. John suspected Clarissa may have just forced her father to accept her request. 'Of course. Mr Leary?'

'Thank you.'

Clarissa put up her parasol and they walked towards Macquarie Street. She was glad of the extra time with John and had flushed with excitement when she'd spotted him outside the church. Her eyes surreptitiously roved over him. He looked good, hard work agreed with him. 'Do you work on Saturdays?'

'I do. Sunday's the only time I have off.'

'And what do you normally do on the Lord's Sabbath?'

'Rest and read. Go for walks.'

'I often think about the voyage. It seemed to go on forever but ended too quickly.' She moved closer to him but not too close to draw her father's attention.

'It would have been a pleasure cruise, Mr Leary,' McGuire said, 'compared to the horror trips to America. I've read reports from passengers' diaries. They called their ships, "coffin ships"'.

'Is that a fact?'

'One in four died in them. It seems the British are far better organised in the conditions aboard their ships compared to the Americans.'

'Our arrangements were passable, Father.'

'Sometimes,' John said, 'I wake in the night and wonder where I am. Then I look around and see the space and the stillness. There's no movement. That's what I miss.'

Clarissa stopped outside the hospital. 'What else do you miss?'

He seemed self-conscious under her stare. He got his thoughts together. 'The dances,' he spluttered.

Clarissa looked surprised and grinned. 'Yes, they were grand.' Then she remembered her father and resumed a straight face. 'It was all strictly controlled, Father.'

'So your mother told me. Were all the passengers on their best behaviour, Mr Leary?'

'Mostly, all, yes.'

'Come on,' her father said. 'Let's cross over.'

On the other side of Macquarie Street, three men and a young lady dressed in high fashion walked towards them.

'It's Mr McCreadie with Mr Higgins, I think,' David McGuire said.

'It is Mr Higgins,' Clarissa said. 'I've seen him at the bank.'

The group stopped as McGuire took off his hat. 'Mr McCreadie.'

John McCreadie copying McGuire's salutation gestured to his companions. 'We've just come from the service at St James'. You know Mr Higgins of course.'

'I do. How are you, Thomas?'

'I'm very well,' Higgins replied. 'This is my daughter Elizabeth.' Both John and David raised their hats. She is an attractive girl, Clarissa thought, as she nodded to her. Early twenties, well dressed and a striking figure. 'And this is a newly arrived client of the Bank's, William Baxterhouse from Dublin.'

'Welcome to Sydney, Mr Baxterhouse,' David McGuire said extending his hand. 'Leary? Are you all right?' John was staring at the stranger as if he'd seen an apparition. His face was pale, his eyes wide.

John shook his head. 'It's the sun, I fear.'

'It must be strong,' Baxterhouse said, 'to trouble a man as big as you.' Baxterhouse stuck his thumbs in his silk-patterned vest. 'Leary? Leary? There was a young man who enquired after me in Cape Town?'

John seemed to recover. 'That was me. Yes, you're from Dublin, as I am. You had a trading house there.'

Baxterhouse nodded.

'And I wanted to know in Cape Town if you were coming here.' He forced a smile. 'You are here of course. I'm in the building game—'

'How did you know I'd left Dublin and was on that warship?'

John seemed flustered, not like anything Clarissa had seen from him. Also he was from Kildare, not Dublin.

Baxterhouse grinned again showing good teeth. 'No matter, you can tell me another time.' He fetched a card from his suit jacket and gave it to John. 'If you want timber, come to me. I can get you good deals from a supplier near me at Darling Harbour.'

'We must take our leave, I'm sorry,' McGuire said. 'Goodbye gentlemen, Miss Higgins.' He took Clarissa's elbow and John joined them.

'Are you feeling better, Mr Leary?' Clarissa asked.

'I am, thank you.'

She wasn't so sure. John had seemed all right up to when that man's name was mentioned. She would love to speak with him alone but that wasn't possible. Still, she knew where he lived and it wasn't far. That was a start. 'They'll have some sort of Christmas dinner in Bent Street, I suppose,' she said. John seemed preoccupied and didn't reply. 'Mr Leary?'

'I'm sorry. Yes, a handsome spread is planned. Donald Watkins will be there. Do you remember him?'

He is still shaken, why? 'I do. Please give him my compliments.'

'I shall.'

McGuire opened the gate to a house. 'This is where we live, for the time being.'

John looked at their home and seemed impressed by the bricks, mortar, lace and finery.

'Goodbye Miss McGuire, Mr McGuire. I hope you and Mrs McGuire have a good Christmas.' John touched his cap. His hand was shaking.

Clarissa noticed it, but smiled and said, 'Goodbye.' That man they'd just met had certainly affected John, but why?

As John left them he didn't notice a curtain move in the upper bedroom window of the McGuire house.

His mind was busy. Maureen's rapist was in Sydney! And not just anywhere—but close to where he worked. Sweat filmed on his back. The rapist was a dapper bastard, good looking, well spoken and well muscled. His vision of the man all these months was nothing like the one he'd just seen in the hot sun. He was a gentleman, well respected, and a businessman with banking connections.

John couldn't face anyone yet, nor eat a barracks' meal so he headed to the quay. In George Street North he stopped at a pub for a pint of porter and sat in a corner facing the street. He gulped the ale. Fate had directed them to meet. John hadn't searched for him. It was frustrating. Not being able to do anything that would be swift, clean justice.

Looking through the window, passers-by became blurred as explosive scenes ran through his head; the hospital, visions of Baxterhouse assaulting Maureen, blood, bruises and battered flesh. He closed his eyes to try to stop the images. Opening his eyes he knew he had to do something, something for his sister. He drank his beer in silence. But what? Assault him? That was futile. He would be arrested and Baxterhouse would be free. But there was one advantage. Baxterhouse had no way to connect John to Maureen. Her married name was Murphy. That was John's ace and he had to guard that card and play it well. If he attacked Baxterhouse, he could well find out that John was Maureen's brother. Baxterhouse had money. John didn't. People in the street came into focus and the voice of reason called him back, easing his breathing. He leaned against the wall and closed his eyes again.

On his journey back to the barracks he forced himself to think about his quarry and resolved to find out all he could about him. His plan now was to bring Baxterhouse down, to ruin him and strip him of everything—legally or otherwise.

Clarissa closed the front door and heard her mother's footsteps coming down the stairs.

'I have to speak with you, Clarissa. Come to the parlour. You were talking to Mr Leary?'

'We met at Mass.' Clarissa took off her bonnet and sat on one of the twin chairs.

Christine McGuire sat straight-backed opposite her. 'Indeed. Did he approach you or did you seek him out?'

Clarissa hesitated but decided lying wouldn't help. She tried to soften the deed. 'Father and I saw him as he left Mass. We went to—'

'So you did meet him. You chased after him like a common girl, in front of our society friends. Who knows what they'll think!'

'I'm not responsible for their thoughts, mother. Father was with me. It was all very respectable.'

'Let me be the judge of that. In future you'll—'

'Christine, please.' Both women looked as David stood in the doorway. 'Clarissa's right. It was nothing scandalous.' He entered the room, closed the doors behind him and went to the fireplace where he took a pipe. 'I met the boy and we had refreshments. We walked home together. That was all.'

Christine raised her chin a little, keeping her mouth in its determined line.

'We're just starting to settle in socially. Now Clarissa goes and ruins it for us. That nice young man, Ian McCreadie— his family is well connected. Why don't you spend some time with him? And he would be a good match.'

Clarissa stood up and offered an olive branch. 'I'll agree to mix more in society, mother, but I'd like to pick the man I marry.'

Her mother bridled. 'Goodness me, the rudeness!'

'Christine!' David said.

Christine looked from father to daughter and picked up a book to read.

David sighed and filled his pipe.

The lighting was dim in the McGuire Sussex Street warehouse and Clarissa took care stepping between the stacks of wire rolls. The last time she'd done so she'd tripped in front of the workers. She spoke to the man at her side. 'How many rolls do we have here?'

'Three hundred give or take a dozen, Miss McGuire.'

'Don't you know the exact number?' The foreman seemed to be frustrated at her firing questions at him, but Clarissa was unconcerned. 'Please get me the right number and those for the previous two months and the turnover. I'll be back tomorrow. Have those figures for me.' The foreman nodded. Clarissa left him and went to the office in the corner of the warehouse. She closed the door shutting off the noise and the faint odour of grease.

'Good morning, Miss McGuire,' a suited man stood and greeted her.

Clarissa sat down opposite him. 'Good morning. Mr Harrison, the foreman has no knowledge of our stock. McGuire's two most important lines are fencing wire and corrugated iron sheeting. Where are the sales reports for the end of November?'

'All's well, Miss. Nothing of significance there.'

'Please let me look at them.'

The manager's eyebrows rose and he lifted a file from a cabinet and returned to the desk. As Clarissa opened the file at the first page, he said. 'I can explain the report. It's—'

'I can read, thank you,' Goodness, these men. God gave me eyes and a brain. After leafing through three pages she stopped. 'Blackwoods are selling twenty per cent more wire than us. Why is that?'

Harrison turned the file around and glanced at it. 'That's only for a month's trading. Overall we're ahead.'

Clarissa opened her bag and brought out her notebook. She

flicked some pages and found the reference she wanted. She looked at the straight-faced manager. 'You're incorrect. I have the last six months' figures and the situation is getting worse. Give me the wire inventory book please.'

Reaching into an adjoining bookcase he placed a ledger on the desk with a bang just as a crane outside dumped another load of wire onto the warehouse floor.

She opened the ledger and read. 'As I thought, stock has increased and that's money lost to us.'

'We can't seem to shift it.'

'Reduce the price below Blackwoods. Offer a one month cost reduction. You'll sell it. If that doesn't work, there are plenty of retailers who'll take our wire, not at full price, and that way we'll get our inventory down.'

The office door opened and her father walked in. 'Is everything all right?'

Clarissa looked at Harrison and waited for him to tell her father the damning facts. He stared at her. Nothing? It was then up to her—

'Miss Clarissa,' Harrison said, 'has some good ideas about saving us money.'

Well, it was one way to save face and she got what she'd wanted anyway. 'I have.'

'Excellent,' her father said. 'Come upstairs. I'd be delighted to hear about them.'

Clarissa nodded a farewell to the manager. Harrison seemed thankful that she hadn't criticised him in front of her father. Maybe she'd get better cooperation when she would be back here tomorrow. Seated in her father's office, she took off her bonnet. 'I haven't done anything special. It's just common sense. I'll write you up some notes, if you could get a clerk to transcribe a copy for me.'

'I'd like to hear them anyway. Anything to reduce our costs is essential.'

'Well, here are my ideas . . .'

Sydney had entered the festive season and John closed and locked the site gate. They'd start up again the day after New Year.

'That'll keep the honest burglars away,' Fruin said. 'That last bit of bracing to the first floor framing was first rate.'

'Thanks.' Fruin was trying hard to be nice for yuletide and John appreciated it. 'Have a good Christmas, Mr Fruin.'

'You too, Leary.'

It was four-thirty and John went to Bent Street and found Donald sitting on the veranda.

'Here you are. Last day at work before Christmas?'

'Aye, and I'm looking forward to tomorrow.'

'We'll have a good time here,' Donald said. 'Free beer, pudding, the lot.'

'We will indeed.'

The next day's bright sun portended a scorcher and the humidity could be sliced with a knife. Thunderstorms were due after the midday meal. John washed, gave a bottle of rum to Donald as a present, wished all the barracks folk a Merry Christmas then headed to Mass.

On the way, he asked the Lord's forgiveness for thinking about a Christmas feast rather than the Saviour's birth. At Mass, the priest intoned the Lord's Prayer but when it got to the forgiveness for his enemies John's piety evaporated. It wasn't possible to forgive Baxterhouse, even today, a day of universal goodwill. The service ended and he greeted people he knew, as he was becoming a regular. He headed towards Hunter Street thinking about Baxterhouse but Clarissa's gate brought him back to the present.

He banged the front door knocker, startling two magpies from a nearby jacaranda. One dropped a dollop of poo next to his boots. Not a bad sign, he hoped. The door opened. 'John Leary,' he said to a servant who took him into the parlour.

Footsteps sounded and there was Clarissa in a navy dress, trimmed in red, with a white collar upon which a necklace glistened. 'This is a surprise. Merry Christmas, Mr Leary.'

'To you as well. I just came to bring you a present.' He brought a wrapped box of chocolates from behind his back. 'Thank you,' she said taking the box and opening it. 'My favourites.'

He sensed she was being polite but he was pleased. Looking at her, he lost his self-consciousness. 'You look in the festive spirit. I tried hard to find snow in Bent Street but I did see a Koala with a Santa hat. And it will be a novelty eating a turkey with lashings of gravy when the temperature in the shade is near boiling.'

Clarissa smiled and moved towards him. 'I'm finding the heat difficult but Mother is finding it harder. We'll persevere, Mr Leary. Now, you have placed me in a most difficult position. I have no present for you. I'm sorry.'

John hadn't expected one. 'That's all right. Please give my respects to your father and mother. I—'

'Mr Leary, compliments of the season.' Startled, they looked up. Mrs McGuire walked towards him.

'And the same to you, ma'am.' John stumbled to find words to overcome his embarrassment and realised that Christine McGuire must have been standing there for some time.

'Mother, Mr Leary brought me some chocolates for Christmas.'

'Very decent of him. Come Clarissa, your guest is waiting.'

That was rude of her but John didn't want to let that spoil his time here.

'I'll see Mr Leary out,' Clarissa said blushing.

Christine McGuire smiled. 'The servant will do that. Goodbye, Mr Leary.'

'Goodbye,' John said and he went out to the hall where the door was opened and closed for him. 'Merry Christmas,' he muttered.

Clarissa was irritated that her time with John had been cut short. She had been about to invite him to dinner. She smiled. Now, that would have put starch into her mother's blouse.

'It's not smiling you should be. Fancy asking him into our house. You had no right.'

'Mother, it's Christmas and—' she was going to say John— 'Mr Leary had brought me a present.'

'I'll not continue this subject. Come.'

Disgruntled, she accompanied her mother through the hallway

and onto the rear balcony where her father and Ian McCreadie were seated in cane chairs. Ian was John McCreadie's son, a tall broad-shouldered man about John Leary's age. Both men stood up.

'Further refreshment, McCreadie?'

'No, thank you.'

'Mr McCreadie is not staying long,' David said. 'We were just talking about their new shareholder William Baxterhouse.'

'David, please,' Christine said, 'no business today.'

'Oh, very well.'

'Thank you,' Christine said. 'Mr McCreadie, surely you can stay for dinner! Your family can spare you and we'd love to have your company, wouldn't we Clarissa?'

'Mother, this is Christmas day and Mr McCreadie should be with his loved ones.'

McCreadie looked at Christine and smiled. 'Your invitation is welcomed, Mrs McGuire. Unfortunately Miss Clarissa is right. I must be on my way. Another time then.'

'I'll see you out, Mr McCreadie,' her mother said.

Clarissa went into the dining room as the shrill of the cicadas punched through the humid air and the potted ferns swayed to the warm nor'wester. White napery highlighted the cutlery that accompanied the Waterford crystal and the silver tureens filled with food. Clarissa thought about John. It was sweet of him to bring her a present and she started to plan how to see him again. She'd write a letter and propose a meeting at the barracks. It would be risky but she had to see him.

'Clarissa, that soup spoon is out of position. It's right in front of you.'

'Sorry, mother.'

'Now, go and get your father. Dinner is ready.'

Christine McGuire sat opposite her husband at the end of the table and the French doors were opened to catch any breeze but otherwise the atmosphere was stifling. Her father said grace and then clasped a goblet filled with ice water and raised it towards his wife.

'Bon appétit and Merry Christmas to us all.'

Clarissa had a bold idea about how to see John. It would mean being chaperoned by the maid but they still could have some private talk. 'Mother, could I have the carriage tomorrow?'

'Why?'

'As the second carriage is being repaired, I'd planned a trip to Bondi Bay.'

'By yourself?' Christine said. 'No, you can't. We have a function to attend.'

'Do we, dear?' David said. 'With whom?'

Christine smiled. 'The Wentworths, a garden party. Don't you remember?'

'That's not till the early evening,' David replied.

'Have you seen Bondi, father? It's quite magnificent with the broiling surf and the wild cliffs.'

'No, I haven't.'

'But the natives,' Christine said. 'Why just last week, yes, there was a disturbance at Ben Buckler. David, please reconsider.'

'Your mother's right, Clarissa. Not by yourself.'

Clarissa was going to reply, but kept silent. She was disappointed but would find another way to see John.

'But *I* can take you to Bondi,' her father said, 'via Point Piper. I'd welcome the fresh air and we can come back to town in plenty of time.'

Christine glanced out the French window then looked back at David. 'If you think that would be all right.'

'Why Point Piper, Father?'

Her father looked at her mother who nodded then he smiled back at her.

'Well, it's a Christmas present to us all. I've purchased a site just up from the water, and that's where our new house will be built.'

Clarissa jumped from her chair and hugged him. 'Thank you, Father.' She looked at her mother whose face was animated. 'You knew and didn't tell me?'

'We were going to tell you later today,' Christine replied.

Clarissa resumed her seat with a beaming face. 'Tell me all about it.'

'I'll tell you in the carriage tomorrow,' her father said. 'Suffice to say I'd been looking at land before you and your mother came to the colony. It's a bit far out and it isn't Macleay Point but it's good. I made a deposit last week. I'm briefing Mr Lewis, the architect, in a few days to start designs for the house.'

Clarissa smiled. Father will need a builder. Good. Another reason to keep seeing John Leary.

William Baxterhouse was raking it in. This was the fourth hand in a row that he'd won—and without tricks. The close humid air wasn't helped by the smoke from assorted pipes and cigars players around the table were indulging in. William's shoulders and arms were sore from an early morning's exercise but he welcomed the pain. It meant he was getting back to his best fitness. The shed beside his boatbuilding business was set up with weights and a punching bag which he worked on each day, hitting its leather skin with closed fists and open palms. Tomorrow night he'd organised a fight at Middle Head with one of George Hough's protégés, an up-and-coming bare knuckle specialist. A big crowd was expected and Baxterhouse couldn't wait. At thirty-five he was old to fight but he still had the skills. But the present must be enjoyed and he patted the thigh of a big-eyed girl sitting next to him. 'Well Mavis, what's the go? Should I cut and run or keep playing?'

He looked around the table but each man failed to match his stare for longer than two clock ticks. 'I'll keep playing then, - gentlemen.'

The Christmas repast with Higgins and his daughter at Glebe had been pleasant, especially with Elizabeth. She was a beauty and, at twenty-two with a rich father, was a catch: a perfect life companion in this new colony. He would relish the courtship over the next six months. 'Two,' he called. He arranged his new cards and placed them face down on the table. He had acquired the shareholding in McCreadie's firm and had won a contract to build six whaleboats for a New Zealand company. Now, he waited with anticipation on the news from his brother, James, in Dublin. Had he been hounded by the creditors? Had he sold the Dublin stock? Thinking of Ireland reminded him of that Leary man and how he'd enquired after him. What was his interest? William knew it probably had to do with his businesses. Leary was from Dublin. Was he a creditor, or representing them? The girl beside him squeezed his thigh, distracting him. 'Steady love,' he said to her.

'Play cards or excuse yourself, Baxterhouse,' one player said.

William laughed. 'All right boys. Let's see what you've got.'

CHAPTER FIVE

'THE TOLL ROAD FIRST, EVANS,' DAVID MCGUIRE SAID TO HIS driver. 'I'll tell you where to stop on the way. Then on to Bondi Bay.'

'I was going to invite Mr Leary today, Father.' Clarissa said as the carriage moved off.

'That's why you wanted the carriage? You wanted to be alone with him?'

'Evans and my maid would have chaperoned us.'

'So it's deception now,' David said. 'I'm disappointed. I really am.'

Clarissa was too. Not because she couldn't see John but because she'd hurt her father. She sighed. 'I'm sorry. But it's nice to be around him as a friend.'

'That's all he is?'

'That's all.'

'I saw your reaction to him outside St Mary's the week before Christmas. Friendships like that turn serious. I'll not have that.'

Clarissa rummaged in her purse as an excuse to avoid his eyes. He could read her better than anyone.

David placed his hand on hers. 'We are different to him.'

'You sound like Mother.'

'You don't mean that. I didn't say we're superior. We're just different. I don't want you getting any ideas about Mr Leary.'

'But it's Sydney father, not Dublin. People aren't so rigid here.'

'That's true, but that doesn't mean standards drop.' David looked out the carriage window. 'So we are agreed? No more Leary?'

Clarissa felt sick. For the first time in her life, she'd have to lie to her father. 'Very well.'

David McGuire said nothing but looked at her. Clarissa counted the seconds before she'd give in and have to tell him her real feelings. 'But then,' David said, 'this trip will give us time to talk about the new house.' Clarissa breathed out. She had survived his scrutiny. 'What are your thoughts on the design?'

'I'm worried about corrosion with this salt air. Corrugated iron could be used for the verandas, the sheets with more zinc coating might do. But slate's the answer for the main roof.'

Clarissa leant forward holding on to a grab handle. 'The drawing rooms must be large and the kitchen well ventilated. So the heat can escape.'

They spent most of the time talking until David looked outside and raised his hand. 'Evans, turn left in about one hundred yards into Wolseley Road.' A minute later, they hung on as the carriage changed direction. It wasn't really a road, more a compacted track. A short time later, David looked out the window again. 'Stop here, please.'

Evans helped them alight. Their land sloped down to the road and they had an uninterrupted view of the harbour. David led the way up with Clarissa following. They stopped on top of a sandstone shelf and her father turned to her.

'So what do you think?'

'Father, it's truly a fine location.'

Surrounded by trees, David looked at the harbour, a hand shading his eyes. 'It is that, a good piece of land. The main vista's to the west, so the verandas will want shading.'

They inspected the site for the next ten minutes then returned to the carriage. 'The architect will have recommended builders,' Clarissa said, 'won't they?'

'I'm sure they would.' David frowned at her. 'You weren't thinking of Mr Leary now?'

'He works for a builder,' Clarissa replied.

'He's still on your mind and that's not good.' He helped her on board. 'Let's leave the selection of builders to Lewis, and for you to consider other men than Mr Leary. Is that understood?'

'Yes, Father,' she said. She was disappointed but there was still hope.

'Bondi Bay now Evans, please.'

Away from the harbour, copses of gums punctuated the sparseness and they kept silent, absorbing the view and the peace. Rounding a cliff top, studded with spinifex, they stopped and the sea met them in all its blueness. To the south, headlands poked their noses into the Pacific like racehorses jumping from a starter's gun and nearer to them, an expanse of white sand like a sash lay between the waves and the inland flora.

Clarissa enjoyed the day with her father. Business talk may have dominated but that was all right. All the while, though, she was thinking about how to get John Leary involved in their new home.

Christine McGuire knew that the occasion had to be planned to the last detail, with the appropriate food and drinks. The scrutiny of many of society's well-connected matrons would be focused on—no—judging her! She had competition and she was determined that *her* party would be the best New Year's Eve party in town. She removed her spectacles and put the list she'd been reading down on the dining room table. 'I'm so excited.'

'Is there much more to do?' Clarissa asked. With all the fuss she guessed her mother wanted them to be noticed by the *Sydney Morning Herald*.

'The chairs. We have to take them out. There'll be more room. Fetch the maid.'

'I'll put up the last decorations.'

'Leave that. Just get the maid then go and change. Goodness me, look at the time. I'll see to the kitchen. Off you go.'

Going to her room Clarissa sat on the bed. How nice it would be to celebrate New Year with John Leary. Clarissa believed she was in love with him and was determined to win him with the same focused attention she gave to her father's business. But did John feel the same way about her? Sitting at her desk she decided to write a letter of New Year tidings to him and request a time when they could meet at the barracks. With that settled she attended to her toilette and prepared herself for the party.

Both men paused as Clarissa opened the office door to them.

'Please come in gentlemen.'

One man moved forward and one hesitated. 'Miss McGuire we had an appointment this afternoon with your father.'

'I know, please take a seat in his office, Mr Penfold and you too Mr Jardine.'

Clarissa stood at her father's desk opposite the two wool merchants. She smiled to herself as they waited for her to sit. They looked awkward in her presence. 'Father had to go home on private business and he gives his apologies.'

Jardine frowned. 'That's unfortunate because we're here to agree the fee we may pay you to manage our wool. We have to sell our clip this week.'

'Indeed,' Clarissa said. 'And my father gave me authority to make decisions on his behalf.'

Jardine's eyes expanded. 'You?'

Clarissa stopped herself from snapping back. But she knew her position must seem odd. Her father warned her about this: a woman right at the core of business. She would have to be on her game in getting the brokerage fee her father wanted. 'Mr Jardine, I do have that authority.'

'Then,' Penfold said, 'I suppose we can continue and see how we go.' He sat back on his seat and steepled his fingers. 'Our estimate of our clip is five hundred bales. On that quantity we're prepared to pay a brokerage fee of one per cent.'

That wasn't too low but she acknowledged it was an opening offer. On that quantity of wool she'd expected to be first offered three quarters of one per cent. 'We are a small house, Mr Penfold. We can move your wool expeditiously and we have an added advantage, we can secure payment swifter than our competitors.'

'How do you do that?' Jardine asked.

'It's one of our features which,' Clarissa smiled, 'we prefer not to tell you—yet. Suffice to say, you get your money quicker.' Clarissa breathed in and exhaled. 'We would like to take your wool and we would charge you a fee of two per cent.'

Penfold looked at Jardine and back to Clarissa. 'We won't pay that.'

Clarissa knew John McCreadie had offered two per cent to these men and had been refused. Her father was willing to accept a half a percent difference to that. 'Mr Penfold, what would you say to one and a half per cent if we can guarantee payment for your wool within fourteen weeks of its landing in England?' This was McGuire's advantage. For a small fee, a clipper ship captain would deliver the receipts in Sydney for deposits made into the accounts the two merchants held with an English bank.

Penfold's eyebrows rose. 'If you guarantee that in writing Miss McGuire, we will accept a fee of one and a half per cent.' Penfold stood up. 'If you would like to draw up the paper, we will sign the agreement tomorrow morning.'

Clarissa opened a folder and withdrew the contract that she had prepared. 'I have it here for you to sign. I'll insert the percentage fee at the bottom.' She added the fee to both copies and handed them to Mr Penfold.

Penfold smiled at her. 'Miss McGuire, you are shrewd. It's been a pleasure to do business with you.' He and Mr Jardine signed both copies and returned one to her.

Jardine stood up. 'My sentiments likewise, Miss. We hope we can do more business with David McGuire or, perhaps in a more charming way, with you.'

Clarissa saw them out and looked at the clock. It was 4.30 pm. She mustn't dally. Grabbing some documents from her desk and two books she hurried out the door.

Sitting in the cab on its way up George Street she knew she was taking a risk. Sydney was a small town in some respects, like Dublin. People saw you. People recognised you. If she was discovered this afternoon in the circumstances in which she placed herself she'd be severely admonished by her parents. There were two subterfuges she was using for her rendezvous and, unlike the *Emily*, they were not copper-bottomed.

Paying the driver she alighted at Phillip Street and walked down to her destination. She felt a combination of excitement and apprehension as she scrutinised every passer-by. There were none who knew her. With confidence she went up the stairs into the immigration barracks. John was there waiting in the common room where they'd agreed to meet. He looked excited.

'Thank you for coming,' he said.

'I cannot stay long. Do they have a noticeboard where advertisements are posted?'

John looked puzzled. 'In the corner, here. Why?'

She followed him to the board. 'We need a yardman for our Sussex Street business and someone from here may want to apply. I have to post this on the board.' This was true and she smiled. 'But not yet. I'm not supposed to see you alone.' She was going to add, *at all* but she kept quiet. 'If anyone I know sees me I can pin the notice and explain meeting you as a coincidence and by the way, here are your books back.'

He took them and grinned. 'Did you like them?'

She looked around. 'Byron especially. Now come over here where we can talk.'

Standing in a corner away from the comings and goings of the busy place, Clarissa was excited being with him, but kept her questions to safe topics. 'Did you pass Christmas well, and New Year?'

'I did, thank you. I can't believe it's halfway through January.'

And nearly three weeks since she'd seen him.

'And you?' he asked. 'I saw your family's New Year gathering in the paper. That must have been something.'

'It was.' She looked around. So far, so good. 'I'm curious. When you met that man before Christmas, a Mr Baxterhouse, you changed. Why was that? Did you know him in Dublin?'

John's face seemed innocent. 'No. It was just the sun that affected me, Miss Clarissa, like I said.'

'Is that true?'

'It is.'

She was sceptical. 'You've been working over two months outside in this heat? You were affected on *that* day?'

'I was, believe me.'

'I have to.' She paused. 'Then why did you say you were from Dublin when your home is in Kildare?'

'Did I?'

'You did.'

He raised his hands. 'Just a mistake. That's all. Tell me. Have you made other friends in Sydney?'

He was changing the subject. He might be lying to her. But why? She let it go—for now. 'Not many friends, really. Mother wants me to mix more in society, as she calls it, but with father's businesses, I don't have much time.'

'How are you coping with that?'

'It's challenging,' she said and smiled. She had missed him.

'I bet it is. A woman ordering all those men around.'

She was ready to take the bait when she saw him grin. She did too. 'When I ask them nicely, they usually do it.'

'You're the boss's daughter.'

'That's probably the reason. But I'm learning.'

'I have to get out of the barracks by the end of January. They only give you three months after arriving.'

He would have his own place where they could be alone. That both unsettled and emboldened her. *What was she thinking?* 'Where will you live?'

'I don't know. Somewhere close to work, I hope.'

A face caught Clarissa's attention and she acted. 'It was nice to see you again, Mr Leary.' Thomas Higgins was looking at her and she moved to the noticeboard. 'Good afternoon, Mr Higgins. I was just about to mount this advertisement for a worker my father needs when I saw Mr Leary.'

Thomas Higgins glanced at John and seemed unsuspecting of her actions. 'Mr Leary.' Taking off his hat he gestured towards the noticeboard. 'I was just about to do the same, but in the Bank's name, of course.' He smiled. 'Always good to offer our future depositors a safe haven for their money. After you, Miss.' Higgins made way for her and he concentrated on the papers in his hand.

Out of Higgins's sight, Clarissa raised her eyebrows and John smiled at her and went back into the building. As she pressed the tacks she wondered how she could meet him again.

'Did you get a bellyfull yesterday at the Foundation Day celebrations?' Harry Dickson asked.

John laughed. 'Of course. God, 1851 already.'

'Oh! I'm short of nails.' Harry said. 'I'll get some.'

'I'll keep going with the bracing.' The first floor framing, the joists, comprised single deep timber beams that were placed parallel and eighteen inches apart and spanned across the room. The end of each beam fitted into prepared masonry slots. To stiffen the deep beams, timber blocks were nailed at right angles between each beam. John placed another bracing block into position and watched his labourer go into the shed. Harry was becoming more of a carpenter's assistant and that helped John do more work. He concentrated and started nailing. He did one more block with the nails he had.

Wiping the sweat from his forehead he thought about Clarissa. It would've been nice to spend Foundation Day with her but that wasn't to be. She'd been astute, he admitted, to spot his reaction to Baxterhouse. It also meant she took notice of him, and that meant she was interested in him. Why otherwise would she risk meeting him unchaperoned? Didn't she realise that any friendship they had could be only that and nothing more? But she might want more. No. New digs, which he needed to find, would make it easier to see her. If she wanted to see him.

To distract himself he glanced at the harbour in its haze. The masts of the ships rose like reeds from a lake. Each ship stood alongside its wharf in Darling Harbour and in Miller's Point, while wagons filled their hulls with goods for England. It fascinated him how much activity there was on the waterfront. This fanned his belief that a few were making profits in the process. Thinking of Darling Harbour reminded him of Baxterhouse and the need to avenge Maureen. John had few ideas.

'Hey, Leary,' Fruin yelled. 'We pay you to swing a hammer, not stare at nothing.'

Harry came up beside him and opened a box of nails. John smothered his reply and went back to work.

William Baxterhouse's cuff brushed the wet ink. 'Please give me another copy. I've smudged this.'

The bank clerk took a sheet and rewrote a copy of the last page of the transport contract. William thought about the previous evening. John McCreadie had invited him to a gentlemen's club in Macquarie Street and had introduced him to representatives from Goldsborough Mort. They had had a delightful evening of food and wines and these men had extended him an invitation to dinner. He was enjoying the benefits of the business fraternity. Thinking of business, he pulled from his suit pocket the letter he'd received that morning and began reading the good news again.

30 August 1850

Dublin

Dear Brother,

I hope this letter finds you in good health. The stock in our

Dublin warehouse was sold five days after you left. I enclose Letter of Credit for £200 that you can take to your bank. It—

'Here you are sir,' the clerk said.

William put James's letter away and snatched the sheet and positioned it for signature. He signed his name. The quill's scratching competed with the din of carts and horses from outside the bank's window. The date? Yes, 17 February, in the year of Our Lord, 1851.

Signing the copy he pushed both back to Higgins sitting opposite him. 'So, you think this is a sound business, like McCreadie's?'

The banker signalled the clerk to leave his office and close the door. Higgins adjusted his suit, tightened his necktie and righted himself in his seat looking at William through spectacles. 'It's a different but a good business. Wagons take the oats from the warehouse to the breweries. The current owner was slipshod in running his wagons to any sort of schedule. It was a profitable business but the breweries often complained about late deliveries and not always the quantity they ordered. The good thing is that all the wagons are only three years old.'

'I've read the financial reports.'

'So improve the discipline of deliveries, Mr Baxterhouse, their timings and loads and you'll turn a better quid.'

'You'll manage the funds and transfer them to the vendor?'

The banker nodded.

'Good. By the way,' William brought out his letter and gave Higgins the Letter of Credit, 'take care of that.' The banker's eyes widened in delight. 'The transport contract is for three years and in that time I'll find another business to build up my cash flow.' He rubbed his hands together. 'All good, all good!'

'Do you want the same lines of funding as McCreadie's? We can do a solid rate. At the moment Bills of Exchange are—'

'I'll let you sort out the details.'

'Very well. The documents we shall retain are the contracts, the mortgages and the guarantees. These will be filed with the McCreadie and boatbuilding documents and a copy sent to your lawyers.'

William pondered about managing the three businesses at once. McCreadie's brokers would take less of his time, as he was a minor shareholder. The boatbuilding business now had a manager, an experienced man called Davies. The transport contract was his and would require a sharp overseer for the loads from warehouse to the breweries. He had to think that through, and where better to find him than the 'Hero'.

Muffled shouts from outside could be heard. Both men looked at each other. The noises intensified.

The banker stood up, alarmed, and went to the door. 'Not a robbery, please God.' He slid open a note-sized panel and looked out.

William was puzzled too. 'What is it?'

'It's not a robbery but something's happening. I'll go and see.'

Higgins closed the door behind him and an excited yell startled William. He'd find out himself and walked into the public chamber and stopped. It was buzzing with noise. Clerks were chatting in pairs with lots of grins and back slapping, customers were racing out the doors and into the street. Deposit slips were being tossed into the air by an ageing matron.

The banker strode up to William, his face awash with excitement. 'I don't know whether it's true or not. I'm trying to verify it. I've sent a boy down to the newspaper office.'

William was exasperated. 'What do you mean?' Higgins looking around excitedly, didn't answer. Grabbing him by both shoulders, William shook him. 'What's happening?'

Higgins held onto his spectacles. 'Someone's discovered gold near Bathurst!'

~

John heard rumours that night about the gold strike, but put it down to beer having the magic to weave fantasy into fact. Next morning the *Sydney Morning Herald*'s headlines cleared the sleep from his eyes quicker than the sight of a pretty girl: 'GOLD DISCOVERED AT LEWIS CREEK.'

John read the article in the common room with the barracks' gang pouring over his shoulder. Everybody spoke at once and John and Donald removed themselves from the huddle. John was excited. 'It's grand. Fortunes to be made, they say.'

Donald sipped his tea and paused as if thinking. 'Terrible news, John.'

'What do you mean?'

'Gold fever's evil. I've an uncle who wrote to me from California in the United States. He said gold ruined more people than made them rich.'

'I don't follow.'

'You see, it's like a drug. It addles ya brain. People just drop everything they're doing, leave loved ones and jobs. They don't care.'

'But if there's money to be made, it's worth it, isn't it?'

'John, you're young. You think like a young man. You think you can do everything and nothing can touch you. As you get older you work things out.' John was unconvinced.

'One of the things my uncle said was that a study or something like that was done after the California strike and guess who made the most money?'

'The man who found the biggest nugget?'

Donald slapped his knee. 'Wrong. It was the merchants selling all the gold fossicking tools and such who cleaned up. There.'

'Is that right?'

'It's what the report said. Shovel suppliers, tent makers. Blokes like that.'

'Well, I'm thinking about going.'

'Right, so how'll you get there? Got the tools, tent? Money for grub?'

John's grin faded. 'Aye, there is all that.'

'Look, wait awhile. Think about it, and keep saving your money. The gold's been in the ground for a long time and it ain't going nowhere. Find out where the best digs are, speak to people coming back. Believe me, it'll help you decide.'

John looked at his friend. It all made good sense but he was impatient. 'I'll think about it.'

John turned the corner from Erskine Street into Day Street. As he got nearer to the site Mr Jenkins and Fruin were yelling at each other. John gave them a wide berth on the way to his work area.

'We can still make the completion date,' Fruin said.

Jenkins had his hand on his hips. 'Tell me how.'

The overseer scratched his head and seemed to weigh up his reply. 'Come over here.' He walked into the space of the future public bar, which now served as a storage area for building materials. Jenkins followed.

John ignored them and got stuck into hauling up the last of the sawn-to-length hardwood floor boards that would be used for the upper floor. Because the site was running behind they had needed to do the floorboards even though the roof was not yet built. Stacked beside John were two big tarps that would cover his work from rain. An hour passed and Harry hadn't fronted and John continued with laying the first of the boards until smoko. Gulping the dregs of his tea he climbed down the ladder when Fruin called him.

'Leary, where's Harry?'

'Haven't seen him.'

'Shite, not another one!'

'Not another what?' John said.

'Pissed off to Bathurst, I'll bet!'

'Dunno.'

The overseer stopped at the foot of the ladder. 'Well, can ya keep going? Got enough to do?'

'Plenty. All the boards.'

'Just keep out of the brickies' way. I'm off to the Annandale site.'

John slogged for the rest of the day doing the jobs of two men. Around knock off time, a shadow came across his vision and looking up he saw Fruin grinning.

'Not bad Leary, not bad, you've done a lot. More than I expected.'

John stretched from his cramped position. 'Where's Harry?'

'I don't know but I'll find out tonight. I know where he lives.'

'Well, if he doesn't front tomorrow, I'll need a hand if you want this lot knocked over by week's end.'

The overseer wasn't looking at John but at his work. He nodded. 'I'll tell you what. Keep going tomorrow. I'll try and find out what happened to that bloody labourer. If he's gone then the day after, I'll bring you another man.'

'Good.'

~

'But I have to have the carriage. It's the nineteenth and Father's expecting me at the meeting. Cabs are too unreliable.'

'I've told you, Evans has gone,' her mother said. 'We're mystified but he may have taken off to follow the misguided souls to the goldfields. Your father has advertised for another driver. All our friends are in a similar situation. Their servants are leaving also.'

'Well then, what do I do?'

'I suggest you wait. Your father will be back at midday and you can discuss it with him. Honestly, these business doings of yours will be the death of me.'

During the meal Clarissa raised the subject with her father. 'The new driver, have you had any applications?'

'I'm looking and trying to pull in a few favours,' David said, 'but it's not been easy. For now we're going to have to make adjustments. Thankfully, our maid and cook are past their prospecting days.' Clarissa smiled. 'And they'll hopefully stay with us. The driver's the problem. Our warehouse is in town but it's the travel to the suburbs that will inconvenience me. Cabs are scarce too. Everyone, it seems, wants gold. This lack of labour is going to get worse. Prices are going to rise as workers become scarce.'

Clarissa nodded. 'After dinner, we should discuss contingency plans if the labour shortage worsens.'

David's face lightened in a smile. 'Something I was going to suggest myself. By the way, I met the architect for the second time yesterday. He's seen the site and has started his design.'

'Very good.' Clarissa reminded herself to speed up her strategy to get John Leary to build their new home.

'Another tea, Mr Baxterhouse?'

William put down the letter to James that he'd drafted. The maid blushed as he scanned her well-developed bosom. He grinned. 'No more, thank you.' Moving to a table near him, she filled the cups of two suited men who were having breakfast together, one holding a newspaper.

William glanced at his letter. There was nothing to add to it. He picked up the newspaper and, pushing his used breakfast plates away, began to read.

'Listen to this and I quote,' the man near him said, '"The excitement of the Bathurst strikes has gripped all Sydney".'

'You see fewer people on the streets, I admit,' his companion replied. 'One shop near Park Street was decked out with blue and red serge shirts from California.'

'It's dramatic,' agreed his companion.

'And this,' his mate said.

William put down his newspaper. The man was about to read it out anyway.

'"One carriage maker has lost ten of his workmen to the diggings, a tailor seven. A vet's assistant has given his employer the option of increasing his pay or losing him to the mines."'

The other man shook his head and continued eating. William was thankful for the silence. There were no big strikes, no sugar bowl-sized nuggets unearthed, but to the souls of Sydney, any dust found would solve their woes. This gold fever would put pressure on prices everywhere. But his businesses were profitable and he could afford to buy a house to reflect his standing, to meet the needs of his wife—Elizabeth Higgins he hoped—and to entertain his friends. A two-storey town house in Chippendale was on the market for a good price and he'd better act before it skyrocketed in value.

He turned another page and glanced at an article in the bottom corner. He read it, and then read it again. A tingling came to his fingers—an opportunity, but how? Then the concept crystallised. Yes! He looked out of the window to the harbour as the heat was burning off the last dregs of the morning mist. Planning was the key but he had to act right away.

The prospectors couldn't get enough kit to dig up their gold! The notice in the newspaper was from Mackays, a retail supplier, which requested tenders from wholesalers for more tools, shovels, tents and other equipment. There was insufficient stock in town it seemed. William suspected there were few companies making such things on a large scale in Sydney. In the medium term there would be a shortage and that was the gold! Forget what's in the ground. The idiots would pay anything to get their hands on the tools to make their fortunes. How could he solve the problem? Yes, he'd stocked picks, shovels and spades as a minor line in his Dublin warehouse. When he'd packed his bag to leave he'd thought about not bringing that price list with him but now he was glad he had. As for tents, he would have to check what they might cost in Sydney.

Getting up he grabbed the newspaper and the letter. Going to his room, he drafted in his mind more things to add to his letter to his brother.

~

Her mother's lips were moving and her eyes closed. Clarissa, sitting beside her, wished her own devotions were as intense. Sighing, she looked down at her missal then glanced up and saw John Leary seated five pews in front of her. Even allowing for the heat, her colour heightened. She juggled her missal and glanced at her mother who was, thank the good Lord, somewhere between heaven and earth and hadn't sensed Clarissa's excitement. How could she meet John with her mother here? She had an idea.

Ian McCreadie sat on her mother's left. It was the fourth time since Christmas that he'd been included in the family outings. Clarissa understood her mother's strategy in trying to get her interested in him. He was acceptable. Ian's father was David McGuire's competitor in the wool broking business and McCreadie's was expanding. It needed an extension to its Market Street warehouse, but not right away. John Leary worked for a builder. The link. Her mother would frown on her bringing business to the Sabbath but she had to talk to John. The Mass ended and Clarissa manoeuvred the four of them so they'd convene at the main doors of St Mary's, spotting John who was just behind them. The sun was bright and she put up her parasol hoping he'd see it. Two heartbeats passed and she heard his voice.

'Miss Clarissa.'

They all turned around as John approached them. A quick glance at her mother told her this would require finesse.

'Mr Leary, good morning,' Clarissa said.

John smiled. 'And to you.'

'This is Mr McCreadie.'

'Good day, Mrs McGuire,' John said and then extended his hand and nodded to McCreadie. 'Where is Mr McGuire?'

'He's in bed with a cold,' Christine said.

'I'm sorry to hear that,' John said. 'I hope he improves and please give him my best.'

'Thank you, Mr Leary.' Christine smiled at him.

Clarissa suspected that her mother was interested in how the men would react to each other. Clarissa took the lead. 'Mr Leary, it isn't done to raise it today but the labour shortage makes it excusable. Mr McCreadie here has to extend his father's wool store and he's looking for a good builder.'

She noted with satisfaction Ian's face changing from a frown to a smile while her mother's registered curiosity.

'Well, yes,' John said. 'Mr Jenkins is a builder. I'd have to talk with him. Here, let's get out of the sun.' He led them into the shade of a tree.

Clarissa wanted to continue talking. 'Mr McCreadie told me about their plans and this is a way to help him. It's so difficult getting people together with the lack of drivers that today may be a good opportunity.' Her mother's curiosity seemed satisfied although she looked guarded.

'Look, Mr Leary,' Ian McCreadie said, 'it's only the middle of February. I don't need the space till next year, even the year after. In fact, we may be able to rearrange our stock to save the cost of building. I just mentioned our expansion to Miss Clarissa some weeks ago.'

'Mr McCreadie,' Clarissa said, 'you know you need it, your store is bursting. That consignment of first grade merino is subject to weather now, as you well know. Those tarpaulins you have covering it are only temporary.'

McCreadie reached up and broke off a dead branch that threatened his eye. 'I know, but I can move that to a rented building. What worries me is building costs will rise due to the labour shortage. How will I know what the final costs on any new building will be?'

That was one of the things about him that irritated her: his lack of confidence. 'More than sufficient reason to use a builder you can trust.' Clarissa gestured in John's direction.

McCreadie looked at John. 'I suppose so. I'll discuss it with Father first and can let Mr Leary know.'

His hesitancy frustrated her. Still, this was business and she knew his business better than he did. She had to. This was one advantage she had. Most men couldn't consider that a woman was capable of planning anything but the household. She had to introduce a lighter note and smiled. 'Very well, look it's not that important. You know your business better than I. Let's not waste any more time discussing it.'

John shot her a searching look and Clarissa guessed he was surprised by her comment but McCreadie seemed to fall for it and his shoulders relaxed.

'I agree, Clarissa,' her mother said. 'As Mr McCreadie said, there's still time for his warehouse or whatever to be built. So, Mr Leary, what are your plans for the rest of the day?'

'Thank you for asking. I'm going sailing this afternoon, Mrs McGuire. Mr Jenkins has a new skiff and he's keen to try it out. I'll say my goodbyes. Mr McCreadie, I'll ask my boss if he can help you. Can he call on you to talk about it?'

McCreadie pulled out a card and gave it to John. He took it and shook the man's hand.

Clarissa was disappointed at the short time spent with John. 'Goodbye. I hope we can meet again soon. By the by, we're getting a new house built at Point Piper. That will mean a good builder. Mr Lewis is the architect. I might ask him to inspect some of Mr Jenkins's jobs, if that's all right.'

'That would be grand,' John said.

'My pleasure.'

'Goodbye, Miss Clarissa, Mrs McGuire. Please give my regards to your husband.'

They watched as John walked away and McCreadie broke the silence of Clarissa's disappointment. 'Such a nice fellow, for a building worker.'

'Yes, he seems to be,' her mother said. 'Come, we must go home. Mr McCreadie, I'm sure you're looking forward to that midday meal with us.'

McCreadie was looking at Clarissa. 'I am that.'

Mackays had given William Baxterhouse a list of what supplies he would need to bid on. William added these in his letter to James. His brother had to come to the colony. But James would need money for purchases. William needed a Letter of Credit to enclose in the letter for the acquisition of the most in-demand items— miners' equipment and hand tools. James would have to scour the Belfast or, if necessary, Liverpool foundries and wholesalers to obtain the equipment and get the load to Sydney via clipper, ideally. Satisfied the letter was in order, William blotted it. James would understand; he knew his onions.

William grabbed the letter to James and going to a cupboard he removed a sealed envelope, left the Hero and set off to see his bank manager in George Street.

'Mr Higgins cannot see you immediately, Mr Baxterhouse,' a clerk said, 'but if you care to wait ten minutes, he'll accommodate you.'

Patience never sat easily on William's shoulders. Twelve long minutes passed and William approached the counter when Higgins appeared.

'A pleasure, as always Mr Baxterhouse, how can the bank help you?'

'In your office, please.'

Higgins settled himself in his chair and William made his request.

'A Letter of Credit? Yes, it's possible, of course.'

'I want it today to mail to Ireland. My brother has to export some equipment.'

Higgins busied himself with pen and paper. 'Any particular type?'

The less said the better, and the more money he'd make. 'Rivet machines. For boatbuilding.'

'Very well, what limit?'

William had thought about this on his way here. He understood how long it would take to get the equipment, plus the distances and time from Ireland. It would take a month for his letter to get there, two months to source and four months to ship, making it late September, October at the earliest, before the goods arrived. He went for broke and wanted the largest shipment possible. 'Four hundred pounds.'

'That's quite a sum. I'll need a director's approval for that which will take two to three days.'

'I don't have that time, Mr Higgins. This order is critical to my business. I need three more machines as demand is rising for boats.'

'That is good but your requested quantum will still take time.'

'All right, all right. What's your daily limit on credit approval?'

'Two hundred pounds.'

William smiled. 'And I can get another two hundred approved tomorrow?'

The banker baulked. 'Yes, that's possible.'

'Get one approved today for two hundred pounds and the other one tomorrow, please. That letter has to leave Sydney tomorrow.'

'It's possible but unusual.'

'Well, do it, man.'

The banker got things moving and within the hour William received the first Letter of Credit. He assembled the documents and would post them tomorrow when he'd got the second Letter of Credit. Pleased with himself and armed with his envelope, he had just one more task to do before dining with Thomas Higgins and Elizabeth. If he added the supply of miners' tools to his burgeoning businesses, he'd have four going concerns: that, and a wool broking partnership, transport wagons and boatbuilding companies. Calling on Mackays in Sussex Street, he placed his sealed envelope in the box marked 'TENDER MINING TOOLS' in the lobby.

'You're keen, sir,' a clerk said and smiled at him. 'It's only the twenty-fifth of February. The tenders don't close for two weeks.'

William waved a goodbye and left. He'd taken a risk because the equipment James was sourcing from the United Kingdom wouldn't come in time to suit Mackays' tender. If he won it, he'd decide then how to get the tools. But at least he'd had a go. And he was sure there would be more demand. A worker at Mackays had also given him, in exchange for ten shillings, the names of two small foundries in Sydney interested in supplying goods. He would set up a plan to thwart them.

CHAPTER SIX

It was near to knock-off time and John positioned a first floor door frame with the help of his new labourer. 'Nail off that temporary brace, Dave.'

The man secured the brace that supported the frame. The brickwork wall could now be built up to each side and on top of the frame, then the temporary brace could be taken away. There were three more to do on that floor and John had started nailing the next frame together when he heard a call. Fruin was waving to him.

'Finish this, Dave, and get Bert to help you. I'll see what Mr Fruin wants,' John said before he climbed down.

'Get this brick order signed by Mr Jenkins,' Fruin said. 'He's in George Street touting for business. Here's the place. Go there and get his signature, then go to the kiln first thing tomorrow. I can't go. I've a few problems to sort out at Annandale.'

John took the paper Fruin handed to him. John remembered his first weeks with Fruin's big carpenter. 'How's Doug Mullins going at Annandale?'

'Struggling as an overseer, but we're short on carpenters. Have you found new digs yet?'

'At Redfern last Sunday. I'll move at the end of the week.'

'Let me know the street and number. Well, John, don't just stand there, get going.'

Ten minutes later he walked up Erskine Street and turned right into George Street, looking for the address. It was McCreadie's the wool broker. Seeing Ian McCreadie with Clarissa at Mass hadn't surprised him. She was attractive, single and came from a good family. McCreadie would be from similar stock no doubt and that would have impressed her mother. But seeing Clarissa again had stirred him. Going to the odd dance with Donald, he hadn't found any girls who interested him like Clarissa did.

Despite his lack of female companionship he was glad he'd been given more responsibility at work, like this brick order. Fruin had made him supervising carpenter for the first floor carpentry and roof, responsible for training up the labourers to assist him, and measuring and ordering the materials needed. For that John thanked the gold strike. Carpenters were scarce as were all tradesmen, with scores of them having raced to Bathurst. There were six building sites in town John had seen abandoned because of the lack of labour, and there were many more, he'd heard. Vacancies were opening up like Doug Mullins's promotion. A good carpenter, but an overseer? John was glad he'd heeded Donald Watkins' advice and remained in town. At last he was on the ladder of promotion.

Lost in thought, John walked right past McCreadie's and was close to Market Street before he backtracked. After going through an anteroom he pushed through a set of doors into a lobby containing two chairs separated by a low table, some paintings on the walls and a counter with a bell. A single door faced him. Ringing the bell, he waited. The door opened and a man appeared.

'I'm looking for Mr Jenkins,' John said. 'I think he's seeing Mr Ian McCreadie.'

The man scanned John's work clothes. 'I'm Mr McCreadie's clerk. And you are?'

'John Leary.'

'Please wait,' the clerk said and disappeared.

John sat on the edge of one of the chairs, conscious of his garb. He looked at the paintings of farm scenes; all sheep and fence posts.

The door opened and Jenkins came out looking a little worried, his face redder than normal.

'Leary. Anything wrong at the pub?'

'No, all's right. Mr Fruin wants you to sign this brick order. I can take it tomorrow to the kiln.'

'Good. Their prices go up on the fifth of March, which is the day after. Give me five minutes. I'm nearly finished with Mr McCreadie about his wool store. Lewis had a look at our site. Thanks to you, we may have a new job. Wait here.'

John sat back down and reached for a newspaper on the table. Good on Clarissa. She was as good as her word. When had Lewis inspected Day Street? John must have missed him. He may have looked at another site Mr Jenkins was building, the Annandale terraces maybe. No matter.

John had little time to read newspapers these days. The silence settled on him and he relaxed absorbing the printed word. He heard the street doors open and close and the door to the lobby open. John glanced at the person. He'd prepared to look away but couldn't. The visitor was William Baxterhouse.

Baxterhouse smiled at him. 'Mr Leary, what brings you here?'

'Kiln order,' John blurted out.

Baxterhouse seemed not to have heard him. 'I'll talk to you later. I've got to see John McCreadie.' He went to the counter and rang the bell. 'Anybody there?'

The same clerk appeared. 'Mr Baxterhouse, how are you! Are you here to see Mr McCreadie?'

'I am.'

'Very good, I'll tell him. Please wait.'

Baxterhouse sat down on the other chair. John pretended to read. 'Kiln order you said? What's that?'

'We need bricks for Day Street. I'm going to St Peters tomorrow.'

'I see.' Baxterhouse grinned. 'Do you box, Mr Leary? You seem to have evidence of it.'

John's shock turned to surprise. 'Bare knuckle?'

'Nothing like it. You'd be good at it.' He paused. 'The last time we met you said you knew I'd left Dublin.' He grinned again. 'So, how did you know?'

John was unprepared for this but he had to say something. 'I was chasing some picks and shovels you might have.' He added another lie. 'Your staff said you were going abroad.'

'Did they now?'

'Yes.'

Baxterhouse paused. 'But Cape Town? That was a long shot asking about me and on a warship? I'm curious how you knew?'

John was now stuck.

'Leary,' Jenkins said as he came into the foyer, nodding to Baxterhouse. 'Got that order? Come over here.'

John thanked the intrusion and went to the counter and in doing so bumped into Ian McCreadie who had followed Jenkins out. 'Sorry, Mr McCreadie. How are you?'

Ian McCreadie smiled at him. 'Well thank you, Mr Leary, but you look peaked. Mr Jenkins is working you too hard.'

'Not hard enough,' Jenkins said and smiled.

'Well,' McCreadie said, 'I've just had a useful meeting. I'm sure your boss will tell you about it.' McCreadie noticed Baxterhouse who'd stood up. 'Hello Mr Baxterhouse, here to see Father?'

'I am.'

'Please come this way.'

Baxterhouse had to pass John. 'Do you still want that timber supplier's name, Mr Leary?'

John was glad that Baxterhouse had forgotten his earlier question instead following up on the timber Baxterhouse had offered when he'd first met him at St Mary's. 'I do.'

'Well, don't stand on etiquette. Come down to my business any time.'

'I will and thank you.' He looked at Baxterhouse's back, presenting a prime target and John clenched his fist, crushing the order. When he opened it, the man and Ian had gone.

'John, are you all right?' Jenkins asked.

'I am.'

'Give me the order.'

John gave him the crumpled paper. Jenkins frowned, straightened and signed it. John pocketed the order as his boss brought out another piece of paper. 'Are you finished for the day on the site?'

'I am.'

'Good. Go to Bourke Street and get this ironmongery order filled and get them to deliver the locks to site. Here's some money for a cab.'

Taking it, John said goodbye and left the building. He wanted space and plenty of it and looked at the address. It was in the Woolloomooloo area of Bourke Street, and after waiting minutes for a cab he decided to walk, setting off up Market Street. Baxterhouse was appearing more often and would continue to do so. He was accomplished, well presented and smart. John had to treat him as a man with whom to do business. That meant talking straight at him with no sign of fear and hesitation, giving the rapist no reason to doubt him. And he'd have to find out more about him and that would cost money. He would have to hire an investigator who could give him information that John could use to bring Baxterhouse down.

After completing his order at the ironmongers he found himself outside the Royal Hotel in Forbes Street. A drink would do the trick. He entered and walked up to the barmaid, 'A pint of Bass, please.'

'Coming up.' She raised and lowered the glass under the tap. The beer overflowed a little as she brought it onto the bar. Her hair was pulled back and she had big, deep-set hazel eyes in a clear face.

'Thanks, luv.' John put coins on the counter, raised the beer and finished it in one hit. Wiping his mouth he put it down and placing both his hands on the bar, he said, 'Another, please.'

He took more time finishing the second beer and sat on a stool in a corner. Noise, people and smoke engulfed him, yet he felt alone.

A man was selling lamb sandwiches. John, waiting his turn, paid for two then bought another beer from the smiling barmaid. At the end of his fourth beer, thoughts of Baxterhouse receded and John was tipsy. The pub was less busy and he was back at the bar speaking to the girl with the smile. 'Nice pub.'

'When you've worked here a while, you get used to it.'

She walked down the bar with a customer's beer and John stretched to look but averted his gaze as she returned to cut some lemons, her back to him. Her well-covered frame was about five feet three. She turned around with the tray and looked straight at him.

His four beers stopped him diverting his eyes. She looked at his empty glass. 'Another one?'

'Please . . . and call me John.'

'Well John, do you want another one or should you slow down?'

'That's not good for business. You . . . you should keep the customer happy.'

The smile went. 'It's all the same to me. When you work behind a bar, you get to know your big drinking types.'

'And those are?'

'Three. Ones that live to drink, ones who are celebrating and ones trying to rid themselves of a demon.'

John grinned. 'Which one am I then?'

The girl picked up a tray of glasses and popped them on the bar. She poured a drink for another customer and returned. 'You've got the clear skin of a light drinker and you're alone, so there's nothing to celebrate. So what does that leave?'

The girl's remark was close to the truth. 'Give me another beer. What's your name?'

'Beth.'

He drank that one and another. The crowd and its noise had now thinned but John wasn't counting his beers, he'd lost count after three. Someone was singing a ballad and John rested his head on the bar. Shuffles came from behind him. Bolts were thrown and he turned to focus. Pub closing maybe, he thought. Turning back he dropped his head back on his elbow. He came out of the dream and felt sick with the bar revolving around two tables in the middle of the tiled floor.

Thinking he was back on the *Emily* he pressed against the bar rail and forced himself upright. There was no one serving but he felt pressure on his shoulder and someone speaking his name from far away. The voice got louder and his shoulder moved.

'John, John, its Beth. Time to leave. I'll help you to the door.'

He turned around and saw nobody but he felt a firm hand around his waist and he giggled. Bending down he noticed the source of his mirth.

'Beth, Beth from the hotel death, coming to...to my rescue!'

'Come on now, not far to go.'

A stronger arm gripped him; likely another person and this time the movement hastened his trip to the doorway. That helper edged him into the darkness and closed the door. John swayed and walked six circular paces back to the hotel's steps. He sat down again and let his head slip back to the door jamb, its coolness pleasant.

Opening his eyes he tried to see. His world had stopped turning but his guts hadn't and feeling the surge approaching he willed himself to stand. Lurching, he made the gutter in time and vomited.

Feeling better but still unsteady, he meandered up Forbes Street and stopped just before William Street. Leaning against a wall, near an alcove, his eyes became drowsy.

~

The sun was bright, the pain throbbed like a steam hammer and his tongue felt dipped in sand. Rolling over, John tried to remember. Where was he?

The pub, that's right. Looking around, each focus accelerated the pounding. He was among old newspapers, empty bottles and crates, all smelling of cat piss.

He rummaged and found his wallet in one pocket. 'That's something.' In the other he found a piece of paper. Focusing on this, he saw the brick order. Shite! What's the time? It was late he sensed. He got up and a sour smell came from his clothes.

The cold water from a nearby tap refreshed him.

~

Beth rinsed the mop, splashing its head back on the tiles and finished the last section of the public bar. She'd leant an ear to more drunks than she'd hot baths but that big young man was different. It was the smile, she knew. Side to side went the mop, removing yesterday's slop.

Her chore was a losing battle. Today's patrons, due in an hour, would stamp her work with their dirty soles. *Yes, I'm easy for a soft smile,* she mused, especially when the whole face lit up, good teeth, eyes and all. John had it but he had a scar as well. A fighter, perhaps, and he probably couldn't read! But his eyes showed intelligence. She rinsed the mop again.

Won't see him again but nice to skip a heartbeat once in a while. Squeezing the mop for the last time she left her floor to await the treads of the thirsty.

~

The St Peters kiln manager wasn't convinced and John tried again. 'Look, I got here late, I know. Isn't there any other way?'

The man pulled his trousers higher. 'Laddie, for the last time. The ovens are loaded, closed and are being fired. If you was here before seven, you'd been orright. We could've fitted your order in.'

John tried to think. His big night had now jeopardised the hotel's completion. Everyone wanted bricks and the kiln manager knew it. Jenkins and Fruin had trusted him, giving him a false sense of his own worth and now he'd made a serious blue. Come on, come on, think. This should be easy. Something came to mind. Yes, it might work. He shook his hangover head. 'The order's for ten thousand first class commons.'

'As I said all commons for this week are now being fired and for customers.'

'Have you got any in stock?'

The manager's leathery face creased in another frown. 'Not the number you want. We've got about half of what you want plus plenty of ordinaries.'

Ordinaries might be all right. They were called that because they were common bricks with minor imperfections. But did Day Street have to have first class common bricks for this order? No, not all, as some will be plastered. The plasterer would kick up a stink because more render would be needed to fill the gaps of the second-class bricks but that was a risk worth taking. 'Right, then let's have all your selects and the rest in ordinary commons.'

The manager scratched his head, and then nodded. 'It's not the bricks you ordered but, yeah, can be done. It'll be cheaper too.'

John thanked him, waited on the loading and hitched a ride on the first brick delivery back to town.

Water from the site tap quenched John's mouth; his fuzzy head now more of a nuisance. He heard a shout.

'Leary,' Fruin said. 'Did ya get to St Peters? Thought you'd be here long before now.'

John looked up and wiped his face. Walking up to the overseer he glanced up to see how Dave and Bert were going. He took a deep breath. 'The bricks are being unloaded now. I didn't get all the selects. I'm sorry. Late night.'

'Bloody hell Leary, that won't do.'

'I think there's a way out—'

'That'll put us behind and it's your balls in the fire. Jenkins gave you more responsibility against my advice. Wait till he hears this.'

'I've got a plan, I tell you.'

'Oh you do, do ya?'

'We can complete the internal first floor walls up to the roof using this order of ordinary commons. They'll be plastered anyway.'

'Plasterer will howl at that. Might cost us a quid.'

'It might, but we can get the next batch of selects in two weeks, from the kiln's next order for the outside walls. They'll be face and will not be rendered. So there's no hold up and we've saved money.'

The overseer frowned and half opened his mouth to object, and then pursed his lips. 'Yeah, could work I suppose,' he prodded John's chest. 'Maybe not the best, but it'll do. Now get your arse back on the roof.'

Jenkins later agreed to the change in plan although John suspected that Fruin probably told him it was his idea. The roof frame was completed awaiting its iron sheeting.

On the Friday night, John took possession of an east-facing

room on the upper floor of an Elizabeth Street terrace. 'It isn't much. But it's mine.' Eight people sharing a bathroom would be hard and John sighed as he remembered the *Emily's* wash-deck pump. For his weekly board and lodging he got a battered two-door wardrobe, a three quarter bed, a bedside table and lockless door. He'd have some privacy at least. Finishing his unpacking, he went downstairs for tea; almost home cooking, very different from the barracks fare. Thoughts of the girl—Beth—at the pub made him want to meet her again. He washed up and put on a clean shirt.

On the way up Liverpool Street, his thoughts turned to Baxterhouse. The previous Sunday he'd scouted out the man's business in Kent Street near Millers Point and found a well-fenced yard and a solid building. But where did the man live? John crossed over William Street and headed to the Royal. If it were in town then he'd want to keep tabs on him and find out his faults and vices. Maybe John could find his friends or, better, his enemies. Work through his enemies to get to him. That way, Baxterhouse suffers and John is not suspected. That was going to be hard.

The pub was packed to the gunwales with patrons spilling out onto the footpaths on the balmy autumn night. Broaching the entrance doors, he peered through the smoke and fought his way through the groups of thirst-quenching workers. He looked left and right. Two women were serving at the bar but no Beth.

One of them, a large-framed woman with reddish-coloured hair came up to him. 'What'll it be, love?'

'Pint of Bass, thanks.'

John paid for the beer. 'Beth here tonight?'

'Haven't seen her, just started my shift and I've been flat out. She might be out the back.' She turned to another customer before John could ask her anything further. Perhaps it was Beth's night off. She still hadn't shown half way through his beer and the big-framed barmaid, who a customer called Mavis, sailed by him again.

'What do you mean out the back?'

Mavis looked at him until his face registered. 'Oh, Beth, yeah in the store room. There's been a big rush on punch. She might be getting more fruit.'

'Well, if you see her, tell her John Leary said hello.'

'Orright, luv,' she smiled as she pulled another beer.

John tried to remember if he'd told Beth his surname. Finishing his drink he'd decided to leave when Beth appeared at the end of the bar. She carried a basket of mixed fruit and heaved the load onto the back bar and started to work on it. John called out to her, 'Beth!'

She turned trying to place him in the crowd and he tried again. 'Beth, it's me, John!'

Beth looked surprised, then smiled and putting down her knife came over. 'Hello. Another one?' John looked down at his empty glass and nodded. Beth poured him a beer. A hair strand hung over one of her eyes and he was glad he'd come. She pushed the beer over to him and he paid her. 'Don't know what's on tonight but the place's a madhouse.'

She turned back to her fruit and John leaned over as far as he could and raised his voice. 'Do you get some time off?'

She looked at the clock, which showed seven-thirty. 'Yeah, get a ten minute one at eight. Why?'

'Just wanted to talk.'

She continued to chop but turned her face around. 'All right, I'll find you at eight, somewhere away from the bar.'

John looked at the clock, which showed two minutes past eight when he felt a tap on his arm. Beth had secured the hair strand and looked freshened up. She sat on a stool next to him with a lemon drink.

'Cheers,' she said, raising the glass. 'Well, did you get home all right?'

He was too embarrassed to tell the truth. 'It's the first time I've been drunk since coming to Sydney.'

Beth looked at him. 'It happens.'

John was glad he came and liked her. He put down his glass and drew a ring on the spilt beer. 'When you get a day off, I'd like to take you out.'

'You mean, you and me?'

'Yes.'

'Why?' she said with a frank look.

She must get a lot of invitations from men. John was attracted to her and he assumed she would go out with him. 'I'd just like to.'

'Where?'

'It's up to you. What do you like to do?'

Beth shrugged her shoulders. 'I love to ride horses but I can't afford it.'

'Well, then, there it is.'

'No, I can't let you. It's too pricey.' Beth strained to glance at the clock, her breasts pushing against her blouse. John diverted his eyes as she spoke to him. 'Time's about up John . . . what's your other name?'

'It's Leary.'

'It's nice of you to ask me but you don't have to.' She got up to leave.

'I know I don't, but can I see you on your day off? Sunday?'

'Not this Sunday as Mum is at home.' She paused, looking hesitant. 'But I'm not doing anything the Sunday after that?'

'That's the sixteenth. All right. I'll come to your place at two and we'll decide then.'

'It's just up the street here, number forty-five.' She disappeared back into the crowd and John smiled to himself. Yes, she's all right. He got up and left the pub.

~

'Mr Higgins,' Baxterhouse remonstrated, 'it's a straightforward banking procedure. You demand that their overdraft is paid in five days.'

Thomas Higgins looked doubtful. 'It is the bank's prerogative, but it's not usual practice. Cullens are trading profitably and there's no reason to call it in.'

Cullens, like himself, was one of the firms tendering for the miners' tools. Overdrafts to these undercapitalised companies were essential for them to survive financially. If Cullens had to pay back its overdraft in full, it would have to withdraw its tender. It would not have the bank's money—the overdraft—initially to make the products for Mackays. One competitor down, one to go. 'But, the bank can call it any time, can't they?'

Higgins squinted at a sun ray reflecting from a nearby window. 'Yes.' He stood up, his hands at his side. 'I haven't the authority to issue such a letter. It'll have to come from a bank director and that will require a history of unsatisfactory trading which isn't the case with that customer.'

'That's too bad.' William thought about the other tenderer, Jackson and Son. He'd have to find a weakness there too, every person had one. 'What do you know about Jacksons? They bank with you, don't they?'

Higgins looked out the window, his poised pen dropping a blob of ink on the blotter. 'Yes, a bigger company, highly liquid. Solid.'

'Who owns it?'

'Father and son run it. Son's unmarried, a bachelor I think. No other children. The father's a bit of a strong-arm. I've seen him in action in this room. His son never says a word. Nervous type, his son, even effeminate one could say. When does your tender close for Mackays?'

'Tomorrow the fourteenth. I'm off to Albion Brewery then to buy a house. Keep honest, Higgins.'

~

It was Sunday 16 March and the day John was to meet Beth. As he finished his midday meal he couldn't take his eyes off the Dublin-postmarked envelope resting against the pepper and salt shakers.

'Thanks Missus for the great meal.'

His landlady smiled. 'You've been ogling that letter so long you'll bore a hole in it.'

John smiled. 'I'll be off then and read it.'

He left the Sunday table, went up to his room, lay down on the bed and started reading. Maureen was coming to New South Wales! He read the letter, dated December 1850, again reliving his excitement.

She'd married a Mr Liam Forde, the brother of Jane, her schoolteacher friend. John was happy at the news. There was demand for schoolteachers in New South Wales and the newlyweds would be here around September. As he placed the letter in a box, his happiness waned. Maureen would be in the colony and so was her rapist.

In the afternoon sun he made his way along Elizabeth Street. It felt something like Kildare, with enough heat, but with an autumn freshness. Looking up he saw St Mary's and his conscience niggled him as he'd missed Mass that morning. It also made him think of Clarissa.

Miss McGuire was attractive, classy, rich and connected. Why hadn't he kissed her when he'd had the chance? It was her social position that had stopped him, no doubt. And that difference was the reason for not telling her his feelings. There was no future there. Beth was working-class—feisty and likeable, and John wanted to take matters further. Months of abstinence were affecting him.

Rounding the corner into Forbes Street, he walked down it noting the numbers. He came to forty-five where two girls were playing hopscotch on the footpath.

'Come to see our sister, haven't ya?'

John looked at the urchin who was about six and saw Beth's features in miniature. The other girl, a year or so younger, stood and stared. 'And you are, Miss?' John asked her.

'Olivia's my name. Livvy to my friends. You're a giant!'

'I am and I'm going to eat you up!' John lunged at the girl who squealed and ran away. He felt the other girl's hands gripped around his thigh.

'You leave my sister alone or I'll bite!'

Looking up at him the other girl had her mouth ready.

'Sarah!'

John turned to Beth who stood in the doorway. 'Leave the giant to me.'

John laughed, extricated himself and walked over to her. The girls were much younger than Beth and he was intrigued, but it would be rude at this time to enquire why.

'Welcome to my two wee sisters, John. Girls, come here.' Both girls stood beside her, holding hands. Olivia had a finger in her mouth. 'Say hello to Mr Leary.'

'Nice to meet you,' John replied.

The sisters remained silent and just stared at him.

'Girls,' Beth remonstrated.

'Hello giant,' Sarah said.

'Sarah!'

Sarah grinned. 'Hello, Mr Giant.'

Olivia waved at him. 'Mr Leary.'

'Do you want to come in,' Beth said, 'or will we go somewhere?'

'We'll go to Hyde Park, if that's all right. There might be a show or two.'

'That'd be nice. Girls, stay indoors.'

'They can come with us,' John suggested.

'Mum's just next door. She won't be long.'

John walked at Beth's side up to William Street noting her light blue dress and fetching bonnet. Not like Clarissa's attire, but Beth still looked good.

'Mum came this morning. She lives in for gentry at Vaucluse. She makes me laugh at some of the things she says about them.'

'The hard times of the rich and famous eh?'

'Something like that. The trouble is there's not much for 'em to do. They've got everybody at their beck and call.'

John thought about Clarissa and her family and he changed the subject. 'Your Da?'

'A roustabout on a station near Scone. Only see him now and again. But he's good, comes home with the bacon for Mum and us.'

'Does he bring home money too?'

Beth's mouth showed a row of white teeth and John returned her smile. 'Anyway what about yourself?' she asked.

'Honest Kildare working boy, you're looking at. I'm a carpenter working on a new pub in Day Street. Fit out's on the go. Hope to finish in three months.'

'When did you come to Sydney?'

'October last.'

Halfway up the hill Beth stopped to allow a carriage to pass and they both turned their faces to avoid the dust. Beth held her bonnet, which had the gratifying effect of accentuating her bosom.

She sighed as they set off again. 'I love to get out in the open air and being away from the smoky pub.'

'Have you always worked there?'

'Mum needs the wages and I work there three days a week. What I'd like to do is care for sick animals, especially horses.'

They crossed College Street and entered the racetrack where a circus camped in one section with its animals being exercised. John smelt manure from the horses. One of these, a broad-headed mare trotted over to Beth, nuzzling into her hand. John was surprised.

'There my beauty.' Beth smiled.

'Where did you learn to ride?'

She continued to stroke the mare's head. 'One summer we went to see Dad at Coonamble. I was eight and he just stuck me on a horse and I had to learn. I love it.'

A man selling ices came by and John bought two. He and Beth sat on the grass and he felt comfortable in her company. A bee hovered near her face. She froze and John whispered. 'Just be very still. Mr Bee is confused. He can't tell the difference between the pretty colours of the ice or the pretty eyes looking at him.'

Beth giggled. The bee held its ground, an inch now from the ice. John brushed it away but it moved closer to her. Beth panicked and fell towards him startling the bee and it flew away. Beth ended up in John's lap laughing.

'Oh you beast! It nearly stung me.' She stopped laughing and looked up at him, her lips parted. He liked her against him, and the smell of her hair shining in the sunlight. John leaned down and kissed her. Beth pressed the back of his head and her mouth opened. His hand travelled from her hip to her breast. Before it got there, she broke away, turned from him and stood up brushing down her dress.

John looked up at her. 'I'm sorry. You looked so good and smelt so nice. I shouldn't have done that.'

Beth smiled down at him. 'Come on, let's look at the other animals and you can tell me about your family.'

William Baxterhouse wanted to be the only supplier of the tools needed for any future tender. And he had a plan to be just that: a meeting with Jackson the foundry owner, one of his competitors for the bid. The clerk showed him into the office and the well-dressed, middle-aged man who approached him was not what William had been expecting. He was tall and heavy-shouldered—looked like he could take a few knuckled rounds before conceding.

He shook William's hand. 'Mr Baxterhouse, Grant Jackson, please sit down. May I offer you some refreshments?' William sat in an armchair facing Blackwattle Bay.

'No thank you and thank you for meeting me.'

Jackson seated himself behind his desk. 'Quite all right. What can I do for you? Your note only raised, if my memory serves me, the possibility of an opportunity to work together. It intrigues me.'

'Mr Jackson, I'm a potential competitor of yours. I lodged a tender with Mackays to supply the miners' equipment, as did your company.'

Jackson looked puzzled. 'A competitor? Really? The only foundries capable of supplying these goods are ours and Cullens.'

'Oh, I won't make the goods here. They'll be imported.'

Jackson's face remained impassive. Very good, William thought, another man might well have shown surprise at this news. A worthy opponent. Silence filled the room broken only by the noises from the foundry. William knew the game had started. Who'll blink first? Jackson did. 'That's interesting. We think we can make any implement in the colony cheaper than an import.'

'Well, I'm here to see if you would accept a small fee for not tendering?'

'I beg your pardon?'

'It's simple. I'm prepared to invest in your company if you withdraw your tender.'

'Withdraw? Why should I do that?' Three frown lines appeared on Jackson's forehead. 'You'd better explain yourself.'

William reached into his suit and withdrew a thick envelope. Standing up he reached across and gave it to Jackson.

Jackson used a letter opener and his face lit up in surprise as he grabbed the cash. 'What's all this about?'

'Please read that letter.'

Jackson did so then looked at visitor. 'I'm supposed to sign this letter withdrawing my bid? This tells me nothing other than what you've told me.' He pushed the contents back across the desk. 'Also, the cash is most irregular. I think you'd better leave.' Jackson stood up.

'I'm a businessman, nothing more. Withdraw your bid and keep the cash.'

'No. Get out. Now.'

William smiled and picked up the cash and letter. Round one to you Mr Jackson, but I'll win this fight. 'Good day.' Maybe Cullen would be more amenable.

~

It was midday and Clarissa wandered around the architect's near-empty drawing office. At times she glanced at her father who was talking to Mr Lewis in the corner workroom. They would be discussing joinery and cabinetwork and she was anxious to be included in that conversation as well, but first things first. She soon found the plans she was looking for. A minute later the senior draughtsman came up beside her.

'I'd like to stay here and study these,' she said. 'You must have important things to do.'

'I was just leaving for something to eat Miss McGuire, and noticed you with these. They are working plans, very technical and require a detailed knowledge of building'.

'I know.'

'But, if you wish to come over here, we've got a collection of artist's coloured drawings of your father's house, showing the general arrangement.'

Containing her annoyance at his presumption of her ignorance, Clarissa replied. 'No thank you. It's the details I'm looking for. These plans are more than adequate.'

'Very well, I'll leave you to your study.'

'Could you give me a pen and some paper?'

He hesitated and Clarissa was going to insist but he looked around. 'I'll get them.'

Clarissa smiled as he left her. Looking back at the designs, her smile changed to a frown. Some basic instructions given to Mr Lewis were not evident on the working drawings in front of her.

'Here you go.' The senior draughtsman placed the pad and pen near her, then left.

Pulling up a stool, she wrote down the date, 24 March, on top of her page and listed the missing items from those her father had briefed the architects to include. Doing so, she had a flash of John's face. Working away for half an hour she didn't hear her father approach.

'Busy my dear?'

She pushed herself up from the table, wiping her hands on a cloth. Her father moved closer and looked at the plans. 'Coming along nicely, Mr Lewis informed me.'

'I don't know about that. Look at what I've written. You told Mr Lewis to include these things in the design and they aren't there.'

Her father frowned and scanned Clarissa's jottings. 'This won't do. I'll see Lewis myself.'

A few minutes later the two men stood beside her. She picked up the list and began reading. After the third item, Lewis interrupted her. 'It seems your daughter has a penchant for design, Mr McGuire. You don't have to waste your time going through these. My draughtsman will complete the plans and I'm sure these things would have been included.'

'Mr Lewis,' her father said, 'it's my house and my money. You've had time to get these drawings done to our needs. I want to go through the list and ensure that all items are addressed and are included.'

'Of course, Mr McGuire,' Lewis replied, 'let's continue.'

It took another hour to complete but Clarissa was satisfied.

'We'll get cracking on this, Mr McGuire,' Lewis said, 'and we'll let you know when the drawings will be ready. About the builders, let's talk in my office.' He smiled. 'Would you like to join us, Miss McGuire?'

'Thank you, I would.'

Seated around Lewis's desk, the architect drew a file towards him. 'Reeds, and two others have capacity and we can add Jenkins to that.'

'Jenkins?' David McGuire asked. 'Who are they?'

'A company your daughter recommended we look at.'

Her father looked annoyed at her and Clarissa jumped in. 'They are the preferred contractor on McCreadie's warehouse extension that Mr Lewis is designing.'

'And their work is first class, Mr McGuire,' Lewis said. 'I've seen it.'

'And the lowest price will win my home?'

'Yes, Mr McGuire, generally, but it's early days. We'll spend more time investigating the financial status of these contractors and other aspects, but all in all, we feel that that process will only be a formality.'

David McGuire stood up. 'Thank you. Come, Clarissa.'

As they walked down the stairs, she said, 'As we agreed, I've spoken to the builders Lewis has recommended.'

'Including Jenkins?'

'Not yet.'

'And?'

'They weren't forthcoming on answers I wanted, but I had—'

'Clarissa, I have doubts about you. You're looking at Leary to build our house? I don't think so.'

'Father, this is business only.' She kept her face impassive and in part she meant what she'd said. 'We want the *best* builder for Point Piper. Jenkins has to pass muster.'

'And that's all there is to this?'

Clarissa had to lie to him a second time. 'Yes.'

'I hope so, for your sake. You were going to say something on the other builders?'

'I've done my own investigations. You know the Thompsons and the Gearys?'

'Yes.'

'Both families had houses built and had briefed architects on what they wanted. But those requirements were not shown on the tender or later contract drawings. Oh, the builders might have been told about them but they didn't include them in their tenders. When the builder is contracted, he then charges a fortune for the item when it appears on the later drawings.' She smiled. 'What we just did in Lewis's office has saved you a lot of money.'

'It has indeed.' Her father smiled.

Clarissa threaded her hand through his arm. She knew she hadn't been completely honest with her father about John but she'd win him around. Now she had to work out a way to see John Leary with a set of the drawings.

Two weeks later and armed with a roll of plans, Clarissa entered a builder's office in Pitt Street, near Campbell Street, and rang the bell at the counter. She'd written to John, care of Mr Jenkins's office, and had received a reply to meet him here today. She was looking forward to seeing him.

A red-headed man came out. His short stature surprised her as untypical for his trade. He was dressed in a pressed shirt and navy trousers. 'I'm Rupert Jenkins.'

'How do you do, Mr Jenkins. I'm Clarissa McGuire.'

'How do you do, Miss McGuire. Right on time. Is your father with you?'

She had expected this. 'No, but he and Mr Lewis are confident I can talk to you about the house design.'

Jenkins eyed the rolled up drawings. 'Sure, you must have some feel for the colours and the furniture, but—'

'I assure you Mr Jenkins, I can answer all your questions on the design, the brickwork, ironwork, levels, soil type, window construction and anything else you'd like to know.'

Jenkins smiled. 'Proper little builder you are. Grand. Come with me to my office.'

Leaving the vestibule and going into a cramped, document-packed but clean office she sat down and handed over her plans to him. Lewis was not ready to tender for some time but she'd asked for two sets of plans for her own use which, as a client, she was entitled to have. She had the spare set of plans hidden at home.

'Is Mr Leary joining us?'

Jenkins shook his head. 'There was a problem on Day Street. We'll get by.'

Clarissa hid her disappointment. She would have to try harder to meet him.

'Do you know him?' Jenkins asked.

'We met on the voyage. Just a fellow passenger.'

Jenkins tapped the desktop as he looked at her. 'We don't build houses as a rule, especially fancy ones, but we'll have a go at this one.' He sat down, put on his glasses, spread the plans out and took a cursory look. Was John disappointed in not seeing her? She hoped so. Or was he trying to avoid seeing her? But he did say that he'd meet her here so her fears seemed unfounded. After a minute Mr Jenkins looked at her. 'These are good. There's a lot of detail.'

'Are there any major problems?'

'Not from what's in front of me. When does the tender start?'

'Early July.'

His eyes widened in surprise. 'It's only the seventh of April now. That's plenty of time.' Jenkins looked puzzled. 'Will these plans change between then and now?'

'There might be more details on cabinet work and the like but no, no big changes.'

'So, Miss, why are you giving me more time and a running start on the other bidders?'

Clarissa knew why. The longer time a builder had with the plans to price, a better bid would result. She wanted to guarantee Jenkins won this bid, but she couldn't say this. And she had to have Jenkins in competition so he would give her the best price. But equally, she wouldn't give these plans now to others and so she told another untruth. 'I'll be issuing a set like this to the other builders tomorrow.'

Jenkins nodded. 'So, we're all equal.' He stood up. 'Thank you for coming in to see me. If I have any questions,' he smiled, 'do I send them to your father, you or Mr Lewis?'

There was only one answer. If Mr Jenkins sent questions to anyone but herself, it would alert them that he had an early start. 'To me, please. I sometimes see Mr Leary at Mass at St Mary's so you could give your questions to him and I'll get them.'

Jenkins smiled. He seemed to have discovered her subterfuge for her visit today but then his face looked innocent. 'That I'll do, Miss McGuire. Now, I'll see you out.'

~

John McCreadie brought his napkin up and placed it on the table. 'That was a delightful dinner, Mrs McGuire. If you'll excuse us, your husband and I have some business to discuss. Miss Clarissa, why don't you and Ian retire to the veranda for a bit?'

'Yes, Mr McCreadie.' Clarissa had eaten her dinner but had been distracted by her meeting with Mr Jenkins that morning. It had been rash to arrange to meet John at Mass and receive his questions on the plans. How was she going to do that? She'd think about that later. Turning to her guest, she said, 'Shall we?'

Clarissa and Ian seated on wicker chairs enjoyed the autumn evening. They bantered with small talk then the conversation took a turn.

'Miss Clarissa, do you find my companionship acceptable?'

'Yes, I do.'

'You are beautiful, confident and caring.'

'Thank you.'

'And over these past three months I've become increasingly fond of you. More, I love you and,' he smiled, 'I would like to ask for your hand in marriage.'

Clarissa turned and stared at him, shocked. 'I beg your pardon?'

His eyes were earnest. 'Will you marry me?'

There it was. 'That's a very serious question.'

Ian smiled again. 'It is and I am serious.'

He was attractive, well suited for her and she did enjoy his company. Assertiveness wasn't his forté but she could live with that. But did she love him? She didn't feel the same way about him as she did John Leary but then a part of her was doubtful if she could win John over. 'Can you give me time before I reply?'

Ian covered her hand with his, which she thought very bold of him. 'All the time you want.'

CHAPTER SEVEN

'It's the eleventh of May and it's Beth's birth*day*,' yelled Olivia, making a rhyme of it. 'Quick Beth, blow them all out!'

Beth grinned at her two entranced sisters, leaned over the cake and blew hard, round and around until all eighteen candles were smoking wisps.

'Yippee!' Sarah said. 'See Livvy, told you she could do it!'

Olivia pouted and wiped a sleeve across her nose. 'Pooh! That's easy. I could blow out a hundred candles.'

Anne O'Hare pushed the knife into the cake. 'Beth gets the first slice. Get me that plate, Livvy.'

'It's delicious,' Beth said taking a bite.

Her mother nodded. 'It should be. It's from France. Madame ordered twelve of them, would you believe? The kind soul offered one to me at a song. I've seem 'em in David Jones for double the price.'

The cake lost some of its flavour. Just for once, especially on her birthday, Beth would've liked to have something that wasn't at a reduced price.

Her mother's obvious happiness struck that thought from her mind. Her Mum was doing it tough, with her wages just enough to pay the rent, and Beth's topping up for food and clothing. 'Good sermon this morning, girls, all about the family. Jesus is with us today, for sure.'

Sarah looked around as if 'He' was behind the door, making Beth smile. 'Go look outside and see if Mr Leary's coming,' she said.

Sarah ran down the hall and out the door.

Anne O'Hare sat down at the table that had more knocks and dents than a butcher's block. She poured herself another cup of tea. 'Where are you off to today?'

'Don't know, Mum.'

'Olivia, go see that your sister don't run off.'

Beth looked at Olivia's shining hair as she flew past.

'And you say he's a carpenter? Well that's something, not like your father's trade. But then, the country's not been the same since the dry of '42.'

Light noises down the hall preceded the thumps of someone heavier. 'Beth, Beth the giant's here!' Both girls rushed past squealing as John loped into the kitchen, grinning.

He stopped at the sight of Beth's mum, doffed his hat and nodded. 'How do you do, Mrs O'Hare.'

'Hello, Mr Leary.'

John turned to Beth. 'Happy Birthday.' He pulled a package from his pocket.

Beth took the present and sat down with her sisters surrounding her. 'Mr Leary, you shouldn't have.' She unwrapped it and held it to the light. 'A hair pin and so shiny. Thank you.'

'It's not gold, of course,' he said. 'But I got it made on site. It's polished brass.'

'It's beautiful. I'll wear it on special days.'

Beth's mum smiled. 'That's a grand present.'

Beth stood up. 'Mum we'll be going.' She gave her a kiss on her cheek.

'Be off with you. I hope to see you again, Mr Leary.'

'Me too, Mrs O'Hare,' John said as he accompanied Beth out the front door.

They headed to Woolloomooloo and Beth was excited. She still could feel John's lips on hers from a week ago, when they'd been down to Circular Quay. All week long, she'd thought of him. Her wants were simple: a good man who earned a good wage, her Mum and Dad taken care of and her sisters too. In just eight weeks and four times together, John seemed just the man. Men like him didn't walk into pubs every day and she didn't want to let him get away. 'So what's on today?'

John kicked a stone into the gutter. 'Well, I'd thought we could go down by the water and then take a hansom back to my place.'

Beth's heart skipped a beat. 'A cab ride. That's posh,' she forced a stern face to cover her excitement. 'And why Mr Leary, would you think I'd go back to your house—alone!'

John appeared shocked. 'No, well, you see, it's only a thought. We could go somewhere else.'

She had pushed too far. 'Let's go to the bay and then back to your place. But you must keep your door open,' she said smiling.

They walked down Forbes Street in the sunlight of a fresh afternoon. 'Have you finished reading that book?' she asked.

'I have.'

'Reading is hard for me.'

'It's something I like to do but not everyone does.'

'I'm sure your sister does, 'cause she's a schoolteacher— and she's coming here. You must be excited.' But John wasn't. His eyes had fired up. 'What's wrong?'

John forced a smile. 'Nothing, come on, let's cross over into the sun.'

Beth ignored his change in mood and after an enjoyable few hours strolling around the Botanic Gardens they took a cab to John's place. She thought the fare too dear, but John insisted—after all it was her birthday. Generosity, another good trait, she thought. Combine that with politeness, ambition, punctuality and a soft touch. He *was* a catch.

She thought about his bedroom. What they could do there both shocked and intrigued her. John led her through the hallway. He glanced into the kitchen on the way. 'Who are you looking for?'

'The landlady. But I think she's out.'

'Why, would she make a fuss?'

'She might.'

'I hope Mr Leary, you don't have a habit of bringing girls to your bedroom.' Beth softened at the look on John's face, a combination of shock and shyness.

'Don't be daft. Up the stairs, first door on the left.'

John followed her up and she sat on a chair John had pulled from the corner.

Sitting on the bed he reached under it and brought up a small box. 'This is my store of treasures. Not much, but it's a link to the old country.' Opening the lid, he took a locket and drew it up for Beth to see.

Getting up from her chair she sat on the bed beside him and looked over his shoulder and smiled at the open door. His treasure box was an odd collection: letters from home, some coins. She took the locket, its green colours catching the glint of the afternoon rays. 'Pretty.'

'Aye. It was my mam's and she loved it. She thought it would bring me luck. I think it has.'

'Are your Mum and Dad in good health?'

'Aye.'

'Are they happy together?'

'Well, they've been married a long time. They don't fight much, but yeah, I suppose they're content.'

'What do you think yourself? Would you marry for love?'

John replaced the locket and closed the box. He looked at Beth and smiled. 'I think love's got to be in marriage.'

'What, like a door in a door frame?'

John's smile broadened and Beth liked that. 'Dad and Mum have had a rocky past,' she said. 'After I was born she left him, had to, as Dad was a drunk.'

'I'm sorry.'

'It's better now but it took Dad nine years to beat it and he has. That's why there's an eleven-year gap between Livvy and me.'

'It's you that interests me, Beth,' John said softly looking at her.

Beth leaned in closer, her eyes looking at his lips.

John said. 'The last time I kissed you, you broke away.'

She raised a hand, extended a finger and placed it on his lips. 'Shush... This time I won't.'

Footsteps sounded on the landing outside and a lady appeared in the doorway. 'Mr Leary, I said that guests were not allowed in my bedrooms.'

John stood up with Beth. 'I'm sorry Missus, we were just talking.'

'Rules are rules,' she said as she stood back to let them pass.

On the footpath outside, John looked sheepish. 'Sorry, Beth. I hadn't expected her to come home. I hope you weren't too embarrassed.'

'Not too much.' It was a shame about that kiss though! Perhaps the landlady's timing was just as well. They could easily have taken things further. She took his arm. 'Let's walk back home. I've had a wonderful day.'

~

William Baxterhouse held onto his hat and walked out of his Kent Street business and into the rain of a wet May morning. A man stepped in his way and William bumped him aside ignoring the oaths fading in the noise of the downpour. 'Shite, weather only for ducks and fish!' he yelled as he got into a hansom cab.

He was not happy. Two breweries he supplied with oats were complaining. Their deliveries were coming in fits and starts and William had to find out why. His cab stopped in Botany Street outside the Redfern yard that housed his wagons. 'Wait here.' He entered the gates as rainwater seeped into his shoes, feeding his foul mood. Confronting the manager in the shed, he came right to the point. 'What's the problem with the deliveries, Mr Myers?'

'Mr Baxterhouse, it's the drivers. Two of them are sick and one's become a drunkard since his missus ran off. We're doing the best we can.'

'That's not good enough.'

'There's not much I can do. I've advertised for more drivers.'

William sighed and sat down. His trouser bottoms were soaked. 'Give the two sick men a day to recover, if not, hire new ones and sack the drunkard. You can drive the wagon in his stead. It's the 15th. In one week I want this fixed and my two breweries on side.' He stood up and clenched his fists, feeling pain from the morning's workout. 'If not, I'll personally come down and force feed *you* a bucketful of oats.'

Myers remained stock still as William left him. Getting back into the cab, William yelled. '*Herald* office,' to the driver. Cullens had won the tender for the mining tools. Like Jacksons they hadn't accepted his cash offer either. Damn them! He should try and bypass Mackays and sell directly. There was some compensation, though, as Mackays had told him there would be more tenders coming, as there wasn't enough supply to meet demand. William had put an advertisement in the papers, just for one week, saying that he could supply tools. People, desperate for goods, were writing to him daily. He couldn't meet their needs—yet. But he had his name out there.

The cab dropped him outside the newspaper office in -O'Connell Street, thankfully the rain had eased. Approaching a counter, he rang the bell and waited. He looked at the clock and drummed his fingers. He rang the bell again. That's bloody odd, ten am and no one's around. He leaned over the ink-stained counter. 'Anyone there? You've got a customer who wants to keep placing his ad!'

A pimply-faced clerk poked his head out from behind a partition. 'Yes sir, be right with you.' The clerk disappeared and William became angry. He was ready to jump the counter and throttle the clerk when the young man came out. 'Sorry sir, but we've had all hands to the pumps. The Melbourne coach mail's just come in and there's been a big strike at Ballarat.'

'A big strike, what sort of strike?'

'Gold, they reckon, bigger than Bathurst.'

William's mouth opened and then closed again. A tingle filled his damp shoes. 'Yes!'

The clerk smiled at William. 'I suppose you'll be off to Ballarat to chance your arm.'

'Maybe.' The news made William rethink his plans. Victoria was a distance but thank God he'd gone for broke and ordered more equipment. He and his brother would clean up.

September couldn't come soon enough with James and his ship full of treasure!

~

John scanned his schedule. It was handwritten on the back of a drawing plan and listed, down the sheet, all the tasks the tradesmen needed to do to complete the works. Alongside each task were the number of days required for each task and the dates that each task had to be done. All tasks were linked to form an overall plan. Some tasks were critical, that is, they had to be done before another could follow, like the bricks had to be built before they were plastered, or render completed, before it was painted. Other tasks were not so important but could be started and finished with more flexibility. The scheduling was a mental challenge for him and he enjoyed it. It was a pity that Fruin didn't share John's enthusiasm for this method of planning the construction. Satisfied that he had the right logic regarding all the remaining tasks, he had recommenced working on the upper window architraves when he heard raised voices. He paused and listened. Jenkins and Fruin were having one of their arguments.

The red-headed builder stood on the footpath fronting his overseer. 'It's the end of May and we're ahead by two weeks. The pub's going gangbusters, so what's your beef?'

'It may look like quality,' Fruin said, 'but at a price. These men here aren't tradesmen, more like apprentices. It's the one or two special men that are holding the whole flaming lot together. Most of the good 'uns have gone to Bathurst!'

'If someone mentions Bathurst to me again, I'll throttle him.'

'It's a fact. The standard's not the same. It may look all right, but it won't last. You'll have a team swarming over it, fixing up the shoddy work.'

'That's your job, Fruin. I'll not have defects on this pub. I've a contract with the brewery and it demands a top finish. It's your problem.'

'Not for long. I'm giving notice from the end of this week. I'm sick of wet nursing would-be tradesmen and clerks.'

Jenkins stood with hands on hips. 'Bloody great! We're nearly finished and here you are pissing off. And what am I going to do next week?'

'That's not my worry. Why don't you get your wonder boy Leary to help you?'

John's grip on the window saved him from falling to the street. The overseer walked away. John kept his head down and counted the seconds till he hoped he'd get the call. He got to nine.

'Leary, get down here. I want to talk to you.'

John leaned out the window. 'Be down in five, boss. Fixing my last casement now.' Four minutes later he faced Jenkins.

'I suppose you heard all that?'

'Aye.'

'Look John, you're good. You've proved that to me. I'm in a spot here and I've made my mind up. The job's yours for a trial period of a month with overseer's pay starting next Monday. You interested?'

John felt a glow, the extra money a bonus. 'I'll take it.'

'I thought you would,' Jenkins said and smiled. 'Don't let me down.'

The rest of John's shift finished in a blur as plans for his future unfolded. He had the same excited feeling he had when unwrapping a much-longed for present.

~

Christine McGuire paced up and down her parlour. 'I don't know what's got into you.' Clarissa didn't know what to say so she kept silent. 'You've been at odds with the world for over a month. Brooding, not accepting any invitations to functions. I can't fathom it.'

Whatever she said wouldn't make a difference to her mother's views on how a young woman should behave. But Clarissa wouldn't go down without a fight. It'd been six weeks since Ian McCreadie's proposal in April and he hadn't forced his suit, but she knew she would have to give him an answer. 'Mother, I don't love Mr McCreadie. It's as simple as that. Marriage without love is meaningless.'

'Love? Dear Lord, what is going on in your mind?' She sighed and took Clarissa's hand. 'Romantic love isn't the stuff of strong marriages. Oh yes, I've read the books.' She smiled. 'I was young once and had the same dreams as you.'

Clarissa was somewhat taken aback at her mother confessing to such tendencies. 'Then you know how I feel or, frankly, don't feel about Ian.'

'I think I do, but affection grows in time, Clarissa. Look at your father and me.' That wasn't a good example but Clarissa wasn't going to argue that now. 'You must be married and Ian is just the person. There's nothing wrong with him, nothing. If not Ian, there's a bevy of well-bred beaux standing in line for you. You can't convince me you can't marry, as you say, *any* of them? Or is it someone else you've got on your mind?'

'There is not.'

'Don't add untruths as well. You can fool your father but not me. The sooner you accept that we will never sanction a union with Mr Leary the better for you.' She squeezed Clarissa's hand. 'Believe me, we are right.'

Clarissa was sure her mother's insistence on her marrying Ian, or someone like him, was to force her to forget John.

'Mr Leary is a hard-working, generous and capable man, but he is not for you.'

There it was. And perhaps she should think of considering other men. If her love for John was real, it would triumph. Still, she had to placate her parents. Clarissa let go her mother's hand. 'I'll accept more invitations, mother. I will.'

'Good.'

Clarissa walked from the room just as her father came in.

'Are you ready? The carriage is here.'

'Please give me a moment.' Upstairs her new maid, Stella, stood ready and opened a coat for her to wear. Stella used to work as a kitchen servant, but since the gold strike, the McGuires had little choice of their staff. 'Thank you. That will be all.'

Clarissa snuggled under the coverlet as the carriage swayed at the force of the wind. Beside her, her father looked from the late autumn sunlight outside, back to her. 'I don't like the way wire is heading,' he said. 'The English manufacturers know the demand here now and they're putting up their prices.'

'But just last week they were stable.'

'The letter I got this morning changes that. Our customers will baulk at paying more, accusing us of profiteering.'

'We need a manufacturer in Sydney.'

'That's who we're going to see.' Clarissa became excited and her father smiled at her. 'And he's got machines that can produce a ton of wire quickly. I've got a rough idea of what we need for the rest of the year.'

'I've got the quantity and gauges we need.'

'With you?' he said surprised.

'In my bag. I keep my own record of what we've sold and what we need.'

'Well done. I'm looking forward to striking a deal. By the by, on our new house, I ran into Mr Lewis the other day and he says all is well. Have you checked?'

'The plans are in good shape, father. I've seen them.'

'It's the middle of May. They should be. Have you spoken to Mr Jenkins about the bid?'

'Yes.'

'Was Mr Leary with him?'

'No.'

'Clarissa?'

'He wasn't, Father.'

'I have to believe you,' he said. 'But you would've liked him to be. He's been on your mind. Is that why you've been morose?'

Clarissa had to get this talk away from John. 'No. It's Mother and her demands for me to marry.'

'Ian McCreadie is not for you?'

Clarissa had to be fair. 'He could be, Father.'

'If he isn't, you'll have to find one who is. I need grandsons, Clarissa. I've got a vision for the future. You're doing a good job but it's only temporary.'

'So, I'm to be discarded?'

He smiled. 'Not for some years yet, perhaps. But one day soon you'll need to find a husband.'

She thought she'd found the one she wanted, but kept quiet. She must meet John Leary and force the issue of his feelings, one way or another.

Lie upon lie Clarissa was telling her parents, and today had been another one: a friend of hers in Miller's Point was ill and needed comfort. Clarissa would see her after the eight o'clock Mass at nearby St Patrick's Church Hill. Her parents had agreed to her going to that church, if she took Stella. Now, clutching her coat tighter to keep out the early June chill, Clarissa, accompanied by her maid, left the Mass. She was taking a risk; she wasn't seeing her friend, rather it was John. She'd written a letter to him, care of the builder's office, and hoped he'd received it

Walking down Charlotte Place, they turned into George Street and entered a tearoom. It had few patrons—fortunately. Directed by a waitress to a table with chairs that faced the street, Clarissa sat down. John came in and Clarissa nodded to Stella who moved to another table close by, but not within earshot. 'Good morning.'

'Hello,' he replied and smiled.

She got the waitress's attention then turned to him. 'Would you like something to drink?'

'Tea would be grand and yourself?'

'The same,' she indicated Stella to the waitress, 'and for my maid too, thank you.'

The waitress took their order and John sat with her. Stella smiled at John and gave Clarissa an excited look. Clarissa felt the same. She should've been more distant with her new maid, but she liked her. A couple entered, all rugged up, their faces obscured and Clarissa was keen to see who they were. They unwound their scarves, and

Clarissa watched them closely. No, she didn't know them, thank goodness.

John pulled out an envelope from his jacket and placed it on the table. 'These are the questions Mr Jenkins has about the house. We talked about them and I've put my two bob's worth in. Hope you don't mind.'

His voice, his smile. She'd missed him. 'Not at all. I'll study them and send my answers to you at the site or Mr Jenkins?'

'Better at our Pitt Street office in my name. The pub's nearly finished and it's chaos there. Your letter might get lost.'

'Pitt Street it is.'

'And I'll write to you with the address of my new lodgings.'

'Good,' she said and smiled.

'I've been made overseer, temporary like, but it's a promotion just the same, with more money. Getting the men to respect me is the hard bit.'

'That's grand and you will.' Clarissa moved her hand closer to his, wanting to hold it and press it to her. The waitress placed their teas on the table. 'On Point Piper, you'll have to have the sharpest price. Your ability to build is unchallenged and you have Lewis's recommendation. It's up to you.'

'I know. Did you talk to the other builders and give them the early drawings?'

'I didn't. I want Mr Jenkins in competition. He still will be, but you got more time.'

'We've already started on the bid.'

'Good,' she said and sipped her tea. Her time could be cut short and so she probed. 'Have you been busy?'

'The pub's been flat out. Not much time for anything else.'

She tilted her head to one side. 'What do you do away from work? Do you ever play?'

'What, like go to dances?'

'Yes.'

'A few.'

At which he would've met girls, and why shouldn't he? 'You

were quite a dancer on the *Emily*.' Clarissa's doubts lifted a little at John's smile. 'There now, something's raised your spirits, at last.'

'You'll always make me smile.'

Clarissa was encouraged. She was getting close, but not close enough. More to do. 'Do you remember when I said goodbye to you on the *Emily*?'

John picked up his cup. 'Yes.'

'I meant what I did that day.' She was emboldened. 'I wanted to kiss you.' It was said, a declaration and she waited.

'I haven't let myself have thoughts of you Clarissa, other than as a friend.'

A disappointing but not fatal reply. 'Why?' But she guessed the reason.

'You're different. You're quality and that's all right. That's how it should be.'

She had been right. But he had said he wouldn't *let* himself have thoughts of her. 'And if you did have thoughts for me?'

'I cannot—'

'If you could have thoughts of me?'

He looked away and Clarissa felt a coldness. He might have met someone else. She hadn't thought of that. She drank more of her tea, which was comforting.

He was looking at her now. 'I can't. I just can't. Look. Society, even here, won't accept it, your mother will fight me and your father will disown you. Three bloody good reasons why.'

She grinned. 'You talk too much.' But what he'd said was right and the hard-headed side of her knew it would be a tough battle. But she would fight that fight, if John was with her. She had to know. 'But you do like me more than a friend?' She now went for broke and took his hand. 'Do you?'

He covered her hand with his. 'I do.'

Her pulse beat harder. His feelings were stated and she had to believe him. Now to dig deeper. 'Do you want to see more of me and get to know me better?'

'I want that too.'

That was enough for now. 'Win this house for me, John. Supervise it and we'll be able to see each other. Is that what you want?'

He smiled. 'It is.'

Clarissa glanced at Stella and caught her eye. 'We have to go. Goodbye for the moment. Keep well until next time.' She leaned closer to him. 'My parents insist I move in society. I'll be meeting more men who may court me.'

John looked worried. That was a good sign. 'Of course.'

'Thank you.' She stood up and when Stella joined her, they left the teashop.

Coming onto site on a mid-June morning, John felt proud of the almost completed hotel. It had been difficult having to step in to the job just as it was finishing, but he sensed the men had welcomed the change. He went inside the public bar, careful not to hinder the workers and their trades. The sparkle of the tiles matched the twinkling brass of the bar rails. 'Looking good,' he said to the gas fitter who was installing the wall lights.

'Thanks, Boss,'

A painter was touching up the cornices and the bite of turpentine and the odour of varnish heralded a new Sydney watering hole.

He felt he'd organised it well. Mr Jenkins was speaking with a Kent Brewery representative in a corner. Threading his way through the workers, he waited until his boss noticed him.

'John, come over here. This is Mr Callaghan. Jim this is my overseer, John Leary.'

'Pleased to meet you, Mr Callaghan.' John said.

'It's more my pleasure, Mr Leary. If you're responsible for this you have my highest admiration. The quality's first class and there's some new things you've done which I'd like to use on our other hotels.'

John's chest swelled.

Mr Jenkins brought up a rolled plan and slapped it with his hand. 'This is what made it easy, Jim. John planned all the stages for the last weeks of the pub's program, all dovetailing nicely. He used labourers for the easiest jobs and wrote it all up.' He hit the paper again. 'It's like the holy grail.'

'That's a great idea,' Jim said.

'Jim, I have to speak to John about a few things.'

'Certainly. I've got to check the beer lines.'

'Come with me.' Mr Jenkins took John upstairs where the fitting out of the bedrooms was in full swing, not quite as finished as downstairs, but getting there. Down the corridor a man was working a plane along a doorframe. John didn't know him and turned to his boss with a questioning look on his face. 'I should have told you,' Jenkins said. 'This bloke has worked with me before and he's good.'

John felt uneasy. The man with the plane looked in his thirties and might be Jenkins's new overseer. His own job was still on trial.

'He's a carpenter, John, Sean Connaire and he's not your boss. The way this pub's being finished is your work. No, you're the overseer—permanent.'

'Thanks, Boss.'

'You've earned it. See that Sean fits the bill. Give him three months. If you think he's all right, which I think he will be, we'll keep him on.' Walking up to the man, Mr Jenkins tapped him on the shoulder. 'Connaire, this is John Leary.'

The man put down his plane and knocked the shavings from his forearm. He stuck out his hand. 'Mr Leary.'

John still kept getting a thrill from older men addressing him this way. It definitely was a sign of respect, as truth soon surfaces on a building site and bulldust was not tolerated. 'Morning. What's your work today?'

Mr Jenkins interjected. 'I'll leave you two to sort things out. John meet me this afternoon. I want to talk about Point Piper.'

'Good.' John turned back to Connaire as his boss left. 'So, where did you work before here?

Connaire leaned back against the doorframe.

'Lots of places, but I just finished a house at Annandale.'

'For Mr Jenkins?'

'No, but he knew of me.'

The man was only five feet five inches tall but his shoulders were wide as a pick handle and moulded from years of labour—a good man to have beside you in a strange pub at closing time. John dug deeper. 'Carpenter all your life?'

Sean paused and looked down. 'Aye, it's an honest trade.'

'Well, Jesus, you and I share that in common.'

Connaire smiled at him. 'He was too good for the likes of me. But I'm content. I've a good wife and four loving children.'

John liked him. A man who spoke his thoughts to another man he'd just met— and a boss. A philosophical sort of man.

He pointed to John's head. 'Nail?'

'Yeah.'

'Nasty.' He tapped his wrist. 'I took one across here. It bled for an hour.'

'A carpenter's risk, I guess. Time to get back into it.'

Connaire picked up the plane and went to work.

John's tasks for the rest of the day were onerous. It seemed all the men wanted their problems solved. If he wasn't arbitrating between painter and carpenter he was soothing the anger of the plumber. Someone had left a valve open in the basement, flooding half the area. He finally sat down and studied the architect's plans for the high-level glass shelves when Mr Jenkins came up beside him. His boss's face had an unfamiliar frown.

'About Point Piper, the McGuire place, I'm not going to put in a bid.'

John was too shocked to say anything.

Seeing John's face, Jenkins said, 'Look, it's nearly knock off. Are you finished here?'

'Er, yeah,' John said, still somewhat dumbfounded by Jenkins's statement.

'Then come for a drink and I'll explain.'

They forced their way through the crowd at the Erskine Street pub, disturbing the smoke from the pipes and cigars. An opening appeared and they lunged for it, using their forearms against the other punters.

Armed with a full beer, Jenkins looked at John. 'How bad would it be if I don't put in a price?'

This wasn't good. His future depended on it but he didn't want to scare his boss. 'It's your business, Mr Jenkins. If you don't price, you don't price, but there could be rumblings.'

'What do you mean?'

'The McGuires know rich people. If word got around that you're not quoting, it could close a lot of doors, a lot of future work. And we have a friend in Miss Clarissa.'

Jenkins grinned. 'She likes you!'

'She thinks she does and she's given me answers to your questions. I have them with me. We have a head start.'

'She probably gave them to all the tenderers.'

John kept silent. 'Maybe. But she's still an ally.'

Jenkins finished his beer. 'I'll think about that. My shout.' He set sail for the bar.

What's his problem? John wondered. He might be worried about stretching his team too thinly. John understood a builder's supervision costs. It was useful knowledge for when he'd have his own company. A small, skilled team of overseers had to run a number of sites. These men could also pick up the tools themselves, if necessary, and fill in any gaps on the jobs. John pondered this till his boss returned carrying the two beers like precious china. 'My problem is that I only have two supervisors,' Jenkins said, handing John his beer, 'you and Mullins. With all the good 'uns off to the gold fields, I can't find the right blokes.'

'But there's opportunity in that. Every builder's in the same boat. The thing to do is train the tradesmen you've got to take on more responsibility. Give your carpenters a bit of a go at running things.'

'That's a thought.'

'Mr Jenkins, if everything's going all right and there's plenty of the right people around, you wouldn't necessarily be making good profits. When labour is scarce, you can price your work up.'

'I know that. But I'm starting two new warehouses soon.'

'You are.'

'I'm at the limit.'

'Not if you take a suggestion.' John said.

'Such as?'

'Day Street will be finished at the end of July, that's one month from now. Before you put me onto the Blackwattle job, which is straightforward, let me train Connaire as a supervisor. You know his work.' Jenkins gestured like he was going to interrupt but John continued. 'If he comes up trumps, then he can supervise Blackwattle, I can go to Point Piper. If Connaire doesn't come up to scratch, then I know I can do Blackwattle and set up Point Piper for a month or two. We can work out then how to find my - replacement.'

Jenkins stroked his chin with his hand. 'You're asking me to take some risk here.'

John went for broke. Point Piper he had to have. Jenkins didn't know it but John wanted McGuire's house as a springboard for his own company. 'Balmain stores will be over then and, I'll do a deal with you. If you can't find another supervisor after two months on Point Piper, I'll do both sites and risk my job on it.'

'Balmain stores finishes the end of September. Doug Mullins will need a job. He can supervise Point Piper while you sort out Blackwattle.'

That wouldn't do, John had to use facts here. 'He could, but I've got the client on side. Doug would be better on Blackwattle until McCreadie's starts.'

Jenkins looked at him for a long time. The crowd had thinned. His boss put his empty glass on a shelf and reached for a stool. 'We mightn't get Point Piper. If we don't, there's no problem but if we do, you'll be on it. Now, go buy me a beer. We've got a tender to discuss.'

~

The twilight settled on the site and John, his breath misting and hands deep in pockets, waited for his boss to lock the site gate.

'Go to Lewis's in my stead. This cold's got to me and I'm going home. They're in Pitt Street between King and Market Streets. They'll have all the final plans there that we have to price.'

'Wrap up warm and drink a whisky, Boss.'

Jenkins grinned. 'I might have two. Off you go.'

John set off. How things can change. Clarissa liked him enough to want to keep seeing him *and* she liked him more than as a friend. That was a revelation that he still found hard to accept. How deep were his feelings? It was flattering that an attractive woman, who, he felt was his social superior, could like him more than as a friend. Was that what he liked about her? Was she a trophy for him? No—in all the time on the *Emily* and now a year on there was a bond between them. Deep feelings he had, but he'd never given them rein, believing that they had no future. Now was another story. But there was risk. She'd said she'd be mixing in society and meeting other men. Was that to make him jealous? He didn't think so as she'd never shown spitefulness, and she'd said that it was at her family's request. But she might fall in love with one of her no doubt many suitors and he'd be left stranded. *She liked him!* It was still a thrill to know that. But if she was seeing others then he would too and tonight he would go to the Royal Hotel and see Beth.

Passing the Erskine Street pub reminded him of Mr Jenkins and that he was using his good-natured boss for his own benefit. That didn't sit well with John. Jenkins was straight and had been loyal to him. John felt he was knifing him in the back. He pushed that thought away and concentrated. Ambition was one thing, getting wealth a different matter. With his promotion a certainty, he could put aside a bit. His new wages could pay for fancier digs, but -Elizabeth Street suited him. Now he had the money to pay someone to get information on Baxterhouse. John tapped the end of a dray as he crossed over George Street. He could live with his sister's rapist being in town, but gnawing at him was that Baxterhouse had got away with hurting Maureen and she was due in Sydney soon. How would she react when she knew Baxterhouse was here? He'd soon find out. He wasn't conscious of the tension in his shoulders until he saw the door of Lewis's architects.

Entering the gas lit lobby he saw David McGuire reading the

Herald. This was a coincidence. McGuire looked at him. 'Afternoon, Mr Leary. Is Mr Jenkins coming?'

Before John could answer him, a man came out of an office and approached them.

John turned to him. 'How do you do. I'm John Leary standing in for my boss who's ill.'

'Robert Lewis, pleased to meet you, Mr Leary. You know Mr McGuire, I understand. Please, let's go into my office.'

Closing the door after them, the architect saw them seated and sat behind a large desk. 'I hope Mr Jenkins gets well soon.'

'I'll pass on your regards, sir. Thank you.'

'You're the fourth and last tenderer for Mr McGuire's new residence' Lewis said, pointing at a table to his right that was piled with documents. 'Those are the drawings showing the architectural layouts, details of wrought iron and structural specifications, all very straightforward. And this,' he picked up a thick document, 'is the contract.'

John would study these in his own time. He wanted proof that Clarissa had been honest about the early plans and that these final ones would be unchanged. Mr Jenkins had agreed to tender, provided John did all the groundwork, preparing the prices and obtaining suppliers' quotations. He'd be a busy boy. 'There's a lot to go through.'

'For a good builder,' McGuire said, 'it should be straightforward.'

Indeed, John thought.

'It's the end of June,' Lewis said. 'And the tender closes in three weeks from yesterday.'

John had a thought. 'I want to win this tender, Mr McGuire and build your house. But I want a square deal.'

'All tenderers will be treated professionally,' Lewis said. 'We thought Mr Jenkins's building work was good, but, he is less known for building prestige houses compared with the other contractors. We'll do the vetting of the bids and make our recommendation to Mr McGuire. Mr Leary, your price may not be the cheapest but it has to be competitive.'

'Of course. Who are the other bidding contractors?'

'I can't tell you,' Lewis said and smiled. 'But knowing you builders, you'll find out.'

'So, it's up to you, young man,' McGuire said. 'Where's Mr Jenkins's office?'

'End of Pitt Street, near Campbell Street.'

McGuire gestured to the pile of documents. 'I can give you a ride down there now, if you wish.'

The offer was too good to refuse. He'd need a packhorse otherwise and he smelt rain coming. 'Thank you, I'd be much obliged.'

'Right,' Lewis said as he started to pass the documents to John. 'Remember, the eighteenth of July at two pm, no later. There'll be a box in the lobby outside to lodge your tender. Good luck to you.'

McGuire took half the documents. 'This way, Mr Leary.'

John, picked up the rest and followed him outside where they turned left.

Twenty yards down Pitt Street McGuire stopped. 'My new brougham, like it?'

Under the gaslight, the paint gleamed and John knew it would've been expensive.

A uniformed man opened the door. 'Come on. Hop on board. Peters, Pitt and Campbell, thank you.'

John felt self-conscious in the leather luxury of the four-wheeled carriage. He was also suspicious of McGuire giving him a ride. It was a favour he didn't think would've been extended to the other tenderers.

McGuire kept quiet till Bathurst Street then he turned to him. 'Let me say first, Mr Leary, I acknowledge your hard work, ambition and other qualities.'

'Thank you.'

'I have a professional interest in your business. It seems my daughter has a different interest in you. I have told her not to see you.'

'I'm not good enough for her?'

McGuire said nothing and looked ahead.

John was about to reply, to defend Clarissa and declare his

intentions. 'We are bound to meet in town. We go to the same church, it's—'

'That's not what I mean. You're not to see her alone or at any time.' He looked at John. 'Is that clear?'

It was. But John had a broader strategy and wouldn't argue with the man now. He had to win the tender, besides Clarissa seemed not without ideas on how they could meet and continue their relationship. 'I respect you Mr McGuire. But I have feelings for your daughter, genuine feelings and I—'

'You're not to see her. Do I make myself clear?'

The carriage was now at Brickfield Hill and it was time to end this. 'Like crystal.' McGuire bridled, but John continued. 'Here will be good to get off.'

'Peters, stop here.'

As the carriage came to a halt John collected the documents. 'I'll get you a winning bid, Mr McGuire. If you accept it, we'll be working together for many months. In that time, you may change your mind about me.'

Before McGuire could reply John nodded a farewell and left the carriage just as the rain started to spit. Scrambling with his load, he made his way to the office knowing that to win Clarissa he had to build her father's house.

CHAPTER EIGHT

William Baxterhouse studied the Bathurst map that the stock and station agent had given him. Three dots along Durham Street indicated opportunities. He had to have a shop with a street frontage and a display area to sell gold fossicking tools to the public, and with a storeroom at the rear. His experience selling directly to people was limited but he knew he could do it, provided he had the right staff and the best outlet. He also couldn't risk supervising the venture from Sydney, which meant Bathurst would take more of his time until he could pass it over to a competent person to manage. Smiling, he circled the middle dot, content it was the right one, wrote down its reference and started to draft a letter to the agent.

Mackays was soon to invite a second tender for tools and James's shipment, on its way to Sydney, would fulfil that. William would win the next tender, but Ballarat was also crucial. *I have to have a secondary supply,* he thought and that supplier would have to be a Sydney-based company. That planning was for the near future. Once the shipment arrived, he'd need armed transport to Melbourne then up to Ballarat, his cargo being as precious as the gold in the ground. If only the Ballarat strike had happened earlier. He could've got James and the cargo to go direct to Melbourne.

~

Walking down Forbes Street in the late afternoon of a July Saturday, John went over his approach to the investigator. His fellow shipboard companion, now senior clerk, Donald Watkins, had provided him with three names. Watkins had used all three in assisting his employer in his new business. John had been able to interest one investigator and his letter to the man had requested a meeting at the Royal Hotel which meant he could see Beth again. Yes, Clarissa liked him and wanted him, but Beth was available now.

John tried to think whether Baxterhouse knew Maureen's maiden name. As far as John knew, she'd always used Murphy, her married name. Pushing open the doors, he entered the cosiness of the hotel. In his note to the investigator, he had described himself and what he would be wearing. Approaching the bar, he felt a hand at his elbow.

'Mr Leary?' John turned and faced a man of about thirty years of age, stocky, dark-haired and sharp-eyed. 'Damien Wexton,' the man said. 'Let's sit down.'

John followed the man to a table away from the window and sat opposite him. He noticed Beth pouring a beer. 'Do you want a drink?'

'Yes thank you, anything but alcohol.'

This surprised John but he went to the bar and Beth came up to him.

She welcomed him with a smile. 'Hello.'

'Hello yourself.'

'What'll you have?'

'A beer and a lemon squash, please.' He tried to get her attention but she concentrated on the tap. 'When do you get off?'

'Five o'clock.'

'Are you going home?'

'I am.'

'Well, I'll wait, if that's all right.'

Beth put both drinks on the bar, collected John's money and smiled again. 'Grand.'

Walking back to the table, he was glad he'd come. It'd been a fortnight since he'd seen her.

Wexton looked at him as he put the drinks down. 'Nice looking girl.'

John sat down and swallowed a mouthful of the ale. 'Aye, she is. Now, let's get down to business. I need to find out more about a Mr William Baxterhouse. He's a gentleman in town with a boatbuilding company in Darling Harbour at the end of Kent Street.'

'I think I've seen his name in the papers.'

'Mr Wexton, it's the stuff that's not in the papers I want to know.'

'I understand. You want all the dirt.'

'I won't tell you your job but this man has an evil side.'

Wexton took a drink and adjusted his waistcoat. 'Mr Leary, you're a new client and you'll have your doubts, that's all right, but I do my job well, and there won't be nothing you won't know about him, including where you'll find his boils and warts.'

'Good, now as for payment.'

'I charge by the day, which includes the night. The rate is ten shillings.'

'Very good.' John pulled out his wallet and put four one-pound notes on the table with a card showing his address. 'That's for eight days work.'

Wexton palmed the money, stood up and put out his hand. 'I'll make an account for this.'

John shook his hand, comforted by the firm grip. 'Meet me next Tuesday fortnight at eight at my digs in Elizabeth Street.'

Wexton left the pub and John glanced at the clock and Beth. He was hungry, so he ordered some food and thought about work. The Day Street job was in good shape and a week from completion. And Sean Connaire was proving a find. The new carpenter was definitely up to being an overseer, so John had no worries that he could handle Point Piper by himself. In five days he had to complete the tender for the McGuire house and check it with Mr Jenkins.

At five to five John went outside to wait for Beth, pulling his coat tighter to fend off the cold. He rubbed his hands together and smiled.

'You look like you've lost a penny and picked up a pound.' Beth's smile was genuine.

'Aye, things are going well, for sure.'

'What's it like to be a boss?'

'It's only been a month, Beth, but I like it.'

'Come, let's go.' She linked her arm in his and they headed for her place.

Closing the front door, Beth went to the kitchen and put the kettle on. 'Give me five minutes. The smoke from the pub stinks your clothes.'

'Aye.' John sat at the table and looked at the dresser. The thought of Beth getting changed upstairs was distracting him. 'Where's the tea and mugs?' he called out to her.

'Cups, left side of the dresser, tea's in the corner cupboard.'

He prepared the brew and waited for the pot to boil, warming his hands at the same time. Beth came into the kitchen just as steam spewed from the kettle. She made the tea and brought the pot to the table where john was sitting. 'So you've been busy.'

'Yeah, flat out. The pub's nearly finished.'

'Good. Where do you go after that?'

'Likely Blackwattle. A warehouse.'

Beth went to a cupboard and brought out a tin, opened it and cut two slices of cake. She put them on a plate and sat down beside him. John was about to speak, when pandemonium broke out.

'John,' squealed Olivia as she ran into the kitchen followed by her sister.

'Boo!' he yelled.

Both girls jumped, screamed and ran from the kitchen.

Beth sat down laughing. 'Stay in the back, girls,' she called out after them. 'Don't go out the front.' She turned to John. 'Eat your cake.'

John ate a slice and drank some of the tea. 'The girls are full of beans.'

'They sure are.'

The warmth of the kitchen, Beth's smile and closeness made him feel like he was at home with his family. She was a friend, a mate, she was someone he could unburden himself to. Being a woman she would understand his anger at Baxterhouse and he needed to get it out of his head. 'I want to talk to you about - something.'

Beth leaned forward, her face concerned. 'From your look, it's serious.'

'I want to punish a man who did a terrible thing to my sister.' Beth put her mug down. John shook his head at his sudden honesty. Had he done the right thing? But he felt better, just a bit, and now he wanted to tell all. 'This man came to New South Wales a little before I did.' John cleared his throat. 'He raped her.'

Beth's mouth dropped open and her shoulders sagged. 'The poor thing.'

'Aye. It's something I'll never ever forget.'

'Oh, John.'

He felt a load slide from his shoulders. Beth got up and hugged him. 'I'm all right,' he said, 'but you're the first I've told.' Beth held onto him and kissed him and he returned it. She broke away, took his hand and looked into his eyes.

'Come,' she said sitting back on her chair, 'tell me all about it.'

John poured more tea for them.

'Have you seen him here, talked to him?'

'I have. I don't know how I did it without hitting him.'

'I know what you mean. But he's guilty. Did your sister know the bastard?'

'The man was her landlord.'

'I know the type. I see them in the pub. They leer at you and make you feel filthy.' She shivered. 'Your poor sister.' Running a hand through her hair she asked. 'Do you know the name of this animal?'

'I do. William Baxterhouse. I want to find out all about him before I deal with him.'

'How'll you do that?'

'What? Find out about him or deal with him?'

Beth shrugged her shoulders. 'Well, both.'

John felt the tendons in his neck stiffen. 'I've met a man today.'

'That one at the pub?'

'It's not cheap, but this man will find out all I need to know about Baxterhouse. That man must suffer by steps to begin with and then . . . I'll enjoy watching all the way.'

'Do you mean that?' Beth said. 'What he did was wrong but—'

'Wouldn't you do the same? I've heard of men who rape young girls, say like your sisters. If a man did that, would you forgive him or punish him?'

Beth didn't look at him. 'There's always the law.'

'And you'd trust the law to get justice?'

'But John—to kill?'

'I didn't say kill.'

'But you would?'

He looked out the window. Could he kill Baxterhouse for what he'd done? Actually, slide a knife into the man or crush his skull with a rock? In Dublin in June last year, he well could have.

'See, you would find it hard.'

'I would not,' he said, but he was unconvinced. 'If you'd seen my sister's torment, you'd understand.'

Beth looked at him for a long time. 'No, I don't believe you.'

'You mightn't know me that well then.'

Beth paused. 'Maybe I don't.'

John took her hand. 'But there's good in me.'

She smiled. 'There is and that's why I like you.'

'You're a good friend, Beth.'

'You didn't kiss me like a friend.'

'You *are* more of a friend to me.'

She smiled. 'I'm glad. These last weeks we've got closer, I think.'

He took her other hand. 'We have. Come here.'

She sat in his lap and kissed him again. Her lips were warm and pliant. He placed his hand on her breast, feeling its firmness and fullness. Beth moaned but eased his hand away.

Olivia came skipping into the kitchen. 'Caught you! Caught you!'

Flushed, Beth stood up and grabbed her sister. 'Manners my girl. You shouldn't scare us like that.'

'You were kissing him.'

'Beth was giving me a hug, that's all,' John said.

'I'll tell Mum,' Olivia said.

Beth smiled and so did John. 'Mum wouldn't be surprised. Now, my young miss, go tidy your room. I'll put the bath on soon.'

Olivia grinned at them. 'Right. Bye, Mr Giant.'

John went to grab her and, squealing, Olivia fled the room.

Beth took the cups to the sink and spoke to him without turning around. 'We were saved again, it seems.' She faced him, looking boldly at him. 'I like you John, but I'll not bed with you. I'm not a doxy.'

'You're not.' He wanted her, but she was the one who started things both in his bedroom and just now.

Moving to the table she took his hand. 'I'll keep a safe distance next time. That's if you want to keep seeing me. But because I'll not bed with you, you mightn't want to see me again.'

'I want to see you again, Beth. I do.'

'That'd be nice. Look, I've lots to do for Mum.'

John looked at her. It took all his willpower not to kiss her again. He got up to leave. 'I'd better go. The landlady keeps a punctual supper table. There are two shows on at the Royal Victoria. One's *Sixteen-String Jack*. It should be good. Would you like to go with me?'

Beth smiled. 'I'd love to. I have next Saturday off.'

'I'll be here at seven o'clock. Now, I'll see myself out,' he said smiling warmly back at her.'

Beth was excited: the Royal in Pitt Street! How fancy. What to wear? Lost in thoughts about dress, the sound of the front door closing returned her thoughts to what John had told her about his sister and the man who'd raped her. Could John really kill the man? No, he was just angry, a deep and bitter anger. If he ever got the bastard, he couldn't do it. She was sure. She shivered. Thank God he'd told her. She'd stop him from ruining himself. That man who raped his sister had to be brought to account, but by the law, not John's way.

Going into the back room she found Olivia reading her book. 'Come on, I'll start the heater and you can help me.'

Lighting the gas, with her sister beside her, Beth could understand what John was trying to do, but couldn't agree with his intentions. This might explain those few occasions when he'd gone quiet. He may have a cruel side. But, most times there was another John and she was certainly very attracted to him. Would she have stopped if Livvy hadn't surprised them just now? She didn't think so. She was weak, but only for him. Other men she'd given short shrift when they'd groped and fumbled with her. She knew John liked her but while his mind was full of plans for avenging his sister, any hope of taking their relationship further was on hold.

As the warm water flowed into the bath, she turned to Olivia. 'Thank you, for your help. Now, go get Sarah and tell her the bath is ready.' As her sister went out, Beth knew that she'd have to be strong and patient when it came to John Leary.

John's grin wasn't lost on Mr Jenkins.

'Yes, my boy you've done a good job and this is something you can be proud of.' Jenkins waved his arm at the customers drinking complimentary grog at the grand opening of Cochrane's Hotel. 'It's the eighteenth of July and the pub's finished ahead of time.'

Jim Callaghan came up to them smiling. 'Gentlemen, on behalf of the brewery, thank you.' He shook both their hands and standing between them slapped their backs.

'Are there more hotel jobs coming up?' John asked.

Jenkins grinned as Callaghan stroked his chin and frowned. 'There might be one or two.'

'We've got a few ideas to save you money,' John said and Jenkins's face took on a quizzical look.

'Oh, aye?' Callaghan said, grinning. 'We're always interested in that.' John ordered them more beers from the barmaid. 'It means us working with your architects during the design.'

The brewery representative looked interested. 'Let's get together soon and talk. I've got to get to Waterloo by twelve. You're welcome to my beer. You've earned it. Again, gentlemen, thank you.'

John turned to his boss. 'I'm going back to the office to complete the tender. We lodge today.'

'I've signed the covering letter already. Two o'clock John, remember?'

'I do.'

~

During intermission at the Royal Victoria Theatre, John and Beth walked down the stairs to the foyer. It was a crowded Saturday night and there were familiar faces: Robert Lewis, the architect, and Thomas Higgins, the banker, accompanied by his daughter, Elizabeth. 'Can I get you something to drink?' John asked Beth.

Beth nodded. 'Thank you, I'll come with you; all these people dressed fancy is too much for me.' She threaded her arm though his and they made their way to the concession. Beth was in a navy dress, not the latest fashion, but acceptable and her proud bosom and attractive features were getting looks from both men and women. John spotted David and Christine McGuire.

'Mr Leary.' A woman's voice spoke to him. He knew who it was.

John turned and there was Clarissa dressed in high fashion on the arm of a military man whose braid and buttons were that of an officer. 'Miss Clarissa, how do you do?'

Clarissa's smile was forced and her eyes hadn't left Beth, taking all of her in. 'I don't have the pleasure of knowing your young lady?'

The possessive term wasn't lost on him. 'Miss O'Hare, this is Miss Clarissa McGuire.'

'Please to meet you. May I introduce, Captain Price?' Clarissa replied, still looking at Beth.

The officer nodded at Leary. 'Good evening, Miss O'Hare, Mr Leary.'

'Did you enjoy the play?' Clarissa said, forcing herself to now look at him.

'I did,' John said, 'although I think Henry Lloyd was miscast as John Rann.'

'A small man, I'll admit,' Price said, 'but you don't have to be tall like Mr Leary here, to be a highwayman, just carry a weapon. What did you think Miss O'Hare?'

'I liked the necklace he stole, it was beautiful. And the ribbons on his knees, very dapper for a robber.'

Clarissa's mouth was drawn tight and she was still watching Beth.

'*The Devil and the Lady* is on next,' John said. 'That should be amusing.'

'Tennyson at his best,' Price exclaimed. 'I'm intrigued to see what sets they'll employ.'

'Please excuse us,' John said, 'we must get our drinks and we haven't much time. Shall we, Miss O'Hare?'

They moved away and Beth giggled. 'Miss O'Hare. How posh. Where did you meet her? She must be rich with that dress. It was full silk.'

'She was a passenger I met coming to Sydney.'

'Do you like her?'

A question John had expected and seeing Clarissa with Captain Price had made him jealous. 'No.'

'Oh. That's good then. Come on, we'll have to hurry if we want that drink before the play starts.'

John got control of himself. Clarissa had told him she'd be meeting men— she had been honest. But when he saw her actually holding onto another man's arm—that was different.

~

In the next ten days John tried to find out what prices the three other tenderers had submitted for the McGuire house, but couldn't come up with anything. On 29 July, he headed home to Elizabeth Street, ate a full meal and waited for Damien Wexton. At eight o'clock promptly, John greeted him and accompanied his guest into the unoccupied parlour of his boarding house.

His visitor took off his hat, put down a satchel and relaxed into the seat. 'Mr Leary, this Baxterhouse is a complex character. A fashionable gentleman and businessman wrapped around a darker core. I've made a single copy of my report. It's easier for me and it gives you peace of mind.'

John hadn't thought about Wexton using any of his information against him. It sobered him knowing he was on a fine line between good and evil. 'I understand.'

'Baxterhouse has debts in Dublin, a good income here from four businesses and social connections. He has a lady friend but still visits the brothels and likes his frolics rough.'

So Baxterhouse's crime against Maureen may not have been a random act of violence? 'Tell me everything you know.'

'He trains as a fighter—'

'He says he likes bare knuckle.'

'I've got it all here, Mr Leary. He's tied one fight and has won one.' He brought from his bag a folder containing clippings from newspapers and scribed notes. 'Here it is.' He held it out to John. 'Please read it.'

For the next few minutes John concentrated on the dossier. 'He owes money in Dublin?'

'Like it says, there's one creditor who's after him and the East India Company is also investigating his Dublin trading company and his family's business in Belfast.'

John continued reading. 'What's his big thing? Gold?'

'Gold. He's leased a store in Bathurst and plans to move up there for three months to settle things in.'

'You've been thorough. Very thorough.'

Damien rummaged in his satchel and removed a piece of paper. 'Here is your receipt for my services to date.'

John accepted it. 'I want you to keep digging. Keep your ears open. If you find out anything, let me know right away.'

'I shall.'

John wanted to celebrate. 'Join me for a drink.'

'Thank you, no. With respect, I find that the information I give my clients frequently results in unhappiness for someone. I'll bid you goodnight.'

As the investigator left his room, John felt a twinge of guilt. Wexton's words gelled with Beth's about the hollowness of revenge.

His conscience wasn't bothered long. Going to the kitchen downstairs he made a pot of tea and returned to his room. He grabbed a thick coat to ward off the chill and smiled; the room's temperature suited him. Reading the report, he began planning his attack.

~

John referred to the drawings, while Connaire checked the set out for the columns at the Blackwattle warehouse site. John hoped to finish early as he had to get away to town this afternoon. Clarissa wanted to meet him and he pressed her note in his pocket. She would ask about Beth and might be angry. She'd been honest with him.

At smoko, with the column check finished, he was thinking about her, when Mr Jenkins came up to him.

'Here's a letter from Lewis. He said he'd tell us in three weeks and it's the eleventh of August today. It's bad news. Read it if you like.'

John wiped his hand on his trousers and took the paper.

Jenkins took his glasses off. 'Bloody Reeds. They've got another one. They're £150 under us.'

'That's low,' John said. 'About twenty per cent.' The McGuire house was the foundation of his future business. Well, no more. He was very disappointed. 'Sorry boss.'

'There'll be others, John. I wasn't keen on doing that house anyway, but that's a rock bottom price. Good luck to John Reed if he makes a quid on this. I very much doubt it.'

'Well, he's got it now.'

'Aye.'

John had an idea. 'Would you let me talk to Mr Lewis?'

'Why? About this? It's gone, don't bother.'

'I want to find out why we were so high, so next time we'll know when we price. I've been here since sparrows, let me leave at two.'

'You'll not get them to change, but have a go. Now, Connaire's waving at us. Get back and help him. We've got a warehouse to build.'

'I'm on my way.'

At two o'clock John left Blackwattle and made his way to town by tram. They couldn't keep meeting like this for long. Rebelling against her parents was one thing, deceit another, and she was seeing him unchaperoned. But Clarissa's confidence in trying to get them accepted by her parents made him believe in her. But first he had to front the architects. Alighting from the tram near King Street he made his way to Pitt Street.

'Yes,' the clerk said, 'Mr Lewis is in and can see you.'

'Thank you.'

Robert Lewis emerged from his office. 'Come in, Mr Leary.' John sat down as the architect closed the door. 'Normally I don't give post-tender interviews but as David McGuire is a good client I will tell you what I can.'

'Reeds' tender was so low. There has to be a mistake.'

'No. We checked all the costs.' Lewis smiled. 'All you builders had to give a detailed price breakdown.'

'I know but in each section you could see where some tenders were high or low.'

Lewis paused. 'Reeds were low in their brickwork allowance but they assured us that they had their prices right.'

'How low?'

'We can't tell you that.'

'Look, Mr Lewis, we both know the rough costs to supply a brick and to lay one. Tell me, was their labour cost low or the material?'

Lewis hesitated. 'Their labour cost was on the money but their supply price was very low.'

'Only two brickworks supply the bricks you specified and we both know their prices to the penny, so Reeds have made a blue.'

'They say that they did a very good deal. Mr Leary that ends the discussion.'

'And the timing to complete the house?'

'You came out trumps on that but we had to look at all aspects of the tender.'

John stood up. 'It's Reeds' job now, but if there's trouble with them, you know where we are.'

Lewis opened his office door. 'We know what we're doing. Good luck on your next bid.'

John left the architect, disappointed, and headed for the Quay. The Point Piper house was gone and that rattled him; he'd have to find another job to make his future. Getting off the tram, he saw Clarissa and that pushed away his anxiety.

'Hello,' she said.

John glanced at the people walking near them. Had they noticed them together? Clearly Clarissa didn't mind. 'Miss McGuire.'

'Come on, we'll sit by the water.' They made their way to a bench just in front of the railing. They sat a yard apart. The smell of the ferry smoke mixed with the tang of the salt water. 'She's good looking, your Beth. Do you like her?'

Straight to the point. 'She's not my Beth. You told me you'd see other men. I'm just doing the same.'

'But I *told* you before I was seeing them. You said nothing.'

That was fact. 'She's a friend I see and take out sometimes.'

'She likes you. I can tell.'

'And Captain Price. Does he like you?'

She kept silent and John guessed that the army officer did. This was silly. 'I wanted to see you today, I did. Now, are we going to fight all the time we have or talk about other things?'

She said nothing for a moment. 'I tried to get you to build the house. I really did.'

'Thank you, but we were beaten by a hellishly low bid.'

'That's what Father said but Mr Lewis is certain Reeds will do the job.' The mention of David McGuire made John feel guilty. Clarissa seemed to guess his thoughts. 'Don't worry. No one knows I'm here, and I don't care if they do see us. This is New South Wales. It's 1851 and women should be alone with whom they please.'

That surprised him but he admired her courage. 'You make it sound so easy. Your father seems like a good man. I admire him and it'll be hard to win him over. But I will if you think the fight's worth it. Do you?'

'That depends upon Miss O'Hare.'

'You want me to stop seeing her?'

'I can't keep putting off suitors forever. I'm to marry and will have to choose sometime soon.' She stood up. 'It's up to you, John. You want to see other women—'

'It's just Beth. No one else.'

She took some time before speaking. 'The risk to both of us is that we'll get deeper in our respective relationships. If you want me, you'll have to do the work to win me, but quickly.'

That was well said. 'So, you want me to fight for you?'

'It's up to you. Now, goodbye.' She turned and walked away.

John felt despondent. How quickly did she mean? If she loved him, she would build barriers to keep the suitors away. So she didn't love him enough to do that? It certainly sounded like it. He got up and left for home, thinking about Clarissa's ultimatum. If he went for broke and concentrated on her and he failed, what then? Nothing but a broken heart. And Beth? He knew how she felt about him, she wouldn't want him after he'd dropped her for Clarissa. It was frustrating, but two things were definite, the first was to make his mark and build a business and second, to get justice for Maureen. Both had to be given priority and women—Beth or Clarissa or someone else—would have to fit into that plan somehow.

Two days after seeing Clarissa, John arrived at Cullen's Blackwattle Bay business, just up the road from his site. John thought of how to approach his meeting with the ironworker.

In investigator Wexton's report, Baxterhouse had tendered to Mackays for the miners' tools and had failed. Cullens had won. Wexton had recommended that John meet Cullen to try and find out more on Baxterhouse. The company was also one of Lewis's preferred suppliers for Point Piper's wrought iron lacework and columns. John had got a price from Cullen for his unsuccessful bid, but had never met the man.

He went in. A clerk looked up at him. 'Mr Leary?' John nodded. 'You're on time. Mr Cullen will see you now.'

John entered an office built in a practical way with every inch utilised. He shook hands with a solidly built middle-aged man of medium height; a man used to physical labour, who'd probably built his foundry from the ground up.

Cullen's face creased into a frown. 'Mr Leary, what can I do for you? You aren't here for my order but you're big enough to work handsomely in my foundry.' He smiled. 'I spoke with John Reed this morning.'

Overcoming his irritation at the Point Piper loss, John posed a question. 'Your wrought iron quotation, was it the same one you gave us?'

'Not a pound more, or one less.'

That still leaves the brickwork costs and Reeds had made an error. They couldn't lay bricks for such a low price. 'Well then. I'm here for another reason.'

Mr Cullen gestured to a chair. 'Sit down, please.'

'I know you won a tender recently with Mackays to supply tools, mining tools.'

The big ironmonger folded his arms 'How'd you get that information, it's confidential—'

'I'm not here for commercial advantage.'

The man paused. 'Go on.'

'Another firm tendered on that same order.'

'Yes, Jacksons.'

'And Baxterhouse.'

'Bloody man.' Cullen's face became guarded. 'You know him?'

'He's not a friend of mine.'

'Good, because I'll have none of him. He tried to bribe me to stop me tendering, bloody cheek. I'm sure he tried to bribe Grant Jackson too.'

'Did he now?'

'I threw Baxterhouse out.'

Cullen seemed big enough to match strength with Baxterhouse and his bare knuckle skills. Well, all that fits. 'I knew of Baxterhouse in Dublin. He's got a reputation.' John stood up. 'You've told me what I need to know. So be warned of him. But thank you.'

Cullen stood up and shook John's outstretched hand. 'Don't worry, I can look after myself. Good day, Mr Leary.'

~

John's first Sydney winter had passed. Now in the first week of spring, the town had turned on a balmy September day. Sean Connaire was a leading hand on Blackwattle with John supervising, as Point Piper was no more. So far so good, except for Connaire's drinking. Although alert on the job and doing everything right, there were times when John knew the man wanted a drink. First thing in the morning and just before knock off, Connaire got testy. His three months' probation was just about up and he had to have a reliable leading hand before he could consider Connaire as a supervisor. John was all set to leave for the builder's office when he heard shouts from behind the wall sheeting.

Connaire was arguing with a carpenter. 'You daft sod, you know what I want. I've told you three times!'

'But it comes out the same. I do it that way all the time.'

'Not on my friggin' sites you don't!'

There was a scuffle and John went behind the sheeting to find him and the carpenter at it. Connaire ducked and weaved landing the odd hit, avoiding damage from his opponent's haymakers. Three other men had come to watch and John had to act. He spotted a mason's hose and releasing a valve drenched both combatants. Spluttering, they turned towards him. 'Connaire, get over here. You Bert, get back and finish your work.' Connaire came over shaking his dripping head. John put a hand on his shoulder and took him out of sight and earshot. 'I've seen this coming. If you don't get hold of yourself, you won't have a future with me.'

Connaire darted a glance at John. 'But he was stuffing things up!'

'I don't care. You have to control the men under you, it's your job. Sean, I've put you forward for a supervisor but, I'm telling you,

you've got three weeks trial starting now. If you can't cut the mustard, you're out.'

Connaire wiped his face on his sleeve and paused getting his breath. 'You've done me a favour and I thank you for it. You've seen me rough in the morning and you've guessed the reason.'

John admired his honesty. 'Isn't that half the battle, knowing yourself?'

Sean grinned and so did John. 'Deep thoughts for a young mind, haven't ya?'

'Like I said, it's up to you,' John stuck out his hand. 'Don't let me down because it's you who'll suffer.'

Sean gripped his hand and nodded. As he walked away, John said, 'And leave that chippy alone.'

John had the next morning off from work, and leaping from the omnibus he ran towards the three-masted clipper at the Quay. From behind a barrier he searched for the face he knew, but there were too many people at the bulwarks and on the gangplank ready to disembark, all excited to be stepping foot onto their new home. A familiar voice called his name but he couldn't place the source.

'Johnny, Johnny, it's me.'

Two men stood aside and let his sister through.

She hadn't changed much, a little thinner but tanned and healthy and she was holding a *baby*. He hugged her and Maureen cried on his chest. Finding her teary cheek, he kissed it. 'You've come. Let me look at you, and who's this?'

'Oh Johnny, it's grand to be here. This is Michael.'

John took a quick look at his nephew then remembering his manners turned to a fair-skinned, light-framed man and said, 'You must be Liam.' The man smiled and John liked him straight away.

Liam pumped John's hand. 'It's grand to meet you at last, John. Maureen hasn't stopped speaking about you.'

John's eyes widened at the baby and his heart beat hard. Maureen wiped away a tear. She hadn't let go of John's arm. 'Well, I'll be,' he said then he had a shocking thought. Baxterhouse. My God, no . . . not his child.

'It's ours, John. Have no fear. Michael was born in May this year, just before we sailed.'

John looked at Liam for any signs of embarrassment at her admission but there weren't any. His sister walked between them and they headed off to Bent Street. John had a thousand things to talk about.

Maureen squeezed his arm. 'Liam and I became friends through Jane just after you sailed. I think she was a good cupid, because Liam asked me to marry him and we did in September. God blessed us because Michael came along so quickly.'

'He's beautiful.'

'We won't be in the barracks very long,' she said. 'Liam's been told of a house in Surry Hills which we can buy and he's got a job with a school.'

'That's grand,' John said not taking his eyes off his nephew. 'Can I hold the little fella?'

'Sure you can,' Liam said. John took hold of Michael as if he was a Waterford vase. Michael opened his eyes and closed them again. 'What a little beauty.'

William Baxterhouse checked the mail coach schedule. He could leave Sydney on a Monday morning at eight and be at Bathurst by three Wednesday afternoon. That suited him because he'd arranged to see the stock and station agent in Bathurst on the Thursday morning about leasing a store. Pushing aside the schedule, he finished his breakfast of fried eggs and bacon and pulled out his gold watch: seven-thirty. In half an hour he had to be in town to sign a new transport contract with a bakery that wanted oats.

He looked out from his dining room in Chippendale to the front garden and made a note for his manservant to arrange more plantings. Hastings seemed to have been a wise choice. He was a former boxer and too many knocks had made him a near simpleton, but an obedient one.

Yesterday afternoon's mail lay unopened on the table. One envelope caught his eye. He opened it; it was bad news. As he expected, it was written confirmation from John McCreadie that their offer to handle a shipment of merino for Goldsborough Mort had been rejected. McCreadie found out that McGuire had succeeded in getting the brokerage. William hated being robbed of income. That had happened in Belfast and the misery that it had wrought still festered. He would sting McGuire somehow.

Hastings entered the room. 'Sir, I've received word that your brother's ship has cleared the heads. Will you require the carriage?'

William's anger at his lost business changed to excitement. 'Yes! It can take me to the bakery first then I'll collect James.'

'Very good, sir.'

Baxterhouse sat back, happier. At last, James was here with his goods.

William spotted James in the queue at the immigration counter. It always struck him as odd that they were so different. James at five feet three inches tall stood six inches shorter than himself, his hair was fair and curly and his eyes blue. His brother loved plays and actors and didn't smoke, but liked a drink. He was their mother's favourite and was very close to her. William hadn't been jealous. James had a talent for design and revelled in cloth selection. He'd been a senior fabric buyer with their father's Belfast firm, Elite Fabrics.

They'd become closer when that business had faltered and it was James's connections in the fashion industry that had kept their income high enough to cover costs. It meant a lot to William that his brother also wanted the business to survive. And they'd sold anything at the time to make ends meet.

Waving, William got James's attention as he arrived at the counter. His brother acknowledged him and grinned back. William loved nobody in this world except this man, and now James was walking towards him, his steps increasing until he had his arms wrapped around him. William's eyes were wet. 'James, James it's grand to see you. Where's your luggage?'

'Not far away, hopefully. God it's hot!'

'It's just the end of September. It gets worse in January when the sweat's dripping off you like you've done thirty rounds.'

James screwed up his face in disdain. 'I'll get an Indian fan over my bed. Trouble will be convincing one of these ex-convicts to pull the damned thing.'

'You'll be staying with me. The ceilings are high in your room.'

'That's comforting,' James said and grinned. 'You're looking in the pink. Things must be good here.'

'I'll tell you all about it when we get home. Now, where's the gear you brought?'

'They're offloading it now.'

William's eyes expanded. 'Then let's follow it till it's under lock and key at Campbell's. Come. While we're doing that you can tell me all about Ireland and how you left it. Here are your bags now.'

At noon, they were seated in the dining room at Chippendale.

'Hastings,' William said, 'bring a bottle of Jameson's and the best side of that lamb I can smell from here. No shirking on the trimmings now.'

'Of course not, sir.'

William leant towards his brother. 'The man's never seen me this happy!'

'I haven't, Mr James,' Hastings said as he left the room. 'I really haven't.'

James sat back and ran a finger around the space between his collar and plump neck. 'God. It will take me ages to get used to this blessed heat.'

'You'll be all right.' William poured two neat glasses of Ireland's own. 'I meant to ask at Campbell's, what were the six numbered boxes I saw?'

'Two sets of new items, extra tents made for the tropics and collapsible cradles for gold panning.'

William rubbed his hands together. 'You heard about Ballarat?'

'I believe it's bigger than Bathurst.'

'We'll talk about that.' William moved back to make way for the lamb roast placed before them. 'But let's start eating.'

William hoed in and James joined him. With his third mouthful safely on its way to his stomach, William dabbed his face with his napkin. 'You said in the carriage that the East India Company had dropped the investigation because of lack of evidence. How sure are you of that?'

'Very. Have no fear about them, but like I said, it's Mr Whitelaw who's on the hunt.'

'That man. He was like a terrier. Did he do the audit?'

'He did and then he acted,' James said and smiled. 'He tried to find you, but you'd disappeared. He set off for America a month after you left, thinking that's where you'd gone.'

William grinned. 'Because of the documents you left around, about New York?'

James smiled as well, 'Must have worked.'

'But,' William said, 'it'll be expensive for him travelling the world to find me. What was my debt to him? A hundred, a hundred and fifty pounds?'

'Not much more.'

'The man's a fool.' William took a sip of whiskey. 'What about Belfast, Elite Fabrics?'

'I had to liquidate that company to buy more of what you wanted.'

'Good man.' William's excitement then became subdued. 'And father?'

'I used some of the money to make him comfortable. He's not with us in mind, brother. He's in his own world. It's for the best.'

William was sad. 'I suppose so.'

'So then,' James said, 'if Whitelaw comes here?'

William split off piece of fat and stabbed at the separated meat. 'Then, we'll deal with him. After we eat we'll look at booking the steam packet for Melbourne. We can also insure the goods.'

'What portion of the gear's going to Ballarat?'

'That's a good question. You better be accurate with the load, because you'll be going with it and setting up in the town.'

James choked on his pumpkin, spitting out a chunk to land near William's glass. 'I'm not going to that Godforsaken tent-rigged city.

A man at immigration told me about it. There's no culture. No music—'

William knew that this would he hard on James. But he could trust no other with the goods. 'It won't be that bad and we'll review the stay after a few months. There's money to be made, dear brother.'

James exhaled. 'If that's what I have to do, I'll do it.'

'Thank you. Next Monday I'm on a coach to Bathurst to look over a store. I want the Ballarat consignment separated by the time I get back on the Saturday.'

James drank another glass of water and finished his meal in silence.

CHAPTER NINE

SEAN CONNAIRE PLACED HIS DRINK ON THE BAR; IT WAS MADE FROM crushed berries and despite its sweetness, it was good. And it was better than the cordials he'd imbibed these last three months. John was right and Sean knew it. Sean's probation was up and he had a permanent job. Now, he had to keep it.

The crowded Royal Hotel struck him as a daft place to join the teetotallers. But, if he could drink juice here and not feel the demon urge, then he was halfway to keeping his work life on track. This wasn't a bad pub, and he was pleased he'd made the move to Woolloomooloo from Miller's Point. The new house was better and Vonnie and the children were happier. He raised the liquid to the ceiling in a salute and wished himself a happy thirtieth birthday.

'Toasting your guardian angel?'

Sean looked at the barmaid, a well-built girl with a cheeky smile. 'Guardian angels don't come here. They keep watch outside.'

'So you can do whatever you want here, I suppose?'

'I still think they can see through the walls.'

She giggled. 'Same again?'

Sean shook his head. 'I'll wait a bit.'

'Yell out if you want another.' The girl busied herself with a new customer.

Sean looked at the clock and thought about his boss. The first time he'd met him he was struck by John's maturity. He didn't mind that he had a younger boss, and thanks to John, he had a better income with his promotion to overseer.

The barmaid came back. 'I haven't seen you in here before. Do you live around here?'

Sean liked the girl. She reminded him of Vonnie. 'We just moved in to Crown Street. Looks like this'll be my local watering hole from now on.'

'Always nice to see a new customer.'

'What's your name, luv?'

'Beth.'

'I'm Sean and I've got to go. See you next time, Beth.'

Sean headed home. It was the first of October and another day free of the grog.

~

In the late afternoon Clarissa stepped down from the cab, a block short of Campbell Street. She was tense. John's last letter had asked her to meet him today at Mr Jenkins's office. It was the tenth of October and it'd been eight long weeks since she'd seen him. Well, no. He'd been at Mass twice but she hadn't been able to talk to him. William Price, Ian McCreadie, and two others had accompanied her over these past weeks to the theatre, tea parties and picnics and despite her trying to have an open mind about each man, she still thought of John. But what of him? Had Beth O'Hare got him entranced? Or another woman? Clarissa would have to try hard today to find out his feelings for her. And their luck may be running out. Her mother had held onto John's last envelope a little too long, recognising, Clarissa suspected, the similarity of the handwriting from his previous six letters. Clarissa was going to say something, when her mother had handed back the letter. Christine McGuire was no fool and Clarissa had an idea about where she could get John to send his next letter.

Entering the front doorway she rang the bell on the counter. Seconds ticked by and Clarissa felt self-conscious. But she shouldn't be, this was her second time here and she was a client, of sorts.

John appeared and she relaxed. He smiled. 'I'm glad you could come.'

'I had to see Mr Lewis about our bricks so I wandered down this end of town.'

John opened the flap in the counter. 'Come in. Mr Jenkins has gone out and we can use his office to talk.' He stood back to let her pass and after closing the door to his boss's office he grabbed a cloth and brushed down one of the chairs. 'Sorry for the mess.'

Clarissa didn't care. There was a comfortable familiarity as if she'd talked to him only an hour previously. She was conscious of his smell and strength; it was all part of his attraction for her.

'Please sit down.' She did and John sat in Jenkins's chair.

'How are Reeds going on your house?' he asked.

'Slowly.' She didn't want to talk about the house yet. Their time was precious to her and she wanted some truths. 'It's been two months since we've seen each other. How do you feel about that?'

He smiled. 'Right to the point. To be honest, I've missed you.'

'Really? How much?'

'A lot, Clarissa, but I have a job to do and money to save. I have to get on with my life.'

'A life of which I'm not a part?'

'That's not fair. Of course you're in it.'

'That's kind of you. Have you seen Miss O'Hare?'

'I have.'

That hurt. But he could ask the same thing of her and her beaux. O'Hare might be kissing him, might be doing more than that with him. She blushed. So why would John want *her*? 'It seems that we're not meant to be anything but friends.'

'That's still good enough for me. I want you to tell me something, if you can.'

It wasn't enough for her. What she felt for John she hadn't felt for any other man. 'What do you want to know?'

'Are you in deep with someone else?'

If she said she was, she would be lying. If she said she wasn't, she would declare herself for him. Price and McCreadie were fine reliable men who would make good husbands. Would John be a good husband? She decided not to lie. 'Not yet.'

'But you're close to being that way.'

'As you are with Beth?'

'Like you.'

So, it was a standoff, she thought. 'What are we going to do then?'

'Your family will not let you marry me.'

'That's your excuse?'

John stood up and came round the desk. He sat on its edge and his closeness affected her. 'Let's not argue, please. It seems pointless trying to see each other like this and at odd times, if we have no approval from your parents. I think we should stop seeing each other.'

He was looking for a way out. He loved Beth, she knew it. He didn't miss her, he was just being polite. If that was the case then she wouldn't beg, but she wanted him to confirm it. 'You think that's best?'

'I think so,' he said. His face was impassive.

'You *think* so?'

'Very well, I know so.'

That was it then. She stood up. 'So you don't want to see me?'

His eyes seemed to show he did want her but he kept quiet. She had her pride. 'Very well. Goodbye, Mr Leary. I trust you find happiness in all that you do.' She turned from him and left the office and saw Mr Jenkins who'd just walked in. 'Good day.'

'Miss Clarissa, hello to you. What brings you here?'

Clarissa put aside her hurt and anger and concentrated. 'Mr Lewis said that I can't have these cream face bricks I want. I'd value your opinion before I have to change to another type.' This was true as she'd just argued that point with the architect this morning.

John came out of the office and Jenkins looked at them each in turn. Clarissa blushed, thinking he might suspect something was going on between them but his face appeared innocent. 'Hello boss, I was just looking for the master order book in your office.'

'I'll get it for you later. Well,' Jenkins said, 'let's all talk about this. What sort of creams, Miss Clarissa?'

'St Peter's specials, I think they were,' John said. 'Smooth face, a touch mottled.'

'They're the ones,' Clarissa said, trying not to let him distract her.

'You can still get them,' Jenkins said. 'But they're scarce. But why does Lewis want to change?'

'I think because of cost,' she said. 'Reeds are saying that they can't get them and are offering a darker coloured one.'

'You stick to your guns, lass. Darker bricks are cheaper. Anything else I can help you with?'

'No. Thank you, Mr Jenkins.'

'Then, if you'll excuse me, I have to do some work. John, see Miss McGuire out. Goodbye, young lady.' Jenkins smiled.

Clarissa left, and as she entered the lobby, John reached for her hand. She pulled hers away. 'Goodbye, Mr Leary.'

Forcing herself not to cry she walked to the door, opened it and stepped into the street. There would be no need for John to send any letters to her now, to any address.

~

John was seated in Cochrane's Hotel reading about a lucky gold strike in the Saturday edition of the *Sydney Morning Herald.* It was becoming a regular event but this find was different. Brian Dawkins, an Irish migrant, had found gold, a lot of it, in one of his claims, near the main Ballarat seam. Overnight Dawkins had become a rich man, one of the few among thousands who tilled, toiled, sweated and broke themselves trying to gather some 'mustard'.

Putting the paper down on the table, he finished his beer and looked around. Business was picking up and John felt important but he was also frustrated. Despite seeing Beth on three occasions, he was missing Clarissa. At Jenkins's office, a fortnight earlier, he'd wanted to test her and when he'd suggested that they didn't see each other, she had agreed. Yes, she'd asked him if he was serious and yes, he had said he was. But was he? He liked her very much, but he knew he had to make a decision and that was not to see her again, or at least not meet and talk with her. And that hurt. There was no future with her because there was no way of getting himself approved by her parents. Meanwhile, Beth was attractive and available and their friendship was developing into something deeper.

Glancing at the date on the newspaper, 25 October 1851, he smiled despite his sadness about Clarissa. It was a year to the day since he'd come to the colony. One year on and Baxterhouse remained unpunished. He ordered another beer at the bar and decided to get drunk. Baxterhouse was growing in wealth and fame. The man had a thriving boatbuilding company, income from a tender he'd won against Cullen and Jacksons, wagons to transport oats, a store and a wool brokerage partnership. All of these, and John had no weapons to attack him.

'It's Mr Leary, isn't it?' Cullen said standing beside him. 'I'll pay for that and I'll have what you're having.'

John's spirits lifted a little at the ironmonger's smile. 'Mr Cullen.'

'Call me Allan. Grab that beer and let's sit down. I want to talk.'

Seated at the table with his beer, Allan Cullen grinned. 'I'm going to make mischief for a friend.'

'Friend?'

'Baxterhouse. The bastard has knocked me off in a tender.'

'Fairly?'

'I don't give a toss for that. I've got enough money to retire from this game. Jackson is different, got loans and debt, but not me. I only stay in it because of the cut and thrust of winning. And now I want to cut and thrust at our friend.'

John's mood lightened. Here was a man who was willing to give the rapist a serve. 'What did you have in mind?'

'The tools business is lucrative, high margins and all that. I've got a ton of stock that I can virtually give away. It owes me nothing.

I'm going to undercut the bastard. I'm going to price my tools so low that he'll have to match my prices.'

'He will. He's tenacious.'

Cullen took a swig. 'Maybe. There's a big tender coming up in Melbourne. The foundries down there are pricing high because they know the demand is good. I'm going to knock Baxterhouse off, every tender he and I compete for, but more than that. I want him to go broke doing so. I want him out of this business.'

John sat back and looked at his drinking companion. A good idea; clean, sharp and painful.

In the Botanic Gardens on a Sunday afternoon, John walked with Maureen while pushing Michael in his perambulator. Her light-sleeved dress and wide bonnet was just the outfit for the end of November. Maureen had recovered from the worst of the effects of Baxterhouse's assault. Her present happiness had come from having a good man, their baby and a new life in a new country.

John seemed to sense her mood for he turned to her and smiled. 'Bit different from the Anna Liffey, isn't it?'

Maureen gazed at the harbour. 'The sun is so blinding, but the heat I love.'

John stopped at a bench shaded by a camphor laurel and sat down. Maureen joined him. Liam couldn't be with them as he was earning extra money tutoring. So it was just the two of them and she was thankful. In the past two months they'd been alone only twice with little time to talk—brother to sister. She wanted to speak about the past and help despatch some lingering demons.

Taking out her handkerchief she dabbed Michael's chin. She then pressed her hands against the bench; the prickly discomfort reminded her that life dealt you pain and that you had to grin and bear it. 'After you left, I had a very hard time. I think, no, I know that I was being strong so you wouldn't worry so much.'

'I did worry. I hated leaving you that way.'

'I know, but when you left, it was just myself and Jane, two women. I loathed all men, Johnny, wanted to be as far from them as possible. I washed twice a day for weeks after you left. I still felt unclean.' John didn't seem troubled by this intimate talk. Talking to him now did help. He covered her hand with his. 'When you left, I didn't know Liam well,' she said.

She helped Michael sit up and he grabbed onto her hands and grunted wanting to get out of the pram. He was a big boy for seven months and could crawl. Maureen pulled him up and sat him on the grass. He gave a little cry and put out his arms to push himself up. He fell back, and again he tried to support himself on all fours.

John laughed. He looked at Maureen whose face was serious.

'Liam loves me completely. That love enabled him to accept something that many men would find impossible.'

John stood up and trailed Michael who was crawling after a butterfly that headed towards a nearby rose bush. John swooped on him picking him up and throwing him into the air. Michael gurgled as John caught him and sat down on the grass.

She got up and sat beside them. Michael was chewing bits of grass and John attended to him. 'Like I said,' she said, 'Liam accepts me with all that's happened. He's quite a man. I'd only known him for a month, but that was enough for us. We met over the following weeks then he asked me to marry him and I said yes. The memory of that bedroom and what I went through still haunts me.'

'I bet. As you had Liam, was that why you didn't try to report Baxterhouse in Dublin?'

She'd found security with Liam, she had to admit. 'Partly, but I still couldn't do anything because the man just vanished.'

'How?'

'I don't know.'

John's face lost its animation and she understood his anger. She still loathed her rapist, but her anger was modified by Liam's love. But like a volcano's lava, her hatred could find a vent.

'That bastard. After he'd disappeared, as you say, did you find out anything about him?'

'His business was sold. Some say he even emigrated, possibly America, although that seems far-fetched.'

John picked up Michael and placed him in the pram. The baby protested his confines but John pushed the pram and he slipped back on the pillow.

Maureen joined her brother and linked her arm in his. 'He'll sleep now. Come, I'll buy you a drink.'

'Maureen, Baxterhouse is a monster from our past and not part of our future.'

She nodded. She was nevertheless pleased with their talk.

~

William Baxterhouse cursed all dumb workers. He'd had enough of this clerk, the third in nearly three months since the store opened in October. The man still didn't know his elbow from his ear. But he had to persevere. The previous two clerks had failed to come up to his standards. 'Promote the panning cradles and the sluice boxes first. Then you sell them all the extras. Got it!' The clerk nodded. 'Well, do that then. We open in five minutes. I'm going to the post office, then the agent, and will be back at noon. Get cracking.'

He left his shop and went outside. Bathurst was frantic and had been since the strike. There were twenty-four pubs and just as many gambling dens to separate the hard working from their spoils. The letter to James, in his pocket, was getting damp from the heat. Pulling it out, he held onto it. It had instructions on profit margins and other matters and he encouraged James to stick it out in Ballarat. In his last letter James had complained that Ballarat was just as he'd said it would be, but worse. William purchased a set of stamps, fixed one onto his letter and posted it.

There was money to be made on property speculation too. McCreadie had told him of a cheap site, not suitable for mining, six miles north-west of Bathurst that would fetch a pretty price on resale. That was the last of the businesses William wanted— land. There was plenty around but at a price.

The stock and station agent offered William a drink of water.

'Not for me, thank you Mr Edmonds.'

He couldn't wait for the pub to open to have a beer, but business first. 'I've seen the property and it interests me. It's on the market for £320. I'm prepared to offer £300.'

'You're too late, I'm afraid. I've already taken a deposit from a client.'

'For what price?'

'I can't tell you that.'

William smiled. 'If it was the asking price, I'm prepared to better that, say £350?'

'I'm sorry, Mr Baxterhouse.' Edmonds smiled. 'The sale has been made and the purchaser has to complete by the end of January by paying the balance.'

'What's his name?'

'It's a Sydney syndicate, wool brokers.'

William moved in his chair. Wool brokers? That's interesting. McCreadie might know them. 'I said, who are they?'

Edmonds remained passive. 'I can't tell you.'

William got up and leaned across the desk. The agent was either brave or stupid for he didn't move. 'You mean you won't tell me.'

The agent kept calm and William sat down; it wasn't worth the effort. He'd try another tack. 'Put my offer to your client.'

Edmonds spread his hands. 'I can, Mr Baxterhouse, but it'll come to nothing unless the purchaser defaults.'

William stood up. 'Just do it, please. Good day.' He picked up his hat and left. The heat in the office had heightened his anger and crossing George Street, he ducked into the Fitzroy Inn's coolness. William ordered a beer and sat in a corner. That land? Who were those brokers? There were at least six in the top range. He would bloody well find out! Despite this setback, as he looked out the window he mused that it'd been a good year. The transport contract was lucrative, with his man installed to run things, more orders for boats, the store here and his tools. McCreadie's shareholding was also paying good dividends.

Christine McGuire locked the door behind her and scanned her daughter's bedroom. She had to find them but wasn't comfortable in the task. It was sad that she had had to stoop to this level to protect her daughter but it was a mother's duty to do that, and so she set to work. Clarissa wasn't due home for an hour. Even though the last letter had been received early October she was certain her daughter was still deceiving her and David. Bed, dressing table, wardrobe, chest of drawers, any one of them could hide them so she dealt with the bed first. Lifting the mattress and feeling under the covers yielded nothing. Smoothing the bedspread she attacked the dressing table and she opened its drawer. It wasn't locked. There would be nothing there and she was right. 'A pity.' She kept looking. The handwriting on the envelopes was Leary's, she was certain and she knew that Clarissa, despite their opposition, was seeing the man. If the letters were here, they would be all together and she kept searching. Nothing found under or on top of the wardrobe so she addressed the clothes inside and riffled through them all. Nothing again. Sighing she sat down on the dressing table seat. The chest of drawers was the last possible repository and if the letters weren't there, they might not be here at all. Clarissa might have them with her. Standing up to search the drawers, something caught her eye. The beading on the seat edge was frayed and she was embarrassed. 'The servants must think we're penniless.' She made a mental note to get the seat repaired. Tucking the offending loose fabric under the base of the seat, her fingers brushed something sharp. There was a piece of elastic tacked to the underside of the seat. Looking under it she found letters bound together and she removed them. Both excited and angry she noticed the last letter was stamped 7 October. Surely Clarissa would have received more letters later than that? It is now the middle of December. Had he stopped writing or was he sending letters now to a different address? She opened the October letter and read a few lines. She didn't want to know the details but going to the last page, she found the author she expected—John Leary. Returning the letters under the seat, she decided what she had to do. Forbidding Clarissa to see the man hadn't worked so she must try another tack.

John was curious about Mrs McGuire's note that she'd sent to him at Mr Jenkins's office. She wanted to meet him. He thought he might see Clarissa, which was both good and bad. It was 15 December and more than two months had passed since their last meeting. Beth was being affectionate but she wouldn't let him go further, hoping, he suspected, that he'd propose to her. And why not? She was more than acceptable. One reason was that whenever he saw Clarissa at Mass his feelings for her were rekindled. It was still hard not talking to her.

Stella greeted him at the front door. 'I'll tell Madame you're here.' She led him to the parlour.

Christine McGuire came in and John stood up as she seated herself on a lounge chair. 'Thank you for coming and I'll get right to the point. I have something for you.'

John was wary. She looked at him and he prepared for another testing time. The clock on the mantle beat out a regular tick.

'Forgive me for asking, but I have a reason. Your wages as a supervisor or whatever you call it, are they substantial?'

He was a little surprised. 'It's a living wage, Mrs McGuire. Being single, I can save some.'

Christine nodded. 'What I am about to offer you is confidential. If you refuse it and discuss our conversation with others I shall deny everything.'

He was intrigued.

'I'm prepared to offer you, from my own income, the sum of two hundred pounds to stay permanently away from my daughter. I know you've been seeing her.' John said nothing. 'I'm right, aren't I?'

'I was seeing her, Mrs McGuire—'

Christine raised her hand. 'I don't want to hear. I have a paper that you can sign. You will agree that it's a handsome sum?'

A handsome sum indeed, nearly two year's wages! The lure was there. John was both flattered and annoyed. 'Mrs McGuire, because you and Mr McGuire won't accept me, I've kept away from your daughter for some time.'

She paused. 'I don't believe you.'

'It matters not to me whether you do or don't. That's the truth. The offer's refused.'

Christine's face creased in frustration and John suspected that she hadn't expected that answer. 'Very well then, four hundred pounds and that's my final offer.'

John felt for the chair behind him and sat. The amount shocked him. He could start a business and run it for a year with that sum. Then anger replaced his shock. 'Mrs McGuire, the answer is still no.'

Clarissa stepped into the room and looked at her mother. John had never seen her so angry. 'I think that's quite enough, Mother.' She turned to him. 'You should leave, Mr Leary, please.'

John stood up.

'I've told Mr Leary not to see you,' Christine said. 'You've been meeting behind our backs. I'll discuss that with you separately. Now—'

'Mr Leary,' Clarissa said, her face crimson, 'I'll see you out.'

John followed her into the hall.

'Clarissa!' Her mother said. 'Come here.'

She ignored her mother and opened the front door for him. 'Our new house is going badly,' she said, her voice just audible. 'See Father, please, and try to fix it.'

She closed the door behind him and John was left wondering what she meant. There was only one way to find out.

Clarissa returned to the parlour, her face flushed with anger. 'I heard everything, Mother. A bribe! Money to keep him away? How could you?'

'It's the one thing he understands, dear.' She sat down and composed herself. 'It surprised me he rejected it.'

Clarissa sat as well, staring at her. '*I'm* not surprised. Mr Leary may have many faults, according to you, but he is honourable. The embarrassment of your grimy offer to barter me off!' She stood up.

'That's the vilest thing you could've done. You don't understand the situation at all, not at all. And, the worst, you don't trust me.'

'And I've got good reason not to. You still see him.'

'I have not, since October.'

Her mother looked at her for a moment. 'If you're right, and as you say, this thing is over. Who ended it? You? Or him?'

'He did.'

'But if he hadn't, you'd still be seeing him. Don't talk to me about trust.' Her mother was right on that. 'He'll think about what I've offered him. He'll change his mind.'

Clarissa turned and walked away. 'This is a waste of time. I'll talk to Father about your *offer*.'

'Talk, talk. I did you a favour, my dear and one day you'll thank me for it.'

'I still can't believe what you did,' Clarissa said and left the room.

Four days later, John waited in the vestibule of the McGuire -warehouse in Sussex Street.

A door opened and David McGuire came out. 'Afternoon, Mr Leary. Come with me.'

Ascending a staircase, McGuire opened an office door, gestured John inside and closed the door. 'Sit down.' McGuire kept standing, folded his arms and leaned again the windowsill. 'Your letter said you wanted to see me. Why?'

'I hear you're having problems at Point Piper.'

'You've been devious, sir, seeing my daughter behind my back. Clarissa confessed all to her mother and me. That's a low thing to do.'

'We like each other's company.'

'That doesn't count. You're unsuitable for her.'

An argument would see this talk brought short. John took a reasoned guess. 'Are you having trouble with the builder?'

'Don't change the subject. You'll not marry Clarissa.' David McGuire looked like he expected John to fight him.

'I understand,' John said and McGuire seemed surprised. 'If I was in your shoes, I'd think the same. I haven't seen your daughter since October the tenth. I told her it wouldn't work, that you wouldn't accept me. But, it didn't need a bribe to keep me away from her.'

McGuire said nothing for a time. 'Christine was being protective. All mothers are. Trust seems the victim here. It matters little when you saw her last. You talk sense about your unsuitability but you're a man who wants things, will fight for what you want, so why did you give up on my daughter?'

McGuire was baiting him now, appealing to his pride.

'Because you're so prejudiced about me.'

'It's not *you* who worries me, Mr Leary. It's my daughter. She demands the best. You're not that.'

'We can argue all day, Mr McGuire. What about your house?'

McGuire exhaled. 'That damned house and that damned builder. Reeds are holding me to ransom and Mr Lewis is not helping.'

'Their brick pricing was low, too low. What do they want?'

'More money. They're complaining about the bricks being unavailable and more expensive. They've stopped work till I agree to pay what they want.'

'What's been done on site?'

'The footings and some walls are up to ground floor level.'

In three month's work, Reeds should've done more than that. It wasn't a lot finished but enough for Reeds to keep David McGuire on the hook and to keep him using them. 'And Mr Lewis? What's he doing about it?'

'Dithering.' McGuire sat down at his desk and leaned back. 'Reeds are in breach of the contract, having stopped work without reason.'

John had an idea. It was a long shot but it might work. 'This will be the first of many times that Reeds will have a go at you. On their two last jobs they hit their clients for extras.'

'Lewis didn't tell me that.'

'Sack Reeds,' John said.

'And then what?'

'We'll finish the job, at Reeds' price.'

'So you can be with my daughter.'

This wasn't working and John stood up. 'I came here to help a friend, Mr McGuire. That's all. There are other builders in town who can help you out. Good day to you.' John walked to the door.

'Mr Leary, wait, please.' He paused. 'I'm in a bind.'

'Go on.'

'The other tenderers offered to complete our house but at exorbitant prices.' John wasn't surprised. McGuire had little choice but to use Jenkins now. It must be galling for the man to have to ask John. 'If you wish to help me, I accept,' he said. 'Does Mr Jenkins know you're here?'

'I'll talk to him. I'm sure I can convince him.'

'Do that,' McGuire said. 'In the meantime I'll write to Reeds and demand they start work again in two days. If not, I'll get rid of them, and I might sack Lewis too for incompetence. This is *business* between us Mr Leary— nothing else.'

'It is, but if Mr Jenkins is to be your new builder then I'm going to see your daughter, chaperoned if you wish.'

McGuire pointed at him. 'You'll see my daughter about the house construction and nothing else. My view is unchanged. I want your word on that.'

John could press for concessions now that McGuire wanted him, but he wouldn't push it, just yet.

'I know my daughter. She's headstrong but it's infatuation, I'm certain.' John was about to interrupt but McGuire raised his hand. 'The house only Mr Leary, and that's all.'

'Write to Reeds and I'll talk to Mr Jenkins.'

'Good day, Mr Leary. You can find your way out.'

Dismissed like a servant, but John didn't care. He would see Clarissa again and he wasn't surprised that he felt good about that.

His shirt stuck to his back in the heat and he concentrated on the blessing. The priest wished everyone Merry Christmas and John moved from his pew. Outside St Mary's, he spotted the McGuires and thanked the Lord that Jenkins had agreed to finish the McGuire's house. Reeds hadn't gone back to work and David had terminated their contract. John had already gone to the site, organised his men and work was now humming. He had taken a risk, promising Mr Jenkins he would do the brickwork at cost price with no profit. John would have to cut his pay to suit. That was all right. He was going to build the Point Piper house and that's all that mattered.

Clarissa saw him, and behind her parents' back, she nodded at him. It was a start.

John made his way to Surry Hills where he shook Liam's hand and kissed Maureen. 'Merry Christmas, everyone.'

In the parlour Michael was playing on the floor with a stuffed toy. John scooped him up and pressed his nose into his nephew's tummy making him laugh.

'Come,' Maureen said, 'let's open our presents before our meal.'

'I could eat a horse,' John said.

The dinner went well, filled with laughter and tales shared of their respective crossings.

John reached into his jacket. 'I got a letter from Ma yesterday, if you'd like to read it.'

'Thank you, Johnny,' Maureen said taking it. 'Any news?'

'They are content and their income is rising.'

'I'm glad,' Liam said.

'Kieran and Vincent have purchased more of the farm,' John continued. 'Alf has a new parish and Mervin had been promoted to assistant manager.'

Maureen's happy face changed. 'Do they ask after me?'

'Ma does.'

'I'm sure Mervin will succeed,' Maureen said trying to overcome her sadness. 'I do wish him all the best.'

Liam reached out and touched her hand. 'We're in Sydney now, dear. All prejudices of the Old Dart don't count here.'

'Indeed,' she said. 'I'll pray for Alf.'

John was glad that Sydney was a new start for all of them, but family was family and old issues, like Maureen's training to be a teacher, were still present. He looked down. 'Either this table has swelled in the heat or it's me. I'd better stand up before I get squashed.'

'I don't think it's the woodwork,' Maureen said and smiled. 'It's a bit cooler now. Why don't you and Liam go outside and I'll get the pudding ready.'

Liam ushered John out to the courtyard. Under the shade of banksia they sat on a bench.

John knew this was the right time. 'Liam, I want a big favour.'

Liam smiled. 'Anything for my brother-in-law.'

'What if I told you something that you must keep from Maureen for her own good?'

Liam waved a fly away from his face. 'If the basis of the secret is legal and moral and Maureen would be protected from it, I'd agree.'

John felt some relief. 'Thank you.' He looked hard at his in-law. 'William Baxterhouse is in New South Wales.'

Liam's eyes rounded. 'How long have you known? Where?'

John sighed. He'd tell Liam enough, just enough. 'Just after I came to the colony. Look, it will do Maureen no good to know now. In time, we can plan how we're going to tell her.'

'She has to know, John.'

'Why? It would only hurt her, and what can we do? We've no proof.'

'But she might find out herself. She's bound to. Sydney's not a big place.'

'I can't help that.'

Liam seemed to hesitate. 'Perhaps it's best to tell her now.'

John shook his head. 'Let's leave it, please. Keep it a secret and then we'll talk about it, in time.'

'I don't like it.'

'I don't either. Do you think it's been nice for me just knowing the bastard's walking around free.'

Liam kept quiet for a moment. 'Where does he live?'

'I don't know,' John lied.

'I'll keep it secret till say Easter, then we'll talk again. If Maureen still knows nothing by then we'll decide. He has to pay for his crime.'

'Fair enough.' He thought Liam naive. Baxterhouse would never be brought to trial, let alone convicted. The man was a wealthy and well-connected gentleman, and there were too many loose ends, not counting the time passed since the crime and the distance between Ireland and New South Wales. They would have no joy dealing with Baxterhouse the legal way. No, his way would be better.

Liam looked him in the eye and said. 'You don't have any wild notion to do something yourself, do you?'

John's thoughts must have been obvious. 'No. Of course I've thought about it, but Maureen's the person to protect here, she's our first thought.'

Liam didn't seem convinced. 'We have to go to the police with this.'

'And you wouldn't want to do something yourself?'

Liam paused. 'I would, you know I would, but it would all turn against us. Let's wait till Easter.'

'Very well,' John agreed. 'Till Easter. But then we decide.'

'Come in,' Maureen called from the rear doorway. 'It's ready,'

~

Clarissa sat opposite her father in his Sussex Street office. It was the day after Boxing Day.

'I've put a deposit on acreage near Bathurst,' David said. 'Good land for breeding. It settles in the last week in January and I want you to go as my representative. Peters will accompany you for protection. I'd like your opinion on the land as well.'

Clarissa was surprised. 'Breeding? But all land there must be being mined, surely.'

'This site's only for grazing.'

'You want to grow wool?'

'I do. It'll be just a small investment but one that could be lucrative.' He reached behind and placed a file on his desk. 'It's all in here, agent's name, location, the lot. The soil's good and the prices are going up ridiculously every month. I don't trust the locals to close this matter. Will you go?'

'Of course, my pleasure.'

'Good. Take Stella for company and watch yourselves. Stick close to Peters.' David finished his coffee. 'Here's the file. Now, let's get on with our work.'

~

Things were quiet in town during the break before New Year, but it was frantic at Blackwattle. The completion date had been brought forward and John was helping Sean. Starting before dawn they worked through two full days. At the end of the second day, when they were cleaning up, Sean said to John, 'We would like you to come to dinner tonight.'

John put his towel into his bag. Sean had been a changed man of late. He was alert and clear-headed. 'I'd like that. Do you want to go from here?'

'Aye.'

They got off the omnibus and walked down Forbes Street. John thought about Beth as the Royal came into view. He'd been with her at a dance the previous evening.

'Come into the pub with me. I have to get something.' John hesitated and Sean seemed to misread this. 'I'm not buying grog. We've none at home. It's something different.'

'All right.'

He hoped Beth was working. She was. They went to the bar where she smiled at them.

'How are you Beth?' Sean asked.

'Dandy, and you and the family?'

'Good as well.'

John chipped in, 'Hello Beth.'

Sean shot a glance at him. 'You know each other?'

Beth beat John to an answer and smiled, 'Oh, John's come in from time to time.'

'Lass,' Sean said, 'a jug of that pineapple juice will do just the trick. Do you have some?'

'You've the luck of our race, Sean. I've just finished making some. Things are quiet after Christmas. I'll get it.'

Sean watched as she disappeared behind the bar. 'Nice looking girl. You should see more of her.'

'I am.'

She brought out the corked jug and handed it to Sean who paid her. 'Happy New Year to you and your family. And you too, John.'

'And to yours, Beth,' Sean said.

On the way out John glanced over his shoulder and found Beth looking at him, before busying herself with cleaning up. Things were different between them; he sensed it, now Clarissa was part of his life again. A week ago, he and Beth had gone to Circular Quay to walk and their conversation had been strained. He was thinking of Clarissa, most times, when Beth was talking to him and she had noticed, he was convinced.

William was back in Bathurst in the New Year and wasn't comfortable. First, Ian McCreadie had told him, on a drinking night in Sydney, that they weren't the Bathurst land buyers. McCreadie had mentioned four other possibilities, competitors of his. William didn't know them well, but he'd find out about them. He wanted that land and he suspected another brokerage was buying land for a grazier. Also, the stubborn agent had still refused his offer until the current purchaser defaulted, which seemed unlikely.

Another niggle also irritated him. He'd lost a lucrative tender in Melbourne to Cullens again. The winning bid was so far below William's price it make him suspicious.

Clarissa, Peters the coachman, and Stella had arrived in Bathurst by coach from Sydney on the Wednesday evening. On the

Thursday in the early morning heat they were walking along Durham Street, looking for the stock and station agent's office.

'My goodness,' Stella said bringing a handkerchief to her face, 'the streets are so dusty, you can taste it.'

Stella was becoming more of a companion than a maid and Clarissa had confided in her about her feelings for John. Stella was sympathetic and sensed John was a good man. 'Here it is, miss.'

Peters waited outside while they went in.

The agent, Mr Edmonds, welcomed them, surprised that a woman was representing the buyer. Sitting in the office, he brought out the paperwork and bank draft. 'Have you brought the settlement monies?'

Clarissa dabbed her forehead with a handkerchief. 'Yes, the cheque, the transfer, power of attorney, deed and survey.'

'My, you're organised. I'll just ensure it's all there.'

It was too hot to fire back a terse reply and Clarissa remained silent.

At the end of thirty minutes, they had a signed agreement. The agent stood up and shook her hand. 'Thank you, Miss McGuire. Have you seen the land?'

'No, and I'd like to.'

'It's about six miles and I've only got a wagon. It's old quality but its seats are well sprung and it's got a canopy of sorts.'

Clarissa didn't expect Bathurst to be filled with broughams. 'That's quite acceptable.'

'Good then. Please wait out the front and I'll bring it around.'

Clarissa and Stella left the office and stood with Peters in the shade of the awning outside. The noise and bustle of the town was omnipresent.

'Do you know where it is?' Stella asked.

'Yes, I looked at the survey.'

'It's grand you can look at a map and find that out.'

'It's not difficult when you know how.'

A man walked towards them who looked familiar. It was William Baxterhouse. He raised his hat and smiled just as the agent's wagon pulled up in front of them. 'Miss McGuire, is it not?'

'It is, Mr Baxterhouse, how do you do.' His time in the colony had tanned his handsome face.

The agent got down. 'Step in ladies, back seat please. Morning, Mr Baxterhouse.' Stella and Clarissa boarded the unpainted but sturdy transport. Peters climbed into the front next to the agent.

'Where are you off to?' Baxterhouse said.

'Mr Edmonds is showing me some land.'

Baxterhouse smiled. 'About six miles from here? Three hundred acres?'

She was about to reply when the agent spoke. 'Just some land, Mr Baxterhouse. Good day.' He cracked the whip.

Clarissa waited till they were out of town. 'I was about to tell him to mind his own business.' But she liked his cheek in asking her.

'I can tell you,' Edmonds said, 'that he was your competitor and was planning to gazump you.'

Clarissa smiled to herself.

Stella leaned in close to her to be out of the agent's hearing. 'He's a good looking man.'

'Stella!' Clarissa remonstrated, but she agreed. He was charming and confident but his dark eyes hinted something of a mercurial temperament. She preferred John's clear open eyes.

William returned to the shade of the awning. She was a pretty woman, that McGuire lass. Maybe he should spread his interest wider than Miss Elizabeth Higgins. It was something to think about. But that was social, land was security. He was now certain that the McGuires were the buyers and that angered him. Being beaten to something always did that to him. It reminded him yet again of Ireland when his so-called friends had lied and cheated him to see his companies falter.

This was the second time David McGuire had bested him and that made William's mind up, good looking daughter or not. It was time to act.

CHAPTER TEN

'I KNOW HER,' CHRISTINE MCGUIRE SAID. 'I KNOW HER stubbornness and her wilful side. These two flaws diminish her otherwise good character and kind nature. You should not have allowed Leary to see her. Not at all.'

David sat opposite her and their parlour was charged with palpable tension. 'I had little option if we're not to pay double to have our house built. I had to use Jenkins.'

'I'd have paid anything to keep Leary away. Surely David, you understand.'

'I do. But money won't work. You've proved that and it seems the young man has morals.'

'He's still unsuitable.'

'It seems that way. But Christine, I don't have the time to attend to the details the builder will want answers on. Twice now Leary and Clarissa have met in Sussex Street and it's just been *business*. To save money, I've paid Lewis for his designs and drawings. That man's no longer involved with the house and Mr Jenkins has told me that he can build from what Lewis has done.'

'Leary will say anything to get to our daughter. You should've demanded Jenkins use some other supervisor.'

'There wasn't one available. And Leary told me differently. He told me he wanted to end it with her. I believe him.' David poured himself another drink.

'I don't.'

Christine didn't want Leary and Clarissa meeting—under any circumstances. She stood up and moved to the open window. The early February heat was stifling and the steaminess almost visible. Taking up her fan, she cooled her face.

'She's so besotted,' Christine said, 'she can't think straight.'

David shuffled the ice in his glass and sighed. 'It's infatuation. He'll do something bad that will make her change her mind.'

'It's not infatuation any longer, David. It's been a year and a half since she met him on the ship. There's no doubt she has feelings for him. Feelings that are forcing her to act with poor judgement.'

'That might be the case, but, I'm certain she'll see him for what he is.'

'I hope you're right.'

David didn't dislike the man, but he was not the man for his daughter. He'd have to look for a way to make Clarissa change her view of the big carpenter.

~

'It's Mr Leary again,' the kiln manager said. 'And with a young lady.'

'Good morning, Mr Barton,' John said. 'This is Miss Clarissa McGuire.'

'How do you do, Miss McGuire.'

'I'm very well, thank you Mr Barton.'

'Here for Blackwattle?'

'Not yet,' John replied. The McGuire house was coming on with the sandstone walls now up to the ground floor. 'We're here to select the Point Piper bricks we ordered. I want all of them delivered by the thirteenth.'

'That's in six days,' Barton said. 'All of them?'

'By the thirteenth of February and of the first ten thousand, let me pick the first thousand at random.'

The kiln manager frowned. 'No cause for that. All my bricks are good.'

'I'll still pick the first.'

The manager paused. 'If you must then. Come with me.'

John hesitated.

'I'll wait for you here,' Clarissa said. 'I've brought the curtain samples to go through.'

He went off and she sat down on a seat in the lobby. It had been a rapid and unexpected turnaround. In two months they'd only met twice but on those occasions it had felt like old times—for her at least. She didn't know about John. Yes, he'd looked at her the right way, but was that just friendship or something more? Her whole strategy was for John to build their house and in doing that convince her parents he was suitable. That strategy had been foiled by Reeds but now it was possible with Mr Jenkins's company taking over the build. She needed to find out how John felt. But, curtain samples first and she concentrated on her task.

Twenty minutes later, John returned and sat beside her. 'All finished?' he asked.

'Yes.'

'Good. Now to Darling Harbour to see some stained timber samples, then on to the site. Let's get a cab.'

'I'm supposed to have Stella with me, but she's in town on an errand for me.'

'Your father wanted a chaperone?'

'Of course, Mr Leary. My father's view is that this is only business. It is, isn't it?' She wanted to know.

'Your father thinks it is.'

'And you?'

'It's not just business.'

This was better. 'It's not?'

'It's a chance to show your parents I'm a decent bloke. By being professional, honest and honourable on this house, I can be closer to being accepted.' He smiled.

Good. 'Why did the kiln manager get upset?'

'It's standard practice. They give you the bricks *they* want which might have colour differences. Sometimes it's too late when they're laid in place to do anything about it. When you randomly select bricks from various batches, they mix evenly when they are laid.'

'Aren't you clever? Here's a cab.' They got on and she had to use tact with her next question. 'You're considering going out on your own at some time, aren't you?'

'Aye, money is the key as it always is.'

'Well, who'll back you?'

'The banks might.'

They might, but her father could too. He always put business before emotion. If she could convince him there was a quid in it for him to back John, he might be interested, but that was for another day. 'I want to know something. About you and me.'

'What?'

'You told me in October you no longer wanted to see me.'

'I did and you know why. Things haven't changed much. Your father is convinced I'm unsuitable for you.' He smiled at her. 'You know, he was surprised when I told him I'd feel the same way if I was him. And he asked me why I hadn't fought for you.'

This was interesting and Clarissa had to ask. 'Why don't you?'

He hesitated, which was disturbing. 'I could.'

He was in love with Beth now. That was it. She wouldn't push him any more.

He took hold of her hand, his touch a pleasant shock. He looked right at her. 'I'll fight for you, Clarissa, if you want me to.'

Well, he'd asked her, and she made up her mind. She pressed his hand and in a quiet voice said. 'I want you to, John. I do.'

He said nothing for some time and the silence worried her. 'It'll be tough and no certainty of success.'

'Fight for me, John,' Clarissa said still holding his hand. 'Do it.'

Up until the end of February John spent most of his time supervising the six bricklayers and their labourers on the McGuire house.

Coming down to breakfast one morning the landlady chastised him. 'You're late and I'm ready to clean up. There are only two fried eggs left. And here's a letter for you.'

'I'm sorry. Two eggs will be good. Thank you.' John sat down and opened his mail. It was from Damien Wexton. He began to read.

Mr Leary,

On a trip to Melbourne and Ballarat last month for another client I found out a bit more on our 'friend'. It's not startling news but, I guess, it's all grist.

Ballarat is like Bathurst but on a grander scale. James Baxterhouse has one of the bigger stores and is doing well, except Cullens beat him to the last tender. While I was there the younger Baxterhouse met up with Brian Dawkins, the man who had that big strike, whom you've probably heard of. They were deep in conversation.

That's about it. I'll not be charging you for this.

Damien Wexton.

John placed the letter back in the envelope. Yes, it wasn't much but any facts on Baxterhouse and his family were useful. He got stuck into his breakfast.

~

'Well Jack,' Baxterhouse said. 'Will you do it?'

Lieutenant Jack Johnson looked down and rued the day he'd got involved with this man. His ship was stationed in Sydney and he was at Baxterhouse's bidding. Now this task, to find someone who'd purchased a Bathurst land site. 'Why don't you wait for the title registration, then you'll know?'

'There are hundreds of land sales to be registered, my friend, and there are too few clerks. It'll take months. Miss McGuire was there with Edmonds the agent. I'm sure she's the buyer or someone close to her. I have to be certain and I can't front Edmonds. He knows me.'

'I'll try.'

'Didn't say it would be easy Jack, and,' he leant forward, 'you don't want to fail me, do you?'

Jack Johnson didn't but his resentment of his blackmailer was intensifying. One day Baxterhouse, one day.

'You have two weeks. Meet me back here at the Hero on the fifteenth of March,' Baxterhouse said.

Jack Johnson wrote to Edmonds in Bathurst purporting to be part of the McGuire business. As a digression, he asked Edmonds if there was more land available for sale. Edmonds had replied that at present there wasn't, thanking Jack for his interest and providing him further details on the land that the McGuires had bought. There was no doubt in his mind that his blackmailer would use this information and now strike at the wool brokers. Another prick to his conscience. Good, innocent people being attacked. Jack was now a part of that and he wasn't happy about it. He knew there was only one way to clear his name and get back some self-respect.

~

John completed sawing to length, the last of the pieces that would be used for bracing the first floor ceiling joists, the sweet smell of the Douglas Fir timber permeating the air. He took a swig from his water bottle and looked out over the harbour from the Point Piper site. It was after nine and Sean was late. That wasn't like him. Work on Blackwattle was ahead of schedule and Sean was needed to help John make up time on the McGuire house. A ladder near him moved, and Sean appeared, unshaven and with bloodshot eyes.

'Sorry I'm late.'

John waited till Sean had buckled on his hammer and nail bag and handed him the end of the second last joist to be installed. John suspected what was wrong but concentrated and inserted the other end of the beam into its masonry slot. 'Want to talk about it?'

Sean remained quiet for a time. 'I've been going good. Then bang. Into the grog.'

'Why?'

'If you're a drunk then you'd know why. It's like a sickness.' He sighed. 'At least the gaps between are getting longer. That's something. And I'm not giving up. I'll keep trying.'

'It's up to you, mate. I can help. Just let me know.'

Sean nodded and drank at length from the water bottle. 'How long will you need me here? I can only give you two weeks.'

'That's enough.'

'But what about us? Going out alone?'

'Been giving it some thought, have you?'

'Since we spoke just after Christmas, I have, and it ain't as easy as you think. I've been working for bosses and the money's good and I'm happy. Why would I want to work for myself with all the worry?'

John readied the last joist and wiped the sweat from his face. The angle of the morning sun dazzled him. 'The time's right and there's money to be made. But I have to be able to trust you.'

'You can.'

'It's not money and effort I'm wanting, Sean. It's reliability. I have to know that you've got this drinking licked. Got it beaten.'

'I have. I have.'

'Time will tell. But anyhow, look at this house. It's quality, not like those dumps at Miller's Point.'

'Not all houses down there are built poor.'

Sean was right but John had to press his point. 'Owners want top stuff and you know you can deliver.'

Sean looked hard at John and rested his hammer. 'It's easy for you. You're a single man. I know you want to get ahead. You're a quick learner, but get a few years under your belt and then decide.'

'I know, I know. But I have to get the business started and you're my key. You can build a whole house, even supervise the plumbers to install a privy. There's a big push for good houses and owners are looking for skilled builders to show off.'

Sean reached for a section of bracing and started nailing. It seemed he wasn't listening. 'I've thought about it,' he said after a while. 'But what happens to Mr Jenkins when we leave? Blackwattle goes till September then McCreadie's will start. He'll be in the shit.'

'He will,' John said, 'and that's something I'll have to work out. Lying in bed at night, I come up with a plan. Then next morning I've changed my mind. That's how I am. Anyway, smarten up. We've got this lot to finish.'

They toiled for the rest of the day finishing a good section of the bracing, with conversation limited to a few words. At knock-off, John looked again at the beauty of the harbour, its natural bush setting still there despite some pockets of development from the building boom.

He turned to Sean. 'Brickies can start here next week with the walls up to the roof. You know, we could be a good team. You make things happen, can kick heads. I'm the quiet one, thinks things through— a planner.'

Sean had packed up and was climbing down the ladder. He looked at John. 'You're a persistent bastard. Tell me more tonight. Your shout.'

'You want to go back to the Royal? After last night?'

'I wasn't at the Royal last night.'

'Do you still want to go there?'

'I'll be right.'

After cleaning up, they went to Woolloomooloo in their wagon.

'Find a seat,' Sean said. 'I'll get the drinks.' John went and sat down and waved to Beth.

Sean brought the drinks back, a beer for John and a lemonade for himself. 'So what's the plan?'

'There's work aplenty. Between the two of us we can make a go of it. I know the pricing side pretty well.'

'And what are we going to do for money for the first six months?'

John took the opportunity and gulped his beer. That was the sticking point. He'd be able to cover most things but cash was a problem, until they got payments from clients.

Sean seemed to take his pause for doubt. 'You've not thought about that, have you?'

He had to be honest, especially with Sean. 'I'd rather us go it alone.'

'That's all good, but be practical. Pride's one thing, business another. If you want me to get serious about going with you, you've got to get money. I've seen more carpenters go broke on their own than I've had blood blisters.' Sean tapped the tabletop. 'What about Mr Jenkins? Why don't you ask him if you can buy a share of his company?'

John hadn't even thought of that then realised a problem. 'If he sold me something, it would be small. I still wouldn't be in charge.'

'We wouldn't be in charge, you mean.'

'Right. There are the banks.'

'They'll bleed you.'

'I'll have to talk to them.'

'Do that, then we'll speak some more.'

'I'd like to finish Point Piper by the end of May and then start on our own sites. Jenkins has been good to me. I'll get him some men when you and I go. Got any ideas?'

Sean scratched his head. 'Get me another drink and I'll think about it.'

Beth smiled as he approached the bar. 'Same again, John?'

'Yes please, and how are you?'

She poured half the beer and prepared the juice. 'Good. Are we all right for this weekend?'

'We are. I'll come around at four o'clock on Saturday.'

Beth completed the drinks then reached out and pressed his hand. 'Grand. I got myself a second job, once a week in town.'

'What?'

'Serving drinks in a fancy uniform to the toffs at the Royal Victoria. Wages are good.'

'How'd you get it?'

'I got a note that someone put a word in for me. Some happy customer here I suppose. I'm not complaining. And you? Have you still got your enemy in your sights?'

John felt like she was baiting him for a quarrel. The last time they'd met she'd tried again to change his mind on his revenge. But he was adamant. 'Yes, and the game's getting interesting.'

He took the drinks, irritated at Beth's attitude. Irritated, because he felt guilty. He should be keeping his mind on Clarissa but he and Beth were still meeting. John admitted his weakness in enjoying the affection Beth was giving him, and although she was passionate she still wouldn't permit him to know her intimately. It wasn't fair on her but he was hedging his bets. Clarissa may not be won and he could still have Beth. But no, he knew that wasn't right.

'Mate,' Sean said as John sat down, 'don't know what you two were sparking about, but you could feel the heat over here.'

'She's all right. A little feisty that's all.'

'About those names. There's McGlinchy, now he's a good head man.'

They talked about the people who could replace them. John found it useful; in some future time he'd have to do this for every level of his career. To grow a company, you had to train the people under you to take more responsibility, then promote them. They in turn would train and promote others.

~

At knock off on the last day of March, John covered the remaining stack of flooring timbers with a tarpaulin. After checking its guy ropes for tension, he left Point Piper in a dray

On the way back down Wolseley Road, he passed a transport wagon heading towards him. The two men on it were unfamiliar to him and he wondered where they were heading. The McGuire house was the only new one being built on the headland. The wagon had high, red-painted sides and when it hit bumps, dust clouds puffed from its tray.

Shrugging his shoulders, he clicked the horses and continued on his way.

~

Clarissa came down the stairs in a lemon silk dress with a matching jacket.

'We're only letting you go unchaperoned tonight,' her mother said, 'because we know Captain Price's family and Ian McCreadie will be there.'

'I know the rules, Mother. Goodnight.'

'Goodnight, my dear,' her father said.

Stella opened the door to William Price.

'You look handsome, Captain,' Clarissa said. 'Is that a new uniform?'

'It is. And you look fetching, Miss McGuire.'

She threaded her arm through his. 'Thank you. Shall we walk?'

'I think we'll take a cab at Elizabeth Street.'

In the foyer of the Royal Victoria they found Ian McCreadie and his well-dressed female companion. Clarissa was glad that Ian had accepted her friendship with Price and that he hadn't raised the matter of his earlier proposal.

McCreadie nodded at Price and turned to his own escort. 'Let me make the introductions. Miss Wentworth, please meet Miss Clarissa McGuire and Captain William Price. Miss McGuire and Price this is Miss Deirdre Wentworth.' Before they had time to smile and acknowledge each other, a bell rang. 'Ah, that's the call, let's go in.'

The show *The Last Days of Pompeii* was entertaining and at interval, they stood with McCreadie and his partner in the foyer.

'Miss Clarissa, are you enjoying the play?'

'It's more than acceptable, Mr McCreadie. A drink would be nice, though. It's so hot in there.'

'I think there's a tray coming around,' Price said.

'Say,' McCreadie said, 'there's that nabob Dawkins. He's with Baxterhouse and Higgins. Would you like to join them?'

'Thank you, no,' Clarissa said. 'They seem already to have attracted a crowd.'

A waitress slipped between them.

'Ah,' McCreadie said staring at the waitress. 'Just the ticket, beer, Price?'

Clarissa was looking at the waitress. It was Beth O'Hare and she'd never looked prettier. Her uniform was navy with a tight-fitting bodice, white trimmed collar, and her eyes were extra bold. 'Miss O'Hare?'

'Good evening, Miss McGuire,' she said as she took a beer from the tray and offered it to Price. 'This is a Bass.'

'I say Miss Clarissa,' McCreadie said as he took a beer for himself. 'You know this creature?'

'Yes,' Clarissa said, still looking at John's friend. The atmosphere between the two women was charged with suspicion but cloaked in good manners. 'How are you, Miss O'Hare?'

'Well, thank you for asking, Miss.'

'And Mr Leary, how is he? I have to get some information from him on the house.'

It was meant to be a barbed question and Clarissa was delighted to see Beth's eyes flash. 'He is well, the last time we met.'

'And that was?'

'A week ago.'

Clarissa called on years of breeding to force a smile, but was upset at what she'd heard.

Miss Wentworth took a cordial from the tray. 'Miss McGuire? What would you like?'

Clarissa turned from the attractive waitress, glad for the distraction. 'Same as you, thank you.'

Beth handed Clarissa her drink and then slipped away to another group.

'She's friends with Leary?' McCreadie said. 'Better watch out Miss McGuire, our Leary's a bit of a wolf.'

'McCreadie,' Price said, 'there's no more to be said.'

Captain Price seemed to be miffed at her interrogation of O'Hare about Leary. Clarissa had some fences to mend. 'Mr Leary is building our house. I want to meet him about some of the details, that's all.' Clarissa sipped her drink and her face was flushed. Her breeding wouldn't let her say more, but she would confront John. There was no formal commitment between them, but if John was fighting to get her, he wasn't showing it. Having a final glance at O'Hare she understood why. John would be attracted to her and she tried not to think what they would get up to together.

People started going back into the theatre. 'I think the show's starting,' Price said. 'Let's go back.'

Clarissa took the officer's proffered arm as they ascended the steps.

In the humid cab ride home, Clarissa waited for the questions to come. William Price was a decent man and she liked him.

'You seemed to take quite an interest in Leary, Miss Clarissa. Why is that?'

'He's building our house and he's got information I want.' She thought quickly.

'About what?'

'Wardrobes. I want to know his timber selection. William, let's not talk about him. When is your next training starting?'

Price smiled, content it seemed that she called him by his first name, a sign of affection. 'Not until next month, Miss Clarissa. I enjoy our times together and to be dreadfully honest, well, I'm going to miss you.'

'That's very bold of you, Captain, but I thank you for the compliment. The feeling is mutual— I enjoy your company.'

At her front door, she turned to him. 'William, when we are alone or out of earshot, please call me Clarissa. Now, goodnight.'

Price bowed to her with a big smile. 'Goodnight . . . Clarissa.'

~

It was a hot and uncomfortable morning as John drove the wagon down Wolseley Road. Getting closer to the house, he smelt a pungent, throat-irritating smoke. He clicked to the horse to pick up pace, his heart beating. Please God, not the house.

There was little timber left untouched, only a spire of smoke coming from the odd piece. The brick walls still stood; their faces blackened and shining and John acknowledged they'd need support. The whole scene looked like a rapacious army had wreaked devastation and then moved on. He saw a movement at the side of the house, and a policeman materialised.

As if sensing someone, the policeman looked up and walked towards him. He carried something. 'Are you the owner?'

John, shocked, tore his face away from the house in its death throes. 'No, I'm the contractor.'

The policeman nodded. 'Well, the owner needs to be here. I'm Inspector Henderson. We had the fire brigade here early this morning but they could do little to save it, just managing to stop the fire spreading to the scrub. Please get the owner here. I'll stay and I'll keep this as evidence.' He held up a metal five-gallon blackened tin. 'It looks like arson.'

~

John, David McGuire and Rupert Jenkins stood in the shade of a gum tree. A wind shift carried remnants of the smoke towards them making McGuire cough. 'I still don't understand it. You say Inspector Henderson suspects arson and the insurance investigator seems to corroborate it. Why would someone do this?'

John was perplexed as well.

'I know you're upset, Mr McGuire,' Jenkins said, 'but we'll have to get cracking supporting what's left standing.'

'Quite, Jenkins. You do that.' He pointed to the house. 'You don't think this was anything to do with you, one of your employees, a dispute perhaps?'

Jenkins looked at John for assistance.

'I doubt it, Mr McGuire,' John said. 'Reeds may be a suspect, but that's a long shot. We'll check it out.'

'The construction is insured and it will be rebuilt,' McGuire said. 'The thing we have to establish is who did this and why.'

'I agree,' Inspector Henderson said as he joined them. 'Do you have many enemies, Mr McGuire?'

'There's conflict in any business, inspector. I can't be responsible for the actions of people if certain of my business decisions don't go their way.'

Henderson brought out a notebook from his back pocket and started writing. 'No one that comes to mind?'

McGuire took off his hat and wiped his forehead with a handkerchief. 'John Reed, perhaps, although it seems unlikely. He was the previous builder I had to sack because of incompetence.'

'Thank you. We'll check on him.'

'Mr McGuire!'

They looked up to see a young man approach them.

'The *Herald's* here,' the inspector groaned.

The journalist put out his hand to McGuire who took it and smiled. 'Tom Baldwin from the *Herald*. Looks like arson pure and simple. Not an April's Fool's joke, that's for sure. Care to comment?'

'Always time for the press,' McGuire said. 'Please come into my carriage and we can talk.'

'Trust Mr McGuire to know what to do,' Jenkins said as the pair walked away.

'Well, what about you two?' the inspector said.

John looked at the policeman, 'Sorry, Inspector?'

'Mr McGuire may or may not have a villain against him. What about yourself or your boss?'

'I'm just a humble builder, Inspector.' John said. 'Small fry.'

'It's the unusual links in arson you have to consider.' The inspector's look tested John, but he held his ground. 'If you think of anything Mr Leary or Mr Jenkins,' the inspector said, pocketing his notebook, 'please report it to the police.'

'Wait,' John said. 'As I was leaving the site yesterday, a wagon passed me and I thought it odd because we're the only site so far north.'

Henderson retrieved his notebook and started writing. 'Any particulars of the wagon you remembered?'

'A transport wagon and it was dusty. Its tray I mean, that's all. It had red sides.'

'Thank you, Mr Leary. We'll make enquiries around here to see if anyone saw it as well.'

'Now,' John said, 'I have a house to save. Good day.'

John and Jenkins went to the ruins and stopped at the base of a propped ladder.

'Get all this squared away,' Jenkins said gesturing to the structure. 'And keep a record. The insurers will want chapter and verse on any cost we have making this mess something graceful again. Come to the office tonight and report.'

'Will do, boss.'

Jenkins left him and John climbed the ladder. He stood on the top of the blackened outside wall, spotted Sean and called out to him. 'Want more help?'

Sean pointed to two men who were helping him with the temporary bracing of the brick walls. 'Mr Jenkins has given us two of his best from his other site. We should have the walls firm by knock off.' Sean cursed. 'The bricks are going to be a bitch to clean, but, insurance won't pay for new ones.'

John agreed. 'At least the walls to the roof weren't up.'

'Any clues on who done this?' Sean asked.

'I'm stumped,' John said, 'but that wagon must have something to do with it.'

They worked on strengthening the walls for the rest of the day.

~

Jack Johnson read the *Sydney Morning Herald's* 2 April edition as he ate his lamb's fry and bacon. Just as he was about to take another mouthful, an article grabbed his attention.

The press had covered the Point Piper fire in detail. Words like 'arson' and 'suspicious circumstances' made his heart sink. Placing his knife and fork down, he pushed his plate aside and put his head in his hands. Patrons at other tables could've been excused for thinking he might have just read unexpected news of a loved one's death.

'Lieutenant Johnson, can I take your plate away?'

He looked up to see the worried face of the maid. 'Yes, of course.'

Jack held his breath as his plate was brought past his nose. *I've got to get out.* Scrambling from his chair he reached the footpath gulping lungfuls of harbour air. Two men were walking towards him. One was Lieutenant Fosdyke from the *Defiant,* who was talking with his companion.

Lt Fosdyke recognised him. 'Jack, you look like you've seen a ghost.'

The informal salutation miffed him, as this man was junior to him.

'I'd like to introduce to you William Baxterhouse's younger brother, James.'

Jack's puzzled look accompanied his outstretched hand. William's brother was diametrically opposite to William. 'It's a pleasure to meet you. Are you new to Sydney?'

'I came here, sir, for a brief time, ere I was off to the primitive interior.'

'I beg your pardon?'

'What he means Jack,' Fosdyke said, 'is that his brother had him in Sydney for five minutes before dispatching him to Ballarat. William's got a store down there that sells tools to the ignorant gold miners.'

'Oh, I see.'

Fosdyke continued. 'Anyway, we're off to a soirée. Would you like to come along?'

Jack hesitated. 'Some other time perhaps.'

'Any time's all right with us, Jack, any time. Come James, we're awfully late.'

'Good morning to you, Lieutenant,' Baxterhouse said.

Johnson watched them go and remembered the *Herald* article. He made up his mind to salve his conscience.

~

Easter Sunday broke clear and crisp for the middle of April and John walked to St Mary's from his digs in Elizabeth Street. He entered the church and through the gaps in the congregation saw Beth with her mother and sisters. It'd been over two weeks since he'd seen her. The less he saw of her the harder he could work on winning Clarissa, who was also at Mass with her family. He tried to distract himself from thinking about the two women by concentrating on the service.

As the faithful thinned out after Mass, Beth smiled at him. He smiled back and glanced at Clarissa who looked at Beth, turned and continued on her way with her family.

'Happy Easter, John,' Beth said. She looked at the departing McGuires then back to him.

'And to you Beth, Mrs O'Hare,' John said. 'If you let your sisters go, will they attack me?'

Both youngsters giggled. 'Come on girls,' Mrs O'Hare said, 'we must be off. Nice to meet you again John, hope to see you soon.'

Beth stayed with him as her family left them. 'What are you doing today?'

'Seeing my sister.'

'How is she? You know since—'

'She's better, thank you.'

There were few people around and Beth came close to him. She leaned forward and kissed him, just a peck but it was nice. 'Can you come to my house this afternoon after your sister's?'

John was tempted but seeing Clarissa had made him hesitate.

Beth seemed to sense this. 'I saw Miss McGuire at the theatre. She was smiling and having a good time with an officer.'

Price, John suspected. Having a good time—grand! 'Who took you to the theatre?'

'Wouldn't you like to know?' she said and grinned. 'I wasn't taken anywhere.' Her face now serious. 'I was there as a waitress. Remember, I told you.'

He held onto her hand, ready to do her bidding. But he couldn't. She smiled at him. 'I can't come back today,' he said, 'but we'll see each other soon.'

She nodded. 'Happy Easter, then.' She touched his cheek and walked away.

He turned and set off for his sister's, knowing that he'd made the right choice, but Beth's kiss lingered and he cursed himself for his weakness. Clarissa wanted him to fight for her, well bloody do it, man! Stop marking time.

Liam recited the Easter Sunday grace. The holy words reminded John of Christmas Day and his promise to his brother-in-law who was now looking at him. Liam seemed to understand John's thoughts.

'Happy Easter everyone,' Liam said. 'Let's hope at next Easter, Point Piper will be finished. John, tell us about the house.'

'Oh, it'll be finished all right, by about September. It's restarted with a vengeance.'

'I trust the security is adequate,' Maureen said as she fed a spoonful of food into Michael's mouth.

'We still have a guard. I think the fire was a one-off thing.'

'Any news from the police?' Liam handed John a platter of roast turkey.

John took a generous helping. 'They're still checking. They suspect arson but John Reed is not a suspect.'

'I hope they find the culprit.' Liam replied tickling Michael's chin. 'He's got an appetite today, dear. That's his second bowl.'

John smiled at his nephew. 'Does the little fella take up much of your time?'

His sister glanced at Liam and sighed. 'I do miss teaching. I can't teach here of course, being married, but I'd love to.'

Liam smiled. 'There might be something you could do, if it's not too much.'

'What's that?' she replied, her face eager.

'John introduced me to Ian McCreadie. His older brother Kevin has two children who would benefit from extra tuition. Would you like to do that?'

Maureen's eyes glistened. 'Isn't he a wonderful man, Johnny? Of course I'll do it.'

'Just a trial to start. I don't want you getting tired or neglecting Michael.'

'I won't, I promise. Thank you again. Now, let's eat before it gets cold.'

After the desserts, Maureen went to clean up and put Michael down. Liam and John went to the parlour for a treat of port and cigars.

'Liam,' John opened the conversation. 'I'm going to form a company and have a crack at building on my own.'

Liam sat back and sipped the port. 'That sounds exciting.'

John savoured the flavour of his own drink as Liam took two puffs on his cigar.

'There's a demand for quality construction,' John said. 'Building companies generate good cash flows and that cash can be channelled into other things.'

Liam blew out a cloud of smoke. 'You know best about such things. But what about capital? I have none to offer, I'm afraid.'

'I'm going to talk to the bank and maybe my boss, but I'll want security. I'm asking if you'll mortgage this house for me. I'll give you part of the company.'

Liam studied him for some time. 'All right.'

'You're very trusting,' John said, the relief draining from him, 'and I won't let you down. The mortgage will be lifted when I get on my feet.' He put out his hand. 'Thank you.'

'You'll succeed because you won't want to fail your sister,' Liam said as he shook John's hand.

'That's true,' John said and smiled.

They talked for the next ten minutes about railways when they heard Maureen finishing up the dishes.

'I've thought about Baxterhouse,' John said. 'I don't want to tell Maureen yet. She seems to be getting over it.'

Liam looked hard at him. 'We'll see.'

Maureen brought in a cup of tea and sat down with them. She smiled at her husband.

'It was a lovely meal,' John said. 'Thank you.'

Two weeks after Easter, in the coolness of late April, John entered McGuire's Sussex Street warehouse and saw Clarissa in the foyer. 'Good morning.'

'Mr Leary,' she said in a businesslike voice, 'have you got the plans for the cabinet work?'

'I have.' John patted his satchel.

'Then come with me.' She climbed the familiar stairs and went into McGuire's office, where John had had his altercation with her father. 'Father's on site looking at all your hard work. Sit down, please.'

John opened the drawings as Clarissa sat in her father's chair. 'All the bedroom wardrobes will be mahogany,' he said. 'The skirtings cedar.'

'Let's have a look, shall we?' Clarissa said.

Thirty minutes later, he underlined the last note on his pad and stood up. 'That's it then. When would you like to meet next?'

She stood up too. 'In future, please don't see me. We'll do everything by correspondence. Good day.'

John was dumbfounded. 'But—'

'Leave, please.'

'Clarissa? What's wrong?'

'You're still seeing Miss O'Hare. You obviously still like her.'

'It was just at Mass.'

'Now you're lying. She told me differently. Your actions are not those of a man who's got me front and centre and is willing to fight for me. Now, for the last time, go.'

John rolled up his drawings and looked at her. 'It's not like that. It's not.'

Her eyes were cold. 'Go.'

He left. As he went onto Sussex Street he felt a hollowness he'd never felt before. He'd been careless and weak with Beth, but wasn't Clarissa seeing Price?

CHAPTER ELEVEN

John left Point Piper with the plumbing plans. Tonight he'd have to list the bathroom fixtures that needed the client sign-off. As promised after their last meeting, he had received a letter from Clarissa with her requirements on the cabinetwork. There was no confusion about what she wanted, but he'd written back asking her to see him again. To date, he had had no response. Foolish and cocky he'd been balancing the emotions of two women and he'd paid the price. He had to see Clarissa, somehow.

Opening the front door of his boarding house in the late autumn dusk he stiffened as he felt a tap on the shoulder.

Facing him was a man of thirty years or more. 'Mr Leary. We meet again.'

John was puzzled, then remembered. He was the officer from the *Defiant* who'd spoken to him in Cape Town. 'Can I help you?'

'It's me who can probably help you. William Baxterhouse may be a common link between us.'

John bristled. This stranger might be in William's employ. Better to meet in a public place. 'Do you know the new pub in Day Street?' he asked him.

'Cochranes?'

'That's it. Meet me in one hour.'

'I'll be there.'

John spotted the officer at a table with an empty glass in front of him. Was this going to be an opportunity or was it a trap to get at him? But then, what wrong had John done to Baxterhouse? Nothing.

The man put out his hand. 'Lieutenant Jack Johnson's my name, Mr Leary. I found that you are Mr Jenkins's supervisor for the McGuire house. What would you like to drink?'

John returned the greeting, got the barmaid's attention and waited till the beers were brought to the table. 'What's your connection to Baxterhouse?'

'Mr Baxterhouse was in Cape Town when you asked about him that day. He's now in Sydney.'

'And I've met him.'

'Right. Well, like most people, I'm flawed. I made a mistake once and I'm still paying for it because at the time, I acted cowardly.'

John took a sip from his beer and waited for the man to keep talking.

'I do Baxterhouse's bidding because of a previous misdemeanour which he's holding over me. Mostly, it's been things like pulling strings to get him a berth on the *Defiant* and other such like which I put up with. But now— that's why I'm here. I'm reasonably sure Baxterhouse caused the fire at Point Piper.'

John held a poker face. 'Why would you say that?'

Johnson looked John straight in the eye. 'Because I gave him all the information I had on the McGuires.'

This was unexpected. Maybe he was telling the truth but John wanted more convincing. 'Why the McGuires?'

'William told me he met Clarissa McGuire at Bathurst. When I gave him the information that it was McGuire who'd bought the land Baxterhouse wanted, I suspected he'd get at McGuire somehow—it's the kind of man he is. Now the fire has happened. That's why I'm here.'

John unwound a little. Johnson's apparent confession could

convict Baxterhouse, so it didn't seem like a trap. 'Why should I believe you? Baxterhouse might have sent you to get at me.'

'Does he have a grievance against you?'

John knew he was on solid ground here. 'No.'

Johnson leaned closer to him. 'I'm telling the truth.'

Yes, you might be. 'Can you prove that Baxterhouse caused the fire?'

Johnson placed his empty glass on the table. 'No I can't, but it's a reasoned guess.'

There was one way to get this man to prove his story. 'What if he tells you?'

Johnson sat back with a quizzical look. 'How do you mean?'

'Why don't you get him drunk and maybe, make him talk. He may boast about it. If he tells you that he did it, come back to me. We'll talk again.'

'It might work.'

'Have you got another way?'

Johnson paused then put out his hand and John took it. 'No. I'd like to nail the bastard for the fire. The police can be involved if I can get the proof.'

John still held Johnson's hand. 'Prove to me you're telling the truth. It's the third of May. Get the evidence and meet me back here in a fortnight.'

John left the pub and walked home. Johnson's story seemed real. Why would the man lie otherwise? It was worth a try.

~

William Baxterhouse relaxed on a couch in the Kent Street club. His left hand held a glass of Bushmills and his right a Havana. On the couch opposite was a man, who, despite his small height, had no fear. Brian Dawkins' childhood in the gutters of Belfast had hardened him to ironstone and that determination had with sweat, effort and a nose for Ballarat gold made him wealthy. He had a cheeky smile and flaming red hair that matched his silk vest. His love was firearms and William remembered his weekend at Dawkins' Oberon property where they'd gone shooting with a cache of fine weapons. A pretty girl sitting by Dawkins' side pressed against him and her hand crept up his thigh. He slapped it away but in a playful manner. The girl pouted.

'It's a good business you've got, Baxterhouse. I've got cash and want to spend.'

He had cash all right. Higgins had perspired in excitement when Dawkins had deposited half his fortune with the bank in Sydney. 'You've told me before and the answer's still no, my friend.'

'That's a pity. Well, if I can't buy into your tools' business what I want is ships to transport them.'

Baxterhouse was interested now. He had no wish to share any of his miners' tools, not yet, but boats were his specialty. 'Ocean--going ships?'

'Have to be, but for the coast from here to Melbourne. I'll need at least three of them and will go to tender.'

The girl seemed bored and sat back admiring her nails.

'How big?'

'Sixty tons each,' Dawkins said and smiled. 'Can you build them?'

'I can.' They were big boats, very big. John Cuthbert, a competitor with a yard not far from him, had plans to build one of similar size, but three, that was a big order. He'd have to tool up, buy cranes and get more equipment and that meant loans from the bank. To get those, Dawkins had to give him an order. 'When do you want them?'

Dawkins slapped the girl's thigh making her jump. He grinned. 'I haven't given you the order yet. But I'm not far away from making my mind up.' He stood up. 'Now, my good wife seeks my company. How are you and Elizabeth? Got that ring on her finger yet?'

'Nearly, Mr Dawkins.'

'Well, don't dally. Her father's a banker. That's always helpful. Let's talk soon at your place. It's the fifth of May and I want those ships built by March next year. Goodnight.'

Baxterhouse waved his arm in farewell. That order he must

have, it would make his fortune. He would see Higgins, but that was for tomorrow.

A smoke layer squatted over the occupants of the adjoining room. He knew all the card players except one, a stranger, who'd glanced his way a few times. Maybe a target whose winning cries threw out a challenge. William wanted to play but waited for a vacant chair. Cullens were killing his tools business and he wondered why he hadn't off-loaded it to Dawkins. Cullen had to be taught a lesson, like McGuire and his house. Fear controlled people and Cullen would feel his wrath. William felt good. He might do the job himself and enjoy the outcome.

A chair became available. William went to the table, nodded to its occupants, cut the cards and dealt. His eyes darted between the cards and the stranger. He missed nothing. The first three hands went by, easy. William then introduced some sleights of hand. These would be detectable by any skilled player. He won the next two rounds, the stranger none the wiser. William upped the ante. Play continued and he started some sophisticated cheating. He won more and his excitement mounted. His winnings piled up. The stranger asked to increase the stake to ten pounds. William nodded—a fool and his money. William won the next two alternative hands. The gamblers at the table had exchanged their places for others, with him and the stranger the only originals. William then lost the next three hands. He wasn't that worried; his confidence was still high.

The stranger placed his cigar on a tray dropping ash onto the baize. He looked hard at William. 'Twenty pounds ante.'

People came to the table from other rooms.

'Too much for me,' one of the two remaining players said. His companion nodded and left with him. It was William and the stranger.

William liked a challenge and still had a few tricks up his sleeve.

'Agreed. Deal.'

The stranger nodded. 'New deck.'

William baulked.

The stranger dealt with skill. William won the first hand. He knew he had this man. The stranger's face started to sweat and he dropped a few cards. Stupid bastard. *I'm going to make the best pile ever.* William dealt. He lost the next hand. No worries. When he'd lost the next three hands, he started to think. Dealing the next hand, he did something untried in New South Wales and a definite winner. He smiled to himself. He discarded the two necessary cards and collected two new ones.

The stranger asked for only one. William raised, was countered, and raised again. William called and the stranger with a calm face showed his cards. William had lost. He banged the table in frustration and a murmur went around the group of spectators.

'Deal.'

The next half hour was disastrous. He tried every trick but lost every hand. He called it quits by accusing the stranger of cheating. He guessed his loss at one hundred pounds. The club's owners, used to William's rages, intervened and ordered him from the premises.

William kept watch on the club's entrance for an hour, cracking his knuckles in excitement. He'd smash the player when he came out. Another hour passed and he felt the cold shoot through him. In disgust he hailed a cab and, under his breath, vowed revenge on the cheating man.

~

A week after he'd met Leary, Jack Johnson was trying to get more drink into his blackmailer to prompt his confession over the fire. Baxterhouse had been in his cups when Jack had arrived at the club.

'I want that thieving bastard caught and dealt with. If you won't, I will.'

Jack didn't doubt him. Over the last half an hour he'd heard the full story including getting a good description of the card-playing man.

'You hearing me, Jack?'

Baxterhouse had received a hit and Jack was pleased. 'I hear you, but my ship sails for Norfolk Island on the twentieth, so I won't be much help.'

'You'll do as you're told. I want him found.' He ordered another drink that went down as well. He was now drunk and restless. 'If you find him Jack, I'll return your gambling receipt. Now, how's that?'

That was encouraging. 'You mean it?'

'I do. You've been a good man.'

Squeals of delight greeted a new arrival at the Kent Street club and they both looked at the source.

Baxterhouse grunted as he seemed to recognise the guest. 'Bloody Fosdyke, raving queer.'

Jack had had his doubts about Fosdyke. Still, he was an able sailor and fighting man. 'Fosdyke, are you sure?'

Baxterhouse hesitated. Then he seemed to make a decision and took a deep breath. 'I am. He doesn't hide his affection for men.'

William's voice carried to Fosdyke who looked at them and seeing Jack, turned away, but Jack had an idea and beckoned the lieutenant over. Fosdyke paused then came, his retinue leaving him for other distractions.

'Ah, Johnson, how are you? And if this is not the estimable Mr Baxterhouse!'

Baxterhouse's elbow slipped on the bar top as he raised himself. 'Fosdyke, get us a drink.'

Fosdyke smiled and glanced at Jack who raised his eyebrows back to him, careful not to let William see him. 'Surely, sir. Same for you, Johnson?'

Jack had to play this game for real. 'Thank you.'

Fosdyke ordered the drinks and returned.

Johnson wanted Baxterhouse to slip up and prodded. 'Mr Baxterhouse got beaten to some good Bathurst land recently.'

Fosdyke looked surprised. 'Really? How sad.'

'Some Sydney toffs beat him to the punch.'

This was the trap. William paused and blinked trying to concentrate. 'I fixed them though. They won't forget me in a hurry.'

'And how was that done?' Fosdyke enquired.

Baxterhouse paused. 'It was done, lieutenant, have no fear.'

Jack was disappointed. 'I'm curious too. How?'

'I burned their new place down,' Baxterhouse said and started to laugh.

Fosdyke smiled. 'That's not a joke. No really, how?'

Baxterhouse moved closer to Fosdyke. 'Yes, I made it all up. There was no ripper of a fire. No fancy house all burnt down.'

Fosdyke was about to say something when Jack placed a finger against his own lips. 'A great blaze William, I agree.'

William stood up, unsteady. I've gone too far, Jack thought. 'How would you know? You weren't there.' William sat down again and closed his eyes for a moment. 'I was though. Saw it from my horse. Boys did a great job, great job.'

Fosdyke's eyes expanded and Jack shot him a warning glance to silence.

'William, I'll go and find your card cheat.'

'Do that, Jack. Now, I'm off.' Turning he slipped and Fosdyke grabbed him to stop him falling. 'Get your hands off me, you sodomite!' Baxterhouse pulled himself together and left the club.

Fosdyke looked chagrined. 'You don't believe what Baxterhouse called me, do you?'

Queer officers were nothing new. As long as they were efficient and brave, Jack didn't care. 'None of my business.' Sodomy was a crime and he could ruin this man's career, but he had a better idea. 'But, did you believe him about that fire?'

'I don't know.'

'He didn't give any other reason or explanation about how he'd got back at those people.'

'Who were those people?'

'Lieutenant, I'm not here to make trouble but I'd like your help.'

Fosdyke's guard seemed up again. 'What? In exchange for your silence about me?'

Jack shook his head. 'I'm not into blackmail, but Baxterhouse is. He seems to know all about you. He'd use it against you. That's his way.' Fosdyke sat up and took notice and Jack continued. 'Do you believe what Baxterhouse just admitted to?'

'It's hard to think he'd resort to arson.'

'But why would he joke about something like that?'

'He was drunk and wanted attention. I heard he'd lost badly at cards here.'

All this was logical and Jack felt his opportunity slipping away. 'Would you be prepared to sign a statement that you heard him admitting to causing the fire?'

'From a drunken man?'

'You wouldn't have to mention that.'

Fosdyke paused. 'How is all this relevant to you?'

Jack had no choice. If he wanted Baxterhouse, he had to take a risk and he still hadn't got back his gambling receipt. 'The man is blackmailing me. It's his way. You'll be next, it's a matter of time.'

Fosdyke finished his drink. 'James is a gentle man. He's told me stories about his brother's penchant for the dark side. Just the facts, yes? That I heard a man I know saying he caused a fire at Point Piper?'

'Thank you. I'll draw up a statement and you can sign it.'

'What has Baxterhouse got against you?'

Jack looked at him. 'Let's just say that I want Baxterhouse out of my life for good. Will you do it?'

Fosdyke put his glass on the bar top. 'Aye, I'll do it.'

~

In a gambling parlour in Pitt Street not far from the Royal Victoria, Jack Johnson ordered a drink and waited till the gambler took a break. Jack knew that if he found William's cheating card shark, he *could* get his receipt back and, at the same time, he'd be subjecting someone else to Williams's malevolence. Yet he'd set out and wasn't optimistic but it took him just three days to find the card player from the description Baxterhouse had given him.

The gambler left the table and Jack intercepted him on his way back from the bathroom. 'Excuse me, sir. Were you at the Kent Street club last Wednesday night?'

'And you are, sir?'

'Lieutenant Johnson. You played a mean hand that night and my friend was upset.'

'I can't remember seeing you there, Lieutenant, but I do remember the man I beat.'

'He's convinced you cheated him.'

The man grinned. 'I don't cheat people, Mr Johnson. Your friend is a good player and he knows a few tricks. His problem is that I know more than he does and he was beaten—cold. Are you here trying for a rematch?'

'That's not my intention.'

'You're in the Navy? A professional man with a reputation no doubt? So why are you associated with Mr Baxterhouse?'

'He never mentioned his name. Neither did I.'

'Go back and tell Mr Baxterhouse that you found me. Now, what is he likely to do?'

'He could well box you up. He is a champion at his trade.'

'He could.' The man was either foolish or very brave. 'So my safety is at risk if you tell your friend that you found me. That doesn't worry me, Lieutenant. In my trade I have to take risks. But if I'm assaulted by your friend, my clients will take action against him in both the criminal and civil courts. Tell your client what you like, but also tell him that I made no money from that table that evening.'

Jack was surprised. 'What do you mean?'

'Just what I said. I work for a firm of debt collectors and I'm under instruction to retrieve a debt that was owed by Mr Baxterhouse in Dublin. My clients are conservative yet they'll use unconventional methods to remedy their debt any legal way they can. In this case they use my services and my talent with the cards. Now, I do have to return to the table.'

Johnson smiled and started to laugh.

'Are you laughing at what I do, sir?'

'Partly, but it's also nice to hear. I think you've answered all my questions Mr . . . ?'

'Barnes is my name, Samuel Barnes. So perhaps your client will not be too inquisitive as to my whereabouts and well-being, Lieutenant Johnson. He might just unearth something of which he thought was well and truly buried in his past.'

'I think that's exactly the case, Mr Barnes,' Jack said still trying to control his mirth. 'I thank you for your information and bid you a good evening.'

Jack left the man with mixed feelings. He was happy that William had got a serve in his hip pocket but equally by not telling him about the card shark, his gambling receipt would still stay with the boatbuilder. He ordered another drink and thought about what he would do. Keep mum. That's what he'd do because there was no guarantee that Baxterhouse would have honoured his agreement.

~

The statement was clear, had been signed on 10 May, and John was satisfied. Jack Johnson was telling the truth and Fosdyke's document backed him up. John looked at the lieutenant sitting opposite him. 'It looks good to me.'

'You can see I'm straight. I'm now going to the police with this.'

John pondered this; it was all about timing. He wanted to get David McGuire's arsonist convicted but not just yet. There may be something that could be done sooner, something done by himself. 'Can you wait?'

'Only as long as Baxterhouse holds power over me. I'm back from Norfolk Island at the end of June and then I'm going to the police. You can see the dates on the statements. If I left it too late, the police might think I was obstructing justice.'

John understood. July was acceptable. 'How's Lieutenant Fosdyke taking it?'

'Pretty well, considering.'

'Well lieutenant, thanks again. I'll let you know when it's the best time to move against him. Your ship sails for Norfolk Island soon?'

'On the twentieth. Oh, and another thing. Baxterhouse lost at cards in a big way; he'll be cursing an empty wallet for some time. He asked me to find the cheat and I did.' Jack smiled.

'Well?'

'The cheat was working for a debt collector.'

'No!'

'He was. Not for money Baxterhouse owed here, but in Dublin.'

John remembered Wexton's report. 'Did he mention a Mr Whitelaw?'

'He didn't. But what he told me was very pleasing to my ears.'

So, another hit against the man and none of it John's doing. Good. 'Send me a note when you're next in Sydney. Look after yourself.'

After Jack left, John started to think. Others were having a go at the rapist, but John wanted to have a go himself. Baxterhouse was being attacked on his tools business, but that still left his three other companies exposed. How to sting the man in one of those? That's what he needed to solve.

~

John left his boarding house in mid-afternoon on Sunday 23 May and made his way to Redfern. After work during the past week, he'd scrutinised the Botany Street business where William Baxterhouse stored his wagons. It was a good place to cause some mischief. The open yard was about one hundred and fifty feet deep. The street frontage contained stables and an office. At the rear boundary of the yard six wagons were packed close to each other and fifty yards from these stood a maintenance store. There was a good eighty feet between the wagons and the stables, and a vacant lot stood on one side of the yard. At around five-thirty each night a man would enter the stables from the street, feed the horses and close up the business.

It was four-thirty now and after checking that the entrance gates were locked, John entered the vacant site adjoining Baxterhouse's, removed some loose fence palings and stepped into the yard. He was on guard, but confident there'd be nobody there. Creeping between the wagons he noticed they were all chained together for security and were in good fettle. Their tray bases were dusty white and touching one he smelt what it could be. A mixture of creosote and . . . not flour, but something. Then he saw them, just a few—oats. And the wagons had red painted sides. One of these wagons had been used for the Point Piper fire, he was certain, and his guilt at what he was about to do was assuaged. Excited now and checking to see that no one was in the front office or stables, he slipped into the unlocked maintenance store and in one corner found what he needed on the shelf at the back— a can of creosote and an empty bottle.

Grabbing both he returned to the middle wagon and unseen from the street he gathered three hessian bags that had been lying on the wagon tray and poured creosote on both sides of the wagon and a dollop on the bags. He knew, as a carpenter, creosote was good to prevent attack from white ants and it was an ideal combustible. He returned the can to its place in the shed. Back at the wagon he placed the bottle near the hessian bags and over them he assembled a pile of combustibles, but not of a size that could look suspicious after the fire. He removed from his pocket a piece of last month's newspaper and a magnifying glass. After shredding the newspaper he placed it on the pile, and using the glass, lined up the sun's rays focusing sunlight to a point on the pile. He started to perspire as the south-westerly wind freshened. Half a minute passed and he was conscious of the time. It had worked three times in the yard behind his boarding house when he'd done trial runs. Deliberate destruction of useful implements was anathema to him but this was a war and he had to win this battle. A wisp of smoke drifted up from his pile and a flame darted. John glanced at the street but it was all clear. The flames spread and the pile took hold, surprising him with its speed, and he stepped back. As the wagons were chained together and their sides close it wouldn't be long before they all took hold. John scrambled between the wheels and left the way he'd come, securing as best he could the loose palings. Peering through these he was both excited and astonished at the blaze he'd created. He didn't dawdle and left. The whole operation had taken less than twenty minutes. Glancing back, a dirty plume of smoke issued from the site. He hoped the horses wouldn't panic. The wagons were not near them and the wind was blowing the smoke away from them. All good.

On the Monday morning, William Baxterhouse stood with his manager, Myers, and a police sergeant looking at the remnants of his six wagons, three of which were destroyed and three -unserviceable.

'It's arson, that's what it is, sergeant.'

'We've been here an hour, Mr Baxterhouse and there's no evidence of that. There is no accelerant, no oil, nothing to indicate a criminal act.'

'What do you mean? Course it's bloody arson!'

'We don't think so. There's no forced entry and it's probably more likely to be a case of spontaneous combustion. Any food product that sits around can cause it. Or more probably that empty bottle capturing the sunlight.' He examined an unburnt section of a wagon's tray. 'Do you use creosote on these boards?'

'We do,' Myers said.

'And have you carted any oils in your business, linseed, etc?'

'Some,' Myers added.

'That might be it then,' the sergeant replied. 'Are your wagons insured?'

'They are,' William said, 'but not my loss of trade. This'll set me back. I still think it's arson and I'll do my own digging.'

'Do that, Mr Baxterhouse, but unless you get evidence of a crime, we'll not act on this other than do a report for your insurers. Good morning.'

William watched him leave. 'I tell you this Myers, this fire was deliberately lit. I don't give a toss what the police say.'

'Bill the stable boy saw the lot when he came.' Myers said. 'There wasn't much he could do about it.'

William kicked a wheel spoke, which splintered into charcoal. 'Someone lit this fire.' Cullen came to mind. Yes, it could well be. 'And someone is going to pay.'

John washed, dressed in his suit, grabbed something to eat and set off from Point Piper for town and the bank. Sean would cover for him if Jenkins asked about his whereabouts. It had been two days since his satisfactory attack on the wagons and if that had been in the newspaper, he hadn't seen it. And other things were happening to Baxterhouse; a big loss at cards and now an opportunity to get the bastard convicted of arson. All that was gratifying after months of frustration but his good feeling dissipated when he thought of Clarissa. His letters to Sussex Street remained unanswered. He was tempted to see Beth but he'd steered clear of the Royal and changed his Mass times at St Mary's. At some time he would have to face her and tell her the truth, but not now.

At the Bank of New South Wales, Mr Higgins met him and invited him into a meeting room. 'What can I do for you, Mr Leary?'

John felt confident. 'I'm a carpenter working for an employer but I want to go out on my own as a builder and start a business.'

Higgins drew up a pad and made some notes. 'You want funds for this business?'

'I have some myself but need more to set up, buy tools, maybe rent a shed somewhere.'

'And jobs? Do you have any that you'll build yourself?'

This was the problem. Jenkins was contracted to McGuire to build his house. It wasn't his.

'No?'

'No. But I'm hopeful.'

Higgins put his pen down. 'Mr Leary, I'd advise you to win a project then we can talk.'

'But how do I win a project if I have little money? My brother-in-law will mortgage his house for me to get loan funds.'

'You have no assets yourself?'

'I don't.'

'The bank can consider lending you funds with property as security. But you are young. Why not wait a few years until you get more experience and save some money?'

That he wouldn't do. 'So how much money could I get for the secured property?'

'That depends upon its value.' He smiled. 'Not from a sale price but the bank values a property at two thirds of what it might sell at private treaty. If your relative is agreeable to that, please get him to write to me with the address of his property and we'll value it. It is unencumbered?'

'What does that mean?'

'It has no mortgage.'

John was unsure.

'Perhaps it would be better if you both came in and spoke with me when you get your first project. Is there anything else I can help you with?'

John stood up. 'No thank you, Mr Higgins. Good day.'

Walking out into George Street, he was disappointed. It wasn't as straightforward as he thought. A project first? Liam's house scrutinised? All very hard. He would have to find another way. He smiled. Maybe he should have taken up Mrs McGuire's handsome offer? No need for banks. But he chided himself. He had made the right decision. Mr Jenkins? Yes, he could talk to him about buying a share of his business. It was worth a go. But Higgins just now hadn't refused him the money so he could, with clear conscience, tell Sean that funds were available. A half-truth at best and, Sean had to be on his side.

William Baxterhouse's recent card loss still galled him but that was tempered as he almost felt the bank notes in his hand; the power he'd have, the property he could buy and the people he could impress. From this, his biggest and most profitable contract, he'd be able to retire in comfort. Not on the level of James and William MacArthur but enough to be respected by them. All this was possible, thanks to the man beside him seated in the bank's meeting room. Brian Dawkins had contracted with him to build his four 60-ton steamers in Darling Harbour. What Dawkins didn't know was that William had kept tabs on the miner. Dawkins had tried to convince John Cuthbert to build his boats but the master boat-builder had offered too high a price. William was now in the box seat.

'It's a big loan, Mr Baxterhouse,' Higgins said. 'The interest payments will be significant and you'll have to carry that interest, compounded, till the last steamer is completed. The bank will extend mortgages over all your assets.'

William knew that was a risk but a small one. He'd tried to get Dawkins to make regular payments to him as sections of the boats were completed but he'd been unsuccessful. If he wanted the contract, Dawkins had said, he'd get one payment at the end. Baxterhouse had consented to that, provided Dawkins gave him a guarantee drawn against his own assets if the rich prospector should default. Dawkins had agreed to this. 'The majority of investment is in cranes, rent, presses and engineering. I've done my own figures,' William said, 'and I agree with yours. But,' he gestured to Dawkins who smiled, 'this gentleman has confirmed his order to me, a copy of which you have.'

'I know.'

'What's your concern, sir?' Dawkins quipped to the banker. 'You have my handsome deposits in your vault. That alone should persuade you of my ability to pay Baxterhouse for my steamers and,' he grinned again, 'after this honourable boatbuilder has deducted his modest profit, you'll get your loan repaid, interest and all, simple and sweet.'

'You make it sound so, Mr Dawkins. Very well, I'm satisfied that all is in order and I'll recommend approval.'

William Baxterhouse thought today, 26 May 1852, was the best day of his life. He couldn't wait to tell Elizabeth the good news. She'd mellowed of late and was allowing him certain familiarities when they were alone. Life was great. More than that, he hadn't forgotten about Cullen and was planning a surprise for the big ironmonger.

Dawkins slapped his knee. 'Grand. Do ya like guns, Mr Higgins? I do, I love them.'

'I can't say that I do,' the banker replied, a little startled.

'You should. I've got a collection that will impress you including a new repeating rifle from America.'

'Quite.'

'Come, Dawkins,' William said. 'Mr Higgins has some paperwork to do and I've got to plan how I'm going to build these monsters of yours.'

'I'll be down at Darling Harbour this afternoon. I have to speak with Mr Higgins now on another matter.'

'Good morning then, gentlemen.' Baxterhouse said and left.

Half an hour later, the banker was imploring the small Irishman. 'It's not impossible, Mr Dawkins, to withdraw half your funds.' Higgins said. 'It's just very unusual. I can give you a Letter of Credit which would be a more suitable alternative.'

'A Letter of Credit will do for the remaining fifty per cent of my funds to be invested.'

'You're putting *all* your funds into this venture?'

Dawkins clapped his hands together. 'The lot, sir, and I've never been more certain of a winner.'

'But—'

'But just the cash for now is sufficient. The Letter of Credit can wait a week or so. This company wants cash up front,' Dawkins said, 'and I don't blame them. There's a queue of desperate Yanks who have greenbacks stuffed in their pockets. Do ya know how big guns are in America, Mr Higgins? There's one in every room and three for each person. The demand is unbelievable. This new repeating rifle will make me a fortune and you as my banker will leverage that cash for your own benefit.'

'But you want to take out so much,' Higgins lamented.

'Don't fret, sir. Those funds will be replaced in the click of a trigger and doubled when I've bought the major share of that company.'

'Which details you will give me in due course. Very well. I'll arrange the transfer authority to our partner bank in America. It will go by clipper.'

'That'll take about seventy days to get to California, if your approval goes today.'

'More likely tomorrow,' Higgins said.

Dawkins smiled. 'Time is money, Mr Higgins.'

'Very well, today.'

'It'll get to California by end of July, give or take a day—grand.'

~

Liam sensed sounds and movement and peered into the darkness. Maureen's perspiring face was creased in stress, her hand clutching the bedclothes. Leaning over her, he focused on the clock. The little hand was on three. 'Maureen.' Her eyes opened and she thrashed out searching, grabbed his hand and hugged him to her. Liam soothed her. 'There, there, it's all right.' Her shivering subsided and Liam kissed her forehead. 'Was it the same as last time?'

She nodded against his chest. 'I couldn't breathe. He was choking me.' She snuggled her face into him. 'Oh God, will I never be free of him!'

Liam stared into the darkness of the ceiling. After some time, Maureen's breathing became controlled. Though he couldn't see her, he knew her eyes were forced open, fearful that to close them would pitch her back into the horror of her Dublin bedroom. The nightmares had lessened over the months but hadn't stopped. He hadn't cared that her assault might affect their relationship. Indeed, it had strengthened it. She might always think that his affection for her was pity and protection rather than love, but he loved her so very much.

The ceiling came into focus and Liam thought about John's promise. Easter had come and gone and Baxterhouse's exposure was still hidden. He resolved to talk to John. Baxterhouse had to be brought to justice.

~

'Thank you no, Mrs Price,' Clarissa said. 'I've eaten two cakes already.'

'Please, dear,' the lady replied. 'You are thin enough to eat a dozen, isn't she, William?'

Captain William Price smiled. Clarissa was beautiful and he was in love with her. 'Are you cold, Miss Clarissa?'

'I'm not, thank you. I enjoy June, and this sunshine today is invigorating.' She looked at the harbour from the veranda of his parents' house at Macleay Point. 'There are a few skiffs racing. Do you sail, Captain?'

'I do indeed. I must show you my boat.'

'You have it here?'

'In the boat shed.'

Clarissa looked at Mrs Price. 'Could I?'

'Of course. William, be careful with our guest.' She smiled. 'Parts of that shed are slippery and I don't want Clarissa falling and hurting herself.'

'Do you think it's wise to go there?' Christine McGuire said.

David McGuire stood up and placed his empty teacup down. 'I'd like to come too.'

Price was disappointed, but didn't show it. He wanted Clarissa alone with him. 'Certainly.' He offered his arm and Clarissa took it and they walked down the lawn where the breeze had picked up. On the harbour side and shielded from view of the house, there was the boathouse with a ramp that ran down to the water. Price let them in.

'What a beauty,' McGuire said. 'It's a twenty-footer, carvel built, isn't it?'

'It is, sir, and she's fast.'

David inspected the boat's rigging and sails. 'Fairly new too.'

'It's just three months old.' Price glanced at Clarissa.

'Father, it's chilly in here. Could you get my shawl from the house? It's near my chair.'

McGuire's look was innocent. 'I'll try to find it.'

When he'd left, Price drew Clarissa to him and kissed her. She didn't resist him but her lips didn't open like he'd found with other girls. Those girls, he admitted, were not of Clarissa's breeding, so that must be the reason.

She broke away and held his hand. 'It's been a nice afternoon, William.'

'Clarissa, you know how I feel about you.'

'I do.'

'Do you feel the same?'

'You can be assured that I value that affection. You are a kind and generous man and fun to be with.'

Nice to hear, but he wanted more assurance. There was a cough outside the boat shed and they separated.

McGuire came inside handing the shawl to his daughter. 'Here you are. Now Price, show me the centre-board and how it operates.'

Behind McGuire, William pressed Clarissa's hand and was excited as she pressed back.

John looked up from the plans and patted Sean on the back. 'Nice easy job for you, mate!'

Sean didn't answer but kept studying the drawings of McCreadie's wool store extension. He had a pad and pencil at his side and was taking notes.

A draughtsman from Lewis Architects, standing at Sean's side, wiped his hands on his dustcoat. 'You see where the old shed finishes.' He pointed at the spot. 'From here it's two hundred feet to the end of the new extension. That's necessary to incorporate the monorail and crane to load the wool bales.'

'I can see that,' Sean said. 'Can you use the end frame of the old store and put it on the end of the new extension?'

'That would save money, yes. Look, it's the fifteenth of June. In two weeks the plans will be finished, then Mr Jenkins can tender in July.'

'It's not up to me. Mr Jenkins will decide.' Sean cast a sidelong glance at John as if to invite him to speak.

'I'll speak to Mr Jenkins,' John said. 'When will the specifications be ready?'

'Like the plans, in a fortnight,' replied the draughtsman. 'We want to start building in August.'

'Very good, come on Sean, we've work to do on Point Piper.'

John held the reins of the dray on their way back to the site. 'Mr Jenkins will price the work. We can then stay with him until

September when Point Piper finishes. Then, with the bank's backing, we can go out on our own.'

'Are you going to ask Mr Jenkins if you can buy a share?'

'Soon, Sean.'

'Good. Have you thought about where we could start?'

'Annandale's a safe bet. I'd also like to try the north side.'

'Transport will be a killer up on the shore. Trails are average. We'll want a heavy dray.'

'There's a lot of kit to get. You're right, a heavy wagon is the go with a spare for breakdowns.'

They kept their silence on the toll road. Alighting from the dray, John's spirits lifted. Point Piper was making progress. New timbers were going up, the roof framing had started and the place echoed to the sound of hammers and saws. John had insisted on a steam pump with a hose connected to the harbour. With this precaution and an expensive night guard, the site was secured. Both were recommendations from the insurers.

John helped Sean on site for the rest of the day. From time to time he thought of Clarissa and how she was faring. His fear now was that she would marry another and he had nothing to convince her otherwise.

~

'Fancy that,' Beth said. The 1852 wall calendar still showed March and she went to turn its pages. 'It's the second of July, for goodness sake.' March reminded her of Clarissa and the theatre. It was obvious that Clarissa liked John. The way she looked at him at Mass was a dead giveaway and yet, was John meeting her? He might be. They'd spent four months together on that ship after all, and, it was now four months since she'd seen John and that upset her. Beth had sent letters to his Elizabeth Street address but they went unanswered. One time she was tempted to go there and demand to know why he wasn't seeing her. But if John wasn't seeing her and wasn't seeing Clarissa, who was he seeing? Sighing, she adjusted the calendar to the right date and turned around to see Sean's smiling face. 'Hello. How've you been?'

'Good, thanks Beth, and yourself?'

Beth ran a cloth over the bar. 'Can't complain. Mum's still busy and Dad's at Ballarat.'

'At the diggings? Is he doing any good?'

'Just started,' Beth said picking up an empty glass, 'but he's making wages. Still in the building game?'

'Aye, pricing a new job for Mr Jenkins. It's McCreadie's wool store at Market Street wharf.'

'Good on you. What'll ya have?'

Sean ran his eye over the bar. 'Just a glass of lemonade, if you have some.'

'I do.' Beth reached down and opened the ice chest. She poured the liquid into a glass and Sean paid her for the drink. 'Sorry if I'm sticking my nose in.'

'It's a nice nose, Beth.'

She smiled. 'You don't drink?'

'Grog?'

Beth nodded.

'I used to lass and sometimes I go back to it, but it does me damage. Terrible damage and not just to me, to my loved ones.'

'I know. My Dad was like that, for nine years.'

'It's a fight I have every day of my life. He's probably the same. Anyhow, did you hear about the fire a ways back at Point Piper?'

'No! Wait a minute, Sean.' Beth turned to a customer. 'What'll it be?' she said to the man.

'A pint of ale, love,' the man said.

'Go on, Sean,' Beth said after giving the man his drink.

'Well, John and me were working on the McGuire's house at Point Piper—'

'McGuire? Miss Clarissa's father?'

'Aye, well it burnt down one night. Police thinks it's arson.'

'Someone having a go at the McGuires, do you think?'

'Probably,' Sean said.

'That's terrible. And how is the missus?'

'She's in grand health. She hates the winter cold but it's nothing like the old country. Can't wait for summer.' Sean drank his lemonade then stood up. 'See you, Beth.'

'Bye Sean. Wait, where is John working now?'

'He's on Point Piper still.'

'Thanks, Sean.'

Sean waved and left. Beth continued to clean up and thought of John. She decided what to do.

Standing outside his Elizabeth Street terrace the next morning Beth shivered in the chill. The sites started at seven and it was six-thirty now she guessed. He must show soon, but he may not. It was a Saturday and he might be somewhere else, snuggled up with another woman perhaps.

Rubbing her hands together, she heard the front door open and close and John walked out. He stopped when he saw her and didn't smile. This wasn't a good sign.

'Hello, Beth. What are you doing here so early?'

He should know why. They'd been close. 'I came to see if you still lived here. It's been a long time.'

John came up to the dray and paused. 'Can I give you a lift to the Royal? It's on the way to Point Piper.'

'It's too early for work but home would be good.'

'I'll harness the horse. Won't be long.' He went down the side of the house and Beth waited and fumed. She'd find out what was keeping him from her. It might be nothing, but it was odd. He mightn't be going to Mass even. She hadn't seen him there for a while.

John brought the horse out and put it into harness.

Beth rubbed the mare's head then took John's hand to climb up to the seat. She sat close and he didn't resist when she threaded her hand through his crooked arm. The warmth was comforting and her old feelings returned.

'I've been busy like,' John said.

Guilt. 'Then why didn't you reply to my letters? I wrote three times.'

They headed up Liverpool Street. 'You did.'

'You got them? Why didn't you reply then?'

'I should have, Beth. I'm sorry.'

She kept silent for some time and just enjoyed his closeness. 'We used to be good friends.' She squeezed his arm. 'And I thought we were more than that.'

'We were.'

'So, what happened? Why aren't you seeing me? What have I done?'

'You've done nothing.'

That was something, but she would've preferred to have caused him some grief so that he could forgive her. 'So?'

'I've got feelings for another girl.'

She took a reasoned guess. 'Miss Clarissa?'

'Aye.' The dray went down College and turned into William Street. 'But she's not seeing me either.'

Beth was a little less anxious now. 'Why is that?'

'I haven't been attentive enough, it seems.'

'Would you like to be?' John kept silent. 'John?'

'Here's Forbes Street. I'll drop you off.'

Beth got down. 'I'm here if you want me, John. Please don't keep away. It's not right. We're still friends even if you feel different about me.'

She walked away without looking back. *I'm going to see him again and I'm going to convince him that I'm the one for him.* That might mean giving him what he wants the most. She wanted a marriage proposal first, then she would share her body with him, but she might take the risk anyway. That little ride from his place had been enough to rekindle her feelings into passion once again.

~

Jack Johnson completed his report on his Norfolk Island inspection, grabbed his hat and made his way to the police station in Phillip Street. It was a temperate day for early July and today his life would change, for the better. He had agreed to go alone and tell his story. The previous night John Leary had wanted to go with him but Jack was insistent. He was the link and it was his mess to put to right. Entering the ground floor lobby he approached the counter. 'I'd like to talk to a policeman about the fire at Point Piper in April of this year.'

'Yes sir. I'll get the responsible officer.'

Five minutes later a tall, thin-nosed, but pleasant-faced officer came up to him. He had a folder under his arm. 'I'm Inspector Henderson and Point Piper's on my beat. You are?'

'Lieutenant Jack Johnson.'

'Please come with me, sir.' Jack accompanied the policeman through a warren of corridors.

'This place is too small for us. We've been trying to get ourselves organised.'

'You have all the forces with you now, I understand.'

'That's right, sir. Two years ago, the Parliament legislated to amalgamate all the colonial police forces into one under the superintendence of an Inspector General of Police, William Spain.' Henderson stopped at an opened door. 'In here, sir.'

The inspector closed the door behind him. 'Sit down, please, and tell me what you know.'

Jack sat opposite the inspector and felt calm. 'I know who caused the fire and the motive. There is however an issue of blackmail.'

Henderson opened his file and brought out a pencil from his jacket. 'Blackmail? Now, how's that?'

Jack's chair had probably seen more grief, torment and fear than he would see in a score of lifetimes. Well, it was going to feel another confession. 'I did the arsonist's bidding because he held a document over me.'

'What sort of document?'

'A receipt for a gambling debt that he paid for me.'

The inspector started taking notes. 'Where and when did this occur, sir?'

'In Dublin in February, 1850.'

The inspector blinked and shot out his arm, his palm facing Jack. 'Please don't continue, sir. I'm only interested in what happens in my town.' He paused. 'But if it's all background on the man, the arsonist . . .'

Jack sighed. He'd have to leave the navy anyway and his pension wouldn't see him starve. Maybe he would get a job on land if the merchant marine wasn't the go. 'Very well, the arsonist's name is William Baxterhouse.'

The inspector put on his spectacles and continued taking notes. Jack looked at the peeling paint in the windowless room then focused on the inspector's long nose. 'And how do you know this, Mr Johnson?'

Jack retrieved his satchel and pulled out some papers while the inspector drummed a pencil on the file in front of him. 'Here are two statutory declarations, one signed by me and one signed by Lieutenant James Fosdyke. Both contain statements of Baxterhouse's conversation admitting to causing the fire.'

The inspector took the statements and read them. 'I take it these statements were made voluntarily?'

'Yes.'

'These are valuable, Mr Johnson. We'll have to get more corroborating evidence, but it's a good start.'

Jack pointed to the documents. 'It's all there, in his words.'

'No doubt, and because you have a witness, it adds credibility. In order to convict Baxterhouse, we'll need more proof.'

'So you can arrest him?'

'Oh yes, we can arrest him and charge him but to convict him we'll have to have something more definite.'

He opened the file and leafed through the sheets. He tapped one. 'The drum that was found at the site. Unusual that, not paraffin, but oil just the same and not just any oil. I got a check done on it. Seems it's a type used for lubricating pulleys and such. All cans are imported under the one licence. Only two things weren't blackened on the can, the letters "B A T H" and three numbers.'

Jack stood up. 'Inspector, I'll try to find something else to help you.'

'Anything at all, sir, but be careful. If Baxterhouse is our man, he's likely to be dangerous. Here, I'll see you out.'

Jack Johnson's back felt nice and straight for the first time in a long time. Yes, he'd have to face a new life but his link to Baxterhouse was now severed. His spine might be more upright but William's reach was long and wide. He had now made himself a target of his blackmailer.

CHAPTER TWELVE

THE SKIFF WENT ABOUT, THE BOOM CRASHED AND THE FORWARD hand's hair flew back in the breeze. If the skipper of that boat loved design, the view of the new house from Blackburn Cove would be as pretty as that from Wolseley Road where John stood.

The dignified scale of the residence relieved John's hangover from the previous night out with Allan Cullen. The house's delicate fascia melded with its curved iron sheeted verandas and slate roof, and the iron balustrades were like a spider's gossamer. The windows and doors punctuated the simple but solid background of cream-coloured bricks. The house was indeed part of the landscape; it didn't compete with it or dominate it. John was proud, very proud.

'Picture postcard, John,' Jenkins said beside him.

'Aye, it is. A fine house for a fine family.'

'We've got some time before we go in. I've been thinking about your future with me.'

John smiled. 'Not letting me go, are you?'

'No, the opposite. What are your plans?'

Now was the time to ask. 'I'd like to have profit rather than just wages. It's my goal to be independent. Would you sell me a share of your business?'

'You're straight up. I'll give you that,' Jenkins said. He looked out onto the harbour before giving John his answer. 'I've never had partners, John. It's one of my rules. I'll make all the money or lose it all. I work alone.' He looked back at him. 'Sorry.'

It was worth a try. 'Fair enough.'

'Good. So what other plans do you have? Are you still with me or do you have plans with the McGuires?'

John smiled again. Jenkins was getting on but he was shrewd. 'I'm not sure. We'll find out this morning.'

'Miss Clarissa hasn't seen much of you, asking for me all these months. Is there something wrong between you?'

'Come on, boss. I'll talk about it later.' They walked up and onto the landscaped front grounds where a gardener was watering the plants in the mid-September sunshine.

Jenkins nodded and took a tighter grip on his satchel. 'I've got another job.'

Now wasn't the time to tell his boss about his future. 'That's grand. Where?'

'Annandale again, another eight terrace houses. I'm waiting for the architect's plans before finishing the bid. With McCreadie's wool store just started, we'll be busy.'

A gravel path led them to the front door, which John opened with a key. When the house was handed over to the McGuires, the lock cylinders would be changed for security. The interior paint smell was still pungent and the windows required cleaning before handover. As he got further inside his anticipation heightened at seeing Clarissa. He was anxious to talk to her, to find out how she was and if she was in love with someone else.

John opened the double doors to the veranda. Clarissa stood there looking out on the harbour, while strolling on the lawns below were David McGuire and Captain William Price. Bloody hell! The officer reminded John of the article in the *Herald* where Price and Clarissa were named at the Wool Graziers' Ball. John had to get Clarissa on her own.

She turned around. 'Good morning, Mr Jenkins.' She looked at him. 'Mr Leary.'

Nothing. Her look was as if she was addressing a tradesman she didn't know.

'Miss McGuire,' Jenkins said. 'I didn't expect you had company. It's still messy inside. If you'd like, we can come back on Monday.'

'No, you're here to do the final inspection and that's what you must do. I want to accompany you when you walk around.'

'That's not necessary,' John said looking at Price who was laughing at something McGuire said.

'I'm the client, Mr Leary. It's my prerogative.'

'Of course it is,' Jenkins said looking at John. 'Perhaps your father wants to join us too?'

'He's left that to me.'

'Grand,' Jenkins replied. 'Do you want both of us? I can stay but John has built this house and knows its paint and plaster, its joists and joinery.'

This would be a test and John hoped she would agree to see him alone.

'I'd prefer Mr Leary only because he'll have no excuse for any defect.'

Jenkins tipped his hat. 'Very good, Miss. John, give our valued client your complete attention.'

'Wait here,' Clarissa said to John as Jenkins left them. She went outside and spoke with her father and Captain Price. Price shook his head and to John's dismay she touched his forearm in an affectionate way. Price then nodded and looked at Leary. Clarissa came back inside. 'Let's start with the upstairs.'

As he followed a pace behind and to her side, the memories of the voyage, her conversation, laughter and dancing came back to him. It was a memory that he hadn't recalled for a while. He'd missed it.

She looked around at him as they climbed the stairs. 'Have you brought writing material?' Damn. Jenkins had it all in his satchel. His hangover had made him forget to ask his boss for it. She rolled her eyes as if he was addled. 'There's some in Father's briefcase. A pencil too?' He nodded. 'Wait here, again.'

As she went off, he thought about her. She was angry with him and that was interesting. If she was in love with Price, she would be her charming self and probably be gentle, perhaps a little sad in telling him she loved the army officer. But she was angry. Yes, he'd forgotten something, but her terse manner wasn't the Clarissa he knew. He would soon find out.

'Here's a pad and pencil,' she said coming back. 'I hope we'll not need to fill its fifty pages. Come.'

This will be good. He entered the date on top of the first page, 18 September 1852, and followed her into the master bedroom.

She looked around and went to the corner and pointed upwards. John looked as well. 'There's scrimming that's been painted over. The plaster has to be sanded and repainted. The second bedroom has the same defect.' She walked to the dressing room and opened the door. Pointing to the bottom hinge she said, 'There's a screw missing there.'

John wrote that down. When he looked up she was looking at him.

'You have kept away.'

He knew what she meant and was relieved she'd made the first comment. 'I did. You told me to.'

'I know. Come on.' They went into the hallway and into the bathroom where she stopped and folded her arms. 'Why did you keep away?'

John was confused. 'Clarissa, you told me to and I did. What do you mean?'

Her lips trembled. 'I didn't think you would. I thought you'd ignore what I said and persist in trying to see me.'

John shook his head. 'I don't understand.'

'No. You don't.'

'So tell me. Tell me what I've done wrong? I've kept away from you. I haven't seen Beth alone. In fact, she came and saw me.'

'I don't want to know.' She pointed to the corner. 'There's grout missing in that skirting tile.' She looked at him. 'And you and Beth are close again?'

John was still writing. 'I told Beth I still had feelings for you and that you didn't want me.'

'You said that?'

'I did. Now, if you don't mind, let's keep going with the inspection.'

'That can wait. I have to know something.'

'What?'

'Don't give me that look!'

'What look do you want? A smile, a laugh, a frown?'

'Sarcastic as well.' She shook her head. 'Three days ago William Price asked me to marry him.'

John was surprised, but then, that's what he had expected. 'Do you love him?'

'I want to know what you think of me.'

'Clarissa.' A voice sounded from downstairs. 'Where are you?'

'It's William,' Clarissa said. 'Stay here.'

She left the bathroom and leaned over the balustrade. 'I'm upstairs with Mr Leary. We'll be about an hour.'

'Can I join you?' John heard him reply. 'Your father has left for the office.' The man must be curious about them being alone. John didn't blame him.

'I'd prefer to instruct the builder by myself,' she said. 'There are a lot of serious problems.' John was curious. There must be many defects, but he didn't think so. 'I really would like you to wait downstairs. If you want to.'

There was a pause. 'Very well. I'll give you an hour.' She returned to John.

'What are these serious issues?'

'John Leary, you're impossible. The house is good. We aren't.'

'We?'

'God save me, man! Captain Price has asked me to marry him. What do you say to that?' Her eyes were bright, her cheeks flushed and there were three lines creasing her forehead.

'I hate it.'

Clarissa closed her eyes for a second. 'At last. And why do you hate it?'

'Because I love you.'

Clarissa closed the bathroom door, came back to him, pulled his face down and kissed him. John's surprise turned to pleasure. Her lips moved with his, her hands pressing his back. It had been months since he had had a woman in his arms but this wasn't any woman and he caressed her.

She leaned her head on his chest and he held it. 'I've wanted to do that for a long time,' she said. 'I'm brazen, I'm sorry.'

John looked into her eyes and saw the women he loved and would forever. 'Will you marry me?'

Her eyes opened as if she'd seen a four-carat diamond. 'Yes, John, oh yes.'

All his doubts, all his confusion and loneliness ended with her words. This was completion, but there were things to talk about. 'How will we marry? You won't be twenty-one till next March, the . . . twenty-second.'

Clarissa smiled. 'You're sweet to remember. Yes, we'll have to work on it.' She removed a piece of paper from the pocket of her dress. 'These are the remaining few defects. Stick them on your pad. There aren't many.'

He took them and smiled. 'How will we win over your parents?'

'We can do anything together, now I know you love me.'

'Let's talk on the bedroom veranda.' Going out into the sun and breeze matched John's good feeling. 'There's a small bit of soffit board that's come loose,' he said. 'I can point it out if your officer comes snooping.'

'He's a nice man, John.'

'He would be. You like him.'

'I'll try to be as gentle as I can. But that's simple to do, though sad for him. What I'm going to do after you leave here,' she pressed his hand, 'which I don't want you to do, is to see Father. It'll be tough but I want to prevail.'

'What if he forbids you to marry?'

She looked at the harbour and tears filled her eyes. She looked back at him blinking them away. 'I don't want to hurt him but, then, we'll wait till after March next year when we can marry.'

'I love you.'

'I know. So, about your future, our future.'

It was now. 'I want my own company. I've seen the bank and I can get funds but Liam my brother-in-law has to mortgage his house to—'

'I've got another idea. I'll get Father to invest in you.'

'With me?' He was astounded. 'Clarissa, it's going to be tough just for us to marry. Your father as my backer? No. I can't believe that.'

'Have faith, my love. Leave it to me. Meanwhile, I must speak with William,' she said and kissed him again.

As he accompanied her down the stairs, he wished her shovelfuls of luck. McGuire wouldn't back him but they could marry in any event. It was a happy day.

~

Allan Cullen left his foundry for home in the late afternoon. His head was better, the hangover from the previous night out with Leary, fading. With his satchel tucked under his arm he set out on his route, ducking through a seldom-used lane as a short cut.

Running footsteps behind him made him turn, but before he did, pain flashed hard in his lower back. Cullen doubled over and fell. His eyes blurred, but he stood up, wavering, and recognised the man.

He was punched again and again. The ironworker was a big man but his assailant inflicted tissue-tearing damage. There was a technique in the assault that was structured and practised. Cullen collapsed again.

'Get up,' his attacker said.

Cullen staggered upright again. But it was only a respite. Two vicious hits to the chin saw him drop again and not moving.

William Baxterhouse adjusted his cuffs and waistcoat, smiled and went on his way.

~

Clarissa sat in a cab on her way to her Sussex Street office. This morning she'd been close to accepting William Price's proposal of marriage, but something had kept her back, something she couldn't define. William had been gallant in accepting her refusal but she'd not told him of John. When John had come today; when he'd been close to her; when he'd spoken and smiled; she realised that it was pointless to accept compromised affection from another. Her future was with the builder but she'd been angry that he hadn't tried hard enough to win her. He'd been too honourable and had stayed away. All was now settled and she was delighted. The cab stopped and she went to see her father. This was going to be her biggest challenge.

David McGuire looked up as she entered his office. She closed the door and sat down. He smiled. 'You look flustered. Is it the heat or did Mr Leary argue about the defects?'

There was little sense in small talk. 'Father, there was no argument.' She exhaled and prepared herself. 'He's asked me to marry him and I've accepted.'

David put his pen down and sat back. 'What? You've done what?'

'I love him and we want to marry.'

'What, just now at Point Piper?'

'Yes.'

'That's ridiculous. You've never said anything these past months. What's happened?'

'I've always loved him.'

'Love?' His face was pale. 'Clarissa, what have you done?'

'Father, it's decided.'

He still seemed in shock. 'Love doesn't make a marriage work. It's compatibility.'

'We are compatible and in love.'

He leaned forward. 'I know now why you wanted to be alone with him today.' He slapped the file on his desk. 'Well, you can't marry him. I'll not allow it.'

'After next year, you won't have a choice.'

David McGuire baulked. He seemed to have forgotten her majority. 'Clarissa, think. Goodness me, he's unsuitable, he really is.

You'll wear the embarrassment of his inadequacies every day of your life. Your mother, your friends, how will they fit in with you two? Your income? How will you live?'

'I'll marry him with or without your blessing.' She stood up and walked from the office.

'Wait, wait.'

She paused and turned to him.

'You liked Captain Price. A good man from a good family.'

'He is but I've refused his proposal.'

David McGuire looked defeated. 'I don't understand you. You're wilful and want your own way.'

'And where do you suppose I got that from. Mother? No. I got that from you, Father.'

'Be it on my head, then. Good God.'

'You have moulded me to be decisive, always, and I am.'

'You're letting emotion cloud your judgement.'

Clarissa gave a faint smile. 'That's one thing I think we can agree on.'

She sat down. 'What's your opinion of Mr Leary as a builder?' David seemed not to hear her. 'Father?'

He shook his head. 'Why?'

'Just give me your opinion, please.'

'He's capable, intelligent, honest and probably not achieving his full potential.'

'Indeed. Now, forgetting my involvement with him.'

'You are involved. You cannot separate—'

'Father, just Leary as a builder, please. He'll make his mark. He's a good leader of men. I've seen it on the site these last six months. The workers there rate him highly. He can achieve and he needs a backer.'

Her father looked puzzled then it seemed to dawn on him. 'Me?'

'You. Now before you get angry again, listen.'

David sat back. 'Go on.'

'It's a good business, construction. There's plenty to do and clients are yelling for quality. The McCreadies, the Prices, Mr Higgins and others have all seen Point Piper and have given it plaudits.' She knew that her father knew this. 'That's John's best reference.' David frowned at her for her use of Leary's first name. 'And there are the commercial buildings, the hotels and warehouses where the profit is handsome. Take a majority interest in his company and watch your investment grow.'

'Be that as it may. You're still going to marry him.'

'Would you back him?'

David looked out onto his warehouse floor. 'That's a very hard thing to ask me.' He looked back at her. 'I can't disassociate you from his potential business.'

'Try, Father.'

'Very well. Yes, I'd back him. With stringent conditions.'

'Thank you. Now, I suggest we think about how we're going to get John into our family the accepted way. I assume you want to be seen by the wealthy colonials that you're willing to anoint an up-and-coming builder and by doing that receive all the praise? Or . . .'

Her father gave her a wary look. 'Or?'

'Or I'll cause a scandal for you, Mother and all your friends and clients in March next year when I marry the man I love.'

Her father shook his head again. 'Negotiate. That's another thing you got from me. God, what did I do to deserve this? You're determined?'

'I am.'

'Very well then.' He looked at her for what seemed forever. 'Tell me how, in Heaven's name, we're going to convince your mother.'

Clarissa's strength slipped from her as she realised he was making a big decision and against his grain. Not about John Leary's future, but her own. She went to him, bent down by his chair and hugged him.

David McGuire looked surprised and then he smiled. 'You think this is going to be easy.'

'You always told me that all worthwhile things require struggle to get.'

'All right, all right.'

Beth prayed for her family during the morning Mass. After the blessing, she went down St Mary's front steps into the spring sunshine and saw him. 'Hello.'

John turned and smiled and she baulked. With that smile, he'd jolted her heart and sent it racing. 'It's nice to see you back at your usual time,' she said.

He looked around. 'Your family?'

'No. It's just me,' she said.

'Are you going home?'

'Aye, it's such a beautiful day. Would you like to join me?'

'I would. Part of the way anyway.'

She walked nice and close beside him down College Street.

He broke the silence. 'So, how've you been, really?'

'Fair to middling. The girls are with Mum today at Vaucluse. The mistress is away so they can play in the garden, which is a treat. Oh, did I tell you, Da's at Ballarat and doing very well.'

'That's grand.'

'Let's hope it lasts. He's sending good cash back to us. And yourself? Is the new home finished?'

'We had the final inspection yesterday. Aye, it is and it's grand, a real picture.'

'You must be proud. And there was that fire.'

'You heard about it? Yeah, it was in the papers.'

'No, Sean told me. Have the police found anything? Who caused it?'

'They have a person of interest and I'm glad,'

'Who?'

'Baxterhouse. He was upset at losing land to the McGuires.'

She stopped walking. 'William Baxterhouse, that mongrel?'

'The same.'

'You're happy about that? Aren't you?'

'Beth, he hasn't been charged yet. The police need more evidence.' John stopped and sat down on a garden wall in the shade.

She flicked away a pebble that lay near her shoe. 'You're not sure though, are you?'

'I'm not. We have some evidence but not enough.'

'But if it's him, he knows you're in Sydney and after him.'

John shook his head again. 'No, I don't think it's that. It's the McGuires Baxterhouse was after. I have met him though.'

Beth swung her head to him. 'When? Where?'

'Outside Mass and at McCreadie's.'

She put her hand on his shoulder. 'Be careful. Are you still wanting him to pay for your sister's attack?'

'Wouldn't you?'

'Yes, but you can't attack him. Don't play by his rules, otherwise you're no better than him. Get him nailed for the fire. That will bring him to task, the lawful way.' John kept silent. 'Surely you know that getting him yourself will not rid yourself of the demon?'

'The demon?'

'That part of you that's eating you up.' John smiled which set off her anger. 'I won't keep seeing you if you keep on with this revenge. It'll kill you.' She felt foolish as a tear filled her eye.

John took her hand. 'Beth, I did want revenge. I wanted to kill the bugger and still do, but there are other ways.'

'What other ways?'

'If I can prove the arson. He'll go to jail.'

'That won't satisfy you.'

'I think it might. He's also getting hits at his money and a fire destroyed his wagons. Anyway it would be foolish to assault him. If I did, I'd come off second best and do myself no joy. I have no proof of the rape, it was in another country and it happened over two years ago.'

Beth's worry diminished somewhat. 'So you won't strike at him yourself?'

'I don't think I will.'

That was something, but it wasn't a solid promise. 'You have friends, I'm sure, and a girl who loves you.'

'She does, Beth, and I asked her to marry me yesterday. She accepted.'

Beth let go of his hand and took a deep breath to control her emotions. When she was sure her voice wouldn't quiver, she said, 'Congratulations.'

'Thank you.'

His look was inquisitive as if he wanted her to be sad, and she was, but she wouldn't let him see that. 'I'm sorry that it can't be you, I am,' he said.

She started to lose control again. This was very hard. 'It's all right,' she replied in the brightest tone she could. 'When is the big day?'

He looked away. 'We don't know.' He looked back at her and grinned. 'I've got to win her father over yet.'

She moved close to him. 'You will and you have much to live for, a wonderful future. Don't throw it away on doing anything foolish about that horrible man.'

John's wide eyes showed surprise. 'You worry about me too much.'

Her self-control was still under test. 'John I like you very much,' she gulped and lied, 'as a friend.'

'I'll keep out of trouble, Beth. Don't worry.'

She wasn't convinced. 'Let others get your man, John. I'll walk the rest of the way by myself. Goodbye.' Turning from him, she set off down College Street. It took all of her control not to bring a hand to her face and wipe away her tears.

John smiled as he felt Clarissa's note in his pocket. It had come, delivered by Stella, on the Monday after he'd proposed. Her father had agreed to their marriage, reluctantly, but John didn't care about that. For the last two days he'd been in a blissful daze. He knocked on his sister's front door in the late afternoon after work.

'Johnny. Quick,' Maureen said as she opened it, 'come in and keep the heat outside.' John smiled and entered the cooler house and gave his sister a hug. 'You're looking well. How are things at Point Piper? Finished?'

He sat down in her parlour on one of the chairs. 'Aye, last Saturday. I'm here to tell you about the McGuires. They have a daughter, Clarissa. She was the one I told you about, the one who came on the crossing with me.'

'I remember. And?'

'I've asked her to marry me and she's accepted.'

Maureen clapped her hands together. 'That's wonderful news, Johnny. Wonderful. But you've spoken little about her. You're a dark horse.' Her smile faded somewhat. 'You don't have to get married, do you? I mean—'

'We don't. Have no fear. No, I love her and she loves me.'

'Grand. When's the wedding?'

'That, we haven't worked out. Probably early next year. I want your help.'

'Surely.'

'I want to buy her an engagement ring. Her family is well off and I can't afford much. What do you think?'

'A semi-precious stone. It doesn't have to be big but it must be quality. I have addresses of some jewellers who could help you. I'll get something to write with.' She stood up. 'In my excitement, I haven't offered you a cool drink. Do you want one?'

'I'm all right.'

'I won't be long.'

John's happiness blossomed. In her letter Clarissa had also said her father had agreed to back him in his new company, but with conditions. That was also encouraging. He was to meet McGuire on Friday, in two days' time.

Maureen returned and started writing. She finished and gave him the note. 'Here you go. Good luck.' She bent down and kissed his cheek. 'Wonderful. Now, I'm sorry but I've got things to do. Tomorrow I'm teaching the McCreadie children.'

John stood up. 'How's that going?'

'It's tiring, but don't tell Liam. The money we get comes in handy. I'll see you out.' She gave his arm a squeeze. 'A married man, grand. I'll invite Clarissa here for tea and we can have a good chat.'

'And tell her all my bad faults?'

Maureen opened the door. 'Maybe. But I want to see what kind of girl has captured my brother's heart. Goodbye, Johnny.'

Kevin McCreadie's children were tired and cranky and by five o'clock Maureen had had enough. They had been hers for the day as their father was at the Homebush Spring Carnival races. She nodded to the maid, 'Right, Dora.'

'Come on children, time for your baths,' the maid said.

Groans greeted them.

'Dora will wash you,' Maureen said, 'and then young Johnny—bed for you.' Susie, the elder was a precocious seven-year-old. A kind of truce existed between them, but they clashed all the time. Today was no different.

'Come on, Susie, let's see how many numbers you can count up to before you hop in the bathtub after your brother.'

'Oh Mrs Forde, we do this every time. Can't we think of something different to do?'

Maureen relented. 'Very well, but I'm coming back in twenty minutes, that's just after five-thirty and I want you ready for your story.'

'When's five-thirty?'

'You know your hours and minutes.'

Susie pouted and Maureen smiled and turned to the maid. 'Give them both a good scrub.'

Dora ruffled the younger McCreadie's hair. 'Especially this one.'

Maureen went to the kitchen and poured herself a cup of tea. Teaching others and raising Michael was challenging, but it did pay well and she and Liam were trying to save. Eating a sandwich, she thought about Johnny and his fiancée. She hoped that he'd found love as she herself had found. It was an essential part of marriage and the foundation on which respect, caring and trust were built. Clarissa was coming to afternoon tea soon and Maureen looked forward to it.

Right, to the children. After cleaning her plate, she passed the boy's bedroom where he was sound asleep. Closing his door she went into Susie's bedroom and was surprised to see her charge smiling and sitting up in bed with a book. 'All ready? What have you got there?' Susie showed her a popular fairy tale. 'Good. I'll read it to you.' Maureen sat next to her and arranged the bedclothes to suit. She started to read the story Susie was eager to hear.

Half way through the first chapter, Susie interrupted her. 'Mrs Forde, did you come from Ireland?'

Maureen put down the book. 'I did.'

Susie nodded and reached over and took one of her dolls from her bedside table, knocking an ornament to the floor in the process. 'Oh dear,' Maureen said. Susie jumped out of bed and disappeared under it. Scrambling up she put the ornament back where it was.

'What is that, dear?' Maureen asked.

'I think it's a gold mine.'

Maureen smiled. 'A little small for that. Let me see.'

Susie handed her the ornament and Maureen marvelled at its weight. It was a miniature panning box made of solid brass. 'It's very pretty. Where did your Mummy get it?'

Susie yawned and frowned. 'Mummy didn't get it. It was a gift from Uncle William, I think.'

Maureen was puzzled. She knew some of the children's relatives, but it could be a close friend. She leaned over Susie and replaced the ornament. Picking up the book she was about to read again when Susie interrupted.

'Yes, it was Uncle William. He gave it to me at my Uncle Ian's office.'

'Does Uncle William have a second name?' Maureen said.

Susie giggled into her doll. 'Yes, it's a funny name. Sounds like something rude.'

'Well, you can tell me.'

Susie's giggling developed into outright laughing.

Maureen couldn't help laughing. 'Come on Susie, out with it.'

'Outhouse, that's what his name is.'

Maureen asked. 'Really, is that his full name?'

Susie put a finger on her chin. 'I think there was a colour in it. Yes, it was black-out house.'

Susie was being silly and now wasn't the time for her to get excited. Maureen wanted her relaxed and picked up the book. 'All right then, now where was I?'

Susie sat up. 'Blaxter house, yes that's it.'

Maureen went cold. It couldn't be, it couldn't. It might sound the same. It's too coincidental, but she had to know. 'Susie, are you sure? It couldn't have been . . . William Baxterhouse?'

'That's it, that's it! You're clever Mrs Forde. Do you know him?'

But Maureen wasn't in Susie's bedroom; she was back in Dublin with Baxterhouse brutalising her. Susie was shaking her. Escaping from her nightmare and forcing a smile Maureen soothed her bedmate. 'If it's Mr William Baxterhouse, yes I've met him. Now Susie, listen. You said you met him at the office where your uncle Ian works.'

Susie stifled a yawn and closing her eyes, softly said. 'Yes. That's where he gave me the brass thing.'

Later, Maureen didn't remember tucking Susie in or dousing the light. Stumbling down the stairs her thoughts were muddled. *Should I tell Liam?* He'd probably go out and kill the man if it is *the* William Baxterhouse. There may well be two men of the same name or Susie was mistaken. This didn't ease her mind. She was certain it was the same man. And what would John do if he found out Baxterhouse was here?

No, this nightmare was one she will have to have again. Confirm it is him. After that, she would decide.

Maureen went home that night and had a restless sleep.

Next morning Liam gave her a worried look. 'Are you all right, you look very drawn?'

She gave him a false smile. 'Just a little feminine trouble, that's all, dear.'

'Well, keep up your strength. This teaching of the McCreadie children isn't too much for you, is it?'

Maureen shook her head. 'They're manageable. Johnny's easy to handle, Susie's a little difficult, but she's a nice child.' The mention of Susie made her feel sick. Thankfully Liam's attention was on his food. Maureen was torn. Should she tell him? After all, he knew all about Baxterhouse. She decided what to do. 'Liam, do you have to be at the school early this morning?'

He looked up. 'Matter of fact, no. Why, is there something you want?'

Maureen starting crying. Liam put his cutlery down, moved around the table and took her in his arms.

'My darling, whatever's the matter?'

Maureen sobbed through her words. 'Susie told me last night that William Baxterhouse is in Sydney.'

'Susie told you? The McCreadie girl?'

Maureen nodded. 'She, she couldn't give me the right pronunciation but it was too much like his name to be a . . . coincidence. It's not a common name. When I said his full name, she agreed. She met him at Ian McCreadie's office. Oh, God.'

'There, there, this still could be some mistake. It just seems so improbable that he'd be here. It might be a different man. Has to be.'

Maureen gave a final shudder and dabbed her eyes with her napkin. She moved over to the sink and got a glass of water. 'I don't think it's improbable. Don't forget John thought that animal could have fled Ireland, and why wouldn't he come here?' Liam sat down, contemplating his half-eaten breakfast. Maureen was puzzled by Liam's reaction. 'What's on your mind?'

Liam shook his head and shrugged. 'It's just so unbelievable he's here!'

'What do you think we should do?'

'Well, if it's *the* William Baxterhouse, we have to find him and bring him to justice.'

Liam's statement jolted her. Up to the present she'd only thought about her past. Now she'd have the burden of facing the future, one fraught with horrible scenes. There'd be police reports, intimate details exposed and possible newspaper enquiries. It was too much.

She stood up, went around to Liam and kissed his cheek. 'Dear, it's a great shock to me. I think we have to find out if Baxterhouse is in Sydney and where he lives. Let's do that first. That's all I can handle now. Also, I don't want Johnny to know. He's likely to do something rash.'

Liam put his hand on hers. 'That's a good plan, one step at a time. It's bad that he should share this town with us.'

Maureen thought the same thing. She needed to be free of the nightmares. A new feeling chipped away at her despair, something positive. At last, the man could be found. She may decide to tell Liam that she'd accept her fate and not take matters further. But she might meet her rapist, perhaps at some social function. Why should he get away with his crime?

'You know, Mr Leary,' David McGuire said, standing by his desk in Sussex Street, 'I've tried to dissuade Clarissa from you, not for any personal reasons, rather that she would be better suited to someone of her own ilk.' Despite his acceptance of John as a son-in-law, McGuire was far from happy with it and wanted to make that point. 'There are three conditions I have for this marriage. These are to protect Clarissa.' McGuire sat down. 'The first, it shall be a formal courtship of say five months. If after that, Clarissa still wants to marry you, then we'll have the wedding. Do you agree?'

That was straightforward. 'Yes.'

'The second, on the deaths of myself and Christine, Clarissa's inheritance will be placed into a trust and is not to be used by you.'

That was hard. How was he going to build, no, to even start his company, if he had no capital? He'd have to work out a way. 'I agree.'

David paused and John guessed that McGuire thought that he wouldn't agree to that.

'And the third?'

'After you're married, any house that I may provide for you will be in my name for a period of ten years. If after that time the marriage is sound, then ownership will be transferred.'

'Agreed.' Again McGuire was tying his hands from getting Clarissa's money.

'I shall have an agreement drawn up to confirm these conditions.'

John's anger at this was mitigated by the thought McGuire was testing him, hoping he'd refuse, confirming to him and Christine that John was just a gold digger. But to him, Clarissa was worth all of these conditions and more.

'Your engagement will be announced this week. I need time to persuade Christine.' McGuire paused. 'We might as well get another matter settled now. You want to start a business?'

'I want to set up my own building company but I have to have capital. I'm asking for your investment.'

'Clarissa said as much. Have you tried the banks?'

'I have, but I've no security and no building projects that I've done on my own.'

'And if I invest? How will I protect my money?'

John had an answer for that. 'There's risk in any new business. But I have a way. Whatever monies you put in will be compensated to you from the profits from the first projects.'

'And if you don't make profits?'

'Then I'll get a job as a supervisor and pay back your investment over time. With you providing us a house I—'

'I said, I *might* provide one,' McGuire said.

'Then I won't have a mortgage responsibility and will repay you in say, five years on my wages.'

McGuire seemed to consider this, then asked. 'I'll have a majority share if I'm to invest.'

'Of course.'

'Let me think on it,' McGuire said, 'but in principle, I agree.' It had been a fair morning all around. There was a knock on the office door. 'I think that's my daughter inquiring after your welfare. You'd better let your soon-to-be-fiancée in.'

John opened the door and smiled. Clarissa smiled too, and came into the office.

'Father, thank you.'

'You mightn't in time, you know. The next few months will tell if this is going to work. It's the twenty-fourth of September, Mr Leary

—John. Come to Point Piper in, say, two weeks.' He looked at his desk calendar. 'Let's make it the tenth of October, a Sunday and we'll discuss the company.'

'You'd better stay for midday dinner on that day, I suppose,' Clarissa said and smiled.

'If your relationship is going to work,' McGuire said, 'which I doubt, we'd better start seeing how you cope with us.' He handed Clarissa a thick file. 'Can you look at that for me? It's a new grazier who wants us to manage his wool.'

~

Clarissa alighted from the cab in Surry Hills on a hot Saturday afternoon. It was eight days since John and Father had met and she was only too eager to accept John's sister's invitation. Clarissa rehearsed her line of questioning. She found herself framing questions as she would to the manager of McGuire Wire and chastised herself. She wanted to get to know John's sister. Tact and politeness were the order of the day.

Mrs Forde greeted her at the door, ushered her in and made her comfortable in the smart parlour. 'What's your choice?' She said standing beside a tea trolley.

'Black tea with lemon, please, Mrs Forde.' It was served in a Royal Doulton tea cup, the spoon in the saucer was silver.

Mrs Forde sat opposite her. 'I was delighted to hear John's news. How long have you two been close?'

'Mrs Forde—'

'Call me Maureen, please, if you are to be my sister-in-law.'

Clarissa smiled. 'And please call me Clarissa.' She sipped her tea. 'We've had a bumpy ride so far. John was finding his feet here and my parents are not happy about us.'

'You're courageous in going against their wishes. I had, still have, a similar issue with my father. You are Catholic? Of course you are. I've seen you in Mass. I trained as a teacher with the Church of Ireland and my father still won't correspond with me. Mother does though.'

'That must be difficult. But did you teach in Ireland?'

'Dublin.' Maureen offered Clarissa a tray of pastries from which she took a rock cake.

'This is very tasty,' she said after taking a bite.

'There's a shop in Macquarie Street where we buy them after Mass.'

'We'll have to go there. They're very nice.' The mention of that street reminded Clarissa of John's reaction when he'd first met with William Baxterhouse. Baxterhouse was from Dublin, yes, but, perhaps Maureen might have heard about him.

'John met a man after Mass once. His name was William Baxterhouse. Did you know of him in Dublin?'

Maureen blinked and her face looked shocked. 'No, I don't. John met that man?'

Goodness, it was the same reaction John had. 'You look surprised when I said his name.'

'It was a stomach cramp I just had.'

'I'm sorry, Maureen, but John had a similar response when he'd met the man.' Clarissa took a chance. 'You know him, don't you?'

Maureen closed her eyes for a second. 'Describe him, please.'

Clarissa did.

'I do know him.'

'I don't mean to pry. I'm sorry if I've upset you.'

Maureen reached out and touched her hand. 'You seem to have my brother's feelings at heart. One day, I shall tell you all and as a woman you'll understand. The frustration I have is that I can't do anything about it here. Give me time and patience.'

'Of course, of course. Let's move on to something simpler. I want to find out things about your brother that only a sister can tell.'

Maureen seemed pleased at the change of subject. She got up and returned with the teapot to refresh Clarissa's tea. 'What would you like to know?'

'John seems well adjusted, ambitious and hard working. Sometimes though, he goes into his own world.'

The front door clicked and Liam brought in his sleeping son.

'Plain wore me out, the little chap. I think he felt like he was Blaxland's assistant, exploring the interior. Good day, it's Miss Clarissa, isn't it? I've seen you at Mass. How do you do.'

'I'm in good health, thank you, Mr Forde, and this is?' She said pointing to the infant.

'Michael John. And congratulations on your engagement. John told us.'

'Thank you,' Clarissa said. 'Maureen and I have just had our first chat, the first of many I trust.'

'It will be,' Maureen said and smiled.

'I'm glad. Maureen sees none too many women. Are you staying for supper?'

'Thank you, no. I have to return to Point Piper. Perhaps next time.'

'Very good. I'll leave you to your chat.'

'Goodbye, Mr Forde.'

'Liam, please.'

For the next half hour Maureen talked about John's early life and his faults and virtues. When it was time for Clarissa to go, Maureen accompanied her to the door. 'Thank you for coming and your understanding. Perhaps in the future I can share my problem with you.'

Clarissa squeezed Maureen's hand. 'I hope so, I truly do.'

Maureen returned to the parlour where Liam was pouring himself a cup of tea. Michael was still sleeping. 'Johnny has met Baxterhouse.'

'When? How do you know?'

'Clarissa just told me. I don't know when he saw him. She didn't say. Why didn't Johnny tell me?'

'To be honest, my dear, I've known since Christmas Day. Your brother and I didn't want to worry you.'

Maureen sat down, her eyes wide. 'Worry me? I'm worried now, Liam. You should've told me, but I understand, I suppose. I was just beginning to get my life together and this happens. Does Johnny know where he lives?'

'I presume he knows where his business is.'

'I'll talk with him. Perhaps we shouldn't find him too fast. I hate the man, but I don't relish the public exposure of a criminal investigation. I may not even be able to prove a case.'

'Let's find him first then we can see how our campaign will pan out.'

'Campaign? Yes, it's that, isn't it?'

~

At midday, Blackburn Cove shimmered and John smiled. One of the McGuires' requirements had been to have a harbour view from wherever you sat in the front of the house. From the study, he had that and more. He looked from the vista back to David McGuire, who was studying the Articles of Association for their new building company. The spacious room comprised a good working desk, three armchairs, a sofa and a table. The high ceilings and fanlights helped to keep the room cool from the outside heat.

McGuire looked up. 'You're lost in thoughts, John?'

'I was thinking. You cross your fingers and hope things will turn out like you'd planned them. This space has. Are the papers all right?'

McGuire nodded and flipped through the pile. 'A few corrections, but they can proceed. I'll advise the solicitors to draw up the final documents, dating them today, the tenth of October. You're noted as a twenty per cent shareholder and Connaire ten per cent with myself holding the balance. The shareholding proportions will be reviewed annually.' McGuire put the papers down. 'When will you tell Mr Jenkins?'

'I'm seeing him tomorrow at the wool store. I don't think he'll be shocked, but he's got to be told.'

'He would have some inkling. You're a young bright man with talent, ambition and, dare I say it, good connections. Chaps like you don't stand around in the sun for long doing little.'

John smiled. 'Yeah, you're right.'

McGuire collected his papers and bound them. 'Before we finish up, I want to tell you that Christine is still, in the least, dubious about you and Clarissa. However, she's agreed to be gracious for the time being and for that I thank her.' Getting up from his chair he walked to the doors. 'Let's go and eat.'

'Thank you.'

Both men went into one of the smaller of two dining rooms where Clarissa and her mother were seated. John felt this next session with Christine would test whether David had been accurate about his future mother-in-law's attitude towards him.

Clarissa smiled. 'Are you finished with business?'

'We are,' McGuire said.

'Good afternoon, Mr Leary.' Christine McGuire's smile seemed at least friendly.

'Mrs McGuire.'

As John tucked into lean ham, roast turkey and vegetables, Christine caught his eye. 'How are your sister and brother-in-law?'

John had a piece of turkey suspended on his fork and was conscious of its size. 'They're both well thank you and little Michael's running around causing mayhem.'

'How old is he?' she said.

'Must be nearly two, I suppose.'

'He seems a dear little fellow,' Clarissa said, 'and Mrs Forde is educated and elegant.'

This was said for John's benefit and he was thankful to Clarissa.

'Wonderful,' Christine said. 'We must arrange to meet with them.'

He thought about the conversation the previous night. Liam had told him Maureen now knew William Baxterhouse was in Sydney. This was serious. Maureen had heard it from Clarissa.

When the meal was over, John was alone with Clarissa. 'Come outside,' she said, 'there's something I want to show you.'

Taking his hand, she walked out of the dining room to the adjoining shaded veranda. John had suggested to McGuire the idea of having some meals outdoors. McGuire had agreed. It was unusual and Christine had said they would be like the natives. Clarissa thought it daring and ideal for the climate. 'The gazebo's the best place.'

Walking down they came to the shade structure designed to be a miniature copy of the details of the main house. It had lattice on three sides and was private.

John took her hand. 'And what did you want to show me?'

She kissed him and broke away. 'That's what I wanted to do.'

The next day, in the mid-afternoon sun at the Market Street site, Jenkins was berating a supplier and John tried to get his attention; but his red-headed boss was not finished yet. John left them to it and sought out Sean who was supervising the erection of hardwood trusses for the first section of roof. 'How's it going?' he asked.

'Not bad.' Sean acknowledged him but concentrated on the crane. It was known as a stiff-legged derrick, steam powered and positioned in the middle of the wool store. It comprised a round base made up of linked beams, in the centre of which a tower, held rigid by guy ropes and struts to the base, supported a jib which could turn and be raised or lowered. Hoist ropes threaded from the steam engine through the tower and at the end of the jib pulleys was a hook. The sling, attached to the hook, lowered the truss to the crew waiting to fix it. Making a final signal to the crane driver, the rigger freed the sling. Sean turned and walked over to him. 'This first bit's the slowest then she should be straight going. The end frame with the wool bale monorail is the hardest. The whole thing has to be framed by February next year and clad by April.'

'I know. Look, I haven't much time. I'm telling Jenkins about us today.'

Sean wiped a hand across his forehead and clucked his tongue. The sun had burnt him to a mahogany brown. 'You're sure about this? Can't it wait a week?'

'I'm sure.'

Sean squatted on his haunches. 'He'll be pissed off. He's counting on me to finish this. I don't feel right leaving him now with you gone as well.'

John had thought the same. 'I'll tell him we're leaving, but I'll tell him you'll stay till February.'

Sean stood up, his knees clicking. 'Oh, old age creeping in, my boy. But yeah, that sounds better. He's been a good boss.'

John knew that too and it wouldn't be easy telling him.

Jenkins walked up to them. 'I can see you now, but let's quit here and go to Cochrane's. Give me two minutes to clean up.'

They set out down Market Street and turned into Sussex Street where the loading of wool bales onto ships was constant and at a pace.

After crossing King Street, his boss opened up. 'So, what's on your mind?'

Jenkins had faith in him from day one and John felt lousy at what he'd have to do. 'Let's wait till the pub.'

'That sounds worrying.'

'Let's get there first.'

They kept silent till they entered Cochrane's and John ordered the drinks.

Jenkins downed half his before speaking. 'I wanted that. Now, about the new site, you know—'

'Mr Jenkins.'

The man's face creased in worry. 'You've got something that's been eating at you, haven't you?'

'You know I asked you about buying a share of your business.'

'And I refused.'

'Well, I'm having a go on my own. I'm leaving your employ.'

There, John had said it and he watched Jenkins's reaction.

His boss ran a hand through his frizzy hair, sighed and looked out the window then back at him. 'I thought as much. When I knocked you back as a partner, I knew you'd be leaving.' John's stomach relaxed a little. McGuire's intuition had been right. Jenkins continued. 'You've got the fire, John. I don't see it in many men but you've got it in barrow loads. I was content to hang onto your tail as you raced along and I benefited, I'll tell you.'

John smiled at the description. 'It's not been easy for me. You've been a great boss.'

'Now, don't feed me bulldust.'

'I mean it.'

Jenkins paused then nodded. 'So, what are your plans? The McGuires are a part of it, I'll bet London to a brick.'

'I'm going to have a go on my own. I'll give you two weeks' notice and I'll want Sean.'

This time Jenkins bridled. 'Now, just wait there . . .'

John put both his hands up, palms open. 'Don't want him right away. He's got to finish the frame on Market Street.'

'That's big of you.'

Silence shrouded them. Jenkins finished his beer. 'That's not on. I can't agree to that.'

John let him have the other barrel. 'Sean wants to come.'

Jenkins's mouth dropped open. 'Shit. I'd better get more beers, this could take a while.'

Sitting back at the table with two fresh drinks, Jenkins seemed deep in thought. 'This is bloody difficult. I'm losing my best two men. My business will suffer.'

'Sean's with you till February next year. From now till then you've got time to recruit and train another. I've got a few names. Two want to work with you.'

Jenkins face lightened a little. 'That's something. Well, I can't chain you down. That's it then. Good luck.'

John brought up his hand over the table and gripped Jenkins's. In the strength of that shake, he felt a bond sealed and held his breath as one part of his life ended and another had begun.

~

Lieutenant Johnson was shore-based as his ship was undergoing a six-month refit. He and John were having a drink at Cochrane's.

'It's the end of October, Mr Johnson,' John said in an officious voice. 'The fire was in April. The police have had six months to find evidence. What are they doing?'

Jack Johnson put his beer down. 'They have the statements but they want more.'

'Did the Inspector say anything? Give you any clues?'

'Only the oil can. Something special about it for lubricating and such.' Johnson went to take another mouthful of beer and stopped in mid-rise. 'Pulleys, pulleys. Like in cranes?'

'Maybe, or anything that lifts things like a spar on a ship?'

'Or a windlass. Like they use in wells and such?'

John nodded. 'More like in mines.'

'Henderson talked about the letters "B A T H" on the oil can. He's doing the check with Bath in England but that'll take time.'

John shrugged. 'Maybe that's not the full name, Bath, windlass, mines. I don't know. There must be a link.' John smiled and nodded. 'Maybe it's Bathurst. William's got a store in Bathurst.'

'That's the link for sure. I'll let the Inspector know. He may be able to prove that Baxterhouse is the sole importer of those cans.'

'It's just an idea.'

'It's the best so far. Let the police take it from here.'

'If we don't get Baxterhouse, he'll still have a hold on you.'

Johnson nodded. 'So I want him convicted.'

'If that happens,' John said, 'he'll tell the Navy about your deal. Would there be a court of enquiry?'

'Likely, and if I'm acquitted that's not the end of it. There'll be a mark on my files with further promotion doubtful. I'll retire a lieutenant.'

Johnson had made a brave stand. A naval career probably finished and now New South Wales was his home. 'What would you do if you resigned?'

'I've known only one life since I was twelve years old and there isn't much else I'm trained for.' Johnson ran a hand through his hair and continued. 'I'll try the merchant marine of course.'

'If that fails?'

'I don't suspect you could steer me in some direction?'

John did have an idea. 'What do you know about being a clerk?'

Jack Johnson smiled. 'Not a lot. But there's plenty of paperwork in the Navy.'

'Would you want to stay on shore?'

'I mightn't have a choice. Yes, I think so. I'll have to train for any job, I suppose. What do you have in mind?'

'I'm going to be busier than a one-armed juggler when the new building company gets going, either being on sites or running between them. I'll want a reliable person in our yard to keep our books and manage our stock and so forth. I'm sure you'll pick it up in no time. Are you interested?'

'It might work,' Johnson smiled. 'If the merchant marine turns me down, yeah, I'll go for it. Thank you.'

John clasped the lieutenant's outstretched hand. 'Done.'

The dust misted from the leather as he hit the bag. Another punch followed and in rapid succession a half a dozen more. The forearm now, each one hitting and grazing and William smiled through his own flushed and glistening face. He loved this. For five minutes he visualised the bag as the big ironmonger, hitting the same spot then mixing it up, higher and lower on his imaginary enemy.

Thirty minutes later, refreshed from a bath and dressed, he left the annexe and went into his adjoining shed. It was seven in the morning and his men would be starting now. Over the past five months and in record-breaking time, he'd managed to cajole, bid, swindle and force his contractors and suppliers to kit out his business for his new steamers and it was all paid for, courtesy of the Bank of New South Wales. William called on his manager. 'Mr Davies, let's have a look at what we've got.'

William was impressed by the machinery that now filled his extended shed. Light used to fill the place, but it was now so packed there was little that filtered through. 'Let's cut more skylights in.'

Davies scribbled on a pad beside him. Overhead, the most expensive item, a large travelling crane was being commissioned.

'When will that be operating?' William asked pointing to the crane.

'In three days, boss. We'll run a ten-ton load as a test.'

'Good.' On one side of his shed stood three presses, fifteen feet tall and twenty feet long, which would make the sheeting for the hulls. Two rivet-making machines occupied the opposite side of the shed, with spaces in between crammed with material and smaller machines: beam benders, splicers and cutting and stamping machines. Walking out into the heat of the last day of October, William glanced one hundred yards to his right where John Cuthbert was building a steam packet. 'That's a pup compared to what we're going to push out of here.'

'We'll be the biggest boatbuilder in Sydney,' Davies said.

'Just about. I want to look at the slipway.' Sixty yards of structure and rails starting from the shed and dipping into the murky low tide stood proud and ready for his new boats. 'All looks well, Mr Davies. All looks well. Now, let's get back and go over the production schedules and manpower. We've got five months to get the first boat off this slipway.' He slapped his manager on the back. 'A great day for Sydney. Mr Dawkins has to see this. I want him salivating for those boats.'

Sunlight bathed the Point Piper house and John thanked God for a fine Saturday. It was 6 November and tonight was the celebration of his engagement to Clarissa. He'd slaved all morning with the marquees, seating and lanterns, and Christine McGuire, despite not being enthusiastic about their union, had been even-tempered and got stuck into all the arrangements—social grace and breeding certainly had their advantages. A young woman of Clarissa's class was supposed to have all the refinements and celebrations the McGuires could muster for such an occasion.

Jim Callaghan, the brewery representative waved at him and John waved back. Callaghan had agreed to supply grog and spirits at good rates. By four o'clock John was exhausted and Clarissa found him lying on his side in the shade.

'Squibbing on the job, are you? Tell me, again, when we are getting married.'

'In February my darling, ninety-six more nights.'

'That's the plan, but my parents are still sceptical, Mother especially. Now, get up, go home and get ready.'

John accepted the congratulations and well wishes of his landlady and left Elizabeth Street in his new formal suit and took a cab, so as to arrive fresh and clean at Point Piper. He found Clarissa checking the seating arrangement.

'I've something for you.' He removed a package from his pocket and offered it to her.

She took it and smiled. 'This is nice.' Taking his hand she walked to the fireplace, reached behind a large vase and handed him a wrapped box about six inches square. 'I've a gift for you as well. Please open it, I don't know if it's suitable.'

John felt the weight and knew it was expensive, his little gift getting lighter by the second. He unwrapped his present to find a dark leather case and he unclipped its brass latch. Inside was a one hundred foot measuring tape from England's best supplier, Chesterman Sheffield. John's eyes popped. 'Oh what a beauty!'

Clarissa's eyes shone with pleasure. 'I'm glad, I am.'

John caressed the tape and marvelled at its workmanship. It would give many years of service. Clarissa opened her present, which was a garnet ring set in a gold band. John watched her for any disappointment, but Clarissa's glistening eyes and smile showed the exact opposite.

By eight o'clock that night, the McGuires were in the vestibule, welcoming their guests. John couldn't stop staring at his fiancée who looked stunning in a Paris-original, blue silk dress that daringly displayed her shoulders. A single diamond, suspended from a near invisible gold necklace, sparkled in the lamplight. Smiling, she greeted each guest as if they were the only ones attending her function.

French wines and champagne went down the wealthy, well-mannered throats and under the steam-driven ceiling fans, the McCreadies, Sean and his wife and the Fordes mixed freely. John's emotions heightened when Maureen and Liam came up to him.

'Congratulations, Johnny. Liam and I are so pleased for you both.'

John shook Liam's hand. 'Thank you, tonight is a big night for all. I'm so excited, I could yell it from the roof gables.'

Maureen smiled. 'Wonderful! I think it's sad that more of our family is not here and I know they'd be proud of Clarissa. We'll leave you to your guests. Have a grand night!'

John watched them walk over and talk to the McCreadies, before his attention was taken with another stranger pumping his hand.

Clarissa felt wonderful. John had joined her for the maiden waltz and she tingled as he put his arm around her, waiting for the beat. Thoughts of the voyage out mixed with the music and how her dream had come true ran through her head. Lifting her dress to advance the first step, she whispered into her John's ear, 'Remember the *Emily* and the dance you organised?'

He squeezed her closer, which sent extra pulses through her. 'Yes, I do.'

They finished their waltz and many more throughout the evening, revelling in the freedom of unrestricted closeness and the conversation and conviviality of their guests.

'Mrs Forde, how nice to see you. And Mr Forde.'

Maureen smiled. 'And you as well, Mr McCreadie. It's been quite an evening.'

'Indeed.' Ian McCreadie waved his arm around. 'Most of Sydney's upper crust is here to celebrate the couple's happiness. Another drink?'

Before Maureen could protest, Ian was off. He returned with his own drink and two flutes of champagne, managing with dexterity not to spill a drop. The three of them repaired to the cooler harbourside terrace, where some of the one hundred or so guests had gone to mingle and round out the evening.

Comfortably seated on a sandstone bench, Maureen decided to get right to the point. 'My husband tells me that Mr Baxterhouse is a shareholder in your firm.'

'Indeed. Why do you ask?'

'Susie, your niece, mentioned him. He gave her a miniature brass panning box and I'd like one. If you give me his address, I'll write to him.'

'I'll do better than that. He's going to be in the office Monday. I'll ask him.'

'No need, just his address would be suitable, thank you.'

'Very well. Chippendale, eighteen Rose Street.'

'Thank you, Mr McCreadie.'

Maureen inwardly blessed herself. She started to work through the details of her next move. She kept smoothing down her dress. Looking up she saw a worried Liam looking at her. She'd have to deal with her husband, but first she must deal with her assailant.

CHAPTER THIRTEEN

On Monday, a week after the engagement party, Maureen told Liam she had an appointment with her doctor. She knew she was pregnant again, but she wasn't on her way to see the doctor. Liam was at home for the morning, preparing the end of year examinations, and would look after Michael.

The jerking motion of the omnibus going down Broadway challenged her nauseous state and only her grip on the rail stopped her from vomiting. Passing St Benedict's on her left, she deflected the good angel darting at her conscience. She should leave vengeance to the Lord, that's what she'd told her brother, and as a Catholic, that's what was supposed to happen. But as a scarred woman who would never forget, she'd have to beat the Lord to His task or —do it for Him. What was she going to do when she got to Rose Street? Stand outside and hope for a glimpse of him? Confront him? That she could do with the gun in her purse. She didn't know, but she seemed to be drawn to him, drawn by a mixture of anger, frustration and a need to know why. Why had he chosen her on that Dublin day? Why her? Just seeing him may answer that question, maybe another step to bringing the mongrel to account.

She saw her stop and alighted. It was nine-thirty and already hot. Baxterhouse mightn't be at his house, but it was worth a try. It was quiet along Shepherd Street with just the odd person sweeping their veranda and a house being renovated.

Her nausea returned and lurching to a garbage bin, she vomited. Embarrassed that someone might've seen her she looked around, but she was alone. A scented hanky helped restore her and she continued walking.

At Rose Street, she stopped to look for the even numbered lots. She found the first house and crossed the street and set off again with a wariness, now that she might well see a carriage, a cab or the man himself walking towards her. Passing the odd numbered houses she continued on her way. There was nowhere to stand and stare, no tree or wagon to hide behind. She slowed her walk outside number fifteen and glanced across the street to study number eighteen.

It was a modest, well-kept two-storey house. She had the advantage now. Baxterhouse didn't know, if he was inside, that just fifty yards outside his home his rape victim was looking at him, evaluating her position of attack and sorting out ways to make him pay. He was the prey now—not her.

Suddenly she felt exposed. The man might well be looking out a window onto the street. Her bonnet was sufficient to mask her face and for that she was grateful. Turning around, she opened her handbag and looked at the derringer. She'd bought it in Dublin, a week after her assault—for protection—but now, she could use it to attack. Her fingers moved towards it and her confidence returned. No, she wouldn't shoot him, but if he'd seen her and was now coming towards her to hurt her again, she would use it. A sense of power filled her, unfelt for more than two years. Yes, it was enough for now, enough for this day. She walked back down the street, confident that this first step in overcoming her nightmares had been successful.

William Baxterhouse looked away from the drawings on his Chippendale study table and rubbed his eyes. A cup of tea was just the ticket. 'Hastings.'

'Yes, sir,' his manservant said as he came to the doorway.

'Tea, please and make it strong.'

'Very good, sir.'

William had been up since dawn reviewing the marine architect's drawings of the steamers' superstructure. His program was going well with two keels and half the hull frame for one boat being made now. By March next year he'd have at least one steamer completed.

Waiting for his tea he went to the window and looked out. The camellias his man had planted were coming on and his garden now befitted a prosperous businessman who had boats, wagons, a wool brokerage, stores at Bathurst and Ballarat—and going well. Cullen had left hospital and was recovering. Perhaps now the ironmonger had learnt his lesson and his place. A woman across the street stood facing his house. Her large bonnet couldn't fully cover her curly red hair but her lower facial features were visible. Was she looking at his house or something on the ground in front of her? Hastings brought the tea in, distracting him.

'Good man.'

William went back to his drawings and after taking two sips of his tea, resumed his work.

Inspector Henderson examined the can. 'The noose tightens, Hopkins.'

'It does, sir,' the sergeant said. 'The Bathurst police have confirmed they purchased that can at the suspect's store. When we compared it with the one found at the fire, it was very similar—both the font of the first four letters of Bathurst are the same and more, it has the same three serial numbered prefix from the -manufacturer.'

'Not quite definite evidence but sufficient.' Henderson handed the file to the Sergeant. 'Prepare an arrest warrant for William Baxterhouse. The charge, arson. I want it ready by tomorrow morning, but date it today, the sixteenth of November.'

The sergeant saluted and left the office.

The next day, Henderson scrutinised the person seated in front of him. He had interviewed many suspects and tried not to prejudice his opinion of their guilt or innocence but he was wrong on only a few occasions. This time it was difficult. Mr Baxterhouse didn't present as an arsonist. The man was an eminent business owner and respected gentleman. It couldn't be him who'd flung the accelerant about at Point Piper, not this gentleman who was dressed in a quality wool suit with a silk waistcoat and starched white cotton shirt. Gold cuff links flashed now and then, and his shoes were handmade and polished. Henderson's confidence in his evidence waned a tad. However, the suspect's eyes were calm. The inspector knew most innocent people were at least anxious in the company of the law. Baxterhouse was not.

He referred to his file and cleared his throat. 'Mr Baxterhouse, you are charged with aiding and abetting a felony, to wit arson at the premises of Point Piper—'

'This is a slur, sir, on my character.'

The inspector continued, 'You are required to attend the Magistrates Court next Monday the twenty-second of November at nine in the forenoon where bail will be set. Failure to attend court will mean immediate arrest and remand.'

'I'm no threat, Inspector.'

'Do you understand, sir?'

'I do.' Baxterhouse stood up. 'Is that all?'

'When bail is posted you will be released on your own surety. You will have to visit this station every week until your trial. Failure to appear as noted will render the terms of your bail void and you will be held in remand. Do you understand that?'

William smiled. 'Yes, is that all?'

'It is.'

'Good day, Inspector.'

Henderson watched him leave. That bloody can had better be the link!

~

Allen Cullen was back at work. Headaches persisted, his left arm ligaments were damaged and a two-inch scar near his eye would be there till he died. Despite all that, he smiled as he read the *Herald* on 18 November: 'Baxterhouse Charged with Arson. March Trial likely.' His grin broadened. In that lane, and through closing swollen eyes, he'd recognised his attacker. After the assault, he'd wanted to go to the police but knew their chance of making a charge stick would be slim. Reading the news again, he kept on smiling. This was nearly as good.

~

John followed Stella into the Point Piper foyer and Clarissa came to greet him, smiling.

'It's been too long, five days, my goodness.'

It had been. He'd seen her a week after their engagement party and here it was 18 November. 'Have you seen today's paper?'

'Yes. Come, dinner is ready.' They walked towards the dining room. 'About Baxterhouse?'

'Yes.'

'Father's seen John McCreadie and they're concerned.'

'Surely, Baxterhouse can't continue as a shareholder?'

'I wouldn't have thought so, but enough of him.' Clarissa stopped him and hugged him. He kissed her. 'I've really missed you,' she said.

They entered the dining room where David and Christine McGuire were seated. The McGuires were at their polite best and after dinner, John and Clarissa repaired to the veranda, where the breeze was pleasant, cooling a setting sun.

'Now Mr Baxterhouse is charged,' Clarissa said, 'can you tell me more about him?'

John decided to tell her part of the truth. 'He was Maureen's landlord in Dublin.'

'I suspected your sister knew him. And what did he do?'

'He caused Maureen and me serious grief. I've been trying to get back at the man since I came here and now it seems he's getting what's coming to him.'

'And you won't tell me what he actually did?'

'I ask for your patience in that, my love. Maureen may tell you as it affected her more than me. The man doesn't warrant attention from us now and for that I'm relieved.'

'All right. Now, on to more important things, our wedding.'

~

Liam entered Mr Jenkins's Market Street site wondering how John had taken the news about Baxterhouse. John and Sean were huddled together talking with the architect. The little group broke up as Liam came up to them. 'Good day,' he said.

John welcomed him with a smile. 'Hello, Liam. How are you and my sister?'

'We're good, thank you.'

'Just a minute.' John grabbed a towel and wiped his hands.

'Have you heard about Baxterhouse?' Liam asked.

'I saw it in the paper and it's good news. I hope the bastard dies in jail.'

That response was expected. 'Maureen saw the *Herald* as well.'

'Well, well,' John said. 'What did she say?'

'The same as you. She's very happy.'

'I'm not happy he's out on bail, Liam. The bastard could do a bolt.'

Liam hadn't thought about that. 'What if he does run?'

'I hope for his sake, he doesn't.'

'Trial's next March, I hear.'

A clang distracted them and they looked up to see a figure standing on a girder. The man raised his sledgehammer a second time. The hammer's arc moved and hit the girder. A second later the clang reached them and the rigger waved his arm to them.

Sean cupped his hands to his face and yelled. 'That's it. No more.'

The rigger acknowledged the order, placed his hammer down and secured the girder to its connecting column. Squeaking pulleys lifted boxes of bolts and connections to fifty or so hands who were working on the other columns.

Liam pointed to two massive beams dwarfing their neighbours. 'What are those?'

'They're the support beams for the monorail which that big hook will connect to. The hook will lift the wool bales onto the ships.' John kept staring at the hook and seemed a world away, then smiled losing some of the tiredness from his face.

Liam looked at him. 'What's on your mind?'

'Nothing.'

'What about Maureen? She knows about the mongrel. Do you think she'll do anything foolish?'

'He's going to jail, Liam. That should satisfy her.'

'You didn't answer my question?'

John smiled again.

'Don't do that. I know Maureen. She won't give up without a fight. I wouldn't be surprised if she's tried to see that man herself. I'm off to school for the last day of term. I'm late already. Don't let Maureen know I spoke with you.'

~

It was late morning on the 24 November and William Baxterhouse returned to Chippendale after reporting to the police station. He couldn't believe his ill fortune. Hastings opened the door. 'Good morning, sir. Are you unwell?'

'Nothing that can't be fixed, Hastings, thank you.'

'Mr Dawkins is here. He doesn't have an appointment but he says it's very important he sees you. I've directed him to your study and have offered him an iced drink.'

'Thank you.' William walked in to find Dawkins holding the model of the new steamer. The real thing was taking form in Darling Harbour.

Dawkins turned to him and placed the model back on its cradle. 'What sort of man, do ya think I am, William? An intelligent man, a sensitive man?'

William poured himself a whiskey and gestured to the bottle but the red- headed Irishman shook his head. 'You're a lucky man,' William said.

'I am that and I'll get lucky again. I had nothing till Ballarat and now William,' he smiled and removed a paper from his jacket, 'I've got nothing again.' He laughed.

'Nothing? What do you mean, nothing?'

Dawkins hit the paper he held with his open palm. 'This just arrived by clipper. In August, the company I had put all my savings into, the company that was going to triple my fortune, the Lewis Jennings Repeating Rifle Company went bust.' He hit the paper again.

'That's unfortunate, but you have other assets?'

The Irishman sat down and shook his head. 'All my savings, William. All. I have none, my friend, none. I'm as poor as a Belfast beggar, but,' he poked a finger at William, 'not for long.'

Sydney was miles away from America and all that Dawkins had lost.

'I'll find more gold.'

That wasn't what William wanted to hear. 'But you have funds here, in New South Wales?'

Dawkins opened his arms to him. 'You're not listening, man. Not a crown. Don't you see, I've got to start again! I've just come from Higgins. The poor soul's face was whiter than a new collar when I left him.'

William felt like two punches had landed on his unprotected stomach. 'No money? None at all.'

'None. You can forget my steamers, friend. Can't buy those now. Best to sell what you have.'

William pressed the desk edge and using it to steady himself he moved towards his customer. 'But your guarantee?'

'It's worthless. You'd better liquidate.'

'Sell? Sell? Two boats are half finished. There's a shed crammed with material and parts. How can I sell?' The bank. He owed the bank and they would demand payment.

'Blame Jennings. They were the ones to go broke.'

William stood upright and anger infused him. 'It was your call to invest. I'll sue you for all my debt, and more.'

Dawkins laughed. 'You don't see, do you? I haven't a farthing.' William lurched towards him with his palms ready, but the Irishman was nimble.

'We don't want to add assault to arson, do we?'

William stopped and glared at his customer. 'Get out! Get out of my house.'

Dawkins picked up his hat and put it on. 'It was a grand ride we had William, grand. Like your fights. You've lost this one but there's more to win. Me, I'm off to Ballarat to chance my arm again. Good day, my friend.'

Hastings came in after Dawkins had gone. 'Can I get anything for you, sir?'

William was shaking. He had cash and gold right here. It wasn't a fortune but it was his. 'Get me the books, all of them, then pack a bag for me. I'm going to a hotel, somewhere, not fancy. I'll send a note where I am and when we're leaving. I want you to stay here. If anyone asks for me, tell them I'm in Ballarat. That should keep them busy till we leave this benighted place. I'll be going in one hour.'

'Very good, sir.'

William did some quick sums, but it was hopeless. If he liquidated the wagons, the stores, the Bathurst stock, McCreadie's wool brokerage, the equity of his house, the plant in his boat yard and all his mining tools, he'd still owe the bank money, hulls-full of it. Time now wasn't his friend and sweat filmed on his back. Going to his study cupboard, he opened it, unlocked the safe and withdrew bundles of notes and three small ingots; there was enough there to live on. This was history repeating itself, he'd left Dublin to make his mark and here he was leaving Sydney—for where? A new start perhaps, and he would take James with him. William was not going to face a trial and go to jail for the fire. What evidence did Henderson have? A sour taste filled his mouth. Despite Dawkins's disaster he was certain others were scheming to bring him down. Between now and his departure, he'd try to find out who they were. Stuffing the gold and notes into a linen bag, he noticed the mail. William pushed three envelopes aside as he smelt demands for his money. The last was a personal letter with no return address. He ripped it open and William's eyes rounded.

The letter was from John Leary and he wanted to meet him alone at the Market Street wool store site at nine o'clock on the evening of 26 November. Perfect. Leary was prepared to tell Baxterhouse who were his enemies.

But why meet on a building site?

William left Skinners Family Hotel the next evening and made his way up Margaret Place, thence to the finger docks at Miller's Point. Experience was telling him that someone he'd crossed was attacking him. Could it be the McGuires, or the docile naval lieutenant, or Cullen? Maybe Cuthbert's had a hand in Dawkins's downfall. The boatbuilder was a competitor, but that seemed unlikely. Yes, it could be any of these or others. His name was black financially and with the law, but he'd been diligent and had made his first appearance at the police station. After he'd left there, he'd managed to avoid the bank's representative standing outside who had a dangerous looking notice in his hand. Bugger these colonials. He had no choice, moving on was his only option, maybe to the islands as a plantation owner. Feeling better, he approached an office at the start of the wharf, its two windows greasy with grime. The door handle turned at his touch and William went to enter.

'What d'ya want?' came a deep voice from behind him.

William looked around to a threatening face then down to a mass of hair that sprouted from a dirty singlet; like a tear in an overstuffed mattress. 'Are you a ship's captain?'

'Master's mate, just back from leave.'

'I see.'

'Want to book passage?'

'I do, for two people. Can you help me?'

'I can.'

'Good. I'm here to get on the first boat to Fiji.'

Hairy Chest looked at him and delivered a mouthful of tobacco juice at William's feet. 'You smell of money. How much would you pay?'

He wanted certainty. 'Twenty pounds for each person.' This was double the normal passage fare. William looked at the open mouth and its assortment of bad and misplaced teeth. A giggle soon followed.

'Forty pounds each and we sail on the thirtieth of this month.'

William became angry and his palms flexed. But hitting the man would do him no good. 'No bloody way!'

The man brushed past him into the office and started to close the door. 'The captain will tell you the same. He's my brother.'

William shoved his boot in the closing space. 'All right.'

~

November had advanced twenty-five days and it seemed like hell had sprung leaks up into Market Street. The heat touched every inch of iron on site, making it kiln-hot to touch. Workmen's eyes, under their hat brims, were stark against their burnt faces.

'What's the matter, mate?' Sean asked. 'Your mind's not on the job.'

John had misread another tape reading and he squinted at Sean through the heat. He nodded. 'Let's have a breather.' It was nearly noon and finding a completed section of roofing they ate their meal under its shade. John leaned back on a sandstone wall. 'I'm going to nail Baxterhouse.'

Sean stopped chewing. 'The mongrel who caused the fire?'

'The same.'

'He's already buggered.'

John tried to ignore him. Despite his best intentions to leave the man to the law, he'd wavered and wanted certainty. 'I've sent him a letter. We'll meet here tomorrow night.'

'What for?'

John kept silent.

Sean shrugged. 'So, it's going to be all on?'

'Aye.'

Sean flung away the dregs of his cup. 'Do you know what you're getting yourself into? The man's stuffed! He's up for arson and he'll go to jail, so what's your rush to finish him off?'

'All well and good. But this isn't any ordinary man. He's like a snake.'

'But a fighting one.'

John had heard the rumours about Baxterhouse's bouts. 'He's still got to be crushed before he runs off. You know he did Cullen.'

'No.'

'Yeah. Mr Cullen told me. But the bastard will run, Sean.'

'To where?'

'I don't know and I don't care. I've spent precious money keeping tabs on him but I can't keep that up till his trial. No, I'm going to see him.'

'And what happens to you if you come out bad? What if you get busted up in a fight or—' Sean turned on him. 'You're not going to do something stupid? Are you? You'd be daft if you did.'

John remembered burning the wagons. 'I want him to know that he didn't get away with what he did.'

'What? The arson? John, leave him alone. The man's in a corner, he's got nothing to lose now. Larkin's seen him fight.'

'I'm taller than him.'

'But, have you ever fought *like* him?'

John knew some punches the bare-knucklers threw, and William was practised. 'No.'

'No. If you come out second best, your life's ended. Kiss goodbye to Clarissa, money, the whole box and dice. Think about that! And why here? Why not at his place? Do ya know where he lives?'

'Chippendale.'

Sean shook his head. 'Well, you've done it now.'

John threw his remaining food in the waste bin. 'If there's a mess on the night, I'll tell the police that Baxterhouse was a burglar. I'll tie him up.'

'That won't work. The man doesn't have to steal.'

'I'll think of something, all right, don't worry.' He paused for a moment. 'I've never told this to any man, but Baxterhouse raped Maureen.'

Sean looked shocked. 'The bastard!'

'In Dublin, just before I sailed. He was her landlord. That's why he's got to pay and big.'

Sean went quiet for a while. 'But he'll go to prison. Yeah, he won't do time for the rape but he'll be locked up for the fire.'

'He's got to be convicted yet.'

'He will be.'

'I'm still going to see him.'

'What time?'

'Nine o'clock.'

'Then I want to be there with you.'

'No!'

'If you don't let me, I'll tell anyone who'll listen, including the police what you're going to do.' John glared at him. 'You have a choice.'

John paused. 'All right. You can come. If things go wrong, just know that I wanted to do this.'

Sean had his third drink for the afternoon and was tempted to have a real one to ward off the worry. John was meeting Baxterhouse tonight. He looked around the bar at the few patrons. Beth was chatting to another barmaid when she caught Sean's eye. 'Same again Sean?'

'No thanks, Beth. Lost me thirst.'

'You've not been yourself, gazing at nothing. Is anything wrong?'

Sean smiled for the first time that afternoon. Once again, Beth had got under his guard. She was a lovely girl and he decided to tell her. 'Do ya remember if John ever told you about a William Baxterhouse?'

It was a while ago, but what John had told her in her house was something she'd never forget. It was for Maureen that she felt. 'He did and a bad piece of work that man is.'

'John told me a secret about his sister that he said he hadn't told to any man. He didn't say if he'd told a woman.'

Beth didn't flinch and Sean was unsure but he continued. 'John is meeting Baxterhouse at nine tonight.'

'He's meeting him alone? Just the two of them?'

'Aye.'

Beth turned to her mate at the end of the bar. 'Sophie, let me have five minutes? It's slow at the moment.' Beth lifted the bar flap and beckoned Sean to a table. 'I knew he'd do something like this. I'll bet that man won't go alone.' Tears filled her eyes.

'What's wrong?'

'Oh Sean, John means a lot to me.'

'And me. Look, Baxterhouse can fight but he'd not suspect John of anything. It's John that we have to worry about. We're going to have to protect the big bastard aren't we? Don't worry, I'll be there to make sure things go right.'

Beth composed herself rubbing her hands on her apron. 'You'll let me know? I have to know he's all right Sean.'

'I'll tell you what. I'll be back here at ten o'clock to put you at ease. It'll be all over by then.'

'And if it's not?'

'Then I'll tell you at your house. Wait up for me.'

Beth stood up and went back to the bar, not looking at him.

Sean stood looking across Market Street at his site. Like any good foreman, he knew every inch of it. The best place to hide was behind the completed store siding, which offered a commanding view of the big-framed building. His watch read ten after six and there was no sign of the night guard who was due now to check all was well. Where the hell is he though? Sean risked exposure but ran across the street and ducked behind the siding to wait. By a lucky coincidence there was a full moon and few of the new roof sheets had been installed. A rattle of a gate alerted him and he kept still as the night guard secured the site.

Digging in his pockets, he took out an apple and banana. Wedging himself into position, he waited; his senses alert for sounds of an intruder. Dead still and it was hard going. Many times in the next hour and a half sounds challenged him, the scurrying of rats, which he'd never got used to, made him tense. A different sound at about eight o'clock alerted him. A shadow seemed out of place in the far row of columns. Squinting, Sean thought he imagined it, but then the shadow moved. Looking at its source, Sean saw a large cat.

His joints now ached. Then he was startled as the front gate opened. John stood in the open gateway and Sean's watch read eight-thirty. John strode the site from one end to the other. Sean slid upright to give himself a rest, his joints clicking in the still silence. Nine o'clock couldn't come quick enough.

~

Maureen knew Liam was uneasy. They'd just completed dinner, but he'd left a lot on his plate. The hall clock struck eight heavy gongs, like counting down to an execution. She shivered and Liam looked at her.

'Are you all right, dear?'

'Yes, yes I think so.' She paused. 'No, I'm not. I want to tell you something that may get you angry.'

Liam pushed his plate aside. 'Go on.'

'I tried to find Baxterhouse myself and nearly succeeded but didn't go through with it.' Maureen folded her napkin. 'I'm sorry for deceiving you, Liam.'

Liam rose from the table and sat beside her. 'I suspected you might do as much and I was worried sick. Do you plan to see him again?'

'No. Not by myself. Thank you for being so understanding. We can talk later, I'll go and see to Michael. He's had a temperature all day and I'm concerned. I'll lie down with him for a little while.'

'Very well.'

Maureen closed Michael's door and crept up to the restless infant. In the darkness she wanted to keep her promise to Liam. It had been a long eleven days since she'd been near her rapist and she was tempted to 'face' him once again. Tempted that is, but would she act on that? Actually confront the man? She wasn't so sure.

~

Beth wiped the glass for a second time and flung the tea towel under the bar. The evening crowd would soon thicken and she had to control her anxiety. It was nine o'clock and in one hour her life could change, forever. She knew it. Her insides were churning, her mouth was dry, but she smiled at the patron in front of her. 'What'll it be?'

'A pint of Bass, thanks love.'

The smell of fresh hops made her heave. Thank God I'm working—it's a bit of a distraction. John was a fool to think he could take on Baxterhouse. And why attack the man? He'd go to jail for arson. But no, John wanted to make sure. Madness. Why couldn't he wait? But it may not be that bad. If things went all right, John would be alive in an hour and Sean would tell her. If not. Well, she couldn't worry about that now. 'Here you are,' she said handing the beer to the customer.

She collected his money and for the next fifteen minutes kept busy, but with a plea to a workmate to take over, she went to the loo. Tears filled her eyes as she stared at the back of the toilet door. You silly, silly girl. Why did you fall for this man? Engaged and all. Will you see him alive again? Or will the police tell you he's dead? Beth washed her face and looked in the mirror.

She returned to the bar where the Royal's crowd had swelled. As Beth served a customer she thought again about John's meeting and spilt more beer than usual. The publican shot her a quick look. Must be wondering if I'm daft or it's the time of the month. She didn't care.

Sophie spoke over the rising din. 'That's the second wrong beer you've pulled! You all right?'

Beth spilt the beer and poured another for the frustrated

customer. 'I am. Rough night last night, that's all.' Hoping this would satisfy her mate, but she knew it hadn't.

She should have gone with them to meet Baxterhouse. John's plan would be too simple, bound to fail. Beth didn't want to look at the clock. But she did—nine forty-five. Now all her experience came into play to stay on the job in hand: pulling beers, wiping up, collecting glasses, flirting with the punters. As time passed, panic now replaced anxiety and she saw blackness ahead. Having John alive was the key. Five minutes to ten. The evening's drinkers kept the pub doors busy and each face made an impression, every face except Sean's.

Ten o'clock passed, her worry cutting sharp swathes in her. She stopped looking at the door but continued pulling beers. At ten-fifteen she accepted the worst. She knew it. At ten-twenty the doors settled and Beth's legs wouldn't support her. Propping both hands on the bar she stared at the closed doors for what seemed an eternity. Sean wasn't coming and the pub was closing in ten minutes. But he still might go to her house. She wouldn't sleep till he had.

~

John saw Baxterhouse first. The rapist strutted as if he knew the site, putting John on alert and he set a course to intercept him. Standing in the centre of the building, John was framed by its structure above and to each side, his body casting a shadow from the moonlight. Pressing his boots into the ground, he wanted Baxterhouse to know who he really was.

Baxterhouse stopped, turned his head a little to one side then started walking towards him alongside an open pit. He stopped ten feet from him. 'Mr Leary?'

John's world came into focus and a peace infused him, his damp forehead cooler. 'It's me.'

'You're going to tell me the cause of all my troubles?'

'I am.'

'Why you? And how much will it cost me?'

'I found out you started the McGuire house fire.'

Baxterhouse paused. 'Supposition.'

'I know the lieutenant. He told me.'

Baxterhouse smiled. 'And you believe him?'

'I do.'

'Then you're a fool. I have money, Mr Leary, more than you know. I'm not into arson. Now, I didn't want to come, but was intrigued by your letter. Who else wants to attack me?'

'The list is long, sir and you already know some of the people. Tell me the time?'

'What?'

'You heard me, Mr Baxterhouse. Read me the time.'

Baxterhouse reached in and brought out his gold watch. 'So it's a game, yes?'

'Nice watch,' John said. 'Where did you get it?'

'It's been in the family for years.'

'You've had it for some time, yes, but it's not yours.'

'It's mine.' The man was adamant.

'Tell me what's on the back of the watch.'

Baxterhouse's eyes twitched. 'There's a "C.M." inscribed on it.'

'You stole that watch and I know from where.'

His opponent's head moved just a fraction. 'No, the watch was my grandfather's on my mother's side. Cedric Maddison.'

It was too much of a coincidence but it mattered naught. 'Mrs Forde is my sister.'

'Mrs Forde? I haven't had the pleasure of meeting the lady.'

'Oh you've met her, sir. She's married, has a husband and son and she used to be Mrs Murphy. Her first husband was called Colin.'

'I knew a Mrs Murphy in Dublin. She was my tenant.'

'That watch in your hand was her husband's. She says you raped her.'

Baxterhouse looked surprised. 'A shocking crime to accuse me of, sir, shocking.' Baxterhouse smiled. 'I know what your sister may be talking about and because she's a lady I'll not share with you the facts of that incident.'

John bridled. There was enough evidence of what happened in

Maureen's bedroom but there were other things, horrible things that shouted violence. 'Oh no, Mr Baxterhouse, you did it.'

'Leary, I like you. I do. You seem a good lad. I've got nothing against you and what happened between your sister and myself, is subject to interpretation. If you must know, your sister hadn't had male company for many months, many months. As a gentleman I'll not say more. In fact, I find this continuing discussion -disturbing.'

'You're a liar.'

Baxterhouse paused. 'Oh, Mr Leary, you disappoint me. Please reconsider what you just said and then retract it.'

'You're a liar, a bloody liar.'

Baxterhouse sighed. 'Then I'm afraid I'll have to teach you manners that will make you see the truth.' Taking off his jacket he hung it on a protruding bolt. 'You're a big boy and you'll give me some sport, I'm sure.' He smiled again. 'I'd suggest you strip down. Blood's a stickler to remove.'

John took off his jacket, tie and shirt and, facing a grinning Baxterhouse, prepared himself. Baxterhouse feinted and John stepped back.

'Have to know when to move, my young friend. Sometimes you don't see what's coming.' Baxterhouse threw a left, his forearm sliding against John's chin, then pain exploded in John's stomach as a right landed there. John stepped back, winded. Another punch and another, this one sent John reeling and blood sprayed in a mist from his mouth.

'Come on, boy. Give me a contest.'

John had to keep his distance and take opportunities as they came. He had reach, age and height over his opponent. He'd have to use those, as Baxterhouse was a specialist. He'd left his ribs exposed and Baxterhouse punched him there but John's straight left jab found its mark at the same time and the rapist's right eye started to close.

'Better, Leary, better.'

For the next few minutes, for every two punches Baxterhouse landed, John scored with one. Bloody cuts obscured John's vision, his nose was broken, and his aching jaw and ribs were tiring him, but he began to pick up the rapist's style; picking the hook-to-hammer-fist punch followed by a trapped-wrist strike where his opponent would protect himself. He pounced when he saw a gap then danced away. Thank God he was fit because he could move in an instant and that saved him further pain.

'Not long now, Leary.' The rapist head butted him and John fell. A boot went into his rib and the pain was excruciating. Rolling away he got up and tackled his opponent crashing them both to earth. Baxterhouse's head hit the ground hard and he became dazed and groggy. John didn't hesitate. With site-hardened strength he pinned the rapist's arms behind him. Baxterhouse came to, spat and heaved and tried to bite him but John smashed his own forehead against the rapist's nose and at the same time wrenched one of the pinned arms so much that it cracked. As Baxterhouse yelled in pain, John released his right hand and rained punches into Baxterhouse's face. He wanted the bastard to pay, pay for all Maureen's misery, pay for the fire and pay for Cullen's attack. Time stood still and the blows hit eyes, chin, mouth, ribs and stomach.

John heard his name being called, but kept on punching. Then he was being pulled back and upright and Sean faced him.

'Jesus, mate, that's enough.'

John shoved Sean away and looked down through his own limited vision at the bloody heap at his feet. Baxterhouse's breaths hissed and bubbled from his mouth and nose. 'The bastard.'

'Aye, and you've made a proper mess of him. He can't die, John. Stand back.' Sean doused the rapist with a bucket of water. Baxterhouse didn't move at first then rolled onto his broken arm. He screamed and passed out. 'Let's get him out of here. I've brought a wagon.' Sean flung John a clean rag.

John refilled the bucket and poured water over himself. It stung in many places but he could just see.

'While you're still hurting,' Sean said, 'I'll fix this.' He placed a finger and thumb on John's nose and John braced himself, knowing what was coming. He'd used the same technique on Kieran after he'd had a fight. Sean pressed and twisted John's cartilage back into place. The pain peaked then settled.

John looked down at Baxterhouse. 'I'll take him to Chippendale.' He wiped himself down and dressed in pain. Before they picked Baxterhouse up, John searched and found the watch. He pocketed it. They carried him to the wagon and covered him with a tarp. 'Let's go.'

On the way, as the pain from John's injuries hit, he realised what he'd done. When Baxterhouse recovered he would accuse John of assault. It would be hard to prove as John would lie and say he was elsewhere and Sean would be his alibi. But it was a risk, a big one, an added complication at best.

'I'll take the wagon home after this,' Sean said. 'I've got to see Beth.'

'At this hour? Why?'

'I told her that you'd be here tonight and I said I'd see her. She'll be worried.'

'Don't go. I will.'

'You're in no state, mate.'

'I'll go there, Sean.'

'You'll go with *me*. You can tell her, then I'm taking you home.'

John nodded. 'Thanks. You reckon Baxterhouse will go for me after this?'

'He might.' Sean smiled. 'But we weren't there, were we? And if we were, we can say we caught and took down a feisty trespasser. But you'd better find a way to tell your fiancée about them cuts.'

John nursed his pain and kept silent.

'I was watching you fight,' Sean said. 'That man sure can. I was going to step in when you were on the ground, but you seemed to go berserk when you tackled him.'

When they got to Rose Street they slowed the wagon. 'It's number eighteen,' John said. 'Let's leave him on the veranda and ring the bell.'

They unloaded Baxterhouse and carried him to the house. He was breathing still.

'Just inside the gate would be best, in sight of his door,' Sean whispered. 'Like he was attacked in the street.'

'Take the wagon to the end of the street. I'll ring the doorbell and come to you.'

Sean moved off and John waited for a bit then rang the bell. Footsteps sounded in the hall and John ran, his sides radiating pain. He was out of sight of the house when the front door opened. Joining Sean at the wagon they continued on their way.

It was about eleven o'clock when Sean and John rode down Forbes Street.

'Just a little bit further, Sean,' John said. 'Let me off here. I'll be about ten minutes.'

John knocked on the front door and waited. The light of a lantern flickered in a window adjacent and a voice asked.

'Who's that?'

'It's me, John. Can I come in?'

The door opened and Beth, carrying the lantern, looked at him. Her mouth opened. 'Oh John! You're a mess, come in. Quickly.'

He entered and went through into the kitchen where Beth placed the lantern on the table, lit the gas flame and closed the kitchen door

'Sit down. I don't want to wake the girls. They'd have nightmares if they saw you.' She put the kettle on, rummaged in some drawers and brought out a bowl, a cloth and some ointment. She scanned his face and grimaced. 'Let me clean you up. What did he do to you? How did you get here? And where is Sean?'

'He's out in the wagon waiting, Beth, and I can't stay long. I fronted Baxterhouse tonight. He found out that Maureen was my sister and what he did to her. We fought.'

'That I can see.' She dabbed at a wound and he jerked. 'Sorry. What happened to him? John, please tell me you didn't kill him? Did you?' She looked at him anxiously.

'The bastard's still alive, and he's beaten up. The trouble is he may have a go at me for attacking him.'

'You were foolish doing that, very foolish.'

'I know, I know.'

She cleaned him up as best she could. 'I'm just glad you're all right. Are you fit to go home by yourself?'

John stood up. 'Sean will take me, Beth, thank you.' He smiled at her.

'What will you tell Miss McGuire?'

'I had a fall at work. I'd better be going. Thanks for this and thanks for being a friend.'

'That's what I'm here for.' She gathered her kit and pausing to check, kissed him on the cheek. 'I'll see you out.'

William Baxterhouse pushed himself up with his good arm and looked at the departing wharf through the porthole.

'Rest sir, please,' Hastings said from the adjoining bunk. 'Those broken ribs won't heal otherwise.'

'I'll mend.' He grinned despite the four-day-old pain from his stitched cuts, chest and plastered arm. 'The boy was good, Hastings, good. I would've taken him out standing up but when he tackled me that was it. Christ, he was heavy.' He lay back. 'I'll let him be, but there's another I have to get— in my own time and in my own way.'

'Mr Dawkins?' Hastings took a stab.

'The red-headed Dawkins.' Baxterhouse closed his eyes. 'Wake me when we get to the island. I could sleep for a week.'

At Cochrane's Hotel, three days before Christmas Day, Sean waited for his partner to order them more drinks and hoped that Christ's birthday would bring his friend some blue sky. They'd heard nothing from Baxterhouse over these past weeks but they'd read he'd failed to appear during his remaining parole and an arrest warrant was out for him. John might be in trouble as the rapist might attack him, but that seemed unlikely.

John brought the drinks to the table with a newspaper. 'I'm glad the wool store's going well.'

'It's a shame that you had that fall there. How are your injuries?'

John smiled. 'Improving.'

'Aye, you know,' Sean leaned closer, 'Baxterhouse might have run.'

'Or he could have gone to ground and be stalking me.' John pulled over a copy of the *Herald* and pointed to an article and read it aloud. '"If Mr Baxterhouse doesn't voluntarily offer up his assets, including his stock at Bathurst and Ballarat by the end of December, the bank will pass them over to the creditors." That was the only thing we didn't know about. Another nail.' John put the paper down. 'I spoke to Maureen about Baxterhouse.'

'Did you give her back her watch?'

John smiled. 'She doesn't want it now as he's touched it. She said I could have it.'

'Right. Did you tell her everything that happened on the night?'

John shook his head. 'Not everything, and as far as she's concerned, he got away.'

'Do ya think she believed you?'

John shrugged. 'I don't know, maybe.'

Sean had to know something. 'You hadn't planned to kill Baxterhouse that night had you?'

John looked at him straight. 'For the last two years I knew I had to get him somehow. I wanted him to pay. He kept to his thieving ways in Sydney and others have made him pay for that.'

'Helped a bit by you.'

'Aye, but the man brought a lot on himself. He had to know who I was and that I'd beaten him.'

'And if I hadn't pulled you off?'

John seemed to think about this. 'I would have stopped. I would have.'

Sean believed him. 'It's finished, John.'

John was quiet for some time. 'The fight's over, yes, but he's still out there, somewhere.'

John concentrated on the space just above Sean's head and Sean guessed his friend was in another place, and would put money on it that it concerned Maureen or Clarissa. Perhaps even both.

The late December air breathed warm and dry through the veranda on a quiet Ballarat street, which was private enough for two men to relax, drinking cold cider.

'Are you disappointed, James?'

James put down the letter he was reading and smiled at his companion. 'About being here rather than Melbourne?'

'Yes.'

'We can always go to the big smoke for some culture.'

'And the loss of the tool business?'

'Ye gods. If I never see another greasy can or grubby pick it'll be too soon.'

'And what about your brother?'

'I'll join him in Fiji sometime.' He tapped the letter. 'And it better be soon. The bank's coming after me.'

~

Inspector Henderson closed the file in front of him and patted his forehead with a handkerchief. This humidity was killing him, he must lodge a request to HQ to stop the compulsory wearing of jackets in summer.

He sighed. An open case like this always frustrated him. Did Baxterhouse leave the colony or was he lying low? Grumbling he looked at all the forms he'd have to fill out including dispatches to other colonies asking them to watch out for his suspected arsonist who had broken bail. Walking to the window on this last day of the year, he looked at the town ready for the festivities.

He had a feeling in his water that he hadn't heard the last of the absconder.

~

John looked down at his polished shoes and back up to the face of his beloved. 'I do,' he said.

Clarissa smiled. Her gown was from Paris with all the trimmings but John was only focused on what the dress enveloped—his girl.

'I now pronounce you man and wife,' the priest said. 'You may kiss the bride.'

John did. Christine welcomed them as they walked down the aisle at St Mary's in the February sunlight, and John smiled and nodded to Sean and Liam. He touched his middle as he passed Maureen and she blushed, acknowledging her pregnancy. Baxterhouse came briefly to his mind but he pushed him away. This was his wedding day, a day he'd long waited for. Nothing was going to spoil that. He knew he'd taken a risk, but Baxterhouse hadn't confronted him and that was good.

Outside, the public wanted its piece of the society wedding. There were journalists and police all crowding them as they climbed into black, polished coaches for the trip to the reception at Point Piper. The rest of the day was a happy blur.

Later in their bedroom, John, dressed in a custom-made nightshirt, went onto the veranda to look out over the harbour. Gum trees rustled in the night breeze and the harbour phosphorescence peeked through the branches where Butcherbirds and Boobook owls twittered their goodnights. John enjoyed a pleasurable shudder. His hand felt the paint's smoothness. He'd made it and vowed that night and for all the nights that God gave them, he would love his Clarissa.

Her hand pressed his back and a perfume tingled his nose. She leaned against him and he looked at his love whose smile told him everything. 'Penny for your thoughts?'

John kissed her on the forehead then her birthmark. 'Nothing important, my precious.'

Clarissa nodded. 'Let's put those on hold for now, my darling. We've a lifetime to talk.'

ACKNOWLEDGMENTS

Grateful thanks must go to Bert Hingley, my literary mentor. His patience, insight and practical advice have positioned this book where it deserves to be.

Cheryl Sawyer, herself a published and respected historical fiction author, gave valuable advice on the women characters and also helped see this book into print.

Final editing credit goes to Kathy Mossop, who helped me greatly in the final run to the line.

The builders of the colony deserve my thanks and admiration. Without their passion, sweat and contribution, their legacy and the world-class quality of today's built environment would not have been possible.

HISTORICAL NOTE

The appreciation of what it takes to create a building from an idea to a physical and useful form has always fascinated me. I've been fortunate to have an affinity with construction and to have been a participant in the industry, from cadet to EGM. In a long career I have celebrated the industry's challenges and triumphs in both the private and government sectors.

In this book, John Leary's assisted voyage from Ireland to New South Wales is faithfully rendered: it was like a 'business-class' journey of today, compared to those taken from the United Kingdom to the United States—these latter vessels were often called 'coffin ships' due to the high mortality rate among passengers.

There are scores of references for mid-colonial Sydney public buildings, churches and chapels. One is a wonderful compilation of drawings by Joseph Fowles, printed by himself in Harrington Street in 1848. His document confirms that St Patrick's Church in Charlotte Place (present day Grosvenor Street) was dedicated in March 1844.

Between King and Market Streets in Pitt Street stood the Royal Victoria Theatre. 'The fronts are bold and lofty faced with fine brick with massive stone dressings and cornices. The spirited proprietor

Mr Moffit deserves great credit for the liberality with which he has contributed towards ornamenting the city.'

Maps of the area of Sydney are also intriguing references. Wells' Map of Sydney 1843 and Woolcott and Clarke's Map of 1834 show that the majority of Sydney's 7,000 houses were still located in the old established area, which stretched from Miller's Point to Sydney Cove in the north to the markets in Campbell Street to the south. The 1851 census counted just over 44,000 people—enough to fill today's Moore Park Sydney Football Stadium. A further 9,600 people lived beyond the boundaries.

Much of the housing was poor and carelessly built. During March and February 1851, a *Sydney Morning Herald* journalist wrote of an area near Parramatta Street hard by the abattoirs on Blackwattle Creek. 'How do they live here? . . . The people cook in dirt—they eat in dirt—and they sleep in it, they are born, bred, they die in dirt; from the cradle to the grave, they pass through life in filth—it was so in the old country.'

Although gas lighting was introduced to the city in the mid-19th century, the streets could be dangerous: hard muggings and prostitutes abounded, especially in the Rocks area.

It cannot be overemphasised how much the Gold Rush affected New South Wales and Victoria. In J M Freeland's *Architecture in Australia, A History*, he says, 'Australian architecture left its innocence behind when gold was officially discovered in May 1851. The immediate effect of the turmoil on architecture was negative. Building virtually stopped. It was in these conditions that many of these substantial business firms of today were founded. In the period 1851 to 1860 the population of Australia trebled to 1.2 million people, Victoria from 76,000 to 540,000!'

The conditions of the 1850s created an over-demand for buildings to an extreme degree. Even iron pot houses were imported as prefabricated units. Mr Freeland also notes in his engaging book that Australian builders developed techniques to suit the local vernacular. 'Ceiling joists (to which modern Gyprock is attached) were used to tie the feet of rafters and so form a simple but effective truss. A simple thing like the humble nail was now being made by factories in England, where machines spewed forth millions of cut and later wire nails at the rate of over 100,000 nails per machine per day. They were regular in size, reliable in quality and cost a fraction of their hand-forged predecessors.'

Sydney was a city on the move. There were countless businesses to do with transport and horses, carriages and harnesses. The colony's 'oxen trail', George Street, rumbled to the sounds of the wool clip being taken to England. The roads were busy enough for there to be a toll road between Sydney and Rose Bay. Parramatta and Newcastle were established towns and Ashfield was a coach stop between Sydney and Parramatta. The city in which Leary's story is set was as rich and dynamic as I have striven to make it.

THE AUTHOR

Michael Beashel is Sydney-born and his Irish forebears immigrated to New South Wales in the 1860s and settled in Miller's Point. He spent his youth in Bondi, is married with adult children and lives in Sydney's inner-west.

Beashel was head of Asset Development for a global accommodation services company registered on the NYSE and has made his mark in some of Australia's iconic construction companies. In Sydney, he has restored government buildings such as the Customs House and the Town Hall, and completed commercial buildings in the private sector. In SE Asia, he managed a construction division that built apartments and hotels in Bangkok and Ho Chi Minh City.

This industry—its characters, clients, trades people, designers and bureaucrats—provides rich material for his writing. He has an eye for the emergence of Sydney's built form, from the early days of the colony to the present, and a love of construction. He says about his writing, 'It's a passion. I revel in using the building industry as a tapestry to weave a great tale seasoned with historic facts and memorable characters. Human shelter is an essential need and I suspect people have a fascination for understanding its context and construction within their societies. Australia still is a young country but there are many, many outstanding building stories.'

Beashel holds a B. App. Science (Building) from Sydney's UTS and is a member of the NSW Writers' Centre. *Unbound Justice* is his first novel and the sequels *Unshackled* and *Succession* complete the Sandstone Trilogy.

Connect with the author

Author Website: https://michaelbeashel.com.au
Facebook: https://www.facebook.com/MichaelBeashelAuthor

Printed in Great Britain
by Amazon

69003570R00196